I0645565

Heart's Desire

BOOKS BY
LINDA HOOVER

Mountain Prophecy

Lighter Than Air

Heart's Desire

Linda Hoover

Copyright 2020 by Linda Hoover
All rights reserved.
Printed in the United States of America
ISBN 978-0-9981806-4-9 (softcover)
ISBN 978-0-9981806-5-6 (ebook)

This is a work of fiction. Names, characters, incidents and dialogues are products of the author's imagination and are not to be construed as real. Any resemblance to actual events or persons, living or dead, is entirely coincidental.

No part of this book may be reproduced in any form or by any electronic or mechanical means, including information storage and retrieval systems, without written permission from the author, except for the use of brief quotations in a book review.

Cover design by Diane Turpin, dianeturpindesigns.com
Formatting by Polgarus Studio, polgarusstudio.com

Boston, February 1880

1

on't worry, nobody knows. The phrase repeated itself in John Phillips' mind like the rhythmic ticking of a clock as he hurried out of his office and headed for the elevator. His valise bumped against his leg with each step. When he arrived, his finger hovered over the button, indecision swirling in his mind.

Maybe I should take the stairs. No, I never do that. Everything has to look as usual. John pushed the button and a bell sounded faintly several floors below. The car made its slow approach while he ran his finger between his neck and tightening collar.

The elevator stopped with a bump and the metal accordion gate across the doorway folded to the side. John's mouth went dry and his heart galloped in his chest as a hideous creature with blood red eyes and razor-sharp teeth stalked toward him, pointing its finger and cackling. He stumbled back, but the creature lunged forward and grabbed his jacket sleeve with its clawed hands.

"Noooo." He twisted and turned, trying to get out of his jacket.

"John, wake up!"

The haze of sleep cleared as John became aware of someone shaking his shoulder. The creature disappeared and he worked to even out his breathing.

"Are you awake?"

He forced words past his constricted throat. "I'm awake, Elizabeth."

"Was it the same dream? You were moaning and thrashing around. I wish you'd tell me what it's about."

"I don't want to burden you with it. Let's go back to sleep." He rolled away from his wife, grateful to be at home in his bed. The situation occurred twenty-five years ago, yet the dream's frequency had increased to several nights a week. He drew in a shaky breath. It took longer each time to calm his pounding heart when he awoke.

John wiped the perspiration from his face with the sleeve of his nightshirt, then pulled the blanket tight around his shoulders. Could this mean he'd been found out?

2

Two days later

Julia Phillips didn't even glance at her friend for fear of losing sight of the handsome stranger she'd been watching. "Sophia, do you see the young man over there?"

The brisk wind blew his golden hair back as his skates flew over the ice with a boundless energy and freedom that filled her with longing.

"The one in the tan coat?"

"Do you think he's anyone we know?"

"I don't think so." Sophia linked arms with her and began skating in the opposite direction. "I don't know why you can't be happy with our circle of friends. It seems you're always looking for someone different."

Julia met her friend's eyes for a moment. "I want to get closer." She skated after him, her hunter green skirt pressing against her legs as she worked her way through the other skaters. Sophia's skates swished behind her.

"Julia, wait!"

The cold, but sunny day had beckoned a laughing, chattering crowd onto Boston Common's Frog Pond. Adults and children in colorful coats, hats and scarves covered the pond, frustrating her efforts to get close to the mystery man. Just when she finally had a clear view, a woman and her two little girls got tangled together and fell in a heap right in his path. He dodged around them, stopped, came back and helped them to their feet.

Julia could see that something more than falling distressed the woman. Grabbing the man's arm, she pointed toward the other end of the pond. "Please find my son. Charlie's wearing a red scarf and black cap." The man took off, his coat flapping behind him as he weaved in and out through the other skaters.

Julia edged closer yet, and watched.

Sophia caught up with her. "Really, Julia, what are you thinking?"

"I want to see how this turns out." A coil of frustration tightened in her middle. Who would believe it'd be such a challenge to get a good look at someone?

Before long the young man came back, holding an indignant little boy by the hand.

"I wasn't lost." The boy's voice carried to his relieved mother and anyone else who cared to listen. "Let me go!"

The mother hurried to her child's side and thanked the young man for his help. Julia saw it all in pieces until a crowd gathered, completely blocking her view.

She drew a deep breath and blew it out, sending her annoyance with it. She turned when Sophia spoke.

"I'm not surprised he caught your attention, but what were you planning to do, introduce yourself?"

Sophia linked arms with her and began leading her across the ice. Julia glanced back at the same instant the crowd parted and the young man looked her way. For a moment his gaze locked on hers. When a group of people moved in front of him again, she realized she wasn't breathing.

Taking a quick gulp of cold air, she let go of Sophia's arm and headed back. By the time she reached the spot where he'd been standing, he was gone. She stood, scanning the skaters' faces until an opening showed he'd left the ice and taken off his skates. After a quick look at his pocket watch, then the skaters, he turned and left, with his swift stride soon taking him out of sight.

With a sigh she went back to where Sophia waited, shaking her head. They glided to a bench to take off their skates. "To answer your earlier question, I look because our friends, with the exception of my cousin Edward, are stuffy. Did you see how gallantly that man helped the woman?"

"Any of the men of our acquaintance would have done the same."

"Possibly, but I've never seen them skate like that." She paused in putting on her boots to stare into the distance. "I can imagine he has some kind of exciting adventure planned. Something that will take him far from Boston."

"It's not as if the young men we know don't leave Boston for an adventure when they finish Harvard, and they're excited about their travels when they come back. You don't give them enough credit."

Julia could hear the chiding in her best friend's voice. She turned and looked into her snapping brown eyes. "Maybe I'm looking for my own adventure. In the meantime, we need to find the new jewelry store my sister, Margaret, told me about."

A bell tinkled as the door to Anderson's Jewelry closed behind the girls, shutting the noise of people and horses outside. Inside, the only sounds were the ticking of clocks on display and a subdued conversation between a customer and the man helping him. The jewelry and watches in their glass-enclosed cases sparkled in the shop's gaslights. Julia went to the nearest case and looked at the selection, hoping for inspiration.

"May I help you?"

She looked up and a jolt of recognition hit her. His face mirrored the surprise she felt, then the young man smiled slowly, showing even white teeth and adorable dimples. Her cheeks grew warm while her addled brain tried to come up with the proper words to form a reply.

"She's looking for a gift for her father," Sophia supplied. Julia nodded.

"Cufflinks are a popular gift. We have some nice ones in gold over here."

The girls followed him to a case displaying cufflinks. Julia looked at the selection, trying to remember what her father already had. "Which pair do you like best?" She couldn't resist gazing at him again.

Their eyes locked for a couple of heartbeats, then after a quick look in the case, he picked out a pair.

"These are probably my favorite. They speak of quality without being ostentatious."

He flashed her a smile and Julia wondered if that's what he thought, or what he'd heard someone else say. It didn't matter, though. They could be lumps of coal and she'd believe him.

"I agree. They're perfect. Thank you for your help Mr…?"

"Anderson. Jacob Anderson. My father and uncle own the shop."

"I suppose that means you'd be here if I were to come again."

"I certainly hope so, but I feel I may have rushed you. Pocket watches are a nice gift." He moved to another case, opened the back and took one out. His fingers brushed hers as he placed it in her hand.

She caught her breath as warm tingles raced from her fingertips to her heart. His eyes widened a bit. *Did he feel it too?* She quickly turned her attention to the watch, but had no idea what it looked like. She could think of nothing but her response to his touch. Would it happen if their fingers met again? She looked up with a smile. "It's nice, but I believe I'd like to see another one."

Mr. Anderson took the watch and replaced it with a different one. Once again, their fingers touched with the same result. Amazing! She would happily have asked to see every watch in the case, but Sophia intervened.

"I think the cufflinks are the best choice. I imagine your father already has a watch."

Reluctantly, Julia turned from Mr. Anderson to her friend and nodded her agreement.

"I'll be happy to show you other gift possibilities if you're not sure."

The slight frown on Sophia's face stopped her from taking his offer. "Thank you, but my friend is right. I believe I'll take the cufflinks."

"Before you go, I need to get your address so I can have your gift delivered."

"Oh, of course." She didn't mind taking one more look into Mr. Anderson's deep blue eyes. "It's Julia Phillips at 5 Louisburg Square. Thank you again for your help, Mr. Anderson. Perhaps I'll see you again."

"The pleasure will be mine."

◦◦◦◦◦◦

Jacob decided he wouldn't wait for her to come back to the store. He'd find out what he could about Miss Julia Phillips and arrange to cross paths with her again soon.

Absently drumming his fingers on the cufflink case, he assured himself he hadn't changed his mind about looking for a farm in Iowa. Jacob had promised his father he'd give the jewelry store a try. It shouldn't hurt to make friends while here.

He crossed his arms, leaned back against the case and thought about his glimpse of her on the ice earlier. And then she'd walked into the shop. Talk about a surprise.

Blonde curls and a pretty face were enough to make her memorable to any man, but he had no explanation for the pleasant tingling that shot through him when he touched her fingers. It'd be easy to feel more than friendship for her if she'd give him the chance.

A voice came from behind him. "You might as well forget her." Jacob turned to see his older brother, Joel. "Women in the upper class only consider upper class men. By tonight she won't remember your name."

"Maybe." Jacob turned for another look at the door she'd just gone through. He didn't want to argue, but he didn't want to forget her either. He'd find a way to see her again and then decide what he wanted to do.

3

Julia and Sophia settled under the fur lap robes and their driver clucked to the horses, setting the sleigh bells jingling as they swished through the noisy streets.

"Sophia, tell me truthfully, have you ever seen a man more handsome than Mr. Jacob Anderson? He has to be at least six feet tall and has such broad shoulders. And did you see those dimples when he smiled?" She rested her head on the back of the seat and sighed blissfully.

Her friend laughed. "Yes, he's quite handsome. I also notice you're having a package small enough to carry, delivered to your door. I don't suppose you used it as an excuse to give him your name."

A tickle in her middle made her smile. "I didn't ask to have it delivered, but I'm sure it'll be fine." Julia ignored Sophia's raised eyebrows. "Do you believe in love at first sight?"

Sophia shrugged and tucked a strand of chestnut hair back under her hat. "I'm not sure there is such a thing. Maybe you should ask your mother."

"Oh, you know what she'll say. Forget love and looks and pay attention to family and finance. I'd rather have love than a fancy family name and money any day.

She gripped Sophia's gloved hand. "Mr. Anderson is the first man to make me feel weak in the knees just by smiling at me, and it's not just his good looks. When our eyes met, I felt safe. It's as if I knew he would be the kind of man a woman could trust with her heart. It has to mean something."

The girls rode in silence for a few minutes as they considered the possibility. "What about God? Do you believe in him, or maybe fate?"

A slight frown creased Sophia's brow. "Of course, I believe in God, but I'm not sure he was responsible for you meeting Mr. Anderson, if that's what you're implying."

"Well, I'd like to think he's more than some being way up in heaven who never pays attention to us. My sister, Katherine, talks about him. Maybe he did want me to meet Mr. Anderson and that's why we went to their jewelry store."

"I suppose it's harmless to daydream about a stranger, but what about Mr. Harris?"

Julia frowned, confused. "What about him? I've already told him I'm not interested in more than friendship. When he spoke to me of marriage, it sounded more like a business proposal."

"He may not have given up the idea. Isn't that him leaving your house?"

As their sleigh approached from the opposite end of the square, the girls watched Lucien Harris come down the steps of the Phillips' four-story townhouse. He put on his bowler hat and stepped into his sleigh with confidence. Even from the distance between them, Julia could tell by his posture and bearing that the visit had gone favorably for him.

A chill ran up her spine. "There has to be a reason, other than me, for him to be there."

Sophia squeezed her hand. "Let me know what happens."

When Julia came in the door, she found their housekeeper, Mrs. Campbell, waiting for her.

"Miss Julia, your mother would like to have a word with you in your room. She'll be up as soon as she and your father have talked."

Julia's apprehension turned to dread. She studied Mrs. Campbell for any sign her fears were justified, but the stout, older woman's pleasant expression told her nothing. She stood, hands folded in front of her, waiting for Julia's response.

"All right. In the meantime, will you please send Millie up with tea?"

"Yes, certainly."

Julia settled in a rocking chair next to her window. Dwelling on the unknown never made her feel better. Instead she turned her thoughts to Mr. Anderson. By the time she became aware of her mother standing in the doorway, she'd convinced herself she had nothing to worry about. Lucien's departure and her mother wanting to talk to her were only a coincidence.

She turned to see Elizabeth Phillips gazing at her fondly. Her mother had fair hair, as did Julia and her sisters, and even though she no longer had a trim figure, and lines framed her blue eyes, she was still a striking woman.

"Have you been standing there long, Momma? I'm afraid I was lost in thought."

"Judging by your smile, it must have been a happy thought. Anything you'd like to share?"

Julia set her teacup aside. "I met someone today, someone who interests me."

"What's his name? Do we know his family?"

"His name is Jacob Anderson. I don't believe you know his family, though. They're somewhat new to Boston."

Momma frowned as she walked around the four-poster bed. She

sat in a walnut side chair opposite Julia and took her time arranging her skirts before speaking. "I have news from Papa."

Was Momma nervous? She couldn't remember a time when her mother didn't get right to the point. Now fear gripped her for a different reason. "Is Papa ill? Has there been a problem at the bank?

"No, it's nothing like that. I guess you could say there's no point in finding out about the young man you met today."

Icy fingers squeezed her heart. "What are you saying?"

"A nice young man, whom Papa feels has great promise, has asked for your hand. Your father agreed."

Julia gripped the arms of her chair. "Did I understand you to say Papa has accepted a marriage proposal on my behalf?"

"Yes."

"May I ask who this nice young man is?"

"It's Lucien Harris. You've been acquainted with him for these last five years. He's practically family. So, you see, it's not as if it's someone you hardly know."

Julia didn't try to hide her dismay, and her mother hurried on. "He spoke highly of you and said he felt sure you hold him in the same high regard."

"No." She hung her head and covered her face with her hands. "Please tell me you're not serious."

Momma gently pulled her hands away from her face. "I'm afraid I am serious. I know you haven't set your heart on any one man, and I don't need to remind you you're twenty-one years old. We were lenient when you turned down offers in the past, but the time has come for you to grow up. Lucien will provide a good home for you. His family name will assure you a place in society and you will want for nothing."

She could only give her mother a blank stare.

"He's not bad to look at."

Her chest tightened with frustration. "Lucien Harris is dull and predictable, and he doesn't care about me. He told me he thinks being an official part of the family would be good for his career, and he'd be able to provide the lifestyle I'm accustomed to."

Julia realized her volume was getting louder, but couldn't seem to stop it. She put her hand on her chest. "I told him I'm not interested. I can't believe he went to Papa anyway. I can't believe Papa agreed without asking me my feelings! Doesn't he care about my happiness? Do you care, Momma?"

"You know I do, but there comes a time when you have to move forward." Momma reached over and patted Julia's knee. "I'm sure you'll grow to care for him. Your sisters made advantageous marriages and they've settled in fine."

Julia gripped her mother's hand. "Momma, it's my heart's desire to marry a man I love, a man who's in love with me. I want to avoid the mistake my sisters made. You can't honestly tell me you think they're happy. Well, Katherine is, but Priscilla and Margaret are only putting on a show. To tell you the truth, I never felt you and Papa were all that happy. Didn't you ever wish you had married a man you loved?"

In an instant, Momma became the take-charge, no-nonsense woman Julia had grown up knowing. She pulled her hand away and stood.

"You're treading into an area that is none of your business. Your papa and I will do what we feel is right for you."

With a heavy heart, she watched Momma leave, then leaned her head against the chair and closed her eyes. Since her parents hadn't made a fuss when she turned down suitors in the past, she'd believed she would be able to choose her own husband in her own time. If a woman couldn't marry for love she shouldn't have to marry at all.

Would she have to leave home to avoid marrying him? What

could she do to earn a living?

She slumped in her chair and twisted her pearl ring around her right ring finger, while she considered her lack of options. She'd gone with Sophia's mother, Mrs. Howell, a couple of times to deliver food baskets to needy families.

The Sewing Circle she and the other debutantes formed at the end of their come-out season came to mind, but she didn't see how she could make a living doing that. The idea was to sew for the poor, but in reality, all they did was roll hems on handkerchiefs and gossip.

Unable to sit still, she stood and paced. Her shoes tapped out a rhythm on the hardwood floor as she walked past her bed and back to the area rug by her window.

Her piano teacher felt she played extraordinarily well, but her parents wouldn't hear of her performing for anyone other than family and friends.

She didn't know of any unmarried, self-supporting woman in her social class. To refuse such a good match would be unthinkable, not to mention ungrateful.

Would she dare join the fight for women's suffrage? That wouldn't provide an income, though.

Marriage seemed to be the only way open to her. Although she desired marriage and motherhood, she wanted it to be to the right man for the right reason.

Collapsing in her chair, she considered giving in to the wave of self-pity threatening to roll over her. It might not be too late, though. Julia straightened. This wasn't the dark ages after all. Surely Papa wouldn't force Lucien on her. If she had to marry maybe she could talk him into letting her marry the man of her choice.

Julia wasted no time going downstairs to the study. She knocked then pushed open the door. Papa stood at the window, hands clasped behind his back, shoulders slumped.

She entered the book-lined room, wrinkled her nose at the scent of cigar smoke, then paused. Should she go to her father or wait until he acknowledged her?

John Phillips was a tall man aging gracefully. Silver threaded his brown hair, but he maintained the vigor and confidence of a young man firmly in control of his life and family. She admired her father greatly.

"Papa, may I speak with you?"

He straightened and turned to face her. "Julia, I didn't hear you come in." He went to his polished oak desk and lowered himself into the chair behind it, indicating she should also take a seat.

Julia sat across from him. He looked sad or tired, or both. Maybe now wasn't a good time to ask him about Lucien.

He took the decision out of her hands when he rested his forearms on the desk and leaned toward her. "Momma tells me you aren't happy with the news, but sometimes parents must make a decision for their child that they feel is best, even if it's not a popular one. Lucien has assured me he cares for you and will make you a good husband. You've known each other for the last several years, and you seem to enjoy his company.

"Because of his connection to my great uncle, we know he comes from a good family. He quickly became an asset to the bank, and I feel he has a bright future. I'm sure you'll get along fine. Lucien will be here tonight after dinner to talk to you himself."

Having delivered his speech, her father leaned back in his chair, as though that settled the matter.

Julia concentrated on making her voice steady. "Did Lucien tell you he had already talked to me about marriage, and I told him no?"

Papa's eyebrows rose. "He didn't mention that. But what could you possibly hold against him? He has all the qualities a father could ask for when thinking of his daughter's future."

She moved to the edge of her seat. "What about love? Shouldn't that be a desirable quality?"

"You've spent too much time reading romances." Papa began shuffling papers around his desk. "Your momma and I have gotten along fine without all that nonsense. The matter is settled. Momma will see to getting out the announcement."

Obviously, he'd made up his mind. She'd been sentenced, but if a pardon was out of the question, maybe she could get a delay.

"Does the announcement have to be made right away?" He frowned and Julia hurried on. "If we wait until summer, we could have a garden party at our country house. That's only four months from now. Surely another four months won't make a difference."

"All right, as long as it's agreeable with Lucien. However, from now on, you should limit yourself more to his company. Do we have an understanding?"

"Yes, Papa."

She left the room grateful for a small reprieve. There was something special about Jacob Anderson, and she meant to find out what before time ran out.

John got up and closed the door behind his daughter, then went back to his desk and rested his forehead on his folded hands on the desktop. The past had indeed caught up in the form of Lucien Harris. John had welcomed the young man into the bank and their family only for him to reveal, today, his relationship to the event of twenty-five years ago. It was blackmail, pure and simple. Make sure Julia became his wife or he'd tell the world what happened.

Sitting up, John scrubbed his hands over his face. Lucien wouldn't stop with the marriage. He wanted something else. John would have to find out what before it was too late.

4

There had never been an afternoon and dinner as long as this. Julia pushed food around her plate, while thinking about what might be her most convincing argument. She couldn't wait to confront Lucien. Maybe he would respond to common sense.

"Julia."

She turned to see her mother studying her. "I know you're not happy with the decision made today, but you've hardly eaten a thing."

"You know I have no appetite when I'm upset Momma. Did you think tonight would be different?"

Papa harrumphed. "That's no way to speak to your mother. I expect better behavior from you. Sulking and petulance won't change anything and will only make you miserable."

She looked from one parent to the other. "I apologize for being rude, but the idea of marriage to Lucien can't make me anything but miserable."

Papa shook his head. "I'd say it's more likely the idea of *marriage* that has you worried. You have a habit of turning everything into a drama."

He tossed his napkin beside his plate and took a breath, but before

17

he could start on a familiar lecture, Julia spoke up, "But, Papa, this could be a mistake."

From the corner of her eye, she saw Momma nod.

Papa looked at Momma in surprise. "Should we go over again, all the reasons why the time has come for Julia to be settled?" Seeming to have forgotten her existence, Papa started the list, ticking each point off on his fingers. "She doesn't know her mind when it comes to men. She could go on having a good time with different young men until she's too old for anyone to notice her. How many proposals has she turned down?"

"Only three."

"Three perfectly good prospects." Papa leaned toward Momma. "You don't want her to be an old maid, do you?"

"Of course not, but it shouldn't sound like a business arrangement either."

"Would you like it to sound like a scandal?"

He got up and paced from the table to the doorway and back. "It's not just a matter of her being settled in marriage. I wouldn't be entirely surprised to wake up one morning and find she had gone off to Europe with Edward for the fun of it."

Julia drew in a quick breath. She couldn't believe Papa had suggested such an exciting idea. His annoying habit of talking about her as if she wasn't there might work to her advantage.

Momma's face flushed. "Surely not. My nephew has more sense than that."

"I wouldn't count on it," Papa fired back. "They're too much alike. It comes from your side of the family, you know. Your brother was just as bad at that age." He stopped pacing and looked at Momma, as if she were at fault for her brother's supposed youthful shortcomings.

She waved her hand in dismissal. "Blaming one side of the family or the other serves no purpose. However, if you think she might do something so foolhardy, then by all means, she must be married. It shouldn't be a problem to wait until this summer to make the announcement, though."

At that moment, the Phillips' butler stepped into the room and announced Lucien's arrival. Julia smiled when her parents looked first at each other and then at her.

Julia turned to the butler. "Please take him to the drawing room, Sanders."

When Sanders left, silence filled the room. She looked at Papa.

He cleared his throat. "I suppose you may understand more clearly now why we feel this marriage should take place. It is an excellent offer and we expect you to tell Lucien you accept his proposal."

Her smile slid away. When she stood, her mother rose as well and started to follow.

Quickly, Papa met them at the door and offered his arm to his wife. "I think we can find someplace else to be."

Momma hesitated, then allowed Papa to lead her to his study. Julia watched them leave with satisfaction. Without her parents in the room she'd be able to speak plainly.

⁓⁓⁓

Lucien prowled the drawing room like a wild animal pacing the perimeter of its cage. Lost in thought, he passed paintings and family photographs, while skirting the many chairs, footstools, tables and curio cabinets that filled the room.

He caught a glimpse of himself when he passed the mirror over the fireplace, came back and peered at his reflection. What did Julia see when she looked at him? A young man of average height with brown hair, brown eyes and features that were all of normal proportion stared back at him. Nothing about his looks should have put her off. Why had she turned him down?

He resumed his trek while contemplating the mystery. She had to see the business advantage. He would be the son her father could pass everything on to. Then he would be in control of all the money. He almost rubbed his hands together like a villain in a melodrama.

Abruptly, he stopped. He had no need to be nervous about seeing her or even worried about what Julia thought? Moving forward again, he had to admit it would make everything easier if she'd be agreeable. He could play the part of patient suitor. The less she knew about the truth of their engagement, the smoother things would progress. Her spirited disposition could be dealt with after their marriage.

Julia entered the drawing room, fully expecting to see Lucien sitting on a sofa wearing a smug smile. When she stepped across the threshold, he ran into her with enough force to cause her to stumble. "Oh my!" He quickly put his arms around her until she was steady, then let go and stepped back.

"Are you all right? Let me help you to a seat." He took her hand, but she pulled it away.

"I'm fine." She sat on a blue velvet sofa, wondering if something was wrong with him.

Lucien followed and sat next to her. He must have felt it would be to his advantage to speak first, because he jumped in with his explanation before she could open her mouth.

"I can see you're upset that I spoke to your father, but I truly believe when you give yourself time to think about it, you'll understand I acted in our best interest. We get along well and it seemed only a matter of time before you said yes."

The man's arrogance was just one of the reasons she didn't want to marry him. "Let me get right to the point. I don't love you, Lucien. Do you love me?"

His Adam's apple bobbed as he swallowed hard. "Well, I'm fond of you and I think you care for me. I'm sure we have what we need to start out."

"I'm sure being fond of each other is *not* enough." She gestured toward him. "You're a nice person, but I don't want to marry you. I won't make you happy. Do you want to be miserable all your life?"

Lucien shook his head and smiled. "How could you make me miserable when we have so much in common? We have the same circle of friends and I'm treated like one of the family. You just need time to get used to the idea. We don't have to announce our engagement right away."

She rose and crossed the room to a window. Snow glittered in the gaslight of the street lamps. The park, at the center of Louisburg Square, appeared quiet and peaceful. The complete opposite of the frustration boiling inside her. Lucien's horse and sleigh stood in front of their townhouse, waiting to take him home. She wished with all her heart he was already in it and on his way. How much longer could she remain polite?

He came to stand beside her. She glanced at him then back outside. "I met someone today. Someone I'd like to know better."

"If he's a Harvard man I can probably tell you about him."

Julia twisted her ring around her finger. What should she say? Neither Lucien nor her parents would approve of Mr. Anderson. It would probably be best to keep his name to herself for now, and move on to the more important issue at hand.

Lucien may not have released her from the agreement, but at least he had suggested waiting on the announcement of his own accord.

With a little sigh, she turned to him. "His family is new to Boston, so I doubt you would know him. However, I don't think marrying me is a good idea when I'm thinking of someone else. I appreciate you being willing to keep the engagement quiet for now. Perhaps some time for both of us to think it over would be best."

"I've already done my thinking. I know you'll come to see I'm right about this."

Julia linked her arm through his and began moving toward the door. "Time will tell. Now, I'd like to say goodnight as I feel a headache coming on."

Lucien stopped and turned to face her, concern evident in his eyes. "I hate to think I might be the cause of your discomfort, but I've observed it puts a strain on a woman when she's unsure of what she wants. The sooner you decide to announce our engagement, the sooner you'll feel better. Good night."

Julia clenched her fists to keep from grabbing one of the decorative pillows from a nearby chair and hurling it at the back of his head. As soon as the door closed behind him, she drew in a deep breath and rubbed her temples. He wasn't going to make this easy.

The next morning, Julia awoke with a smile and leisurely stretched her arms over her head. A young man with golden hair, blue eyes and dimples filled her mind. In her heart she knew meeting Jacob Anderson would turn out to be a life-changing experience, and she tingled in anticipation of where it would lead.

Millie came into the room with a bouquet of flowers from Lucien, and the rest of yesterday's events came crashing in on her. When Millie opened the curtains, Julia sat up with a sigh. She had to figure out a way to see Mr. Anderson again, but another trip to the jewelry store this soon wouldn't be proper. She'd talk it over with Sophia later this morning.

After breakfast, Julia went next door to Sophia's townhouse. As she and Sophia settled in the drawing room she asked, "Where is everyone?"

"Mamma's organizing a charity event, and Papa and James are at the law office."

Sophia set her teacup on the little marble topped table between their armchairs. "Tell me everything. I haven't seen you this upset in a long time."

"First of all, you were right about Lucien not giving up. While we were shopping, he asked Papa for my hand." Julia didn't bother to keep the disgust out of her voice. "Papa said yes. He and Momma feel this is the best thing for me. I tried talking to Papa, but all I could do was prevent any kind of announcement until June."

Sophia regarded her with wide eyes. "I can't believe he accepted without talking to you first. Aren't we beyond that sort of thing?"

Julia pointed her teaspoon at her friend for emphasis. "Twenty-one is older than we thought. It appears we're both in danger of becoming old maids."

"Have you talked to Lucien? Can you make him understand your feelings?"

"I saw him after dinner and told him how I felt. I don't see how he could possibly misunderstand the fact that I don't want to marry him. But there he sat, telling me what a good idea it is and he knew I'd realize it if I'd think about it."

"So, he won't release you from the agreement?"

"He told me he would give me more time to think about it, and in the meantime, he wouldn't say anything." Julia drooped in her chair. "I think that's the best I'm going to get."

"He sounds determined. If someone wanted me that much, I'd say yes."

"That's it!" Julia straightened and scooted to the edge of her seat. "Why didn't I think of it before?"

"What?"

"You and Lucien. You'd be perfect together." Sophia's mouth

dropped open and she began to shake her head. Julia hurried on, "No, hear me out."

Sophia held up her hand. "Lucien isn't interested in me, remember? You can't just transfer his affection from you to me."

"But you two are so much alike. You're both practical and logical and you're much quieter than I am. I know I make him nervous sometimes."

Julia paused and Sophia's silence encouraged her to go on. "You've told me you think he would make a fine husband. You must have some regard for him."

"I said that because I wanted to encourage you to be sensible. But it's true. I do think he has all the qualities needed."

"If I could get him to think of you, would you be interested?"

"Maybe. You obviously don't want him and he would make a better candidate than the other young men I see."

"All right." Julia relaxed back in her chair. "We'll see what we can do. If Lucien changes his mind, Papa can't be upset with me.

Julia refilled her cup. "Now there's something else I want to talk to you about."

"Does it involve Mr. Anderson?"

"Yes. I need to figure out a way to see him again." Julia tapped her spoon on the table as she ran possibilities through her mind.

"You know your parents won't approve." Sophia reached over and took the spoon from Julia. "You'll be wasting your time and possibly getting his hopes up."

"Are you saying you won't help me?"

"I don't want to help you get in trouble." Using her familiar let's-be-sensible tone, Sophia listed her reasons. "What if you get to know him and become attached? You won't be allowed to marry him and you'll probably decide to do it anyway. He won't be able to provide you with the lifestyle you're used to.

"Do you think you could continue to socialize? Most of the families of our acquaintance won't accept your marriage. Your own parents may ostracize you. You would be isolated. I don't think it would be worth it."

"You certainly paint a grim picture, but you're forgetting money isn't important to me."

"What about family and friends?"

Julia's chest tightened. "They're important, but I don't think I can sacrifice my happiness to please them. Are you saying you won't be my friend if I marry him?"

"Of course, I'll be your friend. I would love you even if you married the coal deliveryman. It's just that sometimes you do things without thinking them through." Sophia reached over and squeezed her hand. "I don't want you to end up having regrets."

Sophia's affirmation warmed her. "I appreciate your concern, but give me credit for a little common sense. If I find we have nothing in common I'll drop the idea. Will that make you happy?"

Sophia laughed and held her hands up in surrender. "I give up. I hope neither of us will be sorry."

5

Julia sat at her dressing table while Millie arranged her hair for Papa's birthday dinner. She twisted her ring while thinking about her sisters. What kind of assistance might they give?

Margaret would probably help her. She'd married Steven because it was expected, not because she loved him. Julia went to Anderson's jewelers because Margaret recommended it. If not for that, she wouldn't have met Mr. Anderson. Some of the jittery tension left and she smiled. She could probably count on Margaret.

"That's the first time I've seen you smile today, Miss Julia. You must have had a happy thought."

Julia met Millie's eyes in the mirror. "I did, but it's more of a dream right now. We'll see what comes of it."

Millie secured a crown of curls with tortoise shell combs then moved on to the long ringlets that would cascade down the back of her head.

Briefly, Julia considered Priscilla. She married because their parents convinced her it was financially advantageous to all concerned. Family and finance were the most important consideration according to Momma. If you were lucky, a mutually agreeable relationship followed.

Then there was Katherine. Her oldest sister had the good fortune to fall in love with the right man. The only dark cloud for them had been Katherine's difficult pregnancy and delivery. Grandmother had died giving birth to Momma and Momma's sister had not survived her second child. At least Priscilla and Margaret hadn't had any problems.

Anyway, since Katherine had a happy marriage, she might be willing to help.

Julia sat on a blue damask side chair not far from the drawing room entrance. She kept reminding herself not to fidget while watching for Margaret to come in. Finally, she and her husband, Steven, arrived. After they had a chance to wish Papa a happy birthday, Julia took Margaret off to one side. "Come up to my room after dinner. I have to talk to you in private as soon as possible."

She turned away, but Margaret grabbed her arm. "Wait a minute. You're not going to let me go all through dinner with this mystery on my mind. Give me some idea what it's about."

Julia glanced around to make sure no one could overhear. "I went to the jeweler you recommended and I need to talk to you about someone I met."

Margaret put her hand over her heart. "I thought something terrible had happened. You can be so dramatic."

Julia's eyes narrowed at the mix of amusement and relief in her sister's voice. "I'm not trying to be dramatic. It's important and I need your help."

"All right. I'll be happy to do what I can."

Priscilla and Frank entered the room and spoke to Papa. Then Priscilla made a beeline to Julia as Margaret left her side. "What were you two whispering about?"

"Nothing, Priscilla. Don't worry." Julia attempted to move away but Priscilla blocked her path.

"I worry when it looks as though you're trying to plot something. If it has to do with Lucien, I think you should give it up. Be sensible and marry him. It's a good match."

Julia frowned and leaned close to her sister's ear. "Who told you about it?"

"Momma, of course. She's concerned about you, and asked me to help you see that marrying Lucien is the right thing to do." Priscilla put a hand on Julia's arm, apparently ready to keep her there until convinced.

Julia shook her head slightly. "Momma asked the wrong person. I don't see how you could convince me you made the right choice."

She regretted her words when she saw the stricken look on her sister's face. "I'm sorry, I shouldn't have said that. Please forgive me."

Priscilla's head and shoulders drooped for a moment, then she straightened and met Julia's eyes. "I didn't think it was obvious. But even if Frank and I weren't a love match, I still believe it was the right choice."

"I'm sure it's not obvious to everyone. I see it because I'm your sister."

Pricilla let her hand drop from Julia's arm. "Well, there's more to marriage than momentary heart flutters and emotional displays. Frank is a good husband, in most ways, and a good father. Future children are an important consideration when making your decision. My children are well provided for and will have every advantage. Try to think about something more permanent than emotions."

"I will, Priscilla. I appreciate your concern." Sophia's family came into the room, which gave her the perfect excuse to leave her sister's side.

When Julia reached her friend, Sophia raised her eyebrows in a silent question, but an explanation would have to wait as Lucien joined them.

"Julia, you look well. I hope your headache is gone."

She gave him a polite smile. "I'm feeling better tonight, thank you."

Lucien turned to Sophia. "It's nice to see you. How is your brother getting along at the law office?"

"I think he likes it, although, he still talks more about Europe than his work."

"I can understand that. I quite enjoyed Europe myself. But, there's nothing like getting involved in your life's work here at home."

"It sounds as if you enjoy banking."

"I do, and I enjoy living in Boston. It will always be home for me. Don't you agree, Julia?"

She looked at him for a beat. Did he just tell her what to think? "I'd like to see Europe. Boston is a fine city, but it's not the only place in the world. I wouldn't mind a change, and I don't mean from one townhouse to another. Sophia, on the other hand, would be happy to stay here the rest of her life. Am I right, Sophia?"

"Yes, it's true. I'm quite content with Boston. The city has so much to offer. I always miss it when we go to our country house."

Lucien looked at Sophia as though seeing her for the first time. Interesting. Why hadn't she thought of putting them together before? Maybe she could rearrange the table seating.

She excused herself to speak to the butler, as Katherine come in on Alexander's arm. Julia could tell by her oldest sister's strained smile that something was wrong. She hurried over as Alexander helped her to a sofa, his face lined with worry.

"Katherine, Alexander, it's good to see you." Julia sat next to her sister. "I wondered if you were coming."

"I know we're late. I already apologized to Momma."

Alexander sat on Katherine's other side. "It couldn't be helped. Your mother will understand once you have a chance to talk to her."

"Is there a problem with Alex? He's not ill, is he?" Julia hated to think her nephew might be sick.

"No, he's fine. I'm the one not feeling well. It looks as though we'll be blessed with another baby."

Julia swallowed down a groan. Katherine clearly had mixed feelings and Alexander didn't look happy.

"Maybe it'll be better this time. You've mentioned you believe God cares about us. He'll be with you again, don't you think? And it might be a girl."

"I'd like to have a girl. Thank you for reminding me I should pray instead of worry."

When Sanders stepped into the room to announce dinner, Julia remembered her earlier mission to change seats with Sophia. Too late now, but she'd do her best to throw them together after dinner.

Julia found herself seated between Lucien and Sophia's brother, James. Sophia sat across the table beside her cousin, Edward Harrington, and his younger sister, Lily.

Before Lucien could say anything, Julia turned to James. "Tell me more about France. It sounds so picturesque."

"It's lovely. You'd like it, Julia. With your command of the language, you'd get on quite well there. I'd be happy to take you if you've had a change of heart."

Julia heard a strange choking sound coming from her right. She turned to see Lucien's red face.

"Lucien, are you all right?"

He regained control and nodded. "I'm sorry, the soup started down the wrong way. Nothing to worry about."

"Will you ladies be up for sleighing tomorrow?" Edward asked. "The snow is still perfect for it."

Julia clapped her hands. "I definitely will. How about you, Sophia?"

"You know you can count on me. I wouldn't want to miss whatever you and Edward cook up."

Edward's blue-gray eyes widened. "I don't know what you're talking about. We're always perfectly civilized."

Choking and sputtering sounds came from Julia's right again. "Maybe you better leave that," she whispered.

"How about you, Lily?" James asked.

With a grin, Lily said, "My brother wouldn't dare leave without me. Lucien, can you join us?"

"I wouldn't miss it."

Edward rapped the table with his knuckles. "Good, we'll meet after my morning classes."

Julia gazed at Edward with affection. His easy smile and thirst for fun made him one of her favorite people. And, it didn't hurt that he wasn't the least bit interested in settling down.

Dinner went on, course after course, until they finally got to Papa's favorite dessert, pineapple upside down cake. When they finished, Momma stood and all the ladies rose to follow her to the drawing room, leaving the men to their talk about business and politics.

Julia signaled Margaret to follow her. Once inside the bedroom, Julia closed the door and leaned against it with a sigh. "Dinner went on forever."

"It did seem longer than usual. Now, tell me who this mystery man is. Why does it have to be a secret?"

Julia perched on the edge of her bed and pulled Margaret down next to her. "When you were in Anderson's did you happen to see an incredibly handsome man?"

Her sister's eyes twinkled. "Was he young and tall and did he have blue eyes and blond hair?"

"You left out adorable dimples when he smiles." Julia held her folded hands against her chest. "I've never seen anyone so perfect. You have to help me see him again."

Margaret looked at her as if she had lost her senses. "He might be nice to look at, but he's not in our set. You know Momma and Papa would never approve."

"That's why it's a secret. Did you know Papa accepted a marriage offer from Lucien on my behalf?"

"No, I hadn't heard. But if that's true, why are you trying to see this other man?"

"I don't want to marry Lucien. I've told him how I feel, but he thinks I'll change my mind."

Margaret reached over and gripped her hand. "I'm sorry, Julia. I know what it's like to be obligated into a marriage, but you can't seriously think this man at the jewelry store might be available to you."

"His name is Jacob Anderson. I know Momma and Papa won't consider him eligible, but when I looked into his eyes, my heart told me he's the one I've waited for. Money and family name shouldn't take precedence over that."

Her sister sighed. "I'm sure I could be happy with less money if I'd found my true love. What do you think I can do to help?"

"I won't be able to meet him alone, so if you and I could have outings together where we happen to run into him…"

"I see what you're saying. Where do you plan to run into him? By the way, is he aware of your desire to see him again? What if he isn't interested?"

Julia went to her dressing table and pulled a piece of paper from a drawer. "When the gift I got for Papa arrived, this note came with it. He says he was happy to meet me and hoped I'd have a reason to come to their store again soon."

"I'd say he's interested." Margaret read the note again then tapped it against the palm of her hand as she thought.

"Next week we'll go to the store to shop for earrings. You could mention you'll be at the Wednesday night lecture. If he's smart, he'll get your meaning."

Julia threw her arms around her sister. "I knew I could count on you."

6

When Julia and Margaret joined the ladies in the drawing room, Momma met them with a frown and spoke in a whisper. "I hope there's a good reason for your delay in returning." In a louder voice she said, "Julia, will you play for us? I think the men will be here soon."

Julia took a seat at the piano and played *Moonlight Waltz*. When the men entered, Lucien came to stand beside the piano. As soon as she finished, he asked, "Will you play *Für Elise*?"

She smiled as her hands glided over the keys. This was a favorite. Others gave requests, which she played while trying to locate Priscilla. Ah, over by Edward and Lily. At the end of the current song, she signaled her sister to take over. When she stood, Lucien took her arm and escorted her to a rosewood love seat.

"Have you been thinking about us?"

"Lucien, it could take me months to make a decision. There's no hurry, is there?"

"I suppose not." After a short pause he asked, "How about some tea?"

"I'd like some, thank you."

He filled a teacup from the serving trolley and handed it to Julia.

"Are you planning to go to the Mark Twain lecture Wednesday?"

"Yes, I'm looking forward to it." Julia took a sip and studied Lucien over the edge of her cup. Why did his eyes keep shifting from her to James?

"I suppose you'll be going with your family."

"I'm going with Margaret." She set her cup aside. "Lucien, is something bothering you?"

"As a matter of fact, I'm wondering why you didn't tell me about James Howell."

"What would you like to know?"

Lucien huffed. "I didn't know he had proposed marriage. As your future husband, it seems like something I should know. Why did you turn him down?"

Julia clenched her teeth and counted to ten. "I don't think I need to tell you about other proposals I've had, or my reasons for turning them down."

His eyebrows shot to his hairline. "Other proposals? How many have there been?"

"You're drawing attention. We should talk about this another time." Before he could answer, she stood and made her way to Sophia's side.

Sophia glanced at Lucien. "Is he upset? He's frowning."

"Maybe it would help if you went over and distracted him. Talk about the lecture coming up Wednesday. You're planning to go, aren't you?"

"I assumed we'd go together."

"I think I'll go to this one with Margaret. I'm sure I'll see you there."

"You've told her about Mr. Anderson, haven't you?"

Julia gave her friend a conspiratorial smile. "Margaret's going to help, too."

"Maybe she'll be another voice of reason." Her friend sighed. "At least you're not doing this on your own."

"I do have common sense, remember? Now, go talk to him." Julia gave Sophia a tiny push his direction.

❧

Sophia couldn't help feeling bad for Lucien as she approached him. He had no idea what he'd gotten himself into with Julia. He rose when she stopped in front of him. "You look distressed. I'm a good seem listener. Maybe I can help."

His frown changed to a mixture of hope and doubt. "If anyone can help, it would probably be you. Would you care to sit?"

When they were seated, Sophia looked into Lucien's troubled eyes. She realized in that moment how much she wanted Julia's idea to work. "Tell me what's bothering you."

"I don't understand Julia. I've believed from the time I met her we would be married someday and I thought she felt the same. It makes such practical sense."

"Julia doesn't think that way. Surely you've seen that."

"Well yes, I have, but by now she should be ready to settle down." Lucien shook his head. "Imagine my surprise to find she's had other proposals, including one from your brother."

"Why does that surprise you? She's good company and happens to be attractive. Or haven't you noticed?"

"Of course, I have, but I'm afraid I've done too much assuming."

Lucien leaned his elbows on his knees and stared at the blue and gold patterned carpet. "Apparently my focus has been a little narrow. I've had my life mapped out and have been staying the course for a long time now. According to my schedule, it's time to settle down. I expected Julia to be ready to marry because I am. Obviously, she needs more time. I'll have to be patient, but everyone has their limits."

He straightened and smiled at her with satisfaction. "Thank you for listening. It does help to clarify one's thinking."

"You're welcome. May I make a suggestion?"

"Of course."

"While you're being patient, maybe you should spend time with someone else. If she's not seeing as much of you, she may miss you." Sophia leaned in. "It might speed up her thinking time."

"If you think that'll work, I'll try it."

"Good. By the way, are you planning to go to Mark Twain's lecture Wednesday?"

"Yes, I enjoy hearing him."

"I do too. In fact, I enjoy going to all the lectures. Maybe I'll see you there."

"I'll be sure to look for you."

Sophia glanced toward the door. "It looks like my family is ready to leave. I enjoyed talking to you."

❦

Lucien watched her walk away. If Julia wasn't his ticket to revenge against her father, he'd be interested in Sophia. He might as well enjoy her company until he married Julia.

❦

Julia went slowly down the stairs to the front door with Sophia. "You two looked cozy. And when you stood to leave, his eyes followed you all the way to the door."

Sophia smiled and linked arms with her. "I think you'll find Lucien to be more patient. And I'll have to admit he came to that decision by himself."

"Will you keep him company while he's being patient?"

"I believe I may."

"This couldn't have worked out better. If Lucien's not completely hopeless, he'll see how wonderful you are and forget about me." Julia gave her friend a hug. "I'll see you tomorrow"

At lunch the next day, Momma said, "Edward and Lily mentioned you plan to go sleighing this afternoon. I assume Lucien will be included."

"He said he'd be there."

"You will remember to spend most of your time with him, won't you?" Papa reminded.

Julia focused on Papa. "Lucien has agreed it would be a good idea to wait a while before saying anything. You're still in agreement with that, aren't you, Papa?"

"As long as Lucien is willing, I won't say anything."

She released the breath she'd been holding. "Thank you. Will you and Momma excuse me? James and Sophia will be coming by for me soon, and I need to get ready."

Julia left the dining room, but heard her name and stopped outside the door to listen.

Momma spoke first. "What do you think the chances are that Julia won't fight us down to the last minute about marrying Lucien?"

"You know her as well as I do. She'll fight, but we have to be firm. She doesn't see the future as we do. Someday she'll understand."

She headed to her bedroom more determined than ever. She would win this fight.

Julia sent a silent thank you to the farmers in the area who allowed them to use their empty fields. The blue sky and sunshine made it a perfect day for a sleigh ride. There were only wisps of white clouds here and there. The frosty air made her nose cold, but Julia stayed warm and cozy under the furs in the sleigh with Sophia and James.

She called over the jingling sleigh bells, "Go faster, James. Edward and Lily are going to catch up."

With a laugh and a wave, Edward and Lily's sleigh flashed by, and James slowed their horse. "Well, we were in the lead for a while. Edward's Morgan is impossible to beat."

Edward came to a stop at the designated finish line and waited for everyone else to join Lily and him. James pulled up next to them and Julia couldn't help grinning at Edward's big smile. He put his whole heart into everything he did, including having fun. She admired that about him. Lucien pulled up next, and several others joined them.

"How about a slower ride to give the horses a rest?" Lucien suggested.

Sophia laid her hand on her chest. "That's a good idea. It'll give my heart a rest too. I need to recover from the excitement."

"How about switching partners for a while?" Edward looked at Julia. "You're not tired of excitement, are you?"

Julia longed to jump in the sleigh with Edward, but her father's instructions regarding Lucien made her hesitate. Thankfully, Lucien solved the dilemma. "Would you care to ride with me, Sophia?"

"I'd be happy to." Julia and Sophia briefly squeezed hands, silently congratulating each other. James asked Lily to ride with him, allowing Julia to settle in Edward's sleigh guilt free.

When all were ready, they set off again. While the other couples started off on a more sedate ride along the tree-lined country roads, Edward set a quick pace for another run across the field.

The crisp wind rushed by as the horse sped up. The fluttery feeling in Julia's stomach made her want to giggle. Edward steered the sleigh close to a snow bank and she cried, "Look out!" Icy snow crystals showered over their heads, making her laugh.

Edward laughed with her as he slowed the horse to a trot. "We probably should give her a rest, and it'll give me a chance to ask you something."

7

Edward turned his horse to make the journey back across the snow-covered field, while Julia shifted toward him, giving him her full attention. If his question required them to be separated from their friends, it must be something daring.

"Last night I overheard you tell Lucien and Sophia you'd like to see Europe. You've mentioned it to me too, but I never thought you were serious before now. What I'm trying to say is, why don't you come with me? We'd have a grand time." He reined in the horse, turned to face her and grinned. "What do you think?"

She drew in a quick breath and stared at him. His eyes shone with the promise of adventure, but nothing more serious than that. She relaxed and returned his grin. "Why, Edward, did you just propose?"

HIs grin disappeared and he stammered, "Oh, well, did I? That is, I didn't mean to."

Julia laughed. "Don't worry. I'm teasing." She playfully swatted his arm at his look of relief. "Surely marrying me wouldn't be that bad."

"It wouldn't be if I wanted to get married. You don't know how much you scared me." He laid the back of his hand against his forehead and fell back against the seat for a moment. "It's sweet of

40

you to ask me. I told Sophia the other day it would be fun to go with you."

"Then why not do it? You're not committed to anything here, are you?"

Her hands curled into fists and she closed her eyes a moment before answering. "I am in a way. I'll tell you if you promise to keep it quiet."

"You know you can trust me."

"Papa accepted a marriage proposal from Lucien, on my behalf."

His eyes widened. "Oh no, you two should never be together. What was your father thinking?"

"He's thinking it'll be the best way to make my future secure." She heaved a sigh. "At least they've agreed to give me more time to think about it."

"You can't do it. Lucien is nice in his stiff logical way, but there's something about him that makes me uneasy. It's as though everything he does is part of an agenda."

"You should tell Papa."

"It's nothing I can prove." Edward took both her hands in his. "This is even more reason for you to go with me. You can't marry him if you're in Europe."

Julia looked at him and wondered how her father could have known he might suggest this. The idea of taking off for Europe gave her the same fluttery feeling she had when the sleigh sped through the snow. It would be fun. It would be exciting. But it wouldn't be fair to Edward. "How could I go with you if we're not married?"

"We'll say we're brother and sister. We look similar enough. Just think of the fun we'd have."

"How happy do you think our families would be if we did that? It would be a scandal and you'd be stuck marrying me."

Dropping her hands, he took off his hat and raked gloved fingers through his sandy- blond waves. "Since when did you get so practical?"

"I think Sophia is starting to influence me." Julia smoothed Edward's hair back in place and he put his hat on. "I love that you asked me, though. I'll admit the idea is tempting, but there's something else I want to tell you. I met someone. He's not in our social set, so it'll be a challenge, but Margaret's going to help me."

"Ha. Being practical didn't last long. How is this any less scandalous than going with me?"

"I didn't say I had it all worked out." Julia held his gaze, willing him to understand.

"I want to meet him. If I approve, I'll help too. If it doesn't work out you can come with me. You'd be in trouble anyway."

"Thank you, Edward." Julia threw her arms around his neck and kissed him on the cheek. "You're a good friend."

He returned her hug. "I want you to be happy. Now why don't you tell me about this mystery man while we find the rest of the group?"

∽◦❦◦∼

Julia crossed and uncrossed her ankles and twisted her ring. Did the Sunday morning service always take this long? This day needed to hurry on so she could see Margaret. Thank goodness family gatherings on Sunday evenings were an unbreakable tradition.

At the end of the service, her family left their box pew and joined the other worshipers making their way toward the back of the church. Suddenly, Julia's heart did a quickstep. Had she seen Mr. Anderson?

The people in front of them inched their way down the aisle to the door. When she finally stepped through, Julia scanned the area and spotted him at the bottom of the steps. Mr. Anderson's face lit up in a smile when their eyes met. It warmed her to her toes making her even more certain she wanted to know this man.

When Julia reached him, he took off his hat. "Good morning, Miss Phillips. It's nice to see you again."

Her huge smile wasn't exactly lady like, but she didn't care. "Mr. Anderson. Have you decided to worship here?"

He looked at the building then at her. "Do you come here every Sunday?"

"Yes, I do."

"Then I believe I will, too."

"Wonderful." Excitement stirred as she realized that meant she could count on seeing him at least one day a week. Julia glanced around to see if her parents were watching for her, but they were talking to Papa's brother, Uncle George. "How long have you been in Boston? I don't think I've seen you other than the day we met at your store."

"I've been here a few weeks, but haven't gone out much. Can you recommend something interesting to do?"

Julia smiled at the opportunity he'd given her. "There are lots of things to do, but one I especially like is the lecture series. The next one is Wednesday evening at seven. I'll be going with my sister."

"Do you think I might see you if I attend?"

She'd make sure of it. "I'll watch for you." Julia noticed her mother approaching. "I have to go. I'll see you Wednesday." She quickly headed in the opposite direction.

Jacob watched her go, already looking forward to Wednesday night. Lucky for him his aunt had an interest in upper class activities. He'd have to thank her for pointing him in the right direction this morning.

He took a deep breath of cold air and looked up at the gray sky. Funny. He could have sworn the sun had come out. Maybe being near Miss Phillips had been enough to warm him. Jacob shook his head. He already sounded like a romantic. Smiling, he headed home with a light step.

Momma caught up with her. "Where are you going? The sleigh is over there."

Julia turned to look. "Oh, I forgot."

"It's too cold to spend time outdoors, and it looks like it could snow again. Let's get your father and go home."

Once settled in their four-passenger sleigh, Papa asked, "Who was the young man I saw you talking to after church?"

Julia sighed inwardly. It was too much to hope no one had noticed. "His name is Jacob Anderson. He arrived in Boston a few weeks ago."

Momma waved to an acquaintance in a passing sleigh then turned to her. "How did you meet? Did Lucien introduce you?"

"Do you remember me saying I met someone while shopping with Sophia?"

"Vaguely."

"Well, that's who it was. He asked about things to do in Boston, so I told him about the lectures. I think he's interested."

Papa gave her a nod of approval. "That's fine, dear. If you see him there, be sure to introduce him to Lucien and your other friends."

Julia relaxed. Maybe God did care and wanted this to work out.

Momma's brother, Robert Harrington, lived in a townhouse nearby on Mt. Vernon, and the family planned to gather there tonight. When they arrived, Julia saw Uncle Robert's oldest son and his family had already arrived, as well as Priscilla and Margaret and their families. She'd been disappointed when they received a message from Alexander earlier saying Katherine didn't feel well enough to leave home.

Julia walked by the drawing room where she saw Edward on his hands and knees, giving horseback rides to the little ones.

He wasn't the object of her search, though. She finally found Margaret changing her daughter's diaper in the old nursery on the fourth floor. "Guess who I saw at church this morning?"

Margaret glanced at her with a smile. "Lucien?"

"No silly, Mr. Anderson! I even got to talk to him."

"I thought I might have seen him, but you know Steven. We always have to hurry home right after service."

Margaret straightened her daughter's clothes. Eighteen-month-old Elise wanted to get down and play, so Margaret set her on her feet and they watched her toddle to the toy shelf and pull off a stuffed bunny. She tucked it under her arm and continued to peruse the selection. Without taking her eyes from Elise, Margaret asked, "Did you tell him about the lecture?"

"Yes." She clasped her hands and smiled, remembering how easy he'd made it. "He asked if I could recommend anything to do, so I didn't even feel forward suggesting it. Then, he wanted to know if he would see me there." Julia released a happy sigh. "Isn't it wonderful?"

Her sister turned to her with a slight frown. "You're not forgetting common sense, are you? You sound like a school girl."

"I can't help it. When he smiles my heart melts." Julia picked up her niece and twirled her around the room.

"You sound hopeless already. Did you find out anything about him?"

"Not much. I hope we'll get to talk Wednesday night."

"What about Lucien?"

"The plan is for Sophia to keep him busy." Julia set Elise on her feet then told Margaret about her plan to get Sophia and Lucien together. "So you see, if it works, Lucien will no longer be a problem. I'll be free to marry who and when I want."

Later in the evening Edward took her aside. "I assume Mr. Anderson is the man I saw you talking to after church this morning."

"Yes. He's going to start attending there."

"I wanted to come over and meet him, but Clara and her mother had me cornered. By the time I made my escape, you were heading for your sleigh."

"He'll be at the lecture Wednesday night. I'll introduce you then." Some of her enthusiasm drained away and her shoulders slumped. "That's three days away."

8

Wednesday, Julia dressed with special care. Sparkling blue eyes looked back at her from the hall mirror. Tonight would be fun.

When she went out to the waiting sleigh, her spirits dipped a little on seeing Margaret's husband, Steven. He'd probably spend the entire ride informing her and her sister of everything he knew about the speaker. He defined the word know-it-all. She didn't see how her sister put up with it. The long line of sleighs heading for the lecture hall slowed their progress considerably, which gave him more time to enlighten them. By the time the sleigh came to a stop, Julia had to resist the urge to leap out.

As soon as they entered the lecture hall, Julia scanned the seats and saw James, Sophia, and Lucien had arrived and Edward and Lily were going in their direction. Lucien turned in Julia's direction, waved, then turned back to listen to something Sophia was telling him. Julia sent Sophia a silent thank you, but where was Mr. Anderson? Surely, he'd be here.

As Steven led them to empty seats, Julia felt a light touch on her arm. "Miss Phillips, do you mind if I join you?"

"Mr. Anderson." Pleasure quickened her heart as she turned to face him. "I hoped you'd come. This is my sister and brother-in-law, Margaret and Steven Jefferson."

Steven gave Mr. Anderson a hearty handshake. "Are you new to Boston?"

"How did you know?"

"I haven't seen you before. It's easy to spot a new face amongst the old families. How do you two know each other?"

Julia spoke up. "We met in the store where I bought a gift for Papa. His family is in the jewelry business."

"Ah, import. Did you move over from New York?"

Jacob's eyes widened. "Yes, we did. It's amazing you could know that."

"Not too amazing. New Yorkers sometimes see the sense in moving to a superior city. We should talk sometime. My family made their fortune in shipping. I'd be interested to know what line you use and how you feel about the shift from clipper ships to steam."

"It looks like the lecture is about to start," Margaret said. They took their seats as the lights dimmed.

Julia found it hard to concentrate on the lecture with Mr. Anderson sitting beside her. She kept glancing at him to see if he was enjoying the talk, *and* because she liked to look at him. He met her eyes, more times than not, and smiled. Is the smile because he likes what Mr. Twain is saying, or because he likes being with me? The flutter in her middle led Julia to believe it was the latter.

Jacob glanced at Miss Phillips. Could she hear his heart pounding from her seat next to him? The family's warning about wasting his time faded to the background. From the moment he'd seen her, she'd been on his mind. Right now, the warmth of her arm and shoulder next to his and the delicate violet scent she wore invaded his senses.

Jacob sincerely hoped she wouldn't want to discuss the lecture during intermission, because so far, he hadn't heard a word.

The first hour flew by, and everyone stood for intermission. Margaret directed Steven's attention to some friends a couple of rows over. Before Jacob could start a conversation, he noticed a young man approaching.

"Hello Julia. I knew I saw you over here." He held his hand out to Jacob. "I'm Edward Harrington. Julia's cousin."

"Jacob Anderson. It's nice to meet you." Giving Edward a firm handshake, he got the distinct impression Edward was sizing him up. Hopefully he'd meet with approval.

"Julia tells me your family is in the jewelry business and you haven't been in town long."

Jacob wanted to be honest right from the start. He wouldn't pretend to be something he wasn't, which meant he'd have to correct Mr. Jefferson's misconception.

"My uncle has been in business here for quite a while. He tried for years to get my father to join him, and he finally did six months ago. They changed the name of the store to Anderson's, so the name of the store is new, but not the business.

"Uncle Joshua has no children and wanted the business to stay in the family. There are three of us boys and father felt it would be a better future than farming. My older brother likes it, but I don't think it's for me."

"So, you aren't from New York City?"

He heard the disappointment in Miss Phillips' voice, but it couldn't be helped. "No, my father and another uncle own farms in upstate New York. Tenants are running Father's farm and I helped my uncle until a few weeks ago when I came here. I wanted to please my father and give the jewelry store a try."

A smile lit Julia's face. "Well, I'm sure it will take more than a few weeks to know. In the meantime, you can see what Boston has to offer."

"I'm not in a hurry to leave." Jacob gazed into her shining blue eyes.

Edward gave a discreet cough, bringing Jacob back to surroundings that included more than him and Miss Phillips.

"Mr. Anderson, do you enjoy sleighing?"

"Yes, but I haven't had time since I've been here."

"You should go with us sometime." Julia linked her arm though Edward's. "Edward has a horse that can't be beat."

"I wish I could have brought my horse with me. If you like speed, you'd like riding behind her."

"We go on Saturday afternoons," Edward said. "Why don't you meet us? I'd be interested to know what you think of my mare."

"I will if I can. Thank you for asking."

The people around them headed back to their seats, so Edward left and Jacob and Julia sat down. The second half went by too fast and they headed for the doors.

"I enjoyed Mr. Twain. Thank you for suggesting this. I wonder, though, if we might be able to do something where we would have more time to talk. I would like to know more about you. That is, if you're interested."

"I'd like that. Do you enjoy reading?"

"Yes, when I have time."

"Let's meet at the public library. They have an area where we can talk quietly. Would early afternoon be alright?"

The library. He never would have thought of that. "I'll see if I can on Friday. If not, I'll send a message to your house."

Julia offered him her hand. "Until Friday then."

"Until Friday." Jacob gave her hand a gentle squeeze.

Julia watched him disappear into the crowd, as Steven and Margaret caught up to her.

"Is he gone?" asked Steven. "I wanted to invite him for supper."

While Steven went to get their sleigh, Julia took the opportunity to ask Margaret about Friday.

"I think that would be all right, but are you sure you want to meet him again? You're not letting his good looks cloud your judgment, are you?"

"I don't know enough about him to make a judgment. That's why I need to see him again."

"Do you know enough about what Papa would say?"

"I knew that without talking to him at all. This is about my future, not Papa's."

Elsewhere in the crowd, Lucien told Sophia, "I'm not sure avoiding Julia is making her miss me. She looked perfectly content with that man sitting beside her. Who is he, anyway?"

"You haven't given it enough time. You're being patient, remember?"

"Right, patient, but who is he?" Lucien turned to look at the group around them. "Where did Edward go? He talked to him."

"The last time I saw him, he was headed in the opposite direction of Clara Pennington."

Eventually, Edward rejoined them, and they all went to the Harrington's where they gathered in the drawing room. Edward heaved a sigh. "It's too bad Julia went with Margaret tonight. The evening isn't the same without her."

"Speaking of Julia," Lucien said, "Who was she with tonight?"

"Jacob Anderson. Seems like a nice fellow. I invited him sleighing with us Saturday. Anyone interested in a game of cards?"

Lucien knew he wouldn't get any more information from Edward, so he let it go. Sophia went to the piano and as he wasn't in the mood for cards, he followed her and sat close by. He couldn't help noticing she played as well as Julia. As a matter of fact, he enjoyed it so much he let all thoughts of Julia leave his mind. He didn't think of her again until he left for home.

He tucked the lap robe a little tighter around himself and tried to ignore the vague feeling of guilt nibbling at him. He didn't want to do anything to harm Julia and Sophia's friendship. They all needed to be on good terms after the marriage for his plan to work. On the other hand, Sophia seemed to be encouraging his attention.

Lucien shook his head and sighed, producing a frosty cloud, then turned his mind to the business he'd be dealing with at the bank tomorrow.

Julia sat in her rocking chair, snug in a blanket she'd wrapped around herself, watching snowflakes swirl outside her bedroom window. Tonight had been wonderful. Her hand felt warm and tingly from Mr. Anderson's touch. She still knew only a little about him, though. He had to be able to come Friday.

She folded her hands tightly in her lap. Who was the man behind the beautiful blue eyes and adorable dimples? Would he marry a woman because it was the sensible thing to do? She doubted it. "Sensible" didn't describe what might be happening between them.

After she'd climbed into bed, her mind drifted back to the idea that God might be interested enough in her to have orchestrated a meeting between her and Mr. Anderson. Just to be safe, she directed a thank you prayer toward heaven.

When Jacob entered the family drawing room, his brothers and parents stopped talking and turned toward him. They expected bad news. He had been snubbed, or she hadn't shown up, or something that would prove their point. The middle and upper classes don't mix. Well, they were about to be disappointed. "I'm sure you're wondering about my evening."

His father spoke first. "You don't have to tell us, son. I'm sure we can all be gracious enough to move on from here."

"I want to know," said his younger brother, Jason. "It might not be as bad as you think."

"You're right, Jason." Jacob grinned and sat in a chair close to his brother. "It was wonderful. Not only is Miss Phillips beautiful, but she doesn't seem to mind that we're not in the same social class.

"We sat with her sister and brother-in-law, and they were friendly. I met her cousin, who invited me to go sleighing with them on Saturday. He wants my opinion on his mare. And here's the best part."

Jacob looked at each member of his family. "She wants me to meet her Friday afternoon at the public library. I can get the time off, can't I, Father?"

His parents stared at him in silence. When his father didn't respond, Jacob frowned. "You're not sorry it went well, are you?"

"Oh no, of course not," his mother hurried to reassure him, twisting a handkerchief into a knot in her lap. "We simply don't want you to be hurt. Your aunt and uncle have told us it just isn't done. They've lived here long enough to know these things. Maybe you should give it up now, before you get too involved."

"I appreciate your concern, but just because it isn't usually done, doesn't mean it can never be done. I think I'll take my chances."

His father jabbed a finger at him. "When she invites you to meet her parents, you'll know she doesn't care about class."

Later, Jacob sat in a side chair and watched the snow falling outside his bedroom window. He didn't care what they said. He could understand their desire to protect him, but wouldn't ignore his heart and possibly lose the woman God had chosen for him. He could still feel the warmth of her small hand in his, and knew he could live for these next two days on the sweetness of her smile alone.

He chuckled to himself. Who would have thought he could turn to mush over a woman? Not just any woman, though. When he looked in her eyes it was as if, for a few brief moments, their hearts connected. Leaning his head back against the chair, he closed his eyes and prayed. "Thank you, Father, for bringing Julia into my life. Please guide me. Help me to make good decisions. Amen."

9

On Friday, Julia got in the sleigh with Margaret for a brisk ride to the library. She pulled her cashmere scarf up over her nose and cheeks to protect her face from the stinging wind. Margaret's words were muffled as she spoke through her scarf. "How is Sophia coming along with Lucien? Have you talked to her?"

Julia chuckled, thinking of her plan. "I saw her yesterday. She said he seems to enjoy her company."

"It sounds as though she's making progress."

Julia gave Margaret's gloved hand a squeeze. "I'm glad you're on my side."

"I'm not sure I'm on a side yet, but I think you should have more time."

"You don't know if you like Mr. Anderson?"

Margaret pulled the lap robe up higher. "He made a good impression Wednesday evening, but we still know very little about him. Having this opportunity to talk without a crowd around you should be helpful. I hope he won't disappoint you."

"He won't. I'm sure of it."

When they arrived, Jacob met them at the door. Her pulse quickened when their eyes met. They found a sofa where the three of them could sit comfortably.

Julia smoothed out her skirts. "I'm glad you could get away from your store for a while. I hope it didn't cause you any trouble."

"None at all. I've looked forward to seeing you again, and I'd like to thank you, Mrs. Jefferson, for bringing her."

"I always enjoy an outing with my sister. I may even look for a book while I'm here."

Julia turned to Jacob. "Please tell me about your family. Did you say you have an older brother?"

"I'll be happy to tell you about my family, but first I have to make sure you're clear about me. I'm afraid Mr. Jefferson is under the impression my family is more than it is. I don't want there to be any misunderstanding."

Her admiration for him swelled at his honest admission. "I think I know what you're trying to say, but the fact that you grew up on a farm and your father is now a shop owner makes no difference to me. I'm interested in who you are inside. I want to know about your family, because they have a big influence on making you the person you are. But I also want to know your hopes and dreams."

His eyes widened, then he smiled. "You are a rare person, Miss Phillips. I'll be happy to answer your questions, but I have to ask you one first."

"Okay. What would you like to know?"

"I'm wondering about your parents. Would they approve of you seeing me?"

She groaned to herself. He would have to ask that. "No, they wouldn't, but I don't share their feelings on class distinction." Julia raised her chin a notch and spoke in a firm tone. "I should be able to decide whom I see."

"I don't want you to get in trouble. What do you think, Mrs. Jefferson?"

Margaret laughed. "It wouldn't be the first time Julia found herself in trouble, Mr. Anderson. I wouldn't have brought her if I didn't support her. Our parents will find out about you soon enough, I imagine."

Julia asked, "Are you satisfied?"

Jacob turned back to Julia with a sigh. "For now, but I don't like the idea of going behind their backs."

"We have no choice. I'm sorry." She held her breath. If he left now, she wouldn't blame him. A man should be able to meet a woman's parents and know he had their approval.

Instead of leaving, Jacob started talking about his family. Tension eased as she listened, never taking her eyes from his face.

"My father had four brothers, but only two are still living. I have an older brother, Joel, who is twenty-six, and a younger brother, Jason, who is twenty-one. I was born and raised in upstate New York where I spent most of my life on our farm."

"Do you miss the farm?"

"Yes and no. I missed my family, so I'm glad to be here. I don't think I'm cut out to be a store keeper, though."

"What would you like to do?"

"My uncle has a friend who moved to Iowa about ten years ago. In every letter he sends he talks about what a wonderful place it is. He tried to talk my New York uncle into going out, but Uncle Jared is satisfied where he is. I'd like to see what my uncle's friend is talking about.

"I could have our farm in New York, but I'm afraid Father would think he could still run it from here. He gives the impression no one could do the job as well as he. I want to have a place of my own, be independent. If Iowa is as good as it sounds, I'll probably settle there."

Her heart sank at the excitement in his voice and the sparkle in his eyes. "When would you go?"

"I have no definite schedule. It depends on when I have enough money saved."

Margaret stood. "I think I'll go look for that book. I'll be back in a little while."

After she left, Jacob said, "Your sister's nice. Do you have any other sisters or brothers?"

"I have two more sisters. Katherine is the oldest. She's happily married to Alexander Harrison. Priscilla is next in age. She's married to Frank Jenkins. Margaret follows her and you've met her husband. I'm the baby and a little spoiled," Julia admitted with a grin.

His eyebrows rose. "I haven't seen evidence of that. How have you been spoiled?"

"For one thing, Papa allowed me more education than my sisters. I've had tutors in subjects traditionally reserved for boys. I've had a little more freedom to go out and socialize and, most important of all, I wasn't pressured to marry as young as my sisters were." Because of the way she'd been raised, it made her situation with Lucien all the more puzzling and harder to bear.

"None of that sounds bad. I especially like the fact they haven't made you marry yet. It can't be for lack of offers."

Julia lifted her shoulders in a slight shrug. "I don't want to marry for the wrong reason."

"And you think your sisters did?"

"Katherine didn't. The other two did what was expected of them. I don't intend to make that mistake."

"What did Katherine do differently?"

"She had the good sense to fall in love with the right man. They're devoted to each other."

"May I assume your parents still aren't pressuring you concerning marriage? They don't have someone picked out, do they?"

Julia hated to answer, even though she wanted to be as honest as he had been. Still, she hesitated, looking out the window then down at the toes of her kid leather boots. "Miss Phillips, I promise I won't run for the door if you tell me they do have someone. You obviously aren't happy about it. Maybe I can help."

His desire to rescue her endeared him to her heart. If only he could be her white knight.

After taking a deep breath, she met his eyes. "Yes, they do have someone. It's actually worse than "picked out." My papa has accepted a proposal on my behalf and everyone is eager to make an announcement. It won't be right away, but I'm not sure how long they'll wait."

"Do they know how you feel?"

"I've told him more than once I'm not right for him, but he just tells me that marrying him is the sensible thing to do. He and Papa both think I'll come around." She laughed and shook her head. "Papa should know better."

"It sounds like you have something in mind."

"I do. Unfortunately, it will cause a scandal, and I hate to do that to my family."

Jacob's brow wrinkled. "Maybe we can come up with something else. Will Lucien be sleighing with us tomorrow?"

"Yes. What are you thinking?"

"I'm going to find out what he's thinking. It may be he needs someone to show him what a mistake it would be to marry *anyone* right now."

Julia laughed, as hope bubbled up inside her. "You know, I think we might be a lot alike."

"I look forward to finding out." Jacob gave her a sheepish smile. "I'm afraid I'm going to have to leave it up to you to suggest places to meet."

"I have an idea, but I want to talk to Margaret first. If you'll give me your address, I can send a note to your house."

Jacob gave her an address to a part of the city she'd never been in.

Margaret approached slowly, book in hand. "Are you ready to go? Momma will be expecting us soon."

Jacob and Julia stood and went to the door with Margaret. He assisted the ladies into their sleigh, then hired one to take him back to the store. Meeting Julia had confirmed both his parents' suspicions and his desire. Her parents didn't approve and a future with her seemed out of the question. It wasn't even a good idea. Falling in love would only complicate his plan to go west and start a place of his own. But when Julia had walked into the store that day, his common sense had walked out. He could think of nothing but her.

Once the women were swishing along the streets on their way back to the house, Julia asked, "What do you think now? Isn't he wonderful?"

"He's very nice. I certainly admire his honesty. I hope you were "honest" too."

"About Lucien you mean? Yes, I told him. I also told him I would never let the marriage happen. He offered to help me." She truly hoped he'd be able to.

Margaret's eyebrows shot up. "Is he going to help you to Iowa? You did understand him to say he wants his own farm."

"Yes, I know, but I didn't say I'd marry him. I said he wants to help." Julia sniffed. "Anyway, what's wrong with being a farmer's wife?"

"You wouldn't have the slightest idea what to do." Margaret squeezed her arm. "Promise me you won't do anything out of desperation."

"I won't marry him unless I know I'm truly in love with him, and he with me. Besides, you've never seen me turn down a challenge, have you?"

"Living on a farm may be more challenge than you want. It won't be like going to our house in the country. You'd have to do actual work."

"I can't deny I prefer the conveniences and opportunities the city offers. Cultural and educational advantages, just to name two, are important to me. Maybe he'll decide he likes city life and want to stay here or even go to New York. Besides, you may be lecturing for nothing. He hasn't asked me to marry him. We only want to get to know each other, which is why I'd like to ask another favor."

Margaret gazed at her but didn't say anything. Julia allowed a touch of pleading in her voice. "Will you allow him to call on me at your house? I could tell Momma I'm going over for tea. I wouldn't expect you to let him stay any longer than the proper amount of time, which is way too short, by the way. You don't mind, do you?"

Her sister bit her bottom lip, and a small frown creased her brow. "I never expected this request. However, we should try to make this as proper a courting as possible. You can come on Tuesday. Momma is usually busy at the Women's City Club and I know Steven won't come home. Do you think Mr. Anderson could come then?"

"I'll let you know by Monday. Thank you! Thank you! Thank you!" Julia gave her sister a squeeze.

10

Having Lucien as a dinner guest that evening did nothing for Julia's appetite. If only she could have invited Sophia to attend. Priscilla and Frank were there, but they didn't count as allies.

When dessert had been served, Lucien stood, drawing everyone's attention. "I have some news I'd like to share. Today, I closed the deal on an early wedding gift. I hope you'll like it, Julia." His gaze rested on her for a moment, then took in the others.

Julia stifled a groan. Now what would she have to deal with?

He pulled a document out of his inside jacket pocket, unfolded it and held it up for inspection. It had the word DEED across the top, so either he'd bought a house or land.

Priscilla, who sat beside her, leaned over and gave her a side hug. "This is wonderful. You'll have a nice place to live as soon as you're married."

Papa set aside his dessert fork. "May I have a closer look?" Lucien handed the deed to Papa, then sat and held his jacket lapels with a self-satisfied smile.

Papa turned to her. "Julia, this is for a property in Back Bay. You'll be starting married life in style." He leaned over and slapped Lucien on the back. "Nice work."

"Thank you, sir." Lucien focused on her. "I've spoken to an architect. We'll go soon to talk about what we want. How does that sound?"

Julia managed a small smile. "That's thoughtful." Congratulations came from everyone at the table, but it felt like this "gift" had more to do with Lucien than her. She'd never noticed before tonight how much he liked having the attention focused on him. If his chest puffed out much farther the buttons would pop off his shirt.

When they finished their dessert, Momma stood and the ladies went to the drawing room, where Momma and her sister had only one thing on their minds, planning her wedding.

Priscilla clasped her hands in front of her. "If the announcement is made before everyone leaves for the summer, you could be married in the fall. Your wedding would be the first social event of the season."

"You'll want to be married at the Church of the Advent," Momma said. "Besides being members there, it should be big enough to hold our families and many of our friends."

Priscilla jumped in. "And, October is a lovely time of year for a wedding. It's too bad Katherine won't be able to participate."

Momma spoke. "I'm sure you'll want Priscilla, Margaret, Sophia and Lily to be bridesmaids, won't you?"

Julia lifted her hands palms up. "Don't you think it'd be hard to plan a wedding if we're out of town?"

"We could do a lot of it before we leave." Momma patted her hand. "And, we can always come back a little early."

The pressure inside Julia inched ever closer to the screaming point. Of course, a proper young lady would never scream, nor would her momma be happy if she jumped up and started pacing. Sheer willpower held her in her chair. "Do you mind if we stop talking about this? It's giving me a headache."

Momma and Priscilla gave each other a knowing look, then Momma said, "We don't have to talk about it now, but decisions will have to be made at some point."

The men joined them and Lucien asked Julia to sit with him, a little apart from the others. Julia got them each a cup of tea and waited to see what he had to say.

He set his teacup on a side table and turned back to Julia. "I want to talk to you about the wedding trip. Since I know you're interested in France, we'll go there."

Her conscience nudged her. She should have refused to go along with any of this right from the beginning. If she weren't careful, she'd end up like her sisters. After a short pause she said, "Don't you think it's a little early to plan a trip?"

"It's never too early to make plans. We won't be gone long of course. It will take a while to make the crossing there and back, so we'll take in a few sights, then come home. I don't want to be away from the bank too long."

He picked up his tea cup, leaned back against the sofa and crossed his legs. Julia wouldn't call the little smile he wore smug, but it came close. She wondered if he might be congratulating himself on what he considered his generosity. Time to remind him of her friend.

"I think Sophia would like to see France, too. We've read a lot of the same books and talked about what it would be like to go there. You should talk to her about it sometime."

"Speaking of Sophia, I feel as though I've spent more time with her than I have with you."

"She told me she enjoys your company and admires the way you have a plan for your future. Have you noticed what a sensible young woman she is?"

Lucien looked at her as if he wasn't sure what to say. Finally, he said, "Sophia is nice. I enjoy her company also, but I'd like to spend some time with you. The quintet is playing on Tuesday. I want you to go with me."

Lucien reached over to take one of her hands in his, but she quickly retrieved her teacup.

"All right, I'd like to hear them, and I'll ask Sophia if she can come. I doubt my parents would let us go alone.

A crease appeared between his eyes. "They might, considering the circumstances."

"Maybe, but we don't want those circumstances made public, do we?"

"More *you* don't, than *we*." Lucien set his cup aside again. "You should know your father and I have set a time limit to the waiting. You have until the end of May, three months, to make the announcement."

Exhaustion washed over her. She didn't want to talk about a wedding trip, building a house or listen to any of the other plans Lucien had for their future. She longed for her bed. Mercifully, the evening soon came to an end and she and her parents bid their guests good night.

As soon as they left, Julia headed for the door, but Papa intercepted her. "Julia, wait. I have something to tell you and your mother. Please come back and have a seat."

Swallowing down her frustration, Julia turned, crossed to the sofa and sat next to Momma.

He pulled over a side chair and sat in front of them. "I want you to know Lucien and I have decided the engagement will be made official at the end of May. He feels that should be enough time for you to get adjusted to the idea of settling down."

Julia clenched her teeth. It would never happen.

"Did you also set a date for the wedding?" her mother asked.

"We didn't talk about that. I'm sure once the announcement is made you ladies will have everything under control. I remember what it was like when our other daughters got married." Her father chuckled. "The main thing you needed me to do was stay out of the way."

"That's true. We don't need a man to help us plan a wedding." Momma turned to her. "Do you remember how much fun you had working with the flowers for Margaret's wedding?"

Julia rubbed her temples. "I'm tired and have a headache. If you don't mind, I'd like to go to bed now."

Her father raised his eyebrows. "Wouldn't you like to talk about the evening? I thought it went well.

She squeezed her eyes shut while shaking her head, then opened them and looked first at her father then her mother. "No, there is no point talking about it. The only thing I have to say is, I don't want to marry Lucien now any more than I did last week when you informed me of your decision. Please don't ask me to pretend to be happy. And Momma, don't expect me to be involved in wedding plans."

She angrily brushed away tears and stood. "This marriage is something the two of you want, so I'll let the two of you handle it." She hurried from the room before saying something worse, or breaking down completely. Papa always said women were too emotional and she'd just proven him right.

When she got to her room, Julia welcomed Millie's help with preparing for bed. Once she had her nightdress on, she sat at her dressing table while Millie pulled the pins from her hair and ran a brush through it. The rhythmic brushing soothed her nerves and made it easy to think of other things. Things like Jacob and the chance to see him tomorrow, and hopefully get to ride with him.

Maybe she could talk to him about coming to Margaret's. There were lots of places they could meet. She would need a few moments alone with him to decide what they would do.

In the drawing room, Mr. Phillips stood, leaned a shoulder against the fireplace mantel, hands in his pockets and crossed one foot over the other. "I hoped tonight would bring Julia around, even if just a little."

His wife got out her fan, flipped it open and waved it in front of her face. "It's not going to be much fun planning a wedding when the bride wants nothing to do with it. I don't like to see her so unhappy. Maybe we should give her more time to get adjusted."

"Don't let her theatrics worry you. When she sees the preparations, she'll get excited and want to be involved."

"I hope you're right."

"Aren't I always?"

"Yes, dear." Mrs. Phillips patted him on the arm and left the room. When she'd gone, he collapsed in a chair and rubbed the back of his neck. It had only been a week and Lucien was already getting impatient. His assurances that he'd take care of Julia didn't make Mr. Phillips feel better. No amount of money he'd offered the man to drop the engagement had been accepted.

Mr. Phillips let his head drop against the back of the chair. Apparently, Lucien would rather enjoy the power he felt in holding information over his head. Information that would destroy the credibility he had as an expert in finance and customer confidence in the bank. His family would come to financial and social ruin.

11

"Good morning, Momma." Julia slid onto a dining room chair, took a piece of buttered toast and put it on her plate, then poured a cup of tea.

"Ah, Julia. I'm glad you're here. Mrs. Lawrence is hosting a luncheon today for the Friends of the Library, so I won't be here for the noon meal. What will your day be like?"

"I'm going to Sophia's for lunch and then sleighing with her and James. Will you pass the marmalade please?"

Momma handed it to her. "That sounds like fun, as long as you're back in plenty of time to get ready for the Pennington's ball this evening."

Julia slathered on the sweet fruit spread and took a bite. After she'd swallowed, she said, "Don't worry, Edward is counting on me being there. Half of my dance card has his name on it."

Momma frowned and Julia prepared for a lecture. "You shouldn't be giving that many dances to one person, and you both know it. He needs to stop hiding behind you. I don't know why you let him do it." Her mother poured herself a second cup of tea and then offered Julia the pot.

She took it and put tea in her cup. "I let him do it because he is one of my dearest friends, and he'd do the same for me if I asked. Besides, I like dancing with him."

Julia grinned, but seeing no smile on her mother's face, she said, "Don't worry, he'll let himself get caught when he's ready."

Momma heaved a sigh. "I hope some of your dances are with Lucien. If you're giving half to anyone, it should be him."

"Please, Momma. Let's not ruin a perfectly good morning by talking about Lucien."

"I know he's not your favorite subject, but you can't ignore him."

"He has two dances. I don't plan to ignore him, but if you want to talk about him, I suggest you talk to Papa. I'm not interested."

"Not talking about him won't make him go away."

"Maybe not, but talking about him will make me go away." Julia swallowed the last of her tea and left the dining room.

At Sophia's request, Julia arrived early for lunch. "Come to my bedroom. I want to show you what I'm wearing tonight." A lovely butter colored silk gown with cap sleeves, bead embellishments and a scoop neckline hung on a hanger from the corner of the open wardrobe door. Its full skirt had several layers of soft folds creating a small bustle in back.

"It's beautiful! The shade is perfect for you."

"Thank you. I'm looking forward to tonight."

Julia put her hand on Sophia's arm. "Lucien asked for a dance, didn't he?"

"I told him he could have two and he looked pleased." Sophia smiled as she hung her dress in the wardrobe, and then sat in one of the armchairs close to the iron stove.

Julia sat in the chair across from her, but Sophia's smile had already been replaced with a troubled expression. "What's wrong?"

"I'm not sure if this is the right thing to do. It doesn't seem fair to Lucien."

"Ha! Would you like to talk about what isn't fair? Let me tell you about last night. After Priscilla, Momma and I went to the drawing room, the men decided the end of May would be a fine time to make the big announcement. No doubt they talked about how men need to make the decisions because women have a hard time knowing their own minds."

Julia stood and paced the room. "I tried to tell Papa I'm not ready for marriage and I told Lucien he deserved someone who was. Do you think it made any difference?" Julia stopped to look at her friend.

Sophia opened her mouth, but Julia went on. "Of course not. Papa told me he and Lucien had it settled, and he expected me to be pleased. What do you suppose the chances of that are?"

When she took a breath, Sophia jumped in. "You might as well stop talking to them about it. You can either quit fighting and accept the fact, or continue with your current plan."

Julia plopped back in her chair in an unladylike heap. "To tell the truth, I'm having second thoughts about you and Lucien. I don't know if he'd treat you the way you deserve."

Sophia leaned forward and clasped Julia's hands. "How many proposals have we turned down?"

"Five."

"Right, because we knew those men weren't right for us. Trust me when I say, I'll be careful."

"So, you're willing to keep trying to distract Lucien?"

"Yes. Now tell me about your visit with Mr. Anderson yesterday."

Julia straightened in her chair, happy to share a recap of their conversation, including how Mr. Anderson felt about her parents' disapproval.

"If he knows, then he shouldn't try to see you again."

"We *have* to see each other." Julia scooted to the edge of her seat. "There's a connection between us. I'm sure he feels it too. If it turns out what my heart is telling me about him is true, I'll go anywhere he wants me to go."

"And if that doesn't work out?"

"I have another option. Believe me Sophia, one way or another, I won't be here for a wedding with Lucien."

Fat gray clouds threatening more snow crowded the sky, but they did nothing to dampen Julia's spirits. She couldn't wait to see Mr. Anderson.

As they rode to the meeting spot outside the city, Julia asked James, "How do you feel about the upper and middle classes mixing?"

"I don't know what you mean. The classes mix almost everywhere we go."

Julia leaned forward so she could see him better on the other side of Sophia. "I mean socially. Would it bother you if someone from the middle class joined us today?"

"Would this someone be a she? Because if it is, I'm not interested." James threw her a look that said he couldn't believe she would suggest it.

"No, it's nothing like that. I know you're interested in Lily. He's a friend of mine. I hoped I could count on you to welcome him."

He glanced at her then turned back to the road. "What do your parents think about your friend?"

She hesitated a moment. "They haven't met him yet, but he's very nice. He just doesn't happen to be blessed with old money. That doesn't matter to you does it?"

"I'd like to think I base my opinion of a person on more than how much money he has. I'll give him the same opportunity I give everyone else."

"Thank you. I appreciate it." Julia settled back in the seat with a smile. Now she could count on three people to be nice to Mr. Anderson. Actually, four. Lily was nice to everyone.

When they stopped at the gate by Farmer Hunt's field, Edward, Lily and Jacob were already there, their sleighs next to each other. The two men stood next to Edward's horse. Jacob ran his hand down her neck and shoulder, then stepped beside her. "She's a beauty, and fast. You didn't exaggerate. Morgans are a good choice to pull a sleigh."

"Thank you. I'm happy with her."

Hearing Jacob's opinion made her smile. She knew Edward appreciated the praise from someone who recognized a good horse.

Jacob came over to their sleigh as soon as he finished speaking to Edward. His beautiful dimpled smile was all for her. If she were a piece of chocolate, she'd melt. "Hello Miss Phillips. It's nice to see you."

Julia returned his smile. "I'm glad you could come. I'd like you to meet my good friends."

After James and Jacob shook hands, Jacob turned to Sophia. "Weren't you at the jewelry store with Miss Phillips?"

"Yes, I was. You have a good memory."

"A pretty face is hard to forget."

Edward called to Jacob, and after he'd moved out of hearing distance, James turned to Julia. "He isn't here to see Sophia, is he?"

"Let me out," snapped Julia.

James' eyes widened. "What's wrong?"

"Didn't you just say you'd give him the same chance as anyone else?"

"Well, yes, but…"

"Let. Me. Out."

James helped her over the side and as she walked toward Edward's sleigh, she heard Sophia say, "Stop worrying, James. He's here to see Julia. She said he was her friend, remember?"

"I'll never figure her out."

"You will be nice, though, won't you?"

"Of course, I will. I know how to be a gentleman," James muttered.

When Julia got to the sleigh, she reached up and rubbed the chestnut horse's soft nose. "Sugar is a magnificent animal, don't you agree, Mr. Anderson?"

"Without a doubt." Jacob's eyes shone. "Edward offered to let me try her out."

As Edward helped Lily out of the sleigh, he said, "You should take Julia with you. She can show you where we like to go."

Jacob turned to her with a grin. "Will you help me out, Miss Phillips?"

"I'd be happy to."

As they got settled, Sophia asked, "Has anyone heard from Lucien? He's usually here by now."

"Maybe that's him." Lily pointed up the tree-lined road. Sleigh bells rang merrily as a sleigh approached.

When they got closer Julia recognized Lucien, and he had Clara Pennington with him. Edward groaned and Lily jabbed him with her elbow. Julia couldn't resist saying, "It looks like you're on your own this afternoon."

"Not necessarily. Jacob, you can try my mare some other time. If you hurry and get out, Julia and I can be gone before they get here."

Julia laughed. "Forget it, Edward. Be a man and face her. She's just a girl, after all."

"That girl is relentless."

Clara smiled and waved as they pulled up next to the others. "Hello everyone. I'm glad you're still here. Lucien was afraid you might have left already."

"I saw Clara at the bank with her brother, Ben. He told me he couldn't come this afternoon."

"Sleighing sounded like fun, so I asked Lucien if he would bring me. Isn't it wonderful? We can be together this afternoon and see each other again this evening,"

Lucien got out of his sleigh and came toward Julia and Jacob. Julia tensed. It felt as if the air around them grew colder as he got closer. Each footstep squeaked and crunched in the frozen snow until it drowned out all other sound. When he reached them, his eyes bored into Jacob. "I saw you at the lecture the other night, but haven't had a chance to introduce myself." Holding out his hand to Jacob, he said, "I'm Lucien Harris."

"Jacob Anderson. It's nice to meet you, Mr. Harris."

Edward came to stand beside Lucien. "Julia's going to show Mr. Anderson the roads. He wants to find out if my mare is as fast as the one he left in New York."

"Is that right? Then I trust you'll be careful, Mr. Anderson. I have a special interest in Miss Phillips."

Julia noticed his smile didn't reach his eyes, and his words sounded like a warning. She didn't know whether to be angry or uneasy.

Edward slapped Lucien on the back. "We all have a special interest in Julia." He leaned close and whispered. "You don't mind riding with Clara, do you?"

"Actually, Clara specifically said she wants to ride with you." Lucien gave him a pat on the shoulder. "If Julia wants to ride with Mr. Anderson, then I think I'd prefer Sophia's company."

When Lucien turned and went toward Sophia, Julia let out a sigh of relief. She'd been afraid he might demand she ride with him.

"Oh, Edward," Clara called, "may I ride with you?" She giggled and batted her eyelashes.

Edward looked as if he might bolt for the nearest sleigh and leave by himself, but Lily came over, took a firm hold of his arm and pulled him to Lucien's sleigh.

"Let's go." Julia gestured toward the road. "We'll let them work it out."

As Jacob got the sleigh moving, Edward called, "Try to be back in half an hour. I want to show Clara what a real sleigh ride is like."

12

Giddy excitement filled Julia now that she and Jacob finally got to have this time together. The urge to giggle almost overwhelmed her, but she didn't want to sound like Clara, whom they could still hear. Jacob shook his head and chuckled. "Don't tell me Mr. Harrington is obligated to Miss…?"

"Pennington," Julia supplied. "No, but she would like him to be. We'll follow this road and then take the first turn to the left."

Jacob lightly slapped the reins on the horse's back and the sleigh picked up speed. "What did you mean when you said he's on his own this afternoon?"

"This evening Clara's family is having a ball, and I promised Edward several dances. His main line of defense is trying to avoid her, so he spends as much time with me or out of her sight as he can. This is the first time she's come sleighing, so I suspect Ben, her brother, hasn't told her Edward is part of our sleighing group."

"If Mr. Harrington spends so much time with you, why would Mr. Harris or Miss Pennington think either of you is available?"

"I would guess as long as no announcement has been made, Clara feels Edward is fair game. As for Lucien, no matter how annoying it is, he sees what he wants to see."

Jacob glanced at her. "I know it's none of my business, but what is your relationship with Mr. Harrington?"

"People have been speculating about that for a long time. Some hint about it to our families or even to us. An announcement concerning Lucien and me will come as a surprise."

She thought for a minute about how best to define her and Edward. Finally, she said, "To make a long story short, Edward and I are close and would do anything to help each other."

"Including marriage?"

"Maybe."

Jacob's brow furrowed. "Then—"

Julia held up her hand palm out. "Right now, he's helping by giving you and me time to get to know each other, while at the same time, insuring Lucien and Sophia spend time together." She paused and pointed. "Here's our first turn."

"Somehow I think it would be a good idea to hear the long story." Jacob steered the frisky mare to the left.

Julia gave him a smile. "I'll be happy to tell you sometime, Mr. Anderson."

"Can I ask you a favor? Will you call me Jacob?"

"It hardly seems as if we've known each other long enough."

"All the rest of you are on a first name basis."

"With the exception of Lucien, we've known each other all our lives. Our families have lived in Boston for at least a hundred years. We're either related by blood, by marriage or by a business connection."

"Hmm, sounds exclusive."

"It is. Even if you were from a New York shipping family, it would take my father awhile to adjust to you. Bostonians tend to feel a little superior. You may have noticed it when talking to Steven the other night."

"I guess I didn't. I'd still like you to call me Jacob, though." He flashed her his dimpled smile. "Mr. Anderson sounds so formal and I'm hoping we'll be friends."

Julia didn't mind skipping the formalities. "I'll call you Jacob if you'll call me Julia."

"Okay, Julia. Have you made any progress with Mr. Harris since yesterday afternoon?"

Her smile melted away as she told Jacob the events of the night before. "So, you see, I have three months to change everyone's mind, or to hope Sophia can bring him around. Once we become a public couple it will be a lot harder on everyone when the wedding doesn't happen."

"It sounds as if your father is set on this. Is there any chance he might accept a different arrangement?"

"If I married someone else from our social set before then, or could convince him I planned to, he would have to accept it. It would put him in an awkward position with Lucien, though. I'm afraid it would take him a while to get over it.

"Anyway, I'd never marry someone under those circumstances. When I marry, it will be for love."

"I'm glad to hear it, and as you said, you do have three months. We might change some minds by then." Jacob winked at her. "I haven't had a chance to talk to Mr. Harris yet."

Julia couldn't help smiling as she tucked her hand through the crook of his arm. "Take this next turn to the right and then you can let her run."

When Jacob made the turn, the mare tossed her head, jingling the sleigh bells, and straining against the reins. He loosened his hold and she galloped down the empty road. Trees and fences flashed by as the sled runners swished over the icy snow. The cold wind blowing in their faces took Julia's breath away. She glanced at Jacob to see his reaction, and grinned at the huge smile on his face.

The horse ran for a while, then Jacob reined her back to a slower pace and turned the sleigh around. Chiming came from inside his coat. He unbuttoned it, pulled out a silver pocket watch and released the spring action cover. "Our half hour will be up soon." He tucked it back in and buttoned his coat. "I wonder what Edward has in mind for Miss Pennington?"

Julia pulled the lap robe up higher against the biting cold. "I imagine he plans to scare her into not coming again."

Jacob peered at her, one brow raised. "I'm going to assume you're joking."

Instead of answering his implied question, Julia asked, "How does Edward's horse compare to yours?"

He blinked, then appeared to catch up with the abrupt turn in the conversation. "I think it would be close if we were racing. I see a lot of similarities."

"Will you bring her here?"

"Not if I decide to go to Iowa. I doubt she would enjoy riding on a train."

Julia savored the little time they had left on the ride. The sleigh bells and the clip clop of the horse's hooves made nice background music.

Jacob covered her hand with his where it rested on his arm. "When will we be able to see each other again?"

She turned to him, thankful she and her sister had already discussed it. "Margaret said you may call on me at her house next Tuesday afternoon. Will your schedule be free then?"

"I'll make it work. Won't your mother want to come with you, though?"

"She spends Tuesdays at the Women's City Club. She won't think it unusual for me to go to Margaret's."

Julia gazed ahead for a minute, as an idea formed in her mind. She turned back to Jacob. "You know, it might be a good idea for you to meet Momma. I'm sure someone will take it on themselves to ask my parents about you. If at least one of them has met you they won't be worried. I'll introduce you after church tomorrow. You'll be there won't you?"

"Yes."

"Good. There are a lot of things we can do and if Momma knows who you are, she won't be concerned if we're being seen together." *I hope.*

"What kind of things will we be doing?"

Julia started her list, grateful Boston had so much to offer. "As you already know, we can ice skate at Frog Pond. It's fun to watch the boys sledding on the Common and we could go to see the animals at Deer Park. There are the lectures and also concerts open to the public."

"I know about the concerts. My younger brother took me to one my first week here."

"Did you like it?"

"I liked it, but I'll confess my brother is the real music lover in the family. He was overjoyed about the family's move to Boston. Jason plays the piano beautifully, and since we've moved to the city, he has more time to practice."

"Wonderful. Maybe he could make a career in music."

"He'd like to, but isn't sure how to go about it."

Julia immediately had another idea, and squeezed Jacob's arm in her enthusiasm. "Jason should meet my piano teacher, Mr. Fontello. He could play for him, and if Mr. Fontello thinks Jason has promise he would know how to get him an audition with the symphony. I'll contact him first of the week and see if he'll do it."

Maybe Jacob would find city life more appealing if it helped his brother.

"Let me make sure Jason wants to before you set anything up. I do know he'd like to meet you sometime."

"How about the quintet concert at Chickering Hall Tuesday evening? Lucien made a point of asking me to go with him, but it doesn't mean we can't run into each other."

"I'm sure Jason plans to go." With a grin, Jacob said, "I may become a music lover myself."

As they approached the original meeting place, Julia could see Edward and Clara were already there and Lucien and Sophia were just arriving. Clara chattered happily to Edward who had a pained expression on his face.

Lucien and Sophia laughed together, but Lucien sobered when he saw Julia. "How about a trade? It wouldn't be fair for me to keep Sophia all to myself." He gave Jacob a meaningful look.

Jacob jumped out of Edward's sleigh and hurried around to help Julia down.

"I don't want to trade," Clara pouted. "I want to stay with you, Edward."

"I'm glad to hear that, Clara, because I want to show you what it's like to ride behind a real horse."

Everyone watched as Edward struggled to help Clara find her footing while going from Jacob's sleigh to his. With an expression of grim determination, he climbed in and picked up the reins. Julia tried hard not to laugh as they left. She looked forward to hearing Edward's version of this afternoon's outing.

After they left, Lucien said, "How about it, Mr. Anderson? You don't mind if Julia takes a ride with me, do you?"

Jacob looked at Sophia with a smile. "I'd be happy to have Miss Howell's company if she doesn't mind mine."

"Not at all."

They all got into their respective sleighs and set off. Julia enjoyed a couple minutes of silence before Lucien said, "Tell me about Mr. Anderson."

Julia didn't think Lucien was upset, exactly. Maybe more confused. "I met Mr. Anderson while shopping for Papa's birthday gift. He's new to Boston and asked about things to do. Edward asked him to go sleighing with us today. He's interesting."

Lucien stopped the sleigh and turned to Julia. "Since you mentioned him the other night, I've done some checking. Do you realize his father is a shop owner? And does he have any idea you're already spoken for?"

Julia ignored the first question. "I told him about you." As she looked at him, she realized her mother was right. He wasn't bad to look at. "You know, you have nice eyes."

"Excuse me?"

"Your eyes are the same color as Sophia's. If you two married, all your children would have big brown eyes."

"If I married Sophia?"

"Yes. You would make a beautiful couple. It looked as if you two were having a good time together."

Lucien shook his head. "She's good company, but I plan to marry you." Taking both her hands in his, he said, "I'll be a faithful husband, Julia. You'll never have reason to doubt it."

Julia looked down at her gloved hands, then back into Lucien's eyes. "I believe you, but don't you think it would be easier to be faithful to someone you truly loved? Someone you knew you couldn't bear to be without?"

"I don't think that kind of relationship exists outside of books. I know I care about you, though, and I want you to be part of my life."

Julia didn't have an immediate answer for him, so he went on. "I guess you can look at marriage in two ways. Either it can scare you or you can see it as the logical next step in your life. You're an intelligent young woman. I should think you'd realize you've reached an age when it's time for husband and home."

Her emotions jumbled inside her. She didn't know whether to be angry or sad or laugh at the whole situation. Finally, she asked, "Does this mean you won't consider releasing me from the agreement Papa made with you?"

Lucien frowned and dropped her hands. "I don't intend to change my mind. You need to get used to the idea that I know what's best for you." He picked up the reins and started the horse forward again.

From the set of his jaw, Julia could see it would do no good to argue further. His determination to have her hadn't changed a whit. Well, her determination hadn't changed either. He could never say she hadn't tried to warn him.

Just before they got back to the others, Lucien said, "I don't want you to spend time with Mr. Anderson. We are betrothed, whether it's public or not, and you are no longer free to see anyone you please."

Lucien pulled on the reins, bringing the horse to a stop and helped Julia out. When both of Julia's feet were on the ground, she looked him in the eye. "I will see whom I want. You don't own me and you will never control me."

She turned and marched toward James and Sophia's sleigh. "I need to go home now."

James looked at her, then Lucien and back to her again. His brow creased as he helped her into the sleigh. "Are you all right? What happened?"

"I need to go home." She settled in next to Sophia with a huff. The way the sleighs were situated, she had a perfect view of Lucien, who wore a frown on his beet red face.

Before James got in, he told Lucien, "I don't know what went on between you two, but it should help to know you won't have to take

Clara home. Edward and Lily took her a while ago."

"Good, I don't think I could have tolerated her giggling right now." He glanced around. "What happened to Mr. Anderson? I'd hoped to speak with him."

"He had to go too, and from the look on your face, I'd say now wouldn't have been a good time to talk."

Lucien sighed out a cloud of vapor. "You're probably right. I'll see you this evening."

They all headed back toward Boston with Lucien soon putting distance between them. "He's going a little faster than usual," Sophia said. "I wonder if he's upset about something?"

Julia turned to her friend. "You wonder if he's upset? Would you like to know what he told me?"

"Yes." Sophia's eyes twinkled. "Tell me."

"He told me I'm not allowed to see Mr. Anderson again. Can you believe the nerve?" Julia sat rigid in the seat; her hands clenched in fists.

James leaned forward to see her past Sophia. "Maybe he knows something about Mr. Anderson and is trying to protect you."

"No, he thinks Mr. Anderson might be interested in me and he doesn't like it."

Sophia laughed. "Imagine that."

Julia frowned at her friend. "I'm glad you find this amusing."

"I'm surprised you don't. Are you going to stop seeing Mr. Anderson because Lucien said so?"

"I told him I'd see anyone I pleased. That's why he's upset."

"Since you're going to do what you want anyway, why let him bother you?"

"You have an excellent point." Julia made an effort to relax her tense muscles. "The next time he says something like that, I'll laugh. There's no need for both of us to be angry."

13

Lucien fumed all the way home. Why couldn't Julia be sensible like Sophia? Every time he and Julia were together it ended in a battle. Things definitely weren't going as planned. Her father's assurance about a woman needing a man to make her decisions for her didn't seem to apply to Julia. Somehow, he would have to find a way to deal with her.

After Edward and Lily dropped Clara off at her door, and started home, Lily turned to him. "Would it have hurt you to be polite to her?"

"Humph. She'd never notice. She's too busy talking about nothing. I'm glad to be rid of her." *Someone needed to make an etiquette rule limiting the amount of time a gentleman had to spend with certain females.*

"Julia's friend, Mr. Anderson, is a nice-looking man."

Edward blinked at the abrupt change of subject. "He seems like a decent sort."

"You could lose her. You better stop playing around and get serious before it's too late."

He glanced at her then back to the road. "Lily, you know Julia and I are just good friends."

"Well, I have never seen two friends who are more perfectly suited. If you let her get away, you'll regret it."

"I have school to finish and I'm off to Europe at the end of the summer. This isn't a good time for me to get serious."

"Don't you think she'd wait for you?"

"Maybe I'll take her with me." He gave her a wink.

She swatted his arm. "Can't you ever be serious?"

Edward smiled but didn't answer. Lily was right. He didn't like the idea of losing the relationship he and Julia shared, but her happiness came first. If things worked out for her and Jacob, then so be it. If not, he'd gladly step in. These next several months would be interesting.

The Phillips and the Howells arrived at the hotel for the ball at the same time. The ladies went to a cloakroom to remove their wraps and make sure they were presentable after the ride.

"Do a slow turn for me, Sophia." Julia watched with approval. "Beautiful. That dress is perfect for you."

"You're lovely, too." Sophia linked her arm in Julia's. "Let's go see who's here."

The girls made their way through a crowd to the ballroom. "It appears the Penningtons have a good turnout," Julia said. "It's a good thing we can use the hotel. Can you imagine trying to have everyone in one of our townhouses?"

Sophia paused inside the ballroom and took an appreciative sniff. "I love the sight and scent of fresh flowers in winter."

Julia scanned the large room. Windows, French doors and large mirrors lined the outside walls. The inside walls had fireplaces, with heating stoves in them, spaced evenly with more mirrors. Gaslights and candles provided a soft glow throughout the room. Sofas and chairs lined the perimeter of the room along with tables holding vases of fresh flowers.

The orchestra tuned up at the far end of the room in preparation for the first dance. The ladies in their many-colored gowns and the men in their black evening-wear completed the picture.

Sophia nudged Julia and tilted her head to the right. "Are you ready for Lucien? He's coming this way."

She resisted looking his direction and informed Sophia with a smile, "I'm not going to let him upset me tonight, if that's what you mean." Her smile slid away. "I hope I won't have to spend too much time with him, though."

"Good evening ladies. Julia, may I have a word with you? Please excuse us, Sophia." He led her a few feet away. "I'll get right to the point. Some things were said this afternoon that I'm sure weren't intended to be taken seriously. I'm willing to forget it if you are."

Lucien looked at her expectantly. For a few seconds she was speechless, but quickly recovered and smiled. "I'm glad you've changed your mind. I'll be happy to forget you said anything. It's nice to clear the air, isn't it?"

He frowned. "I think you misunderstood."

"Maybe you can explain it another time. The first dance is about to begin and I see my partner coming."

Lucien turned to see Edward coming toward them with a smile. "Julia, you're beautiful. I love it when you wear blue."

❦

Lucien watched Edward take her by the hand and lead her to the dance floor. She moved easily into his arms and they waltzed gracefully away. To his left, an older lady told her companion,

"Aren't they perfect together? Surely we'll hear an announcement from them sometime soon."

He turned to Sophia. "What does she mean?"

Sophia shook her head. "You're not very observant, are you? For at least a year now, Edward and Julia have been as close to being a couple as you can get without making a formal announcement."

"Why haven't they?" This made no sense. Could he have been so single-minded he never paid attention to what Julia did? Now he'd have to consider Edward a problem to deal with.

"I would imagine it's because they've both been having too much fun to think about anything more serious."

"I'm beginning to see that about her." He turned his attention to the dance floor and watched Julia and Edward glide around the room. "She says the most surprising things."

"Julia is a wonderful person, but she's not sensible or practical. What you can count on, though, is her ability to surprise you. I never know for sure what's she's thinking or what she might do. She and Edward have stories they could tell."

"Hmm." He had better start paying more attention.

Sophia's voice broke into his thoughts. "The second dance is starting and I believe I promised it to you."

Lucien offered her his arm. "Indeed, you did. Shall we?"

As they moved around the dance floor, Sophia said, "Why not try to solve the puzzle of Julia some other time? Just relax and enjoy yourself tonight."

Lucien smiled at her. "That's a sensible suggestion." He made a conscious effort to relax. Sophia was an excellent dancer and when he gazed into her eyes to answer one of her witty remarks, children with big brown eyes came to mind.

When Edward swept her onto the dance floor, Julia breathed a sigh of relief at putting distance between herself and Lucien for a while. She gladly shifted her focus to Edward. "Tell me about this afternoon with Clara."

Her friend grimaced. "The girl is never quiet. She's always chattering, giggling, or screaming. I'm surprised I have any hearing left in my right ear."

Julia tried, but couldn't suppress a chuckle. "I had a feeling you wouldn't take her on a nice gentle ride."

"Once we got behind Sugar, she held my arm so tight I had a hard time using the reins. We didn't go far, because she kept scaring my poor horse with all her noise."

She couldn't help laughing. He sounded so indignant on behalf of his horse. "At least we can hope she won't want to go again."

"Maybe, but this afternoon's ride hasn't slowed her down tonight. She's been doing her best to get my attention. But tell me how it went with Mr. Anderson. He seems like a good man."

Thinking of Jacob made her smile. "We had a nice time. I feel as though I got to know him better. I wish he could be here tonight."

"That's something you need to think about."

"I know, but there are other things we can do. Margaret has been helpful with working out ways we can see each other. We're meeting at her house Tuesday afternoon."

For a little while they didn't speak. The band made it easy to enjoy the rhythm of the dance, gliding, swaying and turning as they moved around the room. Julia could happily dance with Edward all night. Then, he brought her back to reality.

"How are things going with Lucien?"

"Ugh. My father has decreed an announcement will be made by the end of May, ready or not."

"I suppose Lucien is in full agreement."

"Of course, he is. When we were sleighing today, I tried to get him to think about Sophia, but he wouldn't be distracted. I finally came straight out and asked him if he would consider releasing me from the agreement."

Edward gave her a sympathetic look. "I'm sure he said no."

"Not only did he say no, he told me not to see Jacob again."

"I can imagine what you had to say about that." Edward chuckled, then said. "If he's the sensible and practical person we know him to be, he'll quit while he still has some pride left."

Thinking about the conversation made her angry. She mentally repeated her mantra; *I won't let him upset me.* "I'm not counting on it. I'm afraid this is going to end badly."

"Not for you. I promise." He gave her a quick hug before releasing her to Ben.

Julia loved swirling from one dance to the next. She could pretend Lucien didn't exist, until he appeared to claim her for one of the two dances she'd promised him. Her muscles tensed, but she reminded herself not to let him upset her. His style matched his personality, efficient and systematic, with no extra steps to waste time or energy.

Lucien cleared his throat and met her eyes, his expression serious. "Our conversation was interrupted earlier, but I've decided we'll finish it in a more private setting."

"All right." She didn't care if they never finished it. She smiled and said as little as possible for the rest of the song.

Julia and Edward enjoyed the supper dance together, and then moved with the crowd to the dining area. Tables holding a vast array of foods waited for them. Roast beef, turkey and ham, mushroom stuffed artichokes, creamed peas and other vegetables. Rolls, sweet breads, fruits, fancy pastries and much more. They went from table to table until their plates were full, then found a place to sit.

When they were settled, Julia turned to Edward. "I've been

watching you dodge Clara. She is persistent, isn't she?"

"That's one way to put it." Edward frowned. "I don't understand why she keeps pursuing me. There are plenty of other young men in Boston."

Julia swallowed a bite of food. "I'll tell you what her momma's telling her. 'Family name and finance.' You're a good catch, Edward. But that's not the only reason." Julia grinned and nudged him with her elbow. "You're also handsome and a lot of fun."

Edward gazed at her thoughtfully. She covered her mouth with her hand. "Do I have food stuck in my teeth?"

He smiled. "No, something Lily said earlier came to mind."

"About me?"

"About us. We're the perfect couple, you know. She's worried Jacob is going to take you away."

"We're not to that point yet. I should talk to her, though, and warn her about the Lucien problem. I don't want her to be caught by surprise with everyone else."

Julia glanced toward the food tables. "Uh oh, it looks as though Clara has spotted you. She's coming this way. Maybe you could get us something to drink."

"Good idea. I'll be back in a little while."

Clara stopped a moment when she saw Edward leave, then came on and sat next to Julia. "Hello. Are you having a good time?"

"I am. Did you help your mother organize this evening?"

"Yes, it's part of learning to be a wife. I have to know how to do all sorts of things."

"A wife does have many duties to perform."

Clara drummed her fingers for a minute then blurted, "May I ask you a personal question?"

Julia put down her fork and turned to give Clara her full attention. "You can ask. I won't promise to answer."

"Well, it's about you and Edward." She stopped drumming her fingers and twisted them together in her lap.

Julia reached over and put her hand over Clara's. "What about us?"

"Will you tell me why he enjoys your company and avoids mine?"

Looking at the younger girl, Julia wondered where to start. Clara gazed at her as if she could provide the key to happiness. Finally, Julia said, "There can be a lot of reasons why a man is attracted to one woman and not another. Maybe he's partial to a certain hair color, or a woman who is tall or short. He may like a woman who has a lot to say or prefer one who doesn't talk much at all. Sometimes it can be the way a woman laughs that attracts or repels him."

Clara nodded. "That all makes sense, but you're not being specific. Does he like you better because you're taller and have blond hair?"

"To be perfectly honest, he likes me because I don't chase him." So much for trying to be diplomatic.

A small line appeared between Clara's eyebrows. "What do you mean?"

"You're trying too hard. Let him come to you."

"I'm afraid he never will." Clara sniffled. "I know he'd like me if he'd spend time with me."

Julia felt sorry for the girl. She had a serious crush on Edward. "I suggest you consider he might be happy with his life as it is."

"You mean with you? If you two have an understanding, why didn't you tell me to start with?" Clara dabbed at her eyes and nose with her handkerchief.

Giving Clara's hand a squeeze, Julia said gently, "I mean, Edward is more interested in finishing school and going to Europe. Marriage won't be in his plans for a while."

"Are you saying I should wait until he's back from Europe to try to get his attention?"

"I think it would be best."

"Thank you, Julia. I appreciate your help."

From the corner of her eye, she saw Edward standing with a drink in each hand, tapping his foot. He came over as soon as she left and set down their glasses.

"You've saved me again." He lifted Julia's hand to his lips and kissed it. "You're my hero."

Julia laughed. "More than you know. I believe I've convinced her to stop pursuing you. At least for now."

"I don't know how you did it, but I believe you." Edward gave her a grateful smile and kissed her hand again, this time on the palm. "I love you. You know that don't you?"

"I know." She smiled fondly at her friend. "I love you, too."

⟊

Lucien and Sophia sat across the room, where he could keep his eye on Julia. Her behavior with Edward bothered him.

"Are you all right, Lucien? You look like something's troubling you."

"Excuse me?" He turned to look at Sophia.

"I asked if something's troubling you?"

Lucien looked back across the room. "I don't know if you noticed Julia and Edward. Their conduct doesn't seem appropriate."

Sophia patted his hand. "They're close. Nothing is going to change that."

⟊

During his second dance with Julia, Lucien said, "I saw you and Edward in the supper room, and I'll have to say your behavior unsettled me."

Julia tried not to look amused. "Would you like to tell me not to see Edward anymore?"

"Would you pay any attention if I did?"

"No."

"I'm not surprised. I don't think you should act that way after we're married, though."

"Hmmm."

"Is that all you have to say?"

"I have a lot to say. You don't listen."

"Of course, I listen. It's just that in the end, it's up to me to make decisions."

"If you are going to make all the decisions in the end, why should I talk in the beginning?" Julia gave him a sweet smile.

"You are very frustrating."

"I don't plan to be anything else. It's still not too late to change your mind."

Lucien clamped his mouth shut. She smiled to herself. They got along better when he wasn't talking.

14

When Julia entered the dining room the next morning, her parents stopped talking and focused on her with looks of disapproval. Judging by the scowl on Papa's face, she'd be having a lecture for breakfast, along with her tea and toast.

The minute she slid onto her chair Papa began. "Your momma and I are disappointed in your behavior last night. You barely gave Lucien any of your attention. He took me aside to ask about it."

Momma jumped in. "I'm sure he heard everyone talking about what a perfect match you and Edward are." She stirred sugar into her tea, but her eyes never left Julia's face.

Julia took a breath and tried for a nonchalant tone. "People have been talking about Edward and me for a while now. This can't be the first time he's heard it. Would you pass the marmalade, please?"

Papa passed her a small cut-glass bowl. "I assured him there's nothing serious between you."

Julia applied the spread to her toast. "How do you know there's nothing serious between us? Maybe we're waiting until he gets back from Europe to say anything." Momma's brow furrowed and her lips pressed together in a thin line.

Papa shook his head. "I talked to your Uncle Robert about Edward's plans. He felt it'd be quite some time before his son would be ready to settle down."

Momma laid her teaspoon beside her cup. "I'd think if you were more than friends, you would have said something by now."

Julia took a sip of tea. "You're right; we've talked about marriage, but we haven't moved beyond friendship yet. And I don't want to stop being his friend just because it makes Lucien uncomfortable."

Papa frowned. "We're not asking you to stop being Edward's friend. What we are asking is for you to show Lucien some consideration. I must insist we see some changes, starting today." He hit the table with his open hand on the last two words. Julia and her mother jumped.

"I'll try to do better." Julia didn't sound unconcerned this time, more like squeaky with surprise, to her ears at least. It would take a few minutes for her heart to settle back to a normal rhythm. *Lucien better be prepared for more attention. I don't want any more of these kinds of discussions.*

After church Julia spotted Jacob, waiting a short distance from the church steps, and hurried over to him. His smile did funny things to her stomach. "I'm glad you came."

"I wouldn't miss a chance to see you, even if it's only for a few minutes. Do you still want me to meet your mother?"

"Yes, I told her I wanted to introduce her to someone. I think she's over this way."

As she started back toward the church, Jacob caught her hand. "Do we have to go right away? Maybe we could talk for a few minutes."

His blue eyes shone with hope. She squeezed his hand. "I'd like that, but I'm afraid Momma will be looking for me. I've already had one lecture today." She took his arm and led him to where her mother stood talking to Margaret.

The two ladies turned toward Julia and Jacob as they approached. Momma had a reserved smile while Margaret's eyes widened.

After introductions, Momma asked, "How do you like our city, Mr. Anderson?"

"It's an interesting place. My family is quite taken with it, especially my younger brother."

"Why's that?"

"He's good on the piano and hopes to play on stage someday."

The pride Jacob felt for his brother warmed Julia's heart.

With a smile, Momma said, "Well then, he should meet Mr. Fontello. He's helped several young musicians get their start."

"That's what I told him." Julia turned to Jacob. "Have you had a chance to ask your brother about it?"

"He's interested, but feels he needs to practice more before playing for someone."

"You just let us know when he's ready," Momma said. "We'll be glad to contact Mr. Fontello."

"Thank you, Mrs. Phillips. I appreciate you taking an interest."

Margaret gave Julia and Momma a quick hug. "I have to go. I see Steven motioning for me."

"We'll see you at our house this evening, dear." Momma turned back to Jacob. "You mentioned a family, Mr. Anderson. What does your father do?"

"My father and uncle are partners in the jewelry business."

Julia said, "Mr. Anderson's uncle has been here for years, but only recently talked his brother into moving here from New York. It's not surprising his family would like Boston better, is it?"

"No, not surprising at all. Mr. Anderson, it's nice to meet you. I hope we'll see you again."

As the ladies turned to leave, Julia looked back and mouthed the word Tuesday. Jacob smiled as he watched them get in their sleigh and ride away.

"Miss Phillips is lovely, isn't she?"

Jacob turned to see Lucien standing beside him. "Yes, she is."

Lucien gestured up the street with his hand. "Will you take a walk with me?"

Jacob nodded, but from Lucien's unsmiling face and rigid posture, he knew 'no' would not have been accepted as an answer. As they started down Mt. Vernon Street, Jacob planned to take full advantage of this opportunity. They passed by large townhouses while sleighs swished along the street, the horses' hooves making a muffled clip clop on the snow.

"Julia says you're new in town. How long have you been here?"

"I got here a month or so ago." Jacob looked over at Lucien. "I suppose your family has been here for generations."

Lucien's chest puffed out and he gave Jacob a haughty glance. "Most of the old families go back past the Revolution, including Julia's. How did you meet her?"

"She came into the jewelry store looking for a birthday gift for her father. I helped her pick something out."

"I guess it was fortunate for her you were there."

Jacob caught the sarcasm in Lucien's voice, but chose to overlook the jab. "I feel the good fortune was mine. She's a charming young woman and I've enjoyed getting acquainted with her."

"Yes, she is charming. She's also engaged to me. Has she told you?"

"She said her father made an arrangement on her behalf."

With an edge to his voice, Lucien said, "That doesn't make her any less my fiancée." He stopped and Jacob turned to look at him. "I want to be sure there is no misunderstanding about that."

Jacob couldn't blame Lucien for trying to warn him off. If Julia were engaged to him, he'd do the same thing. However, Lucien wasn't Julia's choice and Jacob was determined to do what he could to change Lucien's mind.

"I understand, but do you think marriage is a good idea? Wouldn't working another year put you in an even better position?" Jacob moved forward again and Lucien fell in step.

"Ha. If you're referring to finances, I'm in a position to marry anytime I want. Can you say the same?"

Jacob ignored the question. "Perhaps you might think more along the lines of waiting a while. In a year or so, you both may be more settled, ready to make a commitment such as marriage."

"I see no reason to wait. I have no reservations about marriage, and Mr. Phillips believes it's time for Julia to settle down. My advice to you is to no longer pursue a friendship with her."

Now Jacob stopped, forcing Lucien to turn and face him. "Whatever time Julia and I spend together will be her choice." He looked steadily into Lucien's eyes. "I would never force her to do anything against her will."

Lucien looked back at him for a moment, then turned and strode back toward the church.

Jacob shuddered and started home. He'd never met anyone like Lucien Harris. He could see why Julia felt she might have to do something her parents wouldn't approve of, and he'd like to know what that something was. His gut told him Edward would be involved, but she'd been evasive on that front.

He pulled his hat a little lower on his head then jammed his hands deeper into his coat pockets. Edward hadn't been what he would call possessive the two times they'd been together, but he and Julia had an obvious connection. At least Edward hadn't tried to run him off. That seemed encouraging. On the other hand, maybe he was waiting to see if Julia saw him as more than a passing fancy.

Jacob shivered and noticed he could hear the snow crunch as he stepped on it, but he couldn't feel his feet. Church clothes were not warm enough for a long walk on a winter day, so he found a livery and hired a sleigh to take him the rest of the way.

While Millie helped Julia dress for the evening, Julia recalled the meeting between Jacob and her mother and felt it couldn't have gone better. Momma loved a project, and helping Jacob's brother would insure her blessing on continued contact with Jacob.

It didn't hurt that Margaret had been there and could've said they had seen him at a lecture. Now all she had to worry about was Papa.

At the family supper, Julia noticed her parents were keeping a close eye on her and Edward. Good. Maybe that meant they'd ignore Jacob as a possible threat, and think only of Edward.

"You look like the cat who swallowed the canary," Margaret said, when Julia went with her to the nursery to change Elise's diaper. "Don't tell me Lucien changed his mind."

"Unfortunately, no. But I guess I am feeling a little smug. What did you think about this morning when Momma met Jacob?"

"You're on a first-name basis already?"

"I know we haven't known each other long, but I think of him as Jacob and I like to hear him call me Julia. We would have gotten to that point anyway, so why wait?"

Margaret sat in a rocking chair while Julia leaned against the rail of one of the children's beds that still occupied the nursery.

"The point is, there are rules of etiquette to follow and you're rushing ahead. You need to take your time." Margaret picked up Elise and bounced her on her lap making her giggle.

Julia took a moment to enjoy her niece's laughter, then picked up the conversation. "I don't have much time. Once the announcement is made it will be harder for us to spend time alone. So, what did you think about this morning?" She came and sat next to Margaret.

"It was a brilliant idea. At first, I couldn't imagine what you were doing, but getting Momma acquainted with him will make her a lot more comfortable if someone asks her about him later. Did you plan the part about her helping his brother? That couldn't have been more perfect."

"I thought so, too, but no, I didn't plan it. Isn't it wonderful? It's as if God is giving us his blessing."

Julia couldn't sit still. She jumped up and whirled in a circle, making Elise squeal and clap her hands.

"I don't think God is that interested in us. You were just fortunate." Margaret worked to keep her daughter from bouncing off her lap.

Julia sat and pondered for a few moments. "I'd like to think God has some interest in us. If he doesn't, why should we go to church? Or, why should we bother to pray for Katherine? Our sister needs his help to get through this pregnancy and the delivery."

"I think our family has always gone to church because it's the socially expected thing to do. As for praying for Katherine, if it makes you feel better, you should do it. Just don't expect God to make Lucien go away."

Edward pushed open the door. "Julia, here you are. Lily said she'd seen you two come up here."

As soon as Elise saw Edward, she squirmed off her mother's lap and toddled over to wrap her arms around his knees. "Up!"

Margaret and Julia followed her. Edward laughed and swung the little girl up into his arms. "You're a cutie, Elise, but you're awfully bossy." She grinned and pulled on Edward's nose. "Ouch. What a grip."

Margaret laughed as she took Elise from Edward. "Let's go find something to eat. I think I saw some cookies earlier."

Elise wiggled in excitement. "Cookies!"

"Don't stay up here too long, you two."

As soon as Margaret left, Edward asked, "Why have your parents been watching me all evening?"

"I think they're watching both of us."

"Why? Has Lucien been complaining?"

"Yes." Julia took Edward's hand and led him to the rocking chairs she and Margaret had been using. "Sit and I'll tell you about it."

From the corner of her eye, Julia could see Edward watching her as she took her time arranging her skirts. She looked at the dolls, tea sets and books on the shelves lining the walls, and cleared her throat a couple of times.

Finally, he said, "Julia, you're making me nervous. What did you tell your parent?" "Nothing definite." She turned to face him, pleading with her eyes for him to understand. "It's just that Lucien didn't like our behavior last night, and Papa said he and Momma told him we're nothing more than friends, and I said 'how do you know,' and he said 'your father said so,' and Momma said, 'if we were more than friends we would have said so,' and I said, 'we are friends, but we had talked about marriage.'"

Julia stopped for a breath, then went on. "So, I suppose now they might be wondering if we'll suddenly decide we're more than friends." She folded her hands in front of her chest. "You're not angry with me, are you?"

Edward's eyes had grown bigger as she talked and now his mouth hung open. He sputtered a moment, then said, "Are you saying you led them to believe we might get serious? That my days as a bachelor are numbered?" He stood with a frown and began pacing back and forth. Suddenly he stopped and pointed his finger at her. "You were the last person I worried about giving her parents such an idea."

Julia wanted to cry. She hated for him to be upset with her. "Edward, I'm sorry." She jumped up and went to stand in front of him, but he turned his back to her. "I promise I'll tell them they have nothing to worry about." Then she noticed his shoulders shaking and what sounded suspiciously like someone trying not to laugh. "Oh you!" She planted her hands against his back and gave him a push.

He burst out laughing, spun around and grabbed her in a hug that lifted her off her feet.

"Put me down! I can't believe you did that."

"Oh, come on." He set her down, "You have to admit I was good. Maybe I should move to New York and go on the stage. What do you think?"

"You'd be wonderful," Julia admitted with a laugh. "I'm glad you're not upset."

"Of course, I'm not upset, but I'd think it would be better if your parents weren't wondering about us. You wouldn't want them to suspect you might go with me at the end of the summer."

"Papa already thought of that anyway." She went back to the rocking chair. "Mainly I think if they're paying attention to you, they won't be as likely to notice Jacob."

"You might be right." Edward sat beside her. "I don't mind being a decoy."

Julia leaned over and kissed him on the cheek. "Thank you."

Lily chose that moment to burst through the door with a triumphant smile. "Ha! I knew I was right about you two."

"This is not what it looks like," Julia said.

"Well, you're lucky it was I who found you instead of your mother. She's been quite concerned about where you two could be. Margaret said she might have seen you in the dining room, so while your mother went there, I came up here. If you hurry, she may never know you were spending time un-chaperoned in the nursery."

Edward winked at Julia. "We could tell her we were talking about the future."

Her cheeks grew hot. "You had better not."

15

On Tuesday afternoon, Jacob stood on the porch in front of Margaret's four-story townhouse and stared at the front door. His parents' warnings about an upper- class family not accepting him, replayed in his mind.

What if they were right about Julia only being interested in him as a novelty, and would soon grow bored? They didn't know about her unwanted engagement to Lucien, but if they did, they'd say she was using him somehow. He shook his head to clear away the thoughts. It didn't matter that he stood in front of a house on Chestnut Street in the middle of the Beacon Hill neighborhood. No one there was any better than him. He stepped forward and rang the bell before he changed his mind.

A maid opened the door. He followed her through a small vestibule, then double doors with etched glass windows and into the hall. She took his coat and hat and hung them on the hall tree, then gestured to some chairs on either side of a grandfather clock on the other side of the hall. "Please wait here while I let Mrs. Jefferson know you've arrived."

While waiting for her to come back, he drummed his fingertips on his knees and admired the geometric pattern in the tile floor and the many prints and etchings on the walls. The clock chimed the hour, letting him know he'd arrived on time. He looked toward the stairway to see if the maid might be returning and noticed the handrail, newel posts, and balusters glowed warmly with a gloss varnish. Brass carpet rods held down the stair runner.

Jacob's parents' home was comfortable and his mother had decorated it tastefully, but it couldn't compare to this. Obviously, no expense had been spared here and he could imagine Julia's house must be as grand.

Once again, he heard his mother asking how he could hope to offer her a life in the style she was used to. In truth, he couldn't. Jacob had to admit he could see himself falling in love with her, but would love be enough?

Living in the city all his life would be suffocating, let alone in a house like this one. How could he ask her to do without the luxuries she'd grown up with? Maybe he should leave before it went any further. His body grew more tense by the minute, making it hard to breathe. He stood, and his stiff legs got him almost to the door when the maid called his name. Jacob turned and she motioned for him to follow her upstairs.

When Jacob entered the drawing room, Julia greeted him with a welcoming smile. One look in her eyes and Jacob's doubts and fears vanished like mist in the sun. The vise squeezing his chest released and he took a deep breath.

Julia slid her hand around his arm and spoke as she led him to a silk love seat, near Margaret's armchair. "I'm glad you could come. I hope your father and uncle aren't getting tired of you asking for time off during the day."

"I haven't committed to staying in Boston yet, so they're not being too demanding." He turned to Margaret. "Thank you, Mrs. Jefferson, for allowing me to call."

"You're welcome, but I think you should know it's hard to refuse Julia anything. When she asked, I couldn't say no." She gave Julia an indulgent smile. "I'm fond of her and want to see her happy."

"I wish Momma and Papa still had that problem. But we don't want to talk about that gloomy subject." As soon as they were seated, she turned to him. "Tell me about the jewelry store. Are you growing accustomed to it yet?"

He couldn't muster much enthusiasm for this subject. "It's not too bad for now."

"Tell me more about you. What was it like growing up on a farm?"

Jacob thought back to his boyhood. "We worked hard, but it was fun, too. In the summer my brothers and I would take every opportunity to swim in the creek or go fishing. We would bring home frogs and turtles and Mother would make us take them back." He laughed at the memory. "She really had a fit when we brought home a snake."

Julia's eyes flew wide. "You didn't actually bring a snake home, did you?"

"We caught snakes all the time, but we only showed one to Mother. We were afraid she might die of fright if we showed her any more."

"I wouldn't want to touch one." Julia shuddered. "As a girl, I would go to Frog Pond with Edward and catch frogs, but I stayed away from snakes."

"You've actually touched a frog?" Jacob's eyebrows rose to his hairline. "I'm impressed. The girls around home wanted nothing to do with them."

Margaret chuckled. "Most of the girls around here want nothing to do with them either." She gave Julia a pointed look. "If you have a daughter someday, I hope you'll remember what it was like when she wants to be out at the pond with the boys."

"I'm sure I'll be understanding," Julia said, with a wave of her hand. "What do you think Jacob? Should a girl be allowed to play outside with the boys?"

He didn't hesitate. "If you are an example of how a girl can play outside with the boys and still grow up to be a charming young woman, then I say yes, you should let her."

Margaret nodded her approval. "Good answer, Mr. Anderson."

Julia gave him a pleased smile, but changed the subject. "What did you do about school? Did your mother teach you at home?"

"We went to a one-room school through eighth grade. We were fortunate to have enough hired help that we could go every day. Some of the boys had to stay home and help during planting and harvest."

"Did you stop at the eighth grade?" Margaret asked.

He shook his head. "A town, one day's train ride away, had a high school. When we finished eighth grade we went there and boarded with a family. That's where Jason got more advanced piano instruction. I wish you could hear him. His teacher said he's a natural." He hoped Julia and her mother would be able to help him.

"I'd like to. Maybe he'll play for Mr. Fontello at our house."

"Do you think your mother is truly interested?" He didn't want to get his hopes up on his brother's behalf if the idea was only a passing thought.

"Momma loves a project, especially if it has to do with the arts. If Jason is successful, she'll be able to say she had something to do with it. But the best part is, she won't mind me talking to you because she wants to help your brother." She briefly laid her hand on his arm. "I knew introducing you would be a good idea."

One of the maids rolled a tea cart into the room and Margaret stood. "Julia, will you pour while I check on Elise?"

When Margaret left the room, Jacob said, "Lucien and I had a talk after church Sunday."

Julia gave him a sympathetic look, then went to the tea cart and began pouring. "I hope he wasn't rude."

"He told me it would be best if you and I weren't friends." Jacob shook his head, remembering Lucien's high-handed attitude. "You were right about him. I've never met anyone so determined to have his way. I'm afraid I won't be able to talk him out of anything."

"Don't feel bad. I didn't expect you to." Julia handed him a teacup. "I've resigned myself to the fact that there will be a scandal of some kind over this."

"Does what you have in mind have something to do with Edward?" When Julia hesitated to answer, he said, "I'm wondering if I should expect him to have a talk with me too."

"I don't think you'll have to worry about that. Edward is pretty easy-going." Julia stirred milk into her tea. "But the answer to your question is yes, he will do whatever he can to help me avoid marriage to Lucien."

"I don't suppose you would want to tell me what that help will be?"

"I can't tell you now," she whispered.

As Margaret came into the room with Elise, she asked, "Did you save us any tea?"

Julia turned to her sister and smiled. "Of course, we did, and I'm glad to see you brought Elise with you."

"I hoped you wouldn't mind." Margaret set her daughter down and Elise toddled over to Julia.

"Juwee, up!"

Setting aside her tea, Julia picked up the little girl and gave her a hug. "Jacob, this is my adorable niece. Elise, this is Mr. Anderson. Can you say hello?"

Elise regarded him with solemn blue eyes. He smiled and winked at her. She popped her thumb in her mouth and kept her eyes on him. Jacob chuckled. "I'm afraid I'm not experienced with little ones, but I bet I know what you'd like. How about a cookie?"

Elise bounced on Julia's lap and clapped her hands. "Cookie."

Jacob handed her one from the plate. She leaned back against Julia and munched in contentment.

"Have you had a chance to see the Common or the Public Garden, Mr. Anderson?" Margaret asked, helping herself to a cup of tea.

"I've walked through. My mother is especially fond of Deer Park so I've been there with her. One of my favorite winter activities, as Julia can tell you, is ice-skating. I've been to the Public Garden a few times."

"Maybe we could go this week. People enjoy skating at either place, but my favorite is the Public Garden."

"You name the day and the time and I'll be there." Jacob couldn't think of anyone he'd rather go with.

"We'll plan on Thursday afternoon. I'll meet you at the Charles Street entrance."

Margaret turned to Jacob. "I understand you plan to attend the concert this evening."

"Yes. I am." He wouldn't miss it.

"Well, I suppose you two had better say good-bye until then. Come on Elise, let's see if we can find a book to read." Margaret lifted the little girl from Julia's lap and left the room.

Julia went with Jacob to the door. "It seems like you just got here."

"I agree, but I don't want to argue with your sister. She's been so generous with her time already." Jacob couldn't resist taking her hand in his for a moment. "I'll look forward to seeing you for a few minutes tonight and again on Thursday."

Julia gave his hand a quick squeeze. "As will I. Good-bye for now."

Jacob headed to Beacon Street, where he could catch a trolley, wondering what he'd been so worried about. Julia behaved as warm and friendly as ever. In fact, she seemed as eager to see him as he had been to see her. Everything about her was genuine. He didn't believe she was only casually interested in him, or that she would try to use him to gain some advantage over Lucien.

He turned up his coat collar and put his hands in his pockets. Maybe his parents would feel better about her if they could meet her. Margaret and Mrs. Phillips had been gracious to him; surely his parents could be no less. He would have to ask his mother about it.

Jacob and Jason's sleigh moved slowly along a street filled with sleighs on their way to the concert. "How did tea with Miss Phillips go this afternoon? You still think you can fit in with the upper class?"

"We had a nice time and I'll have to say, as far as classes go, our family seems to be having a harder time than hers." Both men held onto their top hats in a sudden gust of wind.

"You haven't met much of her family. How accepting do you think her father will be if he knows the son of a merchant is interested in his daughter?"

"I get the feeling Julia will do what she wants, regardless of her father's wishes. I think she'll follow her heart."

Jason gave him a meaningful look. "Will she follow you to Iowa? And don't bother to deny you're already thinking about it. I've never seen you like this over a girl."

Jacob smiled and closed his eyes for a minute, picturing Julia in his mind. Looking at his brother he said, "You're right. I've never felt this way about any girl. I can't wait from one meeting to the next to see her again. We haven't known each other long, but I already know she's the one I want to spend my life with." Jacob laughed at himself. "I sound like some hero in a melodrama."

Jason patted his shoulder. "Either you'll end up being the happiest man I know or the saddest. I hope she's worth the experience either way."

"When you meet Julia, you'll see why I can't forget her. Actually, I think Mother and Father should meet her, too. Then maybe they won't keep trying to discourage me."

"If she's everything you say, it would be a good idea. It certainly couldn't make their opinion any worse."

Lucien frowned. "Are you looking for someone, Julia? You can't seem to sit still."

"Oh, I guess I'm just interested in seeing who's here. Have you ever noticed you'll see some people at a concert that you'd never see at a lecture and vice versa?"

Sophia nodded. "I know what you mean. Oh, look. There's Mrs. Pennington and Clara. By the way, what happened with you and Clara at the ball the other night? Was she trying to get advice about Edward?"

Julia finally sat still and gave Sophia her attention. "Yes, and I think I may have gotten her to leave him alone until he comes back from Europe. By then, it may not be an issue."

"What's that supposed to mean?" Lucien asked. "Do you think Edward will come back married?"

"You never know. Of course, Clara may be the one married by the time Edward gets back."

"Well, even if neither of them is married by then, we will be, and Edward will have to take care of himself."

Julia didn't have time to answer because the concert started. There was no point arguing anyway. He'd find out eventually that things don't always go according to plan.

At intermission Julia stood and scanned the crowd. Jacob had to be here somewhere. Suddenly she spotted him with a man that had to be his brother. He was almost as tall as Jacob and had the same blond hair and blue eyes.

"I think I'll move around a bit. You don't mind, do you?" She left without an answer and headed toward the back.

Jacob and Jason stood in the back looking for Julia. "She must have a seat close to the front," Jacob said. "Let's just go up the center aisle and hope we find her." Having made that decision, they turned and almost ran into her.

Jacob blinked a couple of times to make sure he wasn't imagining Julia standing in front of him.

She laughed. "You look surprised. Didn't you expect me to be here?"

Jacob quickly recovered and grinned. "I counted on you being here, but thought we'd have a hard time finding you."

"Then it's a good thing I found you." Julia turned to Jason. "You must be Jacob's brother. You look too much alike to deny it."

Jason smiled. "We've been told that. But other than looks, I'd say we're more different than alike."

"Jacob says you're musically inclined. I'd love to hear you play."

"I appreciate the interest you and your mother have taken in my future. As soon as I feel worthy of an audience, I'll let Jacob know. I'm sure he'll be glad to get you the message." Jason gave his brother a wink.

"Did I tell you we plan to go ice-skating Thursday, Jason?" Jacob hoped Julia hadn't seen the wink.

"No, but it sounds like fun."

"Why don't you come too, Mr. Anderson? My friend, Sophia, will be coming and you would make us an even number. Please say you will."

Jacob enjoyed watching the effect Julia's smile had on Jason. It looked as though she'd won him over.

"I'll make every effort, but I'm not sure if I can get time away from the store as easily as Jacob."

"I don't want to cause a problem with your family. We'll be glad to see you if you come."

Jacob looked over Julia's shoulder and stifled a groan. "I hate to bring him up, but does Lucien know where you are."

"Why?"

"I think he's looking for you. He's coming this way."

Julia's brow crinkled. "Oh dear, how close is he?"

"Too close to avoid, and he doesn't look happy."

"Is there a problem?" Jason asked.

"Tell you later," Jacob said under his breath.

"Here you are, Julia. I'm afraid you left before I could offer to go with you."

"I'm sorry if I worried you, but as you can see, I'm fine. I ran into Mr. Anderson and his brother."

"Yes, I see that." Lucien glanced at the men. "I think it's time to go back to our seats now. We wouldn't want Sophia to worry about both of us." He took Julia's hand and tucked it though his arm, keeping his hand over hers. As he led her away, she turned and lifted her free hand in a quick farewell.

The Anderson brothers watched Lucien usher Julia down the aisle, then, Jason said,

"I can see why you two wanted to avoid him. You didn't tell me she had a brother."

Jacob looked at Jason, considering for a moment. "He's not her brother. He's her fiancée."

Jason's eyes widened. "What! She's upper class *and* engaged? How much more impossible can you get?"

Those who stood or passed near-by turned to look at them. Jacob gripped Jason's upper arm. "Let's go somewhere less crowded."

They made their way through the stream of people returning from the lobby to their seats. Jacob picked up the conversation in a hushed tone. "I know it sounds crazy, but you saw her reaction to him. Her father made the arrangement and she wants nothing to do with it."

Jason shook his head. "That doesn't change the fact that she belongs to him."

"Remember when I said she would do whatever she wanted?" At Jason's nod he went on. "She's tried to talk him out of it, but he won't change his mind. So regardless of what he thinks will happen, she made it clear to me she won't marry him."

"What does she plan to do? Surely it will be a social scandal for her family if she doesn't show up at the church." Jason narrowed his eyes. "Or maybe she's hoping you'll take her west. That would be convenient, since you're pretty sure you'll go anyway."

Anger stirred in Jacob on Julia's behalf. "Does she strike you as the kind of person who would attach herself to someone just to avoid trouble?"

"You never know what a woman might do if she's desperate. I don't know if I trust her." Jason crossed his arms over his chest and waited for Jacob to convince him otherwise.

Jacob replied, hearing the edge in his voice. "That's exactly the kind of reaction I'm afraid our parents will have, so I would appreciate it if you'd keep this to yourself."

"I won't say anything, but it can't be too big a secret if her father has given his blessing."

He heaved a sigh. "It hasn't been announced yet. She talked her father into waiting for a while. Look Jason." Jacob put a hand on his brother's shoulder. "I know it doesn't look good, but I'm asking you to trust me. Julia is not after a ticket west. As a matter of fact, she has a close friend who I'm pretty sure has offered her another opportunity. Somehow, I have to convince her that waiting for me to get enough money and then going to Iowa would be a better idea. I could use someone on my side."

Jason continued to look him in the eye. "Okay, I'll support you," he promised, relaxing his posture. "You've never been wrong about a person's character."

"Thanks." Relief flooded him. "You can see she's special, can't you?"

"She's out of reach if you ask me, but I can see why you haven't let anything stop you. If you win her, she'll be worth it."

16

Julia fumed all the way back to her seat in the front section of the auditorium. As soon as they sat, she turned to Lucien with a frown. "That was rude. I'm sure Mr. Anderson and his brother are wondering at your lack of manners. Not to mention having you lead me away as if I were a child."

"Mr. Anderson and I have already talked," Lucien said, his voice dripping with disapproval. "I have nothing more to say to him, and I certainly can't imagine what I would say to his brother. Furthermore, I wouldn't treat you like a child if you didn't act like one."

Julia stiffened. Of all the nerve. She inhaled, ready to clear up his misguided judgment, when Sophia spoke up. "Maybe it would be a good idea to talk about this later. There will be fewer ears to hear on the way home."

"Fine." Julia stood. "I think now would be a good time to go."

The lights dimmed for the second half of the concert and Lucien patted the seat of her chair. "We'll wait until the concert is over."

Julia sat with a huff and Sophia leaned close. "Take a deep breath and count to ten."

On their way home, Lucien said, "I hope you don't mind if we drop Sophia off before we have our discussion. I'm sure she'd rather not have to listen."

"I agree." No need to subject Sophia to their squabble. "We can talk in my drawing room if you'd rather."

Other than Sophia mentioning the quintet had been exceptionally good that evening, they rode the rest of the way in silence.

Lucien took Sophia to her door and came back to the sleigh. Because Sophia lived next door to her, Julia expected him to help her out, but instead he got back in. "You aren't cold, are you?"

"Not too cold, why?"

"I'd rather talk out here."

She gasped and scooted as far away from him as she could. "You expect me to sit out here in a sleigh, on the street in front of my house, alone with you? What will people think?"

"Ha! It didn't look as though you cared what people might think of you talking alone to a man of recent acquaintance. What do your parents think of him? Do they even know his family?"

"Momma thinks he's nice and no, they don't know his family yet." Julia took her hands out of her fur muff long enough to pull the lap robes closer around her. "As far as talking to someone in a crowded concert hall, I hardly think that qualifies as being alone. I don't understand how that makes me childish."

"I'll be happy to tell you." He held up his gloved fist. "We're engaged." One finger went up. "I asked you not to spend time with him and where do I find you—with him." He raised a second finger. "You seem to have no respect for my authority and your disobedience is childish." Up went finger number three. "Now do you understand?"

Julia stared at him and his three fingers. How could her father ever have believed they would suit? "Tell me something, Lucien. Why do you want to marry me?"

His eyes widened a fraction and he hesitated before answering. "You're interesting to talk to. You're intelligent and I think you would be an excellent mother." He slid closer to her. "I also think you're beautiful and fun to be with, when you're not mad at me. Unfortunately, you seem to be cross with me all the time. What happened to the woman I just described?"

Julia's heart softened a little. "Maybe she's not who you think she is. You wouldn't have to look far to find someone else with all those same qualities, and she's not mad at you."

"You're the one I want."

She shook her head. "People don't always get what they want."

He jerked his thumb toward his chest. "I usually do. There's no point debating an issue that has already been settled. If you would stop fighting it and relax, we could start enjoying each other's company again. Take Sophia for example. She's so even-tempered."

Julia almost laughed. "Why don't *you* take Sophia? She'd be perfect for you."

When he frowned but gave no response, she said, "I'm getting cold. I'd like to go in now."

Lucien heaved a sigh, then saw her to the door.

When Julia passed the drawing room, Momma called to her. "How was your evening? Did you enjoy the concert?"

Julia stepped inside the room. "I enjoyed the concert, but Lucien and I are having a hard time. We've been sitting in front of the house talking, but it does no good. He doesn't understand me and I certainly can't understand him."

Momma considered for a moment. "Maybe what you need is more time alone with him. Sometimes a little affection can get you across the rough spots."

A shudder rippled over her. "Momma, please, I have no interest in being affectionate with Lucien. I'm tired. Do you mind if I go to bed?"

"No dear, that's fine. I'll see you in the morning."

As Julia got ready for bed, she had to laugh at herself. For a minute there she had actually felt sorry for Lucien. How could anyone be so obstinate? The stress making her muscles stiff ebbed away as Millie brushed out her hair. No more trying to do him any favors. If he woke up and realized Sophia was the one he wanted, fine. But if he ended up being thoroughly embarrassed by the end of the summer, that suited her fine too.

The next afternoon, Julia sat at her dressing table frowning at her reflection. Sophia came in and stood beside her. "What could you possibly find to be unhappy about. You look perfect."

She glanced at Sophia and then back to the mirror, turning her head from side to side. "I don't know if Jacob will like my hair this way. I had Millie try something new, but now I'm not sure."

Sophia gave a short laugh. "You'll be wearing a hat, so I don't see what difference it makes. Anyway, I have a feeling Jacob doesn't pay a lot of attention to your hair. He wants to see you."

"Do you truly think so?" With other men, Julia hadn't cared enough to worry about what they thought.

Sophia pulled a side chair over and sat next to her. "Tell me what you think."

"He seems to enjoy the time we spend together." Julia twisted her ring around her finger. "I hope he doesn't keep agreeing to see me because he thinks it would be rude not to."

Laying her hand on top of Julia's, Sophia said, "I think you're finding things to worry about. What do you see when he looks in your eyes? Is it interest or obligation?"

"Definitely interest. No man has ever looked at me the way he does." Julia's cheeks warmed at the memory. "It's as if he sees the real me and wouldn't change a thing. We can talk about anything without him telling me women shouldn't worry their little heads over those issues."

"Then how can you wonder? It's clear he's taken with you. The question is, how far are you willing to let it go?"

Julia gripped her friend's hand. "I've already told you, if my heart tells me he's the one, I'll go to Iowa with him. If he asks me. I still hope he'll decide he likes city life, though."

"So, your heart hasn't decided."

She took the glass stopper out of her perfume bottle and dabbed it behind her ears. "Priscilla told me some things I ought to consider when choosing a husband. Well, choosing wouldn't be the word, since she was actually giving me reasons to accept the choice already made."

Sophia's eyebrows rose. "What did she tell you? I find it hard to believe you would take anything she said to heart. Especially on this subject."

"Priscilla said there's more to marriage than emotions. I should think about future children and what kind of life they would have." Julia turned away from the mirror to give Sophia her full attention. "When I look at Jacob there's no question my emotions are involved. Just thinking about seeing him makes me happy. But I have to ask myself, what kind of life could he offer a child?"

Sophia leaned back, hands folded in her lap. "We've grown up with everything we could want. It's hard to imagine a life with less. To be fair though, there are plenty of people with less money who seem to be just as happy. Maybe it would be more to the point to ask what kind of father he would be than how much money will he make."

Julia leaned over to give her friend an affectionate squeeze. "That's a much better way to look at it. Thank you, Sophia."

Her friend returned the hug. "That's not the only thing, though.

Money shouldn't be the primary concern, but it should be a consideration. If you marry someone in a lower class, you'll have to make material sacrifices."

"When two people love each other they're happy to make sacrifices."

"Easy to say when you don't know what those sacrifices will be."

"Hmm…" Julia drummed her fingertips on the dressing table for a few moments. "We could do some investigating. Maybe visit his mother to see how she lives."

"I suppose it would be a start, but it wouldn't tell you much about farm life."

"We don't know for sure about the farm yet." She glanced at the clock on her fireplace mantle. "Oh no, we're going to be late to meet Jacob."

The girls hurried down the stairs, pausing to say good-bye to Momma, then down the next flight to the hall where they pulled on coats, hats and gloves. They went out into a cold sunny day. As the sleigh glided down the street, Julia said, "By the way, I invited Jacob's brother to come."

Sophia's eyes widened. "Why?"

"Jacob told him we were going and it seemed rude not to include him. Anyway, he's nice and I think he'll be good company."

"Is he the one who plays the piano?"

"Yes, I hope he'll be ready to play for Mr. Fontello soon. I'm anxious to hear him."

When they arrived, they found Jacob and Jason waiting for them at the park entrance. Julia introduced Sophia to Jason and the four started down the sidewalk leading to the lagoon, with Julia and Jacob in the lead.

"I'm glad you suggested skating," Jacob said. "I've always enjoyed being on the ice."

Jason spoke up. "We'd all be at the pond on our uncle's farm every minute we could during the winter. There were times we'd get so cold we could barely walk home."

"I remember." Jacob laughed. "Mother would be worried about frostbite and Father would say, 'If it happens, they'll come in sooner next time.'"

Julia's heart ached for the brothers. "He doesn't sound very sympathetic."

"He expected us to use the common sense God gave us." Jason smiled. "We learned from our mistakes and didn't get into any real trouble."

Jacob turned to her and glanced back at Sophia. "We wouldn't want you to have the wrong idea about our father. If Jason can make a career out of playing the piano, he'll be at every concert. He thinks we should choose our own road in life."

"And if Jacob wants to go all the way to Iowa and buy a farm, when he could have one already established closer to family, then that's all right too."

Everyone stopped and looked at Jason. "Well, maybe none of us want him to go that far, but if that's what he wants, we'll support him."

Jacob grimaced. "Thanks, I'm sure I won't feel guilty if I go."

On arrival at the lagoon, they put on their skates. As soon as they stepped on the ice, Jason said, "I'll race you to the other end."

Jacob frowned at his brother. "We can't leave the ladies here."

"Go ahead," Julia said, waving them off. "We don't mind."

With a grin, Jacob said, "Okay then, just once."

The men took off, coat tails and scarves flying as they dodged other skaters. Sophia shook her head. "Men are boys no matter what class they're from."

Julia and Sophia linked arms and began to skate leisurely in the direction the men had taken. "How did your discussion with Lucien go last night?"

"About the same as it always goes." Julia sighed. "He tried to explain why I need to be loyal and obedient and I tried to point out I wasn't the right choice. I'm afraid I even said he should be thinking of you."

Sophia stopped and looked at her. "So much for subtlety."

"I'm sorry. I know Lucien admires you, though. He thinks you're a wonderful example, and even suggested I be more like you."

"He doesn't understand you need to be yourself. It sounds like Lucien is set on his course and nothing is going to change it."

Julia moved forward again. "I think you're right. It's only been two weeks, but it already feels hopeless."

"If you're not going to change his mind, and you want to avoid arguments, why don't you agree to everything he says? Maybe if he's feeling secure about you, he'll relax more in my company."

"I guess I can try that, as long as I don't have to do what I agree to. I don't intend to stop seeing Jacob."

Jacob and Jason swished to a stop in front of them, a little out of breath. "You two look serious," Jacob said. "No one died while we were gone, did they?"

"No." Julia laughed. "But I'm happy to change the subject."

Sophia said, "What we need is a brisk trip around the pond to clear our heads."

"We'll be happy to oblige you." Jason offered Sophia his arm. She took it and Julia took Jacob's as they started off on a smooth steady pace.

Julia had to admit the exercise, along with the crisp, cold air, helped to lighten her mood.

Jacob asked, "Have you ever danced on the ice?"

"No. I've never heard of it."

"Do you want to try?"

Her stomach flipped over. "I'm afraid I'd make us fall."

"You won't. I'll make sure we stay on our feet." Jacob gave her a reassuring smile.

Both nerves and excitement swirled inside her. If they danced it meant she would be in his arms. And he did promise he wouldn't let them fall. "Okay, I'll try."

Jacob came around in front of Julia, skating backwards, and pulled her into his arms in the official waltz position. He led her around the lagoon as smoothly as if it were a ballroom floor. She heard exclamations of surprise and delight as they whirled by the more traditional skaters.

When they reached their starting point, he spun her in a circle that left her breathless and laughing. "That was fun! Where did you learn to do that?"

"On the pond at the farm. I like to dance and I like to skate, so I decided to combine the two. I'm glad you enjoyed it."

Julia grinned. "Let's do it again."

Jacob bowed. "Your wish is my command." They set off again, passing Jason and Sophia as they went.

When Jacob and Julia came back to the end of the lagoon with a final whirl, Sophia suggested going to a sweet shop for hot chocolate. As they took off their skates, Julia said, "Let's watch the boys coasting on the Common for a while. Do you mind, Sophia?"

"No. That's fine."

The four strolled across the Public Garden to the Common, where the boys flew down the hill on their sleds. Just watching gave Julia a thrill. "Doesn't that look like fun?"

"Yes!" Jacob and Jason both wore big grins.

"No!" Sophia said.

Julia directed her comment to the men. "Sophia fell off and rolled down the hill the one time Edward and I talked her into going. She would never try again."

Sophia sniffed and turned her nose up. "It's not lady-like."

"It's not a problem if you're wearing trousers."

Sophia's eyes locked on hers. "I can't believe Edward's mother never knew you were dressing in his clothes."

"Now wait a minute," Jacob said. "Do you mean to tell me you were actually out in public, dressed as a boy?"

"Are you shocked?" Julia couldn't contain her smile.

Jacob laughed. "No. I guess if you spent summers at the pond catching frogs, it's not surprising you'd be in long pants coasting in the winter."

"You caught frogs?" Jason's eyes were huge.

"To me it wasn't such an amazing thing. The boys I grew up with took it for granted."

Jason crossed his arms over his chest. "I know I've been here less than a year, but it doesn't sound like something a Boston girl would do."

"You're right," Sophia said with a laugh. "All the mommas were shaking their heads and feeling sorry for Mrs. Phillips. Julia was such a tomboy."

Jacob smiled at Julia. "I'll bet no one is shaking their heads now."

"Oh, they're shaking their heads all right, but now it's for a different reason."

17

Jacob and Jason followed Julia and Sophia as they headed for the sweet shop. The shouts and laughter of the boys on their sleds filled the air behind them. Jacob looked at Julia and then at Jason and motioned for him to distract her so he could talk to Sophia.

Jason nodded with a grin. "Miss Phillips, is there any more you can tell me about Mr. Fontello?"

Julia dropped back beside Jason and Jacob stepped up beside Sophia. A quick glance over his shoulder showed him his brother had slowed to put some distance between them.

Jacob offered his arm to Sophia and she slid her hand around it. "It's easy to see you and Julia are good friends. Do you mind if I ask a question?"

Sophia glanced up at him. "What would you like to know?"

Everything. He'd never get away with that, so he said, "This wasn't my original question, but you've got me curious about why mothers are shaking their heads. She appears to be a perfectly charming young woman."

"It's nothing terrible." Sophia's gentle laugh produced a frosty cloud. "They just don't understand her turning down marriage proposals, or why her parents are going along with it."

"I guess her parents ran out of patience." Jacob steered them around an icy spot.

"I'm afraid so, and there will be more head shaking to come."

"Do you have any idea what she's planning to do? Or more to the point, do you know if it involves Edward?"

"Have you asked Julia?"

"Yes, but she's evasive. I know it's probably not fair to try to get answers from you, but she talks about Edward all the time, and I'd like to have some idea what she's thinking."

Sophia glanced over her shoulder, regarded him a few moments, then turned her eyes back to the path. After a few more minutes of silence, he began to think she wasn't going to answer when she appeared to come to a decision. "Edward and Julia are close friends, but it has never been more than that. I don't doubt he would do what he could to help her, but if they've made plans, I don't know what they are. He'll finish school this spring and go to Europe at the end of the summer. I suppose it's not entirely out of the question that she would go with him."

Jacob's eyes narrowed as he considered the possibility. "What do you think the chances are she would do that? Is he going to Europe because it's the tradition for upper-class sons?"

Sophia shrugged. "With Julia, you never know. And he's going because it's felt that touring Europe is a good way to round out a gentleman's education. He'll also be visiting the businesses his father owns. He'll need a good understanding of how things are run on both sides of the Atlantic."

When they stepped into the confectionary, Julia soaked in the warmth and aroma of rich pastry, coffee and chocolate. In spite of the crowd they found a table with four chairs.

She couldn't remember when she'd had such a good time sharing cookies and drinking hot chocolate with friends. It seemed they'd just gotten there when Jacob popped open his pocket watch and sighed. He raised his eyes to hers. "It's three o'clock."

A lump of sadness stuck in her throat and everyone at the table grew quiet. Then Julia gave herself a mental shake. It's not as though they'd never see each other again. She found a smile. "This has been a wonderful afternoon. I think we should skate again on Saturday, instead of sleighing. How does that sound?"

"I like that idea," Jacob said, with a smile for Julia.

For a moment, as they gazed into each other's eyes, Julia felt as if they were the only two in the room.

"I wonder if anyone else will be invited?" Jason remarked.

Julia's cheeks heated. "Of course, everyone's invited."

❦

Julia and Sophia took a sleigh back to Louisburg Square and Jacob and Jason headed to the jewelry store. Jacob had thoroughly enjoyed the time spent with Julia, but almost wished he hadn't asked Sophia about Edward. On one hand knowing Edward and Julia were "just friends" was good, but thinking she might take off with him made him uneasy. He'd suspected they were planning something, but not Europe. How could he hope to compete with that?

Jason nudged Jacob with his elbow. "You look pretty gloomy for a guy who spent the afternoon with the girl of his dreams. Reality setting in?"

Jacob heaved a sigh. "Maybe. I don't know."

"Well, for what it's worth, I can see why you're taken with her. She's a special young woman."

"Yes." A smile stretched across his face. "She is." He couldn't imagine ever being bored in her company.

❦

In the sleigh, Julia turned to her friend. "It appeared you and Jacob were having a serious discussion on the way to Fera's Confectionary. I suppose he wanted to know what kind of risk he might be taking after your comment about mommas shaking their heads."

Sophia chuckled "He asked about that, but he was more interested in Edward. I think he wanted to know if Edward should be considered competition."

"Oh, I guess I do talk about him a lot." She put her hand on Sophia's arm. "Did you tell him we're just friends?"

"Yes, you don't mind, do you?" Her friend paused a moment. "He looked so unsure. I wanted to make him feel better."

"I'm glad you did. Did he seem happy to hear it?"

"He looked relieved. Of course, that worried look came back when I said you might go to Europe at the end of the summer."

Julia's eyes widened. "Weren't you against the idea?"

"I said, if you go, you should be married," Sophia reminded her.

"Well, I suppose it doesn't hurt if a man is a little worried. It keeps him from taking you for granted." Julia relaxed in the seat with a sigh. "I wish Jacob was invited to the Jordan dinner. I'm sure we'd be paired."

Sophia linked arms with her. "That's wishful thinking. What if Lucien has your name?"

Her stomach turned over at the thought, but just as quickly she realized if Lucien's interest was a surprise to her, it surely would be to everyone else. Including Mrs. Jordan.

Julia looked forward to the annual dinner the Jordans held for Boston's old families. Mrs. Jordan enjoyed matchmaking, so as each unmarried gentleman arrived, he received an envelope containing the name of his dinner partner. At a signal from their hostess, the men opened their envelope and escorted that lady in to dinner.

Sophia leaned a little closer as if sharing a secret. "Remember, many of her couples marry within the year."

"Then let's hope Lucien has your name," Julia said, giving Sophia's arm a squeeze.

⚜

At dinner that evening, Julia's mother asked, "When do you think you might see Mr. Anderson again? I'm eager to introduce his brother to Mr. Fontello."

"Sophia and I saw them both at the park today," Julia said with a casualness she was far from feeling. "Apparently, skating is one of their favorite winter pastimes."

"What did you think of his brother?"

"He's a nice young man, and grateful for our interest. He asked me about Mr. Fontello and we talked about what he should play."

"Did he give you any idea when he'd be ready?"

"Maybe another week or two." Julia took a sip of water. "Do you think he could play here? I'd like to hear him."

"I think it would be a good idea to hear him ourselves first." Momma absently twisted the stem of her water goblet between her fingers.

"I hate to interrupt," Papa said, "but have I met Mr. Anderson and his brother? None of this sounds familiar."

Turning to her husband, Momma said, "Now John, I'm sure I mentioned him to you. Julia introduced me to him after church last Sunday. He's a nice young man whose family is new to Boston. He has a brother who's interested in a career on the piano."

Papa's brow furrowed. "You say they're new to Boston?"

"They've been here less than a year." Julia crossed her fingers in her lap, hoping he wouldn't want to get involved.

"Anderson sounds familiar, but I can't recall why. There's no one at the club by that name. I can't think of an Anderson at the church.".

131

Momma laid a comforting hand on his arm. "I'm sure it will come to you dear."

Papa frowned. "I believe it would be a good idea to find out something about this family before you become too involved."

Julia groaned to herself.

"You know, I think we should call on Mrs. Anderson." Momma turned to look at her. "How about doing that next week, Julia?"

"I'd like that." Mamma impressed her. She'd stayed in control and Julia would even get to see how Jacob lived. She only hoped Momma wouldn't scare Jacob's mother. She could be a little overbearing at times.

As they stood to leave the dining room, Papa said, "I'll be at the club this evening."

"All right, John. Have a nice time."

Papa started for the door then stopped abruptly and turned around, causing Julia and her mother to bump into him. "I've got it!"

Momma took a step back. "For goodness sake. Got what?"

"I know why Anderson sounds familiar. There are a couple of Anderson brothers who do business with my bank. They own a jewelry store. The younger of the two came in as a partner less than a year ago. I assume your Mr. Andersons must be sons of the younger brother."

"You're right, Papa. My Mr. Anderson speaks highly of his father and uncle. What do you think of them?"

"I've dealt with Joshua Anderson for years and I believe him to be a gentleman of integrity and good business sense. I'm impressed with his brother too. Moving to Boston to provide financial security for his sons is far-sighted thinking. I predict Anderson's Jewelry Store will be around for a long time."

Julia breathed an inward sigh of relief. "Then you don't mind our association with the family?"

"I don't see any problem. Let me know how it goes with the music, will you?"

Papa left to get ready to go and Julia and Momma went to the drawing room for a quiet evening. Julia couldn't have been happier with the result of their conversation. When Papa said the Andersons were customers at his bank, she knew he'd have a high opinion of them. His bank only dealt with businessmen they had the utmost confidence in.

"It's reassuring that your papa knows something about the Andersons. They sound as though they're a nice middle-class family." Her mother picked up her embroidery, and settled into a wingback chair close to the fireplace. "Do you know how many sons there are?"

Julia sat in the chair across from her. "There are three. The one I met first, Jacob, is in the middle. Jason is younger and I believe he said his older brother's name is Joel."

"Are the other boys interested in the jewelry business?"

"I think the oldest one is." Julia picked up her needlework. "Jacob doesn't know yet."

Momma raised her eyebrows. "Jacob?"

"All these Mr. Andersons are confusing. It's easier for you to know who I mean when I say his first name." Julia gave her an innocent smile.

"Yes, well I see what you mean, but I hope you're calling him Mr. Anderson when you see him. You don't know him well enough to be so familiar."

"He's interesting. I think we could be friends."

"You have enough male friends," Momma said sternly. Ignoring the work in her hands, she went on. "There's no point in encouraging a friendship with someone from his social set. I'm sure Lucien wouldn't approve anyway."

Julia focused on her embroidery. "Well, at least I can be polite and talk to him when I see him. After all, if we're going to help his brother, we're bound to run into each other."

"Look who I found at our front door."

Both ladies turned to see a smiling Papa enter the room with Lucien, who held a large bouquet of flowers.

Julia's heart dropped, but Momma beamed a welcoming smile. "Lucien, how nice to see you. Come over and sit with us."

"Hello, Mrs. Phillips. Hello, Julia." Lucien crossed the room and handed Julia the flowers.

Mama clasped her hands in front of her. "They're lovely. Don't you think they're pretty, Julia?"

She resisted the urge to roll her eyes as she got up to pull the bell cord. "They're nice. I'll have Millie put them in a vase." *And set it somewhere I'll never have to see them.* "Papa, it's fortunate you ran into Lucien. Maybe you can take him to the club with you."

"I think he came to see you dear, not me."

Lucien looked uncertain. "Actually, I hoped to visit with you, but if this isn't a good time…."

"Nonsense," Momma said, "now is fine. When Millie comes to get the flowers, I'll tell her to bring tea."

Julia sat in resignation. Maybe it wouldn't be too bad. Surely Lucien wouldn't be making demands with her momma sitting in the room.

"You know, I don't have to go to the club." Papa also joined the ladies. "How about a game of cards?"

Lucien turned to her. "I'll play if Julia wants to."

"That's fine, Papa. Go ahead and get them." Playing a game might make the time go faster.

They played several games and Julia realized as long as Lucien wasn't talking about marriage, his company wasn't bad.

After the fourth game Momma announced she was done. "Why

don't you two have a nice chat over there while John and I clear this up."

Julia and Lucien went across the room and sat on a sofa. Lucien asked, "Will you be sleighing on Saturday?"

"I'm going skating. Sophia and I went today and decided to go again Saturday."

"Will Mr. Anderson be there?"

"He might be. You never know who you'll see." The thought of seeing Jacob again brought a smile.

"How about a ride Sunday to see the lot?"

Julia's smile disappeared, and she turned to look at him. "The lot where you plan to build?"

He smiled. "Yes, that's the one."

"I've already seen it."

"That was weeks ago, and it won't be long now before the contractors can start the foundation."

"Has anything changed since I last saw it?"

"Well, no."

Julia raised her eyebrows. "Then what's the point?"

"The point is to look at your future address. We can talk about what we want the house to look like." Lucien took one of her hands in his. "We should be sitting down with an architect soon. The plans need to be drawn up."

"Why can't you handle it?"

"It will be your house, too," Lucien said patiently. "I want your ideas."

Julia reclaimed her hand. "Okay, I'll go look at the lot Sunday."

"Good, and I'll let you know when we can meet with the architect."

He must have noticed her parents were no longer in the room, because he moved a little closer. Taking her hand again, he said, "I've enjoyed this evening. It's like being with the Julia I talked about the other night."

"I had fun too, Lucien. As long as you're not saying things to annoy me, we get along fine. As a matter of fact, I have an idea about how we can get along all the time. Would you like to hear it?"

"Not if it involves breaking our engagement." Lucien's tone was light, but he wore a frown.

"The reason we got along so well tonight is because we forgot about being anything other than friends," she said, ignoring Lucien's comment. "If we can agree to be friends, and forget talking about marriage, and whom I can and can't see, we'll get along wonderfully."

Lucien tightened his hold on her hand. "But we're more than friends. I don't want to forget that."

"If you want us to get along, you'll have to think of us as friends. I've always enjoyed your company on that basis."

"You want me to pretend nothing has changed between us, and the end of May, not to mention October, hold no importance for me, for us?"

"Yes." Julia pulled her hand free. "You understand perfectly."

"When do we stop pretending? In May?"

Julia noted Lucien's voice getting a little louder and he looked as though he had a headache coming on. Well, too bad. She wouldn't stop now.

"Naturally some changes will be forced on us when your agreement with my father is made public. However, acting as if we're only friends will still be the best way to be sure we get along. That doesn't mean we can't talk about the house, though. I understand now, it's important." Julia gave him a reassuring pat on the arm.

"Thank you for that concession." Lucien laid on the sarcasm. "What about after we're married. Will we still be just friends?"

"I don't imagine my feelings will change."

He shook his head. "What would be the point of a man and woman sharing a house if they're only friends?"

Julia smiled and relaxed against the sofa. "That's a good question."

Lucien looked into her eyes with what she hoped was resignation. "Is every conversation we have going to end like this?"

"Not if you agree to go back to being friends." She lost her smile. "I can see you're not going to let me out of this agreement, but at least we can spend the spring and summer in peace.

What do you say? Is it a deal?" Julia held out her hand as she'd seen Papa do.

Lucien took her hand and kissed the back of it, then turned it over and kissed the palm. "Here's the deal, Julia Phillips. I'm going to marry you in October. I'll try not to *annoy* you too much between now and then, but I can't promise to think of you as only a friend. Whether you believe it or not, I do care about you." He released her hand and stood. "I'll see you at the Jordan's dinner tomorrow night."

Julia watched him leave with a shiver. When he'd looked at her through narrowed eyes they appeared darker than normal. It made her think of a cat stalking a mouse.

18

Mr. Jordan gave his wife an affectionate squeeze as she stood surveying the tables and settings before their dinner guests arrived. "You're looking satisfied, my dear. Are you thinking about the past or do you have a prediction for this year?"

His lovely wife of thirty years looked up at him, her blue eyes shining. "I was thinking about the past, but I do have a prediction. This is the year Julia Phillips will stop leading the young men on a merry chase. I hear wedding bells for her before year's end."

Mr. Jordan raised his eyebrows. "Are you going to name the gentleman?"

"Do you want the same wager?"

He shook his head. "Tell me his name first and then I'll decide."

"You're not as brave after last year's loss." She chuckled. "Very well, his name is Edward Harrington."

"Ha! I'll be happy to agree to the same wager." He rubbed his hands together. "You're not going to win this one."

"What makes you so sure? Anyone can see they're perfect together." Mr. Jordan stayed at Mrs. Jordan's side while she continued her last-minute walk around the dining room.

"Once he finishes school he's headed for Europe, not the altar."

"Maybe Europe will be a wedding trip." She paused a moment to straighten a fork, then said, "I don't believe I'll change my mind."

Mr. Jordan grinned. "I understand, but I hope you won't mind if I start thinking of a name for my new horse."

"You go ahead, but do it some other time." His wife took his arm. "It's time to greet our guests."

Julia stood with Sophia and James in the green reception room where the unmarried guests gathered. Parents and other married guests mingled in a group a little distance from them. Edward and Lily soon arrived. Edward slipped his arm around Julia's waist and whispered in her ear, "How's my favorite girl?"

"I'm fine. And I'll be even better if my name is in your envelope."

"Isn't this exciting?" Lily bounced on her toes. "It's so much fun to see who Mrs. Jordan pairs with whom."

Edward turned to James. "Do you have your envelope?"

James held it up. "I have it, but I hate to open it. Last year I had Constance Winthrop. I can't imagine why Mrs. Jordan decided we'd make a good couple."

"Sometimes she's very intuitive," Sophia told her brother. "Quite a few couples have married after being paired here."

Julia chuckled and said, "She should have this dinner on Valentine's Day. She's definitely Cupid's helper."

"Whose envelope do you think you're in, Lily?" Edward teased.

Lily blushed. "I hope James has my name."

"I hope so too." James gave her a warm smile, then turned back to Edward. "You appear sure of yourself. What if you end up with Clara?"

"I won't. I have more faith in Mrs. Jordan than that. How about you, Sophia, whom do you want to spend dinner with?"

Julia answered for her. "If Mrs. Jordan is as good as Sophia believes she is, Lucien will be her dinner partner."

Lucien joined the group. "Did I hear my name?"

"Yes, you did." Julia focused on him with a smile. "We were discussing whose envelope we might be in." She let her gaze linger on his eyes. For Sophia's sake she had to be wrong about what she thought she'd seen last night. Tonight, he appeared as usual.

Mrs. Jordan called, "May I have your attention? I would like to ask all the married couples to go in to dinner and all the single gentlemen to open their envelopes."

Nervous laughter, and the rustle of paper filled the room, followed by excited chatter. James had Lily's name. Julia watched them make their way to the dining room with happy smiles. Edward opened his envelope slowly while the two of them watched Lucien open his. She kept her fingers crossed until he pulled out Sophia's name.

"It looks as though Mrs. Jordan thinks you two are a good pair," Edward said. "She's usually right you know."

Lucien looked briefly annoyed, but Sophia's smile brought a genuine smile from him in return. As he offered her his arm, he asked Edward, "Aren't you going to open yours?"

Edward opened it the rest of the way and pulled out Julia's name. "I guess you're stuck with me," he said, giving her a wink.

The little bit of tension in her muscles melted away. "I wouldn't want to argue with Mrs. Jordan."

Lucien and Sophia headed for the dining room and when Edward started to follow, Julia held him back. "That was a warmer-than-usual greeting you gave me. Any special reason?"

"Your parents were watching." He hooked his thumb under his lapel. "I'm doing my job as decoy."

"Ah. What was their reaction?"

He grinned. "You'll probably hear about it later."

"Oh well, the lecture will be worth it, as long as they're not thinking about Jacob."

They entered the dining room, found their place cards and slid into their seats. Julia appreciated the lovely table setting. Crystal goblets sparkled and the silver shone in the light of candles flickering in candelabras spaced evenly down the table. The flowers filling the spaces between them scented the air with their sweet perfume.

As they enjoyed course after course of delicious food, Julia noticed smiles and nods of approval in her direction from several of the older guests. Edward must have noticed too. "It looks as though a lot of people agree with Mrs. Jordan's opinion of us."

"I think you're right. Mrs. Wiggins must be especially happy. She's been asking me for the last few months when we were going to 'stop playing around and get on with it.'"

Edward guffawed. "I've been hearing the same kind of thing from Mr. Bishop. I can count on him to ask me at least once in an evening, 'Son, what are you waiting for?'"

Julia laughed, too. "You sounded just like him when you said that. We're not being nice, though. I feel like we're having fun with their good intentions."

"We are having fun; we're only commenting on their good intentions."

She sobered then, guilt creeping in. If she and Edward were the couple Mr. and Mrs. Jordan wagered on this year, Mrs. Jordan would lose. As much as the two of them cared for each other, their relationship wasn't more than friendship.

Edward set down his goblet and dabbed his mouth with his napkin. "How are things going with Jacob?"

She blinked and returned to the sounds of chatter and clinking of silver on china. Turning toward him, she said, "It's going well, I think. We've been together a few times this week and we've gotten to know each other a little better. We went skating yesterday. He can dance on skates. It's a lot of fun. I know you'll want to try it. Sophia and I are skating tomorrow, too. You'll come, won't you?"

"Of course. It should be interesting to watch Lucien and Jacob together."

They leaned back as a footman placed the dessert course in front of them, then she said, "Lucien and I had a talk last night. I told him if he would treat me as a friend and stop making demands, we'd get along fine."

Edward's eyebrows rose. "Do you think he'll do that?"

"He might. He's tired of fighting every time we're together. We'll see how it goes tonight." The urge to tell Edward about the way Lucien had looked at her last night pushed against her chest, as if the words fought to come out. But what if she was mistaken? She didn't want to worry him over nothing.

After dinner, Mrs. Jordan noticed her husband watching Edward and Julia dancing. Then he went to Edward's father, Robert Harrington. Mr. Harrington laughed and shook his head. After some discussion, her husband sauntered away with a gratified smile. That didn't look good, but most of the time men couldn't see what was right in front of them. With a slight shake of her head, she decided to stick with her decision.

Continuing to scan the room, Mrs. Jordan saw John and Elizabeth Phillips having a conversation with Sophia's parents. John and Elizabeth didn't appear happy. Maybe she could distract them. She hurried over. "Are you folks enjoying yourselves?"

Mr. Phillips gave her his attention. "Ah, Mrs. Jordan, we were discussing your choice of couples this evening."

Mrs. Jordan addressed the Howells. "Aren't Lucien and Sophia perfect together?" She had a good feeling about those two. "Their personalities are similar. I can't imagine them ever having a cross word. I've believed for some time now that they should be a couple, but it wasn't until recently I began to see them together."

Turning to Mr. and Mrs. Phillips, she said, "And then there's Edward and Julia." She held clasped hands over her heart. "They go together like bread and butter. It can't be much longer before we hear an announcement from those two." Mrs. Jordan moved on to other guests, hoping she'd said something to take the frown from the Phillips' faces.

Lucien spotted Julia by the table holding a punch bowl and other liquid refreshments and hurried over. "How about giving an old friend a dance."

Julia set down her empty cup. "I promised the next one to Aaron," she said, indicating the young man beside her.

He focused on Aaron. "You don't mind, do you? I promise to bring her back."

Aaron hesitated. "I had to promise Edward I'd only keep her for one dance."

Julia put her hand on his arm. "I'll still give you a dance. Edward will be fine."

As Lucien took Julia onto the polished oak dance floor he asked, "Shall I add my congratulations to the many I'm sure you've already received?"

"You can if you want," she said, smiling at him. "And may I say what good judgment and insight Mrs. Jordan showed when she paired you and Sophia."

Lucien ignored her comment. "Everyone is expecting some kind of announcement from you and Edward."

"I know, but people don't always get what they want. Sometimes they get a surprise."

His eyes narrowed. "What's that supposed to mean?"

"It could mean any number of things. You know, I think one of our problems is we talk too much. We can't get upset if we're not talking."

He'd never heard anything so ridiculous. "We have to talk to each other," he said, as he continued to guide them skillfully around the dance floor.

Julia raised her eyebrows. "See what I mean? You're getting upset. Maybe we should stay away from each other."

"I am not upset," Lucien snapped. "I fail to see how we could ever learn to get along if we're never together."

"You do have a point. Maybe we should agree on a list of safe topics for conversation. We could talk about how things are going at the bank and with our family members. The weather is always safe and you might want to discuss literature or the latest concert or lecture."

"That list sounds pretty impersonal."

"Those are the kind of things we talked about as friends. I enjoyed those conversations."

"You need to add the house to the list. I talked to Mr. Turner, the architect, today. He can meet with us Tuesday afternoon."

Julia shook her head. "I can't."

A knot tightened in his chest. "Why not? Last night you said you'd talk about it."

"I will. But not Tuesday. I'm free on Wednesday."

He spoke through clenched teeth. "Fine, I'll see if he can do it Wednesday."

The dance ended and Lucien took Julia back to Aaron. Edward stood there, but made no comment when Aaron escorted Julia to the dance floor.

"You look worn out," Edward said, sounding amused. "Maybe you shouldn't dance and talk at the same time."

"It has nothing to do with dancing." Lucien glared at Edward. "Lately Julia wears me out every time we talk. We can't have a relaxed conversation anymore. It seems as if we're always in a confrontation."

"Can I give you some advice?"

"I've known Julia for a number of years now. I'm sure I don't need advice." He turned to watch Aaron and Julia. Her violet dress became part of the kaleidoscope of color the dancers created.

"You may know her, but you don't understand her."

"You're right. I don't." He turned back to Edward. "As a matter of fact, I don't understand you either. I know Julia must have told you about us, and yet the two of you carry on as if nothing is different."

Edward shrugged. "That's because nothing *is* different. The friendship Julia and I share hasn't been changed by the agreement her father made with you."

"I would say it looks like more than friendship to most people."

"Things aren't always as they appear. It certainly didn't stop you from going to Julia's father. Why, all of a sudden do you want to marry her?"

"She's part of my life's plan. I spoke to Mr. Phillips because it's time to make it official. Her father is ready for her to settle down, so he gave me his blessing."

Edward frowned. "What about her plan? She's not ready to settle down and you might not have been her choice anyway. Why force this on her?"

"All women want to marry and have a family. Once she gets used to the idea, she'll be fine."

Edward slid his hands in his pockets. "You're not the first person who's wanted to marry her. You know that, don't you?"

"Yes, but she won't back out this time. Everything is going according to plan."

"Besides the fact that you can't get along." Edward grinned. "You aren't going to tell me to stay away from her, are you?"

Lucien huffed. "I'm sure I'd be wasting my time. At least I know you won't be here past August. How about taking Jacob Anderson with you?"

"That's not very friendly," Edward said, laughing.

Lucien turned back to the dance floor. His aching jaw told him to quit clenching his teeth. When he came up with his plan he hadn't accounted for Julia's resistance or Edward's interference. Or that she might meet and believe herself smitten with another man.

Aaron brought Julia back and she and Edward went to the dance floor. "They go well together, don't they?"

"Perfectly," Lucien muttered.

19

A couple inches of snow didn't keep Jacob or the other young people away from the ice on Saturday. By the time most of the group had gathered only an occasional fat snowflake could be seen drifting lazily in the cold air. Jacob watched for Julia as he and Ben Pennington used brooms to sweep the ice clean. Excitement to see her welled up inside like the bubbles in the carbonated drink he'd enjoyed last summer. No woman had ever made him feel this way. He could only hope she held the same regard for him.

By the time he and Ben headed back to shore more people had arrived. Shouts and laughter filled the air as adults and children called out greetings to one another. Jacob scanned the crowd and saw her. Julia's eyes met his and she smiled and waved. The beautiful sapphire blue coat she wore matched her eyes.

He hurried over to assist her onto the ice. After glancing around, he said, "I don't see Lucien. I suppose it's too much to hope he's not coming."

"He'll be here. He has to work at the bank on Saturdays, and sometimes that makes him late."

"Well, until he gets here, I claim you as mine." Jacob took her hand and maneuvered them through the other skaters to an open area. He bowed. "May I have this dance?"

She gave him a brilliant smile. "I thought you'd never ask."

They assumed the appropriate waltz position and he pushed off. There was no place on earth he'd rather be right now. He breathed deeply; savoring Julia's subtle violet scent mingled with the tangy wood smoke of the warming fires scattered around the lagoon.

Jacob took it slower than they had on Thursday to avoid running into other people, some of whom weren't too steady. He couldn't decide which he liked better, fast or slow. Both had their appeal.

Edward skated into Jacob's line of sight and matched their movements. "That looks like fun. The next dance is mine, Julia."

Jacob brought them to a stop. "You should practice by yourself for a while first. Skating backwards is easy once you get the hang of it, but you wouldn't want to bring Julia down with you if you fall."

Edward eyed them. "This wouldn't be a clever ploy to get me to leave you alone would it?"

"Jacob makes it look easy, but if you practice, I'll take a chance with you."

Edward grinned. "I can't ask for more than that. By the way, Lucien is here."

When he'd skated away, Jacob asked, "Was Edward upset?"

"No, but you can be sure he'll come for me later." Julia heaved a sigh. "We probably should head back though."

⁂

As Lucien sat to put on his skates, Ben took a seat beside him. "It looked as if you and Sophia were having a good time last night. If I were you, I'd think about changing my mind before it's too late."

"Not you too." Lucien groaned. "People I don't even know are encouraging me in her direction."

"If you remember, I expressed reservations when you first told me about your secret engagement. As your best friend, I feel it's my duty to point out the obvious when you can't see it. You and Julia will never get along like you and Sophia."

Lucien felt his friend watching him ruthlessly knot the laces on his skates and turned to glare at him. "I have my reasons for marrying Julia, and I would appreciate it if you and everyone else would leave me alone."

Ben held his hands up in surrender. "You'll never hear another word about it from me. You might be interested to know Julia has been skating with Jacob Anderson since she got here. He seems like a nice fellow. I like him."

"I would like him better if he'd go back to New York," Lucien muttered as he went out on the ice.

◦◦◦◦◦◦

Julia and Jacob met Lucien as he stepped onto the ice. "How about skating with me for a while? You don't mind do you, Mr. Anderson?"

She knew he minded, but what could he do other than be gracious and leave them?

"Yoo-hoo, Mr. Anderson, do you think you could help me? My brother seems to have disappeared."

The three of them turned to see Clara Pennington holding on to a tree at the edge of the lagoon. Jacob hurried over and she immediately let go of the tree and clung to him. Julia hoped Ben would show up soon. She hated to see the look of distress on Jacob's face.

"It looks as though he'll be busy for a while," Lucien said, not bothering to hide his amusement. Tucking her hand in the crook of his arm, he guided them leisurely through the other skaters until they came to Edward lying on his back. "What happened?"

"Edward, are you all right?" Julia knelt beside him and reached to shake his shoulder. His eyes popped open and he smiled.

"An angel." He grabbed her and pulled her down on top of him.

"Good grief, Edward." Lucien helped Julia to her feet. "May I remind you you're not ten years old anymore?"

Edward and Julia both laughed, but as Edward got back to his feet, he managed to answer, "If I were ten, I probably wouldn't hurt so much. You were right, Julia, it's harder than it looks. I *will* figure it out though, and we'll have a dance before the afternoon is over." He skated toward an empty space and tried again.

"What's he doing?"

Julia turned to Lucien, who had a slight frown, probably trying to make some sense of Edward's erratic skating.

"Ice dancing. When he can do his part without falling, he wants to try it with me."

"I don't think today's a possibility no matter how optimistic he is."

After watching him fall again, Lucien asked, "What made him think of it?"

"Mr. Anderson and I were skating that way when he saw us earlier. It's quite enjoyable."

Lucien shook his head and started skating again. "I think I'll save my dancing for the ballroom. It's a lot less painful."

They finished their circuit of the lagoon and found Sophia, James and Lily in conversation.

Julia skated over and linked arms with Sophia. "You all look serious. Has something happened?"

"We're discussing Mr. Anderson's predicament." James said. "He's been saddled with Clara and looks miserable.

With a nod, Sophia said, "I'm sure he'd hand her over to Ben, but he's nowhere to be found."

Lily chimed in. "Ben has made himself scarce. I saw him once with Samantha earlier and haven't seen him again."

The five of them skated together until they caught sight of Jacob and Clara. Jacob did his best to keep her from falling, while she alternated between squeals and giggles.

"Poor Mr. Anderson." Julia's heart ached to think he'd been stuck with Clara all this time. "Lucien, maybe you should give him a break."

He held up his hands, palms out. "No, thank you. Clara's not my problem, and I don't blame Ben for wanting to avoid her."

"I'm going to find him." Julia broke away from the group and Lucien followed. When she found him and Samantha, she said, "You look as if you're having a nice time."

Ben stopped with a smile. "Yes, actually, I am. It's nice to be able to skate without someone hanging on my arm. I don't think Clara will ever learn to stay on her feet. I wish she wouldn't insist on coming."

Julia planted her fists on her hips. "Do you even know where she is?"

Ben laughed at her stern expression. "Of course, I know. I've been keeping an eye on her. Your friend, Jacob Anderson, has been quite chivalrous. She's in good hands."

"Well, don't you think he's been doing your job long enough? Why don't you give him a break?"

He sighed. "What I need to do is find her a husband."

Lucien gestured toward Jacob. "How about Mr. Anderson. He's not engaged, is he Julia?"

She dropped her hands to her sides. "No, he's not, but I don't think he'd be interested."

"Ha. My parents would never approve a match between them anyway."

Julia huffed out a breath. "Why not? He's a perfect gentleman."

"Not exactly old family, though, is he?" Ben leaned closer. "I can't imagine your parents giving him their blessing."

"Papa happens to think highly of his family."

"That's probably because they do business at his bank. Otherwise I doubt he would know who they are."

A shrill squeal made them all cringe, then look at Ben. "Well, I guess I'll go relieve Mr. Anderson. Maybe I can talk Clara into going home and then come back without her. Would you be willing to help, Samantha?"

"Yes. Maybe if we keep her between us, we can get her off the ice."

As soon as Ben had taken over, Jacob skated to Julia's side. "She wore me out. This isn't a good place for her to catch a husband. Everyone's afraid of her."

"Clara is one of those girls who will have a better chance in a drawing room or ballroom," Lucien offered. "Especially if she loses that giggle."

Jacob briefly touched her arm. "I have to leave soon. Will you go around with me one more time?"

"I'd be happy to." She glanced at Lucien. "You don't mind, do you?"

They waltzed away before he could form an answer. Julia had a schoolgirl urge to giggle over the idea of getting away with something, in spite of what Lucien had just said about Clara.

She swallowed it down and asked, "Have you seen Edward?"

"Once in a while. It takes a lot of concentration to keep Miss Pennington upright."

"I'm sorry you had to deal with that. The reason I asked about Edward is he's been working hard. I expect he'll want to try a turn with me before we leave."

"Tell him not to go too slow or too fast. That will be safest to start with."

"Do you have to go? We're all going to Sophia and James' later for hot chocolate. I hoped you would come with us."

"I would enjoy more time with you, but I need to get back to the store."

Disappointment made her throat ache, but she didn't say anything else. Instead, Julia allowed herself to relish the feel of Jacob's arms around her and the gentle swaying of the dance as they glided over the ice. All too soon they were back to the benches.

Jacob sat and exchanged his skates for his boots. He stood and gave her hand a gentle squeeze. "I'll look for you after church tomorrow."

Edward whooshed to a stop beside Julia. "I'm ready! I haven't fallen once in the last fifteen minutes."

"That's great," Jacob said. "Remember what I told you, Julia."

Edward and Julia waved and started on their way. "Jacob said to tell you not to go too fast or too slow."

"All right, but you need to relax. I feel like I'm trying to dance with a broom."

A nervous laugh slipped out. "I'll try." Julia wasn't as convinced as Edward that they'd have success, but she did her best to be flexible. After skating for several minutes without falling, she said, "This is wonderful, Edward. Is it worth all the falling?"

"It's worth it, but I have to tell you, dancing with you is a lot more fun than by myself. Are you ready to warm up?"

"Yes, please." They headed toward one of the fires set around the lagoon for the skaters to warm themselves. The dancing orange and yellow flames beckoned them closer. Edward helped her to a bench then sat beside her.

"Maybe we could meet Wednesday afternoon. My classes are over early and I wouldn't have to share you with anyone."

"I'd love to, but I told Lucien I'd see the architect with him on Wednesday." She held her gloved hands toward the fire enjoying the warmth on her hands and face.

"That sounds serious. You're not considering…"

"No, I'm not. I'm going to get Sophia's ideas and act as though they're mine. I felt as if I had to be agreeable on some point, and the house isn't too personal, since I won't be living in it."

"Well, how about tomorrow afternoon?" Edward twisted around to warm his back.

"I can't, I'm riding with Lucien to see the lot. I'm sorry." She turned her back to the fire as well.

Edward turned to her with a frown. "Lucien is starting to get on my nerves. It's bad enough I have to share you with Jacob on Saturdays, but now Lucien wants to take up your time.

"You know I'd rather be with you than Lucien." She turned and put a reassuring hand on his arm. "If the appointment Wednesday isn't going to work out, I'll let you know."

"Okay." He held his hands out to the fire again. "I'll probably be too sore to move tomorrow anyway."

Julia lay on her back in bed that night, replaying the afternoon in her mind. Jacob was by far the best part, and not just because of his beautiful blue eyes, handsome face, or those broad shoulders. His fun-loving spirit, kindness and consideration were only a few of the things that drew her to him. Too bad he'd been stuck with Clara for so long. Even though she'd see him tomorrow after church for a few minutes, Tuesday is what she looked forward to. Margaret would give them at least an hour together, hopefully. She couldn't wait to tell Jacob.

And then there was Lucien. She had to admit he hadn't been bad.

None of the time spent with him had annoyed her. With any luck, tomorrow would be the same. Thank goodness she'd been able to spend enough time with Sophia to get some house ideas. If Lucien asked, she'd be ready.

Julia rolled to her side, snuggled into the soft mattress and pulled the comforter up to her ears. She smiled as her thoughts drifted back to Jacob. Hopefully she'd see him in her dreams.

After church the next morning, Julia paused to take a breath of fresh air. The clear, crisp day, wasn't so cold that everyone wanted to hurry home. She saw Jacob waiting for her at the bottom of the church steps and hurried down. As usual, his smile, when he greeted her, warmed her to her toes.

"What have you planned for us this week?"

"Tuesday we can go to Margaret's again. Maybe she'll give us an hour this time."

"We've known each other for another week." His eyes twinkled. "Maybe that will make a difference."

Julia grinned. "I'll be sure to mention it." She led them further into the church yard to get out of the way of people still coming down the steps. The tall oaks and hickories stood dark and skeletal against the snow and gray sky. Looking at them made her shiver.

She turned back to Jacob. "Momma plans to call on your mother this week. She'd like to meet her since we've taken an interest in your brother. Do you know if one day is better than another?"

Jacob gave her an embarrassed grin. "I think she's home most of the time. I haven't paid much attention to what she does."

"Don't worry, Momma will work it out. I'm excited to meet her. If you and your brother are anything to judge by, I'll enjoy knowing her as well."

"Thank you for the compliment. I have to tell you, though, Mother will be nervous about meeting you. She's a wonderful person, but not sure what to expect from someone of the upper class. My aunt and uncle have filled my parents' minds with doubts about the two classes being any more than business associates."

This gave her pause. "Your parents don't approve of your friendship with me, do they?"

He hesitated. "They're concerned."

"Oh no. I didn't think about it going both ways. Do they know how much time you spend with me?"

Jacob slid his hands in his coat pockets. "I've never kept it a secret. My parents don't tell me what to do. They just make sure I know how they feel about it."

"Do you think your mother won't like me?" Now she'd be nervous, too.

"I don't know how anyone could not like you. However, I think your mother will be what she expects. No offense."

Julia shook her head at her own short sightedness. "I've never thought about how I or my family might be perceived. I hope that doesn't make me a snob."

"It makes you sweet." He reached for her hand and gave it a quick squeeze.

Suddenly Edward joined them. "Your momma's coming. Look happy to see me."

Julia obliged by taking his arm and smiling up at him. "You're taking your job seriously."

"I enjoy it." Edward winked at her. "Jacob, I have to tell you, before yesterday my backside hasn't had that much contact with the ice in years."

"You caught on quickly, though. I assume you managed to stay on your feet when you and Julia tried it together."

"Here you are Julia." Momma gave her and Edward a slight frown. "Did you know Lucien is looking for you?"

"No, I haven't seen him." Julia glanced around relieved when she didn't see Lucien anywhere near.

"How is your brother coming, Mr. Anderson? Will he be ready soon?"

"It shouldn't be too much longer, Mrs. Phillips. He's been practicing every day."

"Good. Did Julia tell you we'd be calling on your mother?"

"Yes, she did."

"Let her know we'll come by tomorrow afternoon. I look forward to meeting her. Also, you might like to know my husband speaks highly of your father and uncle."

"Julia, it's time we left. Gentlemen, we'll see you another time." Her mother gave the men a slight nod and Julia followed her to where her father stood talking to a family friend.

❧

Jacob watched Julia and her mother walk away. "Mrs. Phillips doesn't leave you with any question about who's in charge, does she?"

Edward laughed. "If she's on a mission, the best thing you can do is stay out of her way. She gets things done. If she says she can help your brother, you can count on it."

"We appreciate her making an opportunity possible." Jacob looked to see if Julia was still there and saw Lucien talking to her. She smiled and it looked as if she agreed to something. Then Julia left with her parents. Jacob turned back to see Edward studying him.

"Do you have a sleigh or can I give you a ride?"

Jacob didn't know if he wanted a ride. So far Edward had been friendly, but Jacob couldn't tell what he was thinking.

Edward smiled. "Don't worry, I won't give you a stay-away-from-Julia talk."

Jacob returned the smile with relief. "In that case, a ride would be nice."

When they were on their way, Edward asked, "What do you think of Boston, now that you've been here a while?"

Jacob looked at the three-story townhouses lined up along both sides of the street, like tall fences crowding him in. People and horses were everywhere, making for constant noise, especially in the merchant area around the jewelry store. Even the parks were crowded. He couldn't even imagine what a racket carriage wheels on bricks would make when the snow melted.

When he took a while to answer, Edward chuckled. "Is it that hard to decide or are you afraid you'll hurt my feelings?"

"I'm trying to sort it out." He heaved a sigh. "It's a big change. I'm used to a lot more space around me. Even the houses are sandwiched together here. The city is interesting, though. There are a lot of things to do and see. It's easier to get what you need or want. I guess the best part would be the people I've met."

Edward glanced at him. "People like Julia?"

"Yes, especially Julia. I've never met anyone like her."

"She finds you interesting, too."

"What do you think of that?" Jacob mentally prepared himself for a negative reply.

"I haven't decided yet. Julia mentioned you're thinking of going west, to Iowa. Wouldn't it be easier to take over your father's farm in New York?"

"It would, but as long as my father is living, and I hope that's a long time, he'll feel he can tell me how to run it. My uncle, in New York, has a friend that makes Iowa sound like a good place for a man to start a place of his own."

Edward's brow furrowed. "Don't you enjoy working with your family?"

"My family isn't the problem. It's the location. I would rather the city be a place I visit from my home in the country. How about you, do you plan to stay in Boston?"

"I haven't thought seriously about it yet. My family would like for me to stay here, but there's a lot more to the world than Boston."

Stores and businesses stood along the sidewalk now. Soon they'd pass the Public Garden and arrive in his neighborhood. The rowhouses were smaller there and if you traveled further in you'd see single and two-family homes, each on a little parcel of land. "Sophia told me you're going to Europe."

"Yes, in August. If I like it, I may stay a while. I tend to make up my mind as I go."

A twinge of jealousy shot through Jacob. "It would be nice to have that freedom."

Edward turned to him. "It's not as if you don't have a choice. You can stay or go."

"That's true."

"If you go to Iowa, when do you think it'll be?"

"I'd like to go this summer, but I don't know if I'll have the finances that soon. It also depends on how things are going here. There's my address." He pointed to a two-story townhouse. "Thank you for the ride."

"You're welcome. I'm sure I'll see you again." The horse tossed her head and snorted, blowing a cloud of fog in the air as Edward turned the sleigh around and headed back up the street.

As Jacob went slowly up the steps, he realized Edward had been true to his word. He hadn't tried to discourage him about Julia. But Jacob felt as if he'd been through an interview, and he still didn't know what Edward thought of him. He couldn't worry about that now, though. His immediate concern was telling his mother to expect visitors tomorrow. So much for her choosing the best day.

As they finished lunch, Julia said, "Lucien will be stopping by to take me to look at the lot for the house he plans to build. I don't imagine we'll be long."

"That's a splendid idea, just splendid." Papa beamed at her. "Take all the time you need."

"I'm so glad you two are thinking about your future," Momma said. "I don't mind telling you Mrs. Jordan had us a little concerned by her choice of couples Friday night."

Julia looked at her relieved parents for a moment. "I'm afraid you've gotten the wrong impression. Mrs. Jordan couldn't have been more right in her choices. The only reason I'm going with Lucien today is because I'm tired of fighting him on every issue. He pointed out the house would need to be started as soon as we have a thaw, and there has to be a plan if they are to start. We will meet with an architect, possibly on Wednesday." Julia patted her mouth with a napkin then laid it by her plate.

Papa's smile faded. "Well, it's good he wants you involved in designing the house you'll live in. Maybe you'll surprise yourself and actually get interested in the project."

"I should get ready. He'll be here soon."

She excused herself then paused outside the door. Eavesdropping was bad manners, but she knew she'd be the subject.

Her mother sighed. "I should have known better than to get my hopes up."

"At least she's beginning to realize it's useless to keep fighting." Papa's chair brushed over the carpet as he came to his feet. "Helping to make decisions on the house may be just what she needs."

"I'll be glad when the wedding's over. I'm going to be a nervous wreck until then." Momma's chair slid back.

"Don't worry my dear, she'll do the right thing."

Julia hurried up to her room, leaned against the closed door and sighed. If only she could get them to change their mind about the "right thing" before the announcement in May. She didn't want to cause a scandal for her family when she left.

20

Julia studied the new houses and empty lots as the sleigh swished down the streets of the Back Bay neighborhood. She tried to muster up some interest, but knowing she had no real investment in this place made it difficult.

Lucien stopped the horse beside a lot that appeared identical to the others they'd passed. "Well, here we are. What do you think?"

"It's a nice location."

"We're not far from Margaret. You could visit her whenever you liked."

Her fists clenched inside her fur muff. "I imagine we would have a lot in common. Are you thinking three stories or four?"

Lucien launched into a description of his plans. "The architecture will have to go with the houses on either side, of course. I'm thinking three floors not including the attic. I want rounded bow windows with decorative ironwork and a single front door."

"Do you want sidelights at the door?"

He looked at the front doors of the houses already along the street. "I'm deciding between sidelights or a transom."

She had to admit he'd put a lot of thought into it. "Those all sound like good ideas."

He turned to her, his smile bigger than usual. "I'm surprised you're being so agreeable. Not that I don't appreciate it. I want you to have as much say about the inside as possible, so be thinking about what you'd like."

When they returned to Julia's house, Lucien said, "I'll let you know about Wednesday with Mr. Turner."

Julia remembered the possibility of ice-skating with Edward. "Do you think you could let me know by tomorrow evening?"

"I'll stop by and tell you personally." He helped her from the sleigh.

As soon as her feet touched the sidewalk, she stepped away from him. "I don't want you to go to any trouble. A note will be fine if you're busy."

"I won't be too busy for you." Lucien smiled as he walked her to her door. "You might as well get used to seeing a lot of me. I don't plan to be one of those husbands who stays at the club all the time. I'm sure you'll be a lot more entertaining than a bunch of older men smoking cigars."

"I'll see you tomorrow night then." Julia closed the door behind her. *Well, isn't that wonderful? Who has been giving him lessons on courting?*

The family went to Uncle George's that evening. Edward and Lily wouldn't be there, since they were on Momma's side of the family. Since Papa was the youngest in his family and she the youngest in hers, all the cousins were older. Julia didn't have much in common with any of them, and their main interest in her seemed to be finding out the status of her pending old maidhood. Thankfully Margaret would be there.

When Julia stepped into the drawing room, she saw Katherine.

The rose-striped satin dress she wore complimented the green velvet settee she sat on. Julia hurried over with a light heart. "I'm glad you're here." She sat next to Katherine and gave her a hug. "How are you feeling?"

"Not well, but I'm tired of not seeing the family. Alex misses his cousins, so I insisted Alexander bring us."

"I've missed you too."

"Margaret says you've met someone. I want to hear about him."

Julia glanced around at the aunts, uncles, and cousins sitting or standing about the room, then leaned closer to her sister. "Did she tell you he's a secret?"

Katherine's eyes sparkled. "She did, and that makes me even more interested."

No one seemed to be paying attention, so Julia told her about meeting Jacob, the time they'd spent together and finished with, "No man has ever made me feel the way he does. When he looks into my eyes it's as though my heart is responding to his. Did you feel that way with Alexander?"

Her sister smiled and breathed out a soft sigh. "Yes, I know what you mean. It's too bad Mr. Anderson isn't in our set."

"Would it have made a difference to you? Would you have given up Alexander for that reason?" Julia needed to hear her sister's answer. Katherine's perspective would help form her decision if it came to that.

"Probably not. I can't imagine living without him. I'm glad you're trying to get to know Mr. Anderson, though. Some women make decisions based solely on their emotions, and live to regret it."

"He wants to go to Iowa and live on a farm. That scares me. I believe living in the city would be better. If he truly loved me wouldn't he want to stay here? Or maybe if I loved him, I would want to go."

From the corner of her eye, Julia noticed a painting above them she hadn't seen before. She turned to get a better look and stifled a gasp. It depicted a lovely landscape of green pastures, a large pond, trees and cows. There were other small details, but she couldn't get past the cows.

Her sister continued to speak, giving her good advice. No doubt advice she needed to hear, but her brain couldn't get past those cows, which would live on a farm, which is where Jacob wanted to live. Should she consider it a sign or some kind of message?

"Julia." Someone patted her arm. "Julia." She tore her eyes from the painting to see her sister regarding her with a slight frown.

"Katherine, look at this."

She obliged by twisting around to view the picture. "This is different. I wonder how many paintings Uncle George acquired this time?"

Julia turned to her. Obviously, Katherine didn't get it. "Look at those," she said, jabbing a finger at the cows.

"They're nicely done, but I don't know why you find them so fascinating…Oh, this is a picture of a farm." Her sister turned to her. "What are you thinking?"

Julia frowned as they straightened around. "Don't you think it's odd that we were talking about possibly moving to a farm, and here we are sitting under a picture of one?"

Katherine took both of her hands and looked in her eyes. "I wouldn't jump to conclusions. Let me finish. Taking your time to make a decision is smart. If all these feelings are being brought on by nothing more than his good looks, they'll go away. If you still feel drawn to him after you've found out as much as you can, I'd say it's serious."

With a sigh, Julia said, "There's something else to consider. Did Margaret tell you about Lucien?" At Katherine's nod, Julia went on.

"I can't take a lot of time making up my mind about Jacob. You're right about emotions being tricky. I don't want to be confused by my need for rescue from an unwanted marriage."

Her sister released her hands to push stray strands of golden hair back from her face. "That *is* a serious consideration, and yes, Margaret told me of Lucien before she said anything about Mr. Anderson. I expected her to follow that by telling me you and Edward had decided to make it official. What does Edward think about Lucien?"

"He thinks it would be a mistake. If things don't work out with Jacob, he wants to take me to Europe."

Katherine's eyebrows shot up. "A lot of people will be upset."

Julia lifted her shoulders in a helpless gesture. "People will get over it. They won't be surprised if I take off with Edward, rather than marry Lucien. What will shock them is if I marry Jacob. I may not be forgiven for that, and it would cause a scandal I don't want Momma and Papa to have to deal with." She paused. "Of course, Jacob hasn't asked me, so it may never be a problem."

"It sounds like a lot to pray about."

Julia's eyebrows rose. "Do you believe God cares about something like this?"

"With all my heart." Katherine took Julia's hands in hers again. "I want to tell you about someone I met. Alexander's Aunt Maude from New York visited us a few months ago, and what she told me about God changed my life. He loves us, protects us and provides for us."

Julia tilted her head. "We do that ourselves. The men provide the money and we spend it."

"God makes it possible for men to earn money. But that's not the best part. He loved us so much He sent His only son, Jesus, to die for us. If we believe in Him and ask Him into our hearts, we'll go to heaven when we die. So, you see, no matter what happens here, we can know we have a better life waiting for us."

The warm light shining in her sister's eyes told Julia she believed every word she said. "I thought you just had to be good to get to heaven."

Katherine shook her head. "God wants to be more than someone we think about on Sunday morning or someone we pray to when there's a problem. He wants to have a personal relationship with us. He cares about our everyday lives."

"Do you think God will help me get out of the agreement Papa made with Lucien?"

"I don't know what He has in mind for you, but I do know He wants you to trust Him to take care of you. I can't tell you what peace of mind it has given me to turn my worries over to Him."

Julia didn't know what to think about all of what Katherine had said, but she didn't like the idea of sitting back and hoping God would arrange her life to her satisfaction. "It sounds like you're happy, Katherine, and I'm glad. I'll think about what you've told me."

Margaret approached them. "Do you feel like eating, Katherine? It's time to go down to supper."

Alexander joined them, ready to assist his wife. "I'll try to eat something," she said as Alexander helped her up. "We should talk again, Julia. Come and see me."

Margaret held Julia back as most of the others filed out of the room. "She talked to you about God, didn't she?"

"Yes, she seems convinced."

"She told me about Him when I visited with her Friday. I suppose it's natural for someone in her condition to think about God and prayer."

"You don't believe any of it?"

Margaret snorted. "I can't see what God has done for me. As far as I can tell, we take care of ourselves."

"Are you two going down to the dining room or are you going to stay here and talk?" Steven asked, as he came to join them.

Margaret took his arm. "I don't know why we need God when we have men telling us what to do."

Steven puffed out his chest. "God gave us the responsibility to tell you what to do. I'd hate to think what the world would be like if women were in charge."

Margaret turned to Julia and rolled her eyes. Julia had no trouble imagining Lucien saying the same kind of thing.

On Monday afternoon, Julia spent extra time on her hair and dress. She wanted to look nice but not pretentious. Hopefully, Momma wouldn't intimidate Mrs. Anderson. She wanted Jacob's mother to like them.

When Julia and Momma arrived at the Anderson townhouse, they were shown to the drawing room without delay. The rooms were nicely furnished and decorated. The floors had carpet and the usual assortment of knick-knacks, photographs and paintings filled the room. Even though the house was smaller than theirs, it didn't seem as though it would be much of a step down.

Irene Anderson was a small woman with the same bright blue eyes as her sons. Her smile appeared a little uncertain as she greeted them and invited them to sit on the settee while she sat in an armchair close by. "It's good of you to call on me. Jacob speaks of you often."

"He's a nice young man," Momma said with approval. "He seems exceptionally proud of his brother. I look forward to meeting the young man and hearing him play."

"Jason feels he'll be ready by the end of the week. You're welcome to come back to hear him."

"That will be fine. Shall we make it Friday?"

"I'll let Jason know." Mrs. Anderson sat with stiff posture and twisted a lace handkerchief in her lap, until a serving girl brought in a tea tray. The girl set it on an occasional table next to Jacob's mother and left. Mrs. Anderson's body appeared to relax as she reached for the teapot. Julia guessed she may have been relieved to have something to do with her hands.

As Momma accepted a teacup and saucer from Mrs. Anderson, she said, "I understand you're somewhat new to Boston. How do you like our city?"

"I'll confess there are times I miss the country, but Boston is an interesting place. I'm glad Jonah, that's my husband, decided to move here." She handed a cup to Julia, then offered her and Momma a plate with shortbread cookies, coconut macaroons and lemon tarts. They each took one and set it on their saucer next to the cup.

"Our oldest son, Joel, likes working in the store far better than on the farm. And of course, Jason is thrilled to have more time on the piano. We hope your Mr. Fontello will like what he hears."

"I'm sure an appointment can be made for next week sometime. We'll be sure to let you know."

Mrs. Anderson looked at Julia. "Perhaps your daughter can tell Jacob. They see each other fairly often."

Julia's cheeks warmed. She'd said little up to that point. Her mother tended to run a conversation and she'd found it best not to interrupt. Now Momma looked at her with eyebrows raised. Time for an explanation.

"It's true, we do see each other quite a bit. We seem to have a habit of being in the same place at the same time. I enjoy his company, Mrs. Anderson. He's a perfect gentleman." She smiled and took a sip of tea.

Momma studied her for a moment then asked Mrs. Anderson, "What about your middle son? You haven't said if he plans to stay here."

Mrs. Anderson stirred a lump of sugar into her tea as she talked. "Jacob enjoyed farming and he's thinking about going west to settle. We'd prefer he stay here, but we want him to be happy. Do you enjoy the country, Miss Phillips?"

The abrupt change of subject took her aback, but she answered with enthusiasm. "Oh yes, I look forward to going to our house in the country every summer. Surrounded by trees and flowers rather than buildings is refreshing. I can see why you would miss it."

"Have you ever been to a farm?"

"No, but I'm sure they're nice." Julia hoped that was the proper thing to say about a farm. She couldn't help feeling Jacob's mother was sending her a message.

"They are a lot of work," Mrs. Anderson countered. "Life in the city is much easier."

Momma stepped in. "When do you think your son will go, if he decides to?"

Mrs. Anderson shifted her focus back to Momma. "He has no definite plans. He doesn't have enough money saved yet." She continued to stir her tea even though the lump of sugar must have dissolved a while ago.

"Well, we'll wish him the best if he goes. Won't we, Julia?"

"Of course." Julia took another sip of tea, then smiled agreeably.

In the sleigh on the way home, Momma turned to her. "Tell me I have no reason to worry about you and Mr. Anderson."

"What makes you say that?" Julia hoped she sounded unconcerned.

"I got the feeling Mrs. Anderson believes there's more to your relationship with her son than casual acquaintance. Why do you suppose that is?"

Momma's eyes were intense. Julia knew from past experience that her answer better satisfy, or the subject wouldn't be dropped. It might even make its way to her father.

"Edward met him the night I saw him at the lecture, and he invited him to go sleighing with us. He's been included in the group since then, so I see him every Saturday, and briefly on Sundays." Julia forced herself to maintain eye contact.

"That better be all it is." Momma looked away to adjust the lap robe, then said, "Mrs. Anderson seemed a little nervous. I hope we didn't make her uncomfortable."

"At least we were invited back to hear Mr. Anderson play."

"Yes. I look forward to that."

Julia thought she might melt into a puddle of relief. Having to explain the times she'd seen Jacob to Momma had been unexpected. She hated being misleading, but after the conversation they'd just had, clearly she'd never be able to see Jacob with her parents' approval. And she had the feeling Mrs. Anderson didn't approve of her. Maybe because of her answer to the farm question. Julia dearly hoped the next visit would go better.

21

Jacob hadn't seen his mother until the family sat down for dinner Monday evening. He wanted to ask about the visit with the Phillips's, but his father beat him to it.

Helping himself to the baked beans the Bostonians were so fond of, his father asked, "How did your visit with the upper class go this afternoon, Irene?"

"It went well." She turned to Jason. "I invited them to come back Friday to hear you play. You'll be ready, won't you?"

"I'll be ready by Friday, but what we all want to know is, what did you think of Miss Phillips?" He gave Jacob a wink.

"She's a pretty little thing, but I can't imagine her on a farm. She has never even been to one."

Jacob laid down his knife and fork. "That doesn't necessarily mean anything."

His mother focused on him from across the table. "Miss Phillips wouldn't have the first idea what to do. If you're thinking she might be willing to go with you, Jacob, you better be prepared to hire help to do everything."

"I don't think you're giving her enough credit. She's smart and isn't afraid of a challenge."

"I won't debate her intelligence, but I doubt she'll ever be able to handle real work. She'll get tired of it and want to come home to Papa's big house and money." She plopped a spoonful of mashed potatoes on her plate and passed the bowl to Joel.

Jacob shook his head, "She won't do—

Mrs. Anderson held up her hand, palm out. "That's not the only thing bothering me. Miss Phillips didn't appear comfortable with her mother knowing how much time you two spend together. As a matter of fact, I could tell Mrs. Phillips was surprised to hear about her seeing you at all."

"I told you her parents would never approve." His father pointed his fork at him for emphasis. "Going behind their backs isn't honest. You'd best forget about her. She'll only bring you trouble."

"There are a lot of girls back in New York who would be glad to go to Iowa with you," Joel said, helping himself to the roast beef. "Any one of them would be a good wife, and the kind of help you'd need to start a place of your own."

Frustration welled up inside Jacob. "I'm not looking for just any woman to start a farm and family with. I wasn't looking at all, but on the day Julia walked into the store, she walked into my heart. I wish you all would give her a chance. You're my family and what you think means a lot to me."

"She's a nice person," Jason said, around a mouth full of food. He swallowed, then continued. "On the afternoon we spent together, I could see how well the two of them got along. And it's not as if he's proposed yet. As far as I can see, he's not rushing into anything."

His father shook his head. "That's all fine and good, but it doesn't change facts. I don't know how we're to give her a chance if we never socialize. I may get on well with Mr. Phillips when I see him at the bank, but I don't anticipate a dinner invitation."

Jacob drummed his fingers on the table. His father was right. He looked at Jason and had his answer. "How about Friday?"

His father frowned. "What about Friday?"

"Maybe you could be here Friday when Julia and her mother come to hear Jason. That would at least give you the opportunity to meet her."

"Okay son, I'll be here Friday. I want you to promise me though, that you'll think carefully before making her any offers."

"Don't worry. I plan to be careful." Dinner conversation moved on to other topics, but Jacob didn't join in. He had counted on his mother seeing what a special person Julia was. At least she had time to get to know Julia better since he didn't have the money to go anywhere yet.

Tuesday afternoon Julia paced back and forth in front of the window, waiting for Jacob to arrive.

"Stop looking out the window," Margaret said. "Come sit beside me, and tell me how your visit with Mrs. Anderson went."

She sat with a sigh on the blue brocade settee next to her sister. "I suppose it went all right, other than the fact Mrs. Anderson seemed uncomfortable having us there. She mentioned the fact that Jacob and I see a lot of each other and caused Momma some concern. I'm pretty sure Mrs. Anderson doesn't like me." She heaved another sigh.

"Now why would you say that?"

The sympathy in her sister's voice warmed her. "She talked about Jacob wanting a farm and asked me if I liked the country. Then she wanted to know if I had ever been on a farm, and when I said no, her expression said that's exactly what she expected me to say. I don't believe she thinks I'm good enough for her son." Julia couldn't sit still. She stood and went back to the window.

"Obviously Jacob is interested in you, so his mother naturally wants to know if you could make him happy. She probably thinks you wouldn't know how to be a farmer's wife, and she'd be right."

Julia turned back to Margaret, hands on her hips. "It's not as if I'm incapable of learning. Anyway, surely there will be servants to do the work."

"You can't count on it. If you want a house full of servants you need to stay in the upper class." Margaret patted the seat beside her and Julia slowly went back.

"His mother had a nice house and domestic help."

"His mother isn't just starting out," Margaret reminded her. "Why don't you see if you can get Jacob to tell you about farm life. Ask him what kinds of things his mother did? You need to have some idea of what you're considering."

"You're right, I'll do that." Julia didn't like a situation being out of her control, so she appreciated Margaret's suggestions. The idea that Jacob's mother might think she wasn't good enough for her son unnerved her.

The maid came to the door and announced Mr. Anderson's arrival.

Julia met him at the drawing room door, unsure if his mother may have influenced him against her. The warmth of his greeting was all the reassurance she needed. She returned his smile as she took his arm and led him to a sofa. Before sitting, he directed his attention to Margaret. "Hello Mrs. Jefferson. It's kind of you to allow me to visit again."

"We're glad you could come. We were discussing yesterday's visit. Julia didn't have a chance to tell me if your brother will be playing for Momma soon."

"They have agreed on Friday afternoon. Father and I will be there as well. I want him to meet you, Julia." Jacob took a seat next to her and gave her his full attention.

Julia was hesitant. "Do you think he should? I'm not sure I made a good impression on your mother."

"I'm afraid she makes assumptions based on her ideas rather than on individual merit. I hope she wasn't unkind." Jacob's eyes brimmed with concern.

"No, she didn't say anything out of the way." Julia briefly laid her hand on his arm. "I could just tell I fell short."

"I'm sorry she made you feel bad. As far as I'm concerned, you're perfect," Jacob said with a smile.

Julia laughed. "Thank you, however, I'm sure I'm not perfect. As long as we're being honest about our mothers, you might as well know Momma is concerned about the amount of time we might be spending together. I'm afraid she's guilty of making assumptions too."

"I'm glad you're still willing to see me. I've enjoyed getting to know you."

"I enjoy our time together too." Julia accepted a cup of tea from Margaret. "I don't think I'll have to worry about Momma though, because she's more concerned about Edward right now."

"I meant to ask you if she talked to you about Friday night," Margaret said. "You and Edward were quite the couple. Mrs. Jordan went around telling everyone she was sure you'd be making an announcement soon." She offered Jacob a plate of teacakes and he took two.

Julia quickly filled Jacob in on the event Friday evening, and finished with, "Mrs. Jordan means well, but she and everyone else are in for a big surprise. And yes Margaret, Momma and Papa both gave me the expected lecture."

"Speaking of Edward, he gave me a ride home from church Sunday," Jacob said, then popped one of the teacakes in his mouth.

"He didn't give you a hard time, did he?"

Jacob swallowed. "No, but he said he hasn't made up his mind about me. He obviously cares a lot about you. I can see why you trust him."

She smiled. "He's a good friend. I like it that he's looking out for me." Her smile disappeared. "I have to disappoint him tomorrow, though. He wanted to go skating, but I have to go with Lucien to see the architect about the house. Edward has never had to share my time so consistently with other people. He's getting tired of it."

"Did Lucien stop by last night?" Margaret asked, then took a sip of her tea.

"Oh yes, and he told me I need to get used to seeing him. He plans to come by often." Julia shook her head. "It wasn't too bad, though, since we kept the conversation on general topics. The only annoying thing was how positively smug he looked when he found out I gave up an outing with Edward to go with him Wednesday. He can't wait for Edward to be gone."

Margaret grinned. "I wonder how smug he'd look if he knew you were keeping company with Mr. Anderson this afternoon."

"He'd be furious because he had an appointment already set for today, and I told him I couldn't make it."

Jacob cleared his throat. "Does Lucien have any idea how many people are plotting against him? I'm starting to feel a little bit sorry for him."

Julia shook her finger at him. "Don't you feel sorry for him, Jacob. He's had more than his fair number of chances to back out of this." She drooped a little. "I do feel bad for Momma and Papa though, because I know they have my best interest at heart." Julia straightened her shoulders. "I don't feel bad enough to go through with a marriage I don't want, though."

"Tell me about the house you're seeing an architect about," Jacob said.

"Lucien bought a lot not too far from here as part of his settling down plan. He wants the house started as soon as the ground thaws, but he doesn't have a plan yet. He wants me to be in charge of the interior since he believes I'll be spending so much of my time there. We see Mr. Turner tomorrow to work out details."

Margaret poured more tea for everyone. "It's generous of him to give you so much freedom with the house. Do you have any ideas?"

"I got some from Sophia. I'm pretty sure I know enough about what she likes to plan it so she'll feel it belongs to her. I still believe she'll be living in it someday."

"Do you want to be involved in planning the house you'll live in?" Jacob asked.

"The man I share that house with is my first concern. I'll worry about the rest later."

"Tell us about farm life, Mr. Anderson. Julia and I have never been to one."

Julia glanced at her sister. Margaret must have decided she wasn't going to get around to asking. "Yes, tell us what a woman does there." She set her teacup down and fixed her gaze on Jacob.

<hr>

Jacob set his cup aside also, and considered where to start. His mother had worked hard and it wouldn't be fair if Julia didn't know. He just hoped she wouldn't lose interest in him when she found out what farm life involved. Julia and Margaret watched him expectantly, hands folded in their laps.

"I have to be honest; I don't know what all my mother did. The obvious things were cleaning the house, doing laundry and getting meals. She spent a lot of time in the kitchen, even though we had a girl who helped.

"She did some things outside too, such as feeding chickens,

gathering eggs and milking, besides tending the garden. Of course, my brothers and I helped with all of that until we left for high school. When we got out of school, we mostly helped our father in the fields and with the other work. Actually, the best way for you to learn about a woman's life on a farm would be to talk to a woman who is living on one now."

Julia and Margaret's expressions went from smiling interest to wide eyes and slack jaws. The reaction he'd been afraid of.

"I had no idea." Julia's hands were no longer folded loosely, but clenched together. "Your mother said it was a lot of work, but I never imagined all of that."

Margaret reached over and patted Julia's hands, her face pale. "It's a lot to think about, isn't it?"

"I'm thinking of attending the lecture tomorrow evening. Do you know the subject?" He hoped changing the topic would take the uncertainty out of Julia's eyes.

She stared at him for a moment, her eyes blank, then blinked. "I believe it will be a dramatic reading of some of Charles Dickens's works."

"I'll look forward to that." Jacob smiled, trying to coax Julia's smile to return. "Will you be with Lucien, or do you think we might be able to sit together again?"

Julia avoided eye contact while answering him. She'd never done that before. "My parents are planning to attend, so I'll go with them. I'm sure Lucien will sit with us, but that doesn't mean I can't see you too. A lot of our friends will be there."

He turned to Margaret and mouthed the word help.

"I'm going to check on Elise. I'll be back in a little bit." She stood and left the room.

Jacob slid closer and took Julia's hand. She looked at him with troubled eyes. His heart ached, thinking of what that might mean.

"I've scared you, haven't I?"

She drew a shaky breath. "Margaret's right. It's a lot to think about. That doesn't mean I don't want to continue our friendship, though. I still want to know your hopes and dreams."

"I suppose it's hard to imagine yourself in that lifestyle." Jacob held her hand a little tighter.

"It is right now. It's so far removed from anything I've experienced. I think talking to a woman who is living happily on a farm would be a good idea. I would like to get her perspective."

"I wish I could take you to my uncle's farm so you could talk to my aunt. She's always lighthearted. I'll try to find someone closer, though."

"I'd like to see where you grew up. Maybe someday that'll be possible."

"Maybe, but let's talk about now. What do you want to do Thursday?"

"Why don't we meet at Deer Park? We can walk and talk, and when we get cold, we can get a hot drink."

"I'll plan on that."

Julia returned to her usual cheerful mood, and they enjoyed trouble free conversation for the rest of Jacob's allotted time. As he left, he sincerely hoped she meant what she said about wanting to continue their friendship. Her behavior toward him at the lecture Wednesday evening would be a good indication.

After Jacob left, Margaret asked, "Are Lucien and his new house starting to look better?"

"No, but comparing a life of hard labor to one of travel and ease is making Edward and Europe look a lot more tempting. I think that would make me a coward though. Knowing farm life is hard doesn't change the way I feel about Jacob. If I decide I truly love him, having to work shouldn't matter. I'm sure I could get along."

"As I keep saying, it's a good thing you have some time to think about it."

Lucien steered his horse around the corner and pulled to a stop at the sight before him. He didn't believe he'd be noticed, but he was close enough to see Jacob Anderson leave Margaret's townhouse, get into a waiting sleigh and ride away. His hands tightened on the reins.

If he hadn't been in the neighborhood and decided to use the street Margaret lived on as his route back to the office, he wouldn't have known. No doubt Margaret and Julia were conspiring together to find ways for Julia and Mr. Anderson to spend time together. He took a deep breath and blew it out to release some of his anger, then got his horse going again.

Honestly, it didn't surprise him. Julia defied him at every turn, but he wouldn't be made a fool of. Everything he'd planned and worked for counted on his relationship with her appearing legitimate. He spent the rest of the ride mulling over a way to put a stop to this without letting Julia know the true purpose of their engagement.

22

Wednesday morning, Lucien stopped to see Steven, Margaret's husband. Steven and his father used offices in a building on State Street. On entering the building, he draped his black wool overcoat over his arm and removed his Homburg. The elevator carried him to the fifth floor and opened onto the reception area for Jefferson Shipping. Lucien approached a polished mahogany desk across from the elevator and spoke to the secretary, a stern woman with graying hair pulled into a tight bun. "I have an appointment with Steven Jefferson."

Steven stepped through the doorway of a corner office and motioned for him to come in. "Good morning." He shook Lucien's hand and closed the door. "Please take a seat. What can I do for you?"

Lucien settled into the chair as Steven went to the other side of the desk and sat. "I'd like to make you aware of something I hope you'll keep between the two of us."

"Intriguing." Steven rested his arms on the desk blotter and leaned toward him. "I'm good at keeping confidences. You can tell me without fear."

Lucien crossed his legs and relaxed in his chair. "It has to do with Jacob Anderson. Julia said you met him."

"Yes, a few weeks ago. His father is in the jewelry business. Nice fellow."

"Did you know his father is a merchant? He and his brother own a jewelry shop in the business district."

Steven's eyebrows lifted. "You don't say. That's not the impression I got."

Lucien closed his eyes and shook his head briefly. "Mr. Anderson is good at letting people believe he's more than he is. More to the point, he has befriended Julia and Margaret, and Margaret has had him and Julia in your home for tea."

Steven straightened, a small crease between his eyebrows. "She entertains many different people, struggling artists, poets, those who have talent and a desire to achieve their goals. Margaret does a lot of charitable work as well. Something about Mr. Anderson must have sparked her interest to help."

This wasn't the reaction he'd expected. Now he had no choice but to tell him the truth. "Here is what I need you to keep between us. Julia's father has given me his blessing to marry her. The announcement will be made in May. In the meantime, I see no reason for Julia to spend time with Mr. Anderson. I believe his intentions are more than friendship."

"Ah, I see." Steven smiled and nodded. "You want me to tell Margaret not to have Julia and Mr. Anderson at the house at the same time."

"Precisely, although I hope you won't be angry with her. You would be doing me a favor. And one more thing, please leave me out of your explanation."

Steven relaxed his posture. "I won't upset her and I'm happy to do this for you. Anyone can see you're the better choice as a husband for Julia."

Lucien smiled. "That's what I'd like to think. He stood and

extended his hand, which Steven shook. "I appreciate your time and help in this matter." He left, satisfied that one of Julia's allies had been eliminated.

❦

Julia stepped into a noisy, crowded lecture hall Wednesday evening. It seemed most of Boston wanted to hear from the works of Mr. Dickens. She had barely entered the room with her parents when Edward took her hand and pulled her arm around his elbow.

"Hello, Uncle John. I'm taking Julia with me. We have seats toward the front." Her parents frowned but didn't say anything as Edward guided her away.

"Are you on the job?" She smiled with raised eyebrows. "Or is there some other purpose for ambushing me and dragging me off?"

Edward stopped and faced her in a side aisle. "There's something you should know before you see Lucien. I don't know how, but he found out you were with Jacob yesterday afternoon, and he's not happy. Is Jacob coming tonight?"

"Yes, I had planned to watch for him before finding the rest of you." Julia looked back toward the doors. "I'm afraid he won't see me in this crowd."

Edward glanced toward the doors, then back at Julia. "Maybe it would be better if he didn't."

She frowned. "If Lucien is that upset, I shouldn't sit with him. We could end up causing a scene. I'll go back and look for Jacob and we'll sit somewhere else."

Edward quickly grabbed her hand as she started to leave. "He's not going to like that either." He turned her around to face him, not the doors. "You'll probably be better off trying to placate him for now. I know you don't like it, but he feels he has the right to restrict your company to him."

"This is ridiculous." Julia resisted the urge to stamp her foot. "Things have been going so well these last few days. He must have found out after our appointment with Mr. Turner, because he didn't say a thing this afternoon."

"Let me take you to where the group is sitting. I'll look for Jacob and tell him what's going on. Maybe you can see him at intermission."

Julia reluctantly agreed and took Edward's arm. He escorted her to the next aisle. When they got close, she saw Sophia sitting beside Lucien, trying to engage him in conversation. He didn't look happy. When they got close, he glanced up and stood.

"Save me a seat," Edward said. She watched as he headed back up the aisle.

When she lost sight of him, she turned around to find Lucien standing in front of her. She pasted on a smile. "Hello Lucien, quite a crowd tonight, isn't it?"

Lucien didn't return the smile. He simply ushered her to the empty seat on Sophia's right, then sat to her right. A quick look at Sophia confirmed her friend's concern. Turning back to Lucien, she decided on the direct approach and spoke to the side of his head. "You might as well tell me what's bothering you."

He continued to stare at the stage with his arms crossed. "What's bothering me isn't on our list of safe topics."

"I think you better tell me anyway."

Lucien turned to her, put his arm on the back of her seat and leaned close so he could be heard above the crowd. "You spent yesterday afternoon with Jacob Anderson. I had to reschedule an appointment so you could have tea with someone who is not even in our class. It looks as though he's more important to you than I am. That bothers me."

Julia looked at him with surprised admiration. She had to give him credit. He manner was discreet. She strove for the same level of calm he displayed. "My appointment to have tea with Mr. Anderson was set before you told me about Mr. Turner. I enjoy visiting with him and Margaret, and didn't want to cancel."

"Does Steven know Margaret is entertaining men from the middle class?"

Be civil. "Steven met Mr. Anderson a couple of weeks ago and liked him. He hasn't objected." She forced herself to keep her eyes on Lucien, when she wanted to turn around and look for Jacob.

"Just the same, I can't imagine the purpose of the visit."

"We're friends. Did you know on Monday, Momma and I called on Mrs. Anderson?"

"Yes, you told me Monday evening. However, I find it hard to believe your mother approves of you seeing Mr. Anderson socially."

Julia did a quick count to ten. "It was tea at Margaret's. We didn't attend a dinner together. Let's be reasonable."

"As long as we've left the safety zone, I'd like to say it doesn't seem unreasonable to ask you to limit your company to me. You may consider him a friend, but he might have other ideas."

"I understand. I'll try to be more sensitive to your wishes."

Lucien's eyes widened. "You will?"

"Yes, now let's talk about something else. Did you tell Sophia how our meeting with Mr. Turner went?"

"She asked me about it just as I saw you."

Julia turned to Sophia and gave her an enthusiastic account of the meeting that afternoon. She'd been able to pass on all of Sophia's ideas and knew her friend would be pleased with the result.

Jacob came into the hall, in time to see Julia and Edward disappear into the crowd. When he finally spotted her, it looked as if she and Lucien were having a cozy chat. Then she turned to Sophia and they began a lively conversation. He watched, willing her to turn around and see him. After a while he had to admit she didn't plan to look for him. Jacob turned with a heavy heart and plodded toward the doors. He didn't blame Julia for wanting to stay with the people she'd grown up with. Jacob couldn't compete with the kind of future Lucien or Edward could offer.

Julia saw Edward come back as the auditorium darkened. He sat in the empty seat she'd saved between her and Sophia, and shook his head at her silent inquiry. He leaned close. "We can try at the break." She nodded and they turned their attention to the stage. The only thing keeping her from turning around for one last look was the lack of light.

At intermission, Edward leaned over her and spoke to Lucien, "Julia and I are going to see her mother. She told me before the program started, she wanted to see Julia during the break."

"Is that all right?" Julia looked at Lucien, waiting for permission to leave.

"Uh, yes, that's fine."

As Edward led Julia to the back, she asked, "Did Momma really want to talk to me?"

"No, but we can talk to her, just in case he asks. You're planning to go to Sophia's, aren't you?" She nodded. "We'll tell her now, so you don't have to look for her afterward."

"Okay, but where do you think Jacob is? He has to be here." She scanned the crowd for a tall man with blond hair.

"Did everything go all right yesterday? Maybe you said something that made him think you'd lost interest."

"He told me about farm life and I said I couldn't imagine myself doing that. He looked unhappy so I tried to reassure him I still want to be friends." She began twisting her ring. "Maybe he didn't believe me."

Edward took both her hands in his. "We don't know why he's not here. Something might have come up. Do you plan to meet tomorrow?"

"Yes, at Deer Park."

"If he doesn't show up there, and you don't get a letter explaining why, I'd be inclined to think you're right. But don't jump to conclusions tonight."

Julia's mother stepped out of the crowd and swatted Edward on the arm with her handbag. "Will you two break it up."

"Ouch. What's in that bag?" Edward rubbed his arm.

Julia smiled at Momma's flustered look. "We came to tell you we'll be going to Sophia's after the lecture."

"I hope Lucien will be going."

"He'll be there. He'll probably walk me to our door afterwards."

Edward grinned. "Unless I beat him to it."

Her mother frowned and pointed at Edward. As she drew a breath to speak, Julia's father joined them. He didn't look pleased either, but before he could say anything, Mr. and Mrs. Jordan stopped next to them.

Mrs. Jordan beamed. "Here's my couple. How are you two enjoying the reading?"

"It's interesting," they said at the same time. She and Edward looked at each other and laughed. Her mother threw up her hands and looked at the ceiling.

Mrs. Jordan jabbed her husband with her elbow. "See what I mean? Perfect."

Squashing down the urge to keep laughing, Julia said, "We should get back. It's nice to see you."

The two of them looked for Jacob as long as they could, then went to their seats. Lucien stood when he saw her. "Did you talk to your mother? You were gone the whole intermission. Did you have a hard time finding her?"

"We found her. I told Momma I'd be going to Sophia's later."

She turned to the stage, aching with disappointment. Edward whispered in her ear, "Don't worry. I bet you'll see him tomorrow.

Later that evening, at the Howell's, Sophia took Julia aside. "I didn't see Jacob there tonight."

"I didn't either." Julia dropped onto a side chair. "I'm afraid he may not be interested in seeing me after I told him I couldn't imagine myself on a farm."

Sophia sat next to her. "I'm glad to hear you've come to your senses. Not so long ago you said a farm would be a challenge you could handle. What changed your mind?"

"Jacob described some of the work his mother did on the farm. I had no idea it would be so much." She stopped and looked at her friend with suspicion. "What do you mean, come to my senses? You don't expect me to forget the man, who might possibly make me happier than anyone on earth, just because of some hard work, do you? Surely you know me better than to think I would give up and marry Lucien."

With a grimace, Sophia said, "I'd rather you wouldn't marry Lucien, but I wish you would stay in our social set." She reached over and patted her hand. "I've done some reading about farming, and I hate to think of you working your life away. Do you realize you might actually have to touch a cow or some other animal?" Sophia wrinkled her nose.

Julia shook her head, dismissing all of that. "What about following my heart?"

"Follow it in another direction. You said you'd like to travel. Why don't you go with Edward? It's obvious to everyone you two enjoy each other's company."

She gazed at Sophia for a few moments. "I'm supposed to meet Jacob at Deer Park tomorrow. You'll still come with me, won't you?"

"Yes, of course, I'll go with you, but if he's not there, will you consider giving him up?"

"If he's not there, I'd say he's made the decision for me."

23

On Thursday afternoon, Julia and Sophia set out for the park. "I'm amazed at how well you and Lucien got along last night."

Julia chuckled. "It's thanks to you. I finally decided to take your advice and be agreeable."

"I hope he won't hear about your meeting this afternoon, assuming Jacob will be there."

"I hope he will be. If Jacob thinks our friendship is a mistake, I want to hear him say it."

When the girls arrived at the park, Julia scanned the area. No one fit Jacob's description. A knot formed in her chest making it hard to take a deep breath. She couldn't believe he would stop seeing her without a word. "Do you mind waiting a bit? He must be running late."

"I can wait."

Jacob finally finished with the indecisive customer and hurried to Deer Park. He hated to be late, but after last night, he didn't have much hope for Julia to be there. The sense of connection between them must have been one-sided. It disheartened him to think his parents might be right. Yet he couldn't believe she would stop seeing him without an explanation.

When he got close several groups of people caught his eye. A couple of women stood a little apart from the others. Their hair color was right and one of them wore a sapphire blue coat. His heart sped up.

Jacob took one more step forward, then stopped. What explanation could he give for last night? Should there be an explanation from Julia? If he cared about her, the kindest thing to do would be leave this sweet woman in the upper-class, and stop torturing himself with possibilities. He'd made up his mind to leave when the two women turned around. Julia. When she saw him, her face lit up with a smile and she came toward him. He went toward her like a moth to a flame. Maybe he would torture himself a little longer.

⁂

As soon as Julia reached him, she said, "I was afraid you weren't coming."

"I'm sorry to keep you waiting. I couldn't get away from the store as soon as I wanted."

They searched each other's eyes, not speaking. Finally, Julia said, "I didn't see you last night."

He sighed and dropped his chin to his chest. "I was there for a while." He raised his head and met her eyes. "It looked as if you and Lucien were getting along better than usual. I didn't want to disturb you."

She frowned, trying to think what he could mean. The quiet conversation they'd had about her seeing Jacob came to mind. That could have looked like an intimate chat. Her brow cleared. "So, you left?"

"As much as I enjoy a dramatic reading, I'm more interested in seeing you. I didn't see a reason to stay."

Julia reined in her frustration. "Edward looked for you. If you'd stayed, he would have explained what Lucien and I were talking about."

"What were you talking about?"

She took his arm. "Come on. I've left Sophia standing back there on the path long enough."

They joined Sophia and continued as a threesome. Julia turned to Sophia. "Jacob said he came last night, but only stayed long enough to see how well Lucien and I were getting along."

Sophia looked at Julia and chuckled, then spoke to Jacob. "If it wasn't for Julia's ability to handle an argument with the skill of a diplomat, it would have appeared much different."

He turned to Julia, frowning slightly and she said, "Somehow, Lucien found out we had tea with Margaret Tuesday. He didn't like it, but I turned things around and now he thinks I'm being agreeable."

"At least, that's what he'll think until he hears about today," Sophia quipped.

A mixture of relief and concern crossed Jacob's face. "I never would have guessed."

Julia gazed up at him. "What *were* you thinking?"

"I thought you'd decided your life would be better without a farm boy."

She stopped. "When I didn't find you at intermission, I thought you'd decided life would be better without a city girl."

A slow smile lit up his eyes. "I guess we were both wrong."

The three of them continued to stroll until they got cold enough to look for a shop selling hot chocolate. When they found one, they bypassed the pastry case and sat at a table, ordered hot chocolate and chatted amicably over their hot drinks. The clock hanging on the wall at the front of the shop showed Julia the thirty minutes she'd allowed herself to stay were up.

When they stepped outside the shop, Julia's heart skipped a beat. Ben Pennington and Samantha stood by the door waiting to go in. Ben appeared surprised to see Jacob, but quickly hid it, giving them all a friendly greeting.

Once the door closed between them, Sophia tilted her head toward the shop. "What do you suppose the chances are you'll have a visit from Lucien tonight?"

Jacob stepped closer. "I don't want to cause problems for you."

Julia noted the worry lines on his forehead. "It'll be fine. I can handle Lucien. If we have an opportunity to talk tomorrow, I'll tell you about it."

He hesitated. "All right. I'll see you tomorrow."

On the way home, Julia said, "You're disappointed, aren't you?"

"Yes, but Jacob is such a nice man. I can see why you might consider giving everything up for him."

After dinner that evening, Julia and her mother settled in the drawing room. Julia curled up in the corner of a settee, eager to start her copy of *The Bostonians* by Henry James, while her mother sat in a rocking chair, working on embroidery. Sanders soon came to the door and announced, "Mr. Harris is here to see Miss Julia."

"Bring him up," Momma said, "and ask Millie to bring tea." Sanders nodded and left.

Julia sighed. She hoped he'd be as calm tonight as he had been last night. It wouldn't do for Momma to hear about Jacob.

She watched him closely when he entered the room. He smiled as he sat next to her, giving the appearance of a man satisfied with life.

Maybe Ben didn't talk to him. Tea arrived and after chatting for a while, Momma excused herself.

Now I'll hear about it.

Lucien put down his teacup and turned to her. "I hoped she'd give us some time alone. Ben told me he saw you and Sophia with Jacob Anderson today. Originally, I thought he was attracted to you. Now I'm wondering, do you suppose he's interested in Sophia?"

His obvious concern took her off guard. She never dreamed he'd come up with that possibility, but it could work to her advantage.

"If he is, he hasn't told me. It wouldn't be surprising, though. Sophia's attractive and good company. I've noticed Aaron and Tyler have been giving her a lot of attention."

Lucien brushed a nonexistent piece of lint from the sleeve of his jacket. "Does she seem to be attracted to anyone in particular?"

Julia set her teacup aside. "Well, now that you mention it, she did say there was a man she wouldn't mind spending more time with."

He leaned toward her. "Did she tell you who it is?"

Julia put her hand on her chest. "You want me to share my best friend's confidences?"

"No, no, I understand you can't do that." He sat back. "It worries me she might be thinking of Anderson. If she is, her parents will be quite upset."

"Does that sound like something she'd do?"

Lucien hesitated a moment. "No. In the conversations we've had she's been quite sensible. That's one of the things I admire about her."

"What else do you admire about her?" Julia reclaimed her teacup and saucer and took a sip.

Lucien relaxed. "As you said, she is attractive. I enjoy talking to her, and I like her sense of humor."

"I've heard the other men mention those same things." She leaned toward him. "I will tell you this. Sophia is more ready to settle down than I am. It wouldn't surprise me if she married before the year is over. That man will be extremely fortunate."

Julia smiled to herself. Lucien didn't look at all happy with that information. He drummed his fingers on his leg as he thought about it.

Sanders came to the door again. "Mr. Harrington to see you Miss Julia."

She laughed. "I can see that."

Sanders turned to see Edward looking over his shoulder. "I told him I knew the way," Edward said with a grin. Sanders left, shaking his head.

Setting her tea down, she jumped up, gave Edward a quick hug and led him to where she and Lucien sat. "Would you like some tea?"

"I'm sure he won't be staying," Lucien said, frowning. "I should think one male visitor at a time is enough, and I arrived first."

"You may have been here first, but I'm her favorite." Edward made himself comfortable in an armchair across from them. "I came to see how your day went, Julia."

The look on Lucien's face caused Julia to struggle with her composure. She wanted to laugh out loud at Edward's outrageous behavior. "The day went well. Sophia and I had an outing in the park."

"Was Mr. Anderson with you in the park as well?" Lucien asked.

"That's where we first saw him. We walked together and ended our time over hot chocolate." Julia handed Edward a cup of tea.

"What do you think of that, Edward?" Lucien asked. "Our Julia and Sophia spent the afternoon with this Jacob Anderson. Are you aware he's in the merchant class?"

Edward looked to her, eyebrows raised.

"We saw Ben as we left the shop."

"Ah, I see. What do I think?" Edward took a sip of tea. "I think Jacob Anderson is a decent fellow, regardless of being from the merchant class. As far as I can tell, there's no reason for them to shun his company."

"Ben believes there might be a mutual attraction between Sophia and Anderson. Have you noticed anything to suggest that?" Lucien focused on Edward, waiting for a reaction.

Julia could almost see Edward's mind adjusting to this new line of thinking. "Stranger things have happened. Maybe our main concern should be what will make Sophia happy."

Lucien waved the thought away. "Women are happy when they are protected and well provided for. As men, it's our responsibility to do that."

Edward glanced at her. His lips quirked up at the corners when she put her hand to her mouth, pretending to cover a yawn. "Is that what you believe, or what you've heard the older men saying?"

Lucien looked down his nose at Edward. "Sensible men know it to be true." He relaxed back, and crossed his legs. "I suppose Julia has you believing in some happily-ever-after, fairy-tale marriage."

Edward set his cup and saucer on the small marble-topped table beside him. "I think you should be in love with the person you marry, if that's what you mean. If you don't have mutual love and affection, I don't know how either of you could be happy."

"Of course, it's best if you admire and care for the other person. Affection, on the other hand, is yours by right of marriage."

Julia cleared her throat, reminding the men of her presence. She had no desire to hear Lucien's thoughts on a man's marital rights.

Her mother chose that moment to re-enter the room. "I'm sorry I was gone so long. Are you having a nice chat?" The men stood as she crossed the room. Her eyes widened when she saw Edward. "Sanders didn't tell me you'd come. How long have you been here?"

"Not too long. You needn't worry, though. Julia has been the perfect hostess."

Momma sat in the armchair on the other side of the table holding Edward's tea. "I hope we're all getting along." She looked at Lucien, then Edward.

He winked at her. "I can get along with almost anyone."

"As can I." Lucien crossed his arms over his chest.

To Julia's amusement, they continued to make conversation until it became clear both Lucien and Edward were determined to out stay each other. Finally, her mother made a point of looking at the clock on the fireplace mantel and stood. "It's getting late, gentlemen."

"Want to walk me to the door?" Edward asked Julia, his eyes twinkling.

"She can walk Lucien to the door," Momma said. "You don't need an escort."

The three of them went downstairs, with Julia holding Lucien's arm. When they got to the door, she let go. "Good night, Lucien. Thank you for coming, and thank you for your concern for Sophia."

"You're welcome. I'll see you soon." He retrieved his coat, hat and galoshes from the hall tree, put them on, then went through the double doors to the vestibule and on out to his sleigh.

Julia turned to Edward and he pulled her into a tight hug. "He's bad for you. Don't lose your determination," he whispered. He kissed her on the cheek and let her go. "I'll see you at dinner tomorrow night."

❦

Lucien waited outside, his toe tapping the snowy sidewalk. The minute Edward came out the door, Lucien confronted him. "Apparently I need to remind you Julia is engaged to me. I'm beginning to make some progress in winning her over, and you're not helping." Lucien jabbed his finger at Edward on the last three words.

Edward slapped Lucien on the back. "You're just going to have to win her in spite of me."

Lucien watched Edward get into his sleigh and leave, then slowly climbed into his. He ignored the bitter night air and thought about the evening. It would be nice to see Julia's face light up with a smile when she saw him. He wondered what it would be like to hold her in his arms. Other than on the dance floor, the closest he'd come to any kind of intimate contact was holding her hand, and she didn't even seem comfortable with that.

He sighed, and icy vapor hung in the air before him. Sophia always appeared happy to see him. His eyes lingered on Sophia's house, one door down. But what about Jacob Anderson? Did she look happy to see him, too? He shook his head. These kinds of thoughts would derail his plan. If he wanted to avenge his father, he needed to stay the course.

24

At breakfast the next morning, Momma said, "You seem distracted today, dear. Things went well with Lucien last night, didn't they?"

Julia brought her focus from the two ladies in a rose garden picture over the buffet back to the conversation. "Oh, Lucien? Yes… fine."

"Your tea will be too cold to drink if you pour any more milk in it." Momma helped herself to a honey nut muffin. "I can't tell you how surprised I was to see Edward in the drawing room when I came back last night. I felt sorry for Lucien having to compete with him. You should have told Edward you'd visit with him tonight at your grandmother's dinner."

Julia smiled, remembering Edward's visit. "I wasn't about to send him off. He hardly ever gets to visit during the week. Anyway, I prefer Edward's company to Lucien's. He makes me laugh."

Momma frowned while buttering her muffin. "Well, it's not fair to Lucien. I'm sure you've told Edward that you and Lucien are betrothed. He shouldn't continue to call on you."

"I'm looking forward to this afternoon, aren't you?" Julia smiled at Momma and added a piece of bacon to the untouched food on her plate.

"Changing the topic doesn't change facts. You need to be more respectful of Lucien's feelings. And yes, I am looking forward to this afternoon. I sincerely hope the young man plays as well as we're anticipating. I've contacted Mr. Fontello to make an appointment."

"Will he have time next week?"

"Tuesday afternoon is the only day he has free. That means I'll have to miss going to the Women's Club. But if Mr. Fontello likes him, it'll be worth it."

After breakfast Julia went to Sophia's. They settled in the drawing room in the armchairs near the fireplace, and Sophia said, "I assume Lucien visited last night."

"He did, and you're never going to believe what he said." Julia still couldn't get over the absurdity of the notion.

"What?"

"He's concerned that you and Jacob might be attracted to each other." She laughed when Sophia's mouth dropped open.

"Why?"

"That's the way Ben saw it, and reported it to Lucien. Lucien wanted to know what I thought."

Sophia's eyes widened. "You set him straight, didn't you?"

"Well, not exactly. He didn't like the idea, so it seemed like a good opportunity to make him jealous."

"Not to mention, to keep him from worrying about you and Jacob," Sophia said with a twinkle in her eye. She shook her head and relaxed.

"I mentioned Aaron and Tyler, also. I wanted to give him several people to think about." Julia gave her a conspiratorial smile. "If he thinks you're interested in making a commitment to someone, it may help him realize that *someone* should be him."

"You didn't tell him anything specific?"

"Only that there was someone you wouldn't mind spending more time with."

Sophia sighed. "Okay, but promise you won't add to that."

"I promise," Julia said solemnly, holding up her right hand.

"All right, then. That should be fine."

Julia and Momma were finally on their way to Jacob's house. Julia didn't know if her uneasy stomach had more to do with being excited to see Jacob or nervous about meeting his father. He probably wouldn't like her any more than Jacob's mother did.

Momma must have sensed her agitation, because she said, "You're not the one auditioning, dear. Why are you so fidgety?"

"Mr. Anderson will be there."

"Which Mr. Anderson? I assume you mean other than the son who will play."

She tried to twist her ring, but her gloves were in the way. "I mean Mrs. Anderson's husband."

"I don't know why that should bother you. Your papa said he's a good man. He's no one to be afraid of. You don't need to worry, though." Momma patted her hand. "After next Tuesday, I don't think we'll have much contact with the family. Jason Anderson will have to take it from there."

She gave Momma a small smile. She didn't know about the rest of the family, but she certainly planned to continue seeing Jacob. If only they didn't have to work against the silly class issue.

When they arrived, Mrs. Anderson greeted them as before and invited them in. Jacob and his father stood and approached when they entered the room. Julia noticed Jacob and Jason looked a lot like their father. She hoped their personalities were similar.

Jacob introduced his father to Momma first. Mr. Anderson smiled. "It's good to meet you, Mrs. Phillips. My wife and I appreciate your interest in Jason." Then he turned to Julia. "I'm happy to meet you as well, Miss Phillips." His emphasis on her name with a serious gaze quieted the room. She met Mr. Anderson's stare with a tentative smile and he gave her a reserved smile in return. His tone didn't sound like he disapproved, but it wasn't a ringing endorsement, either.

Jason charmed Momma with his manners and his appreciation. "Let's hear what you've been working on young man."

Without further ado, Jason sat down and played. There had been no exaggeration about his skill. Both Mr. and Mrs. Anderson watched their son with pride. They had a right to be proud. Julia had no trouble imagining how happy Mr. Fontello would be when he heard Jason.

When Jason finished, Momma cried, "Marvelous! You must play for Mr. Fontello. He can hear you at our home on Tuesday afternoon. You can come, can't you?"

"I think so." Jason looked at his father. Mr. Anderson nodded. Turning back with a smile, Jason said, "Tuesday will be fine."

Momma spent the rest of their visit talking to Jason about how many years he'd studied piano, who his teachers had been, and what his goals were. Before they left, she invited the Andersons to come with Jason on Tuesday.

"Mr. Fontello wants to have a private audition," she clarified, "but we can be nearby and listen."

"I don't think I'll be able to get away from the store," Mr. Anderson said, "but Irene and Jacob are free to go."

"Fine, that's settled." Momma handed Mrs. Anderson her calling card. "I've written our address on the back. Please come at 2:30."

Julia managed to remind Jacob, without her mother noticing, they were going skating the next day. She'd have to fill him in on Lucien's visit then.

After Julia and her mother left, Jacob and his family starred at each other without speaking until Mrs. Anderson said, "It kind of feels like a whirlwind blew through, doesn't it?"

"I like Mrs. Phillips," Jason said with enthusiasm.

His mother gave Jason a hug, his father pumped his hand and Jacob slapped him on the back. Mrs. Anderson said, "I knew you had special talent."

"I guess meeting Julia was a fortunate thing for the two of us." Jacob grinned. "She's not so bad, is she father?"

"She's a beautiful young woman." Mr. Anderson thought for a moment before going on. "She seems sweet, but her mother is somewhat overwhelming. It's hard to say much about Miss Phillips."

Jacob looked at his father with raised eyebrows. "But what is your initial impression?"

"If I were to go on looks, I'd say she's a refined lady who will have no idea what to do if expected to work."

"There's more there than you can see."

"I hope so, son. I hope so."

"April is such a muddy month," Lily complained. Julia and Sophia looked over at the drawing room window where Lily stood. Rain ran in little rivers down the glass, making the world beyond it a blur.

"April is almost over," Julia said. "Now come back over here and sit down. You're supposed to be helping me with this handwork."

Lily heaved a sigh and came to sit next to Julia on the settee. "James and I were going on a picnic tomorrow. I don't see how we'll be able to now." She picked up her embroidery hoop, and half-heartedly got back to work.

"It's a little early for picnics," Sophia said, from one of the upholstered armchairs across from them. "I'm surprised James agreed to it."

"Falling in love does funny things to one's common sense." Julia patted Lily's arm.

"I guess you should know." Sophia softened her comment with a smile.

"Be nice, Sophia. I think Julia and Jacob are incredibly romantic, even though I still believe you should be with Edward, Julia. I don't know how Uncle John and Aunt Elizabeth could ever have agreed to pair you with Lucien." She waved her embroidery hoop toward Sophia. "Anyone can see he is much more suited to Sophia."

Sophia chuckled and looked up briefly from her work. "I'll have to say since you mentioned I might be interested in someone he's been more attentive."

Lily snorted. "It's beyond me how a person can be so blind. Or maybe stubborn is a better word. But since we know there isn't going to be a wedding, why do we have to do this embroidery?" This time she waved her hoop at Julia.

"I do plan to get married. I just don't know when."

"Or to whom." Sophia arched a brow. "Has Jacob said anything to give you hope?"

Julia stopped stitching and looked at Sophia. "Not yet, but we're spending as much time together as we can. I know he cares for me. Sometimes I feel he'd like to say more, but he's holding back."

"Maybe he's worried about what he has to offer," Lily said. "He's been to Margaret's, and here for his brother's audition. He may not think you'd consider going with him to a farm, especially since you keep trying to get him to think of staying in the city."

"I'm sure that's part of the problem," Sophia said, letting her work rest in her lap. "Even if he continued to work with his father, he wouldn't be able to provide the kind of lifestyle you're used to."

Julia laid her own work down and looked at her friends. "To be honest, we haven't discussed it much. I mention how nice it would be to raise a family here and he talks about how much he enjoyed growing up in the country. At any rate, he did tell me he doesn't have enough money to settle down right now. So even if he does want to marry me, he can't afford it."

"You want to marry him though, don't you?" Lily asked. "You two have your hearts in your eyes when you look at each other."

Julia didn't hesitate. "I love him. Even if he never changes his mind about a farm, I'd be willing to go just to be with him."

"Maybe you should tell him," Lily said.

"I'm afraid he'll think I'm asking him to marry me so I can get out of my situation with Lucien. He offered to help, but never suggested marriage."

Sophia nodded. "Julia's right. She should wait for Jacob to ask."

"What if he doesn't?"

"Well…" She hesitated to mention Edward. His attitude and actions toward her hadn't changed, but he hadn't said anything else about her going with him either.

"Edward will," Lily said with confidence. "I know you love Jacob, but surely you must have some love for Edward, too. You're so much alike. Think how romantic it would be to run off to Europe and get married."

The thought made her smile. "It does sound exciting. And you're right, I do love Edward, but I'm not *in love* with him. He's not in love with me."

"I know he won't let you marry Lucien." Lily clenched Julia's forearm. "If he asks you, you'll go, won't you?"

"Where will you go?" Momma asked, as she came into the drawing room.

All three girls jumped. Julia hoped they didn't look guilty. "Momma, it's good to see you up. Is your headache gone?"

"I'm feeling some better." She settled into an armchair. "I hoped visiting with you girls might help me forget about it. How's the work coming?"

"We're making progress," Sophia said, "but it's a good thing we have plenty of time. You might have had to ask the seamstress to do the embroidery, too."

"My momma taught us a woman did the fancy stitching on her trousseau herself. I'm sure Julia will be happy to help you two when the time comes, and from the look of things, I'd say it won't be much longer before we hear something from you, Lily."

Julia and Sophia smiled at Lily and she blushed. "James and I are getting along well. If he asks, I'll say yes."

"Do you hear that, Julia? Lily is ready to make a good marriage without any fuss at all." Momma gave her a meaningful look.

"Why don't you ask her why she would say yes?"

"I'm sure she can see it's the sensible thing to do."

"They're in love, Momma." Julia returned Momma's meaningful look.

Momma turned to Lily.

"It's true. I wouldn't consider marrying him if we didn't love each other."

"It's nice you feel that way now, dear, but there's more to marriage than emotions. James comes from a good family and you'll be well provided for. The fact you already care for each other is a head start in many unions."

"You won't talk about this to anyone, will you, Aunt Elizabeth? James hasn't proposed yet."

"His mother and I feel it's only a matter of time. Don't you agree Sophia?"

Sophia chuckled. "If the perpetual smile on his face is anything to go by, I have to agree."

"I'll bet there aren't any mommas predicting an announcement from Lucien and me," Julia said dryly.

Momma picked up her embroidery hoop. "Speaking of you and Lucien, we need to schedule more fittings with the seamstress. She'll have a lot to get done over the summer. And how is the house coming?"

"It looks like a big mud hole. I don't know why Lucien gets so excited about it. He wants to drag me over there to look at it every chance he gets."

"Men do tend to get excited over little things, but it'll be more interesting when the walls start going up."

"We'll see." She concentrated on her stitching and not Momma.

"By the way, Julia, Mrs. Wiggins said you and Jacob Anderson were seen at the public library again the other day. You two seem to run into each other a lot. Doesn't he have to work at the store his father owns?"

"He doesn't have to work all the time." She glanced at her friends, hoping they might come up with something to distract Momma.

"I don't think you should be seeing so much of him. It doesn't look good. More and more people are beginning to mention it. I'm surprised Lucien hasn't said something to you."

"Lucien isn't worried about Jacob. You shouldn't be either." Now she gave Momma her full attention. "You know what a nice person he is, and you know his family."

"While I do think he and his family are good people, they aren't in our set. You need to be more careful, especially after the announcement is made in a few weeks."

"Papa has never objected."

"Papa isn't aware. It takes men longer to hear things. When he does, you can be sure he won't approve. And I certainly hope you and Edward will change your behavior after the announcement. Sooner would be better."

"I've told you I prefer Edward's company. I don't know why everyone keeps insisting Lucien and I go through with this."

Momma leaned toward her. "If you and Edward want to do more than make me nervous, why don't you say so?"

The silence in the room grew uncomfortable as everyone waited for her answer, but all she could do was shrug her shoulders. "We don't have anything to say right now."

"Julia, invitations to the engagement party go out next week. The event will be held two weeks after that. Now is the time to say something."

She knew Momma was frustrated, but so was she. "I know. But all I can tell you for sure is I don't want to marry Lucien."

"Your father is set on this marriage. In three weeks, your betrothal becomes public. There will be no turning back. I suggest you stop being obstinate and adjust your thinking to acceptance of matrimony."

They worked in silence until Momma said her headache had returned and went back to bed.

Lily turned to her. "Are you sure you can't say anything to Jacob?"

"I'm sure. If he wants to marry me, he'll have to ask."

25

Julia sat brooding in a wingback chair by the fireplace in the drawing room, her embroidery in her lap. Last night's tedious planning dinner replayed in her mind. Lucien, Priscilla, Frank, Margaret and Steven rounded out the group. They covered everything from names for the guest list, to what food to have on the menu.

She hadn't said much, and she could tell Momma thought that best. Having Margaret there helped. At least someone could sympathize with how she felt.

The boring dinner wasn't the only thing bothering her. The plan to meet Jacob at the Common had to be canceled, again, because of the rain. She felt like a prisoner trapped inside with her embroidery hoop chained to her wrist.

At least she'd see Jacob at the concert tonight. That fact alone kept her from going stir-crazy. Jason would make his first stage appearance, and no matter what, Julia planned to sit with Jacob. People could do all the talking they wanted.

"You're not as pretty when you frown," Papa said, sitting down in the chair across from her with a newspaper.

"I don't feel like smiling right now."

"I should think you'd have a lot to smile about. Last night's planning session was productive. You'll have a nice engagement party."

"That doesn't make me feel like smiling. As a matter of fact, I may have a headache that night." Julia rubbed her temples, knowing it wouldn't be imaginary.

"You'll be in perfect health that night," Papa said sternly. After a few minutes of silence, he said, "I know what should make you smile. Hearing your friend's brother at the concert tonight."

She straightened in the chair and found herself talking to the back of the newspaper. "I'm going to sit with Jacob. This opportunity for Jason is partly because of me, and I want to be with a family member."

Papa lowered the paper enough to look at her over the top. "I understand dear, just make sure it's all right with Lucien." He raised the paper back up.

"I talked to him last night." She reached for her book. Reading should help pass the time. If only she could concentrate.

◦❦◦

Edward walked past the drawing room door and Lily called to him. He backed up and stepped in the room. Lily sat on a brocade sofa, a book in her lap. "I'm glad you're home. I want to talk to you."

He crossed to the sofa and sat next to his sister. "This sounds serious." He grinned. "I'm not in trouble, am I?"

She lowered her voice. "Do you know where Momma and Papa are?"

"I saw them in Papa's study."

"Good, I want to talk to you about Julia." Lily laid her hand on his arm. "I'm concerned about her."

His smile disappeared. "What's wrong?"

"Sophia and I were at her house yesterday, working on her trousseau."

"Ha. I can't help you with that."

"Be quiet and listen." Lily squeezed his arm. "Julia doesn't know what her future's going to be, and I can tell her parents are wearing her down. She's getting a little anxious. The formal announcement is in three weeks, you know." Lily gave him a pointed look.

"I know the schedule. What do you want me to do about it?"

"Do you remember when you said you might take Julia to Europe with you?"

"I did?" Edward tried to remember when he might have mentioned that to Lily.

She flipped her hand. "Well, I know you were joking, but I think it's a good idea. It would be a romantic adventure." He didn't comment, so she added, "I know you care about her, even though she said you don't love her."

He shook his head. "You must have misunderstood. She knows I love her." Edward gave her a reassuring smile. "I think you're more worried than she is. But if it'll make you feel better, I'll promise you Julia won't marry Lucien."

Lily threw her arms around him. "I knew you would rescue her."

He returned her hug. "Are we counting Jacob out?"

"No, but Sophia and I are beginning to think he'll never get around to it. We all hoped things would be settled before the party. Aunt Elizabeth as much as told Julia if she wanted to make any changes, now's the time. Although…" She gazed over his shoulder and tapped her chin with her index finger. Bringing her focus back to him, she said, "Aunt Elizabeth told Julia her father is set on the match with Lucien, so there won't be any changes regardless."

Raising his shoulders in a shrug, he said, "Julia has given her parents plenty of warning. It'll be up to them to handle the situation when things don't go their way."

She sighed. "You're right, I have to stop worrying about it. I'm going upstairs and choose which dress to wear tonight."

Edward smiled at his sweet sister as she left the room. James would be lucky to have her.

His smile faded, and he slumped back on the sofa. What did Lily want him to do? Remind Julia she had another option? Take Jacob aside and tell him to get on with it? He felt helpless sitting around waiting for Jacob to do something. Even if it didn't happen before the party, they'd have the summer to get something worked out.

He sat up and leaned forward, resting his forearms on his thighs. If they didn't have a plan in place before August, he wouldn't hesitate to step in. He doubted he'd ever find another woman as perfect for him as Julia.

Julia arrived at the concert hall with her parents to find Jacob waiting for her. Momma had taken to calling him Jacob a month ago and greeted him warmly. Julia had introduced him to Papa after church one Sunday, and they seemed to get along fine.

"Well, Jacob, is your brother ready for his big night?" Papa asked.

"He's a little nervous, but confident. To be part of an orchestra, and even to have a solo performance, is a dream come true."

"I'm sure he'll make us all proud."

Julia smiled to herself. Papa had begun to feel he could take some responsibility for this evening.

"I know he will," Momma said. "You two enjoy the concert. You know where our seats are."

Her parents left them and Julia turned to Jacob. "Are we sitting with your family?"

"You don't mind, do you?"

"Not at all." She took his arm with a smile.

"Good. We have seats close to the front. Should I have saved one for Lucien?"

"No, I told him I'd be sitting with you and he said okay. We've been getting along so well it makes me wish I'd pretended to be agreeable right from the beginning."

"I think you've done the right thing. No one will be able to say you didn't tell him how you felt from the beginning."

When they arrived at the seats, Mrs. Anderson's eyes widened and her mouth fell open for an instant. Mr. Anderson and Joel immediately stood and greeted her.

"It's nice to see you all," Julia said. "You must be so proud of Jason tonight."

"Yes, proud and nervous." Mrs. Anderson twisted a handkerchief in her lap. "I want everything to go perfectly."

Julia smiled. "I'm sure it will. He says he practices for hours."

"That's true," Joel said. "I hear music in my dreams."

Everyone laughed and settled in their seats.

Jacob leaned close to Julia and whispered, "Mother didn't think you'd sit with us."

"She appeared surprised," Julia whispered back. "I hope she'll come to like me."

"I like you." Jacob smiled and squeezed her hand.

"I like you, too." *Tell me you love me. Tell me you don't care what our parents think, because you know we'll be happy together.*

Julia sighed mentally. "Katherine would like to meet you. I told her we would come Tuesday. Will that work out for you?"

"It should. I'd like to meet her, too. You've said so many nice things about her."

"We won't be able to stay long because she doesn't have a lot of strength. And I should warn you she'll talk about God."

Jacob's eyebrows rose. "I don't have a problem with God."

"I don't either, but sometimes I get a little uncomfortable with how personal she wants to make him. You'll see what I mean."

"I'm sure it'll be fine. Now I have something to ask you." He hesitated for a moment before going on. "My family planned a reception for Jason tonight after the concert. Several friends have been invited, as well as my aunt and uncle, of course. Do you think you might be able to come?"

Julia could see hope and doubt waging a battle in Jacob's eyes. "I would love to come, but of course I'll have to ask my parents."

"You could bring someone with you if that will make them feel better."

"I'll mention it if they're reluctant." She thought for a moment. "Maybe Edward can come. We'll ask at intermission."

⚬⚭⚬

"Do you know where Julia is?" Ben asked as he took a seat next to Lucien.

"Yes, she's with Jacob's family."

Ben leaned toward him. "Doesn't it seem a little unusual for her to sit with them instead of you? I'm sure I'm not the only one who saw her over there."

Lucien faced Ben. "We discussed it last night. Her family had a lot to do with Jason Anderson getting a seat in the orchestra, and she wants to be supportive."

Ben humphed, but kept his thoughts to himself, which was fine with Lucien.

Edward sat in the row ahead of him with Lily and James. When Mrs. Wiggins passed by, she made an abrupt stop and peered at Edward over the top of her spectacles. "Where is Julia?"

"She's sitting with another friend tonight."

"It won't do to let a lovely young woman like that out of your sight for long. Other young men might get ideas."

"I'm not worried. But thank you for the advice." When the elderly lady moved on, Edward turned around with a grin. "I guess you're not worried either."

"In a few more weeks, people won't be directing those remarks to you," Lucien said evenly. "I hope by then, you will have the grace to step out of the picture."

"We'll see," Edward said, with a maddening smile.

Until Lucien had decided to put his plan into action officially, he had never run into anyone who infuriated him more than Edward. His jaw ached and he made a conscious effort to relax. In a few months the man would be gone. He could tolerate him until then.

At intermission, Julia and Jacob found her parents talking with Edward's mother and father. "I have a question for you. A reception is planned for Jason at the Anderson's home and I'm invited. May I go?"

Her parents hated to appear as snobs, so they started giving excuses for why it wouldn't be a good idea. "You've already promised to go to the Pennington's for supper, haven't you?" Momma asked.

"I'm sure they'll understand."

"That's an unfamiliar part of town," Papa said.

"I'll make sure she gets home safe and sound," Jacob assured them.

"Well, I don't know." Her father had worry lines on his forehead. "Have you spoken to Lucien?"

"Not yet." Her hands tried to curl into fists of frustration, but she forced them to remain loose.

"Why would she talk to Lucien?" Edward's mother asked. "How

about if she takes Edward? Would that make you feel better?"

"Yes, that's the ticket," Edward's father said. "Take Edward. He can be a chaperone."

Her mother sagged in defeat. "I suppose."

"Thank you, Momma, Papa." Julia and Jacob left to find Edward before her parents could change their minds.

"They didn't like it."

"No, but I'm going. Remind me to give Aunt Rose a big hug later."

Edward stood in a group of people that included Lucien so she would have to send a messenger. She scanned the people around them and saw Margaret coming toward her.

"Hello, you two. Isn't the concert wonderful? Your brother is playing beautifully, Jacob."

"Yes, he's doing well. He'll be featured in a solo part after the intermission."

"I'll look forward to it." Margaret looked around. "How did you manage to lose Lucien?"

"Papa and Lucien said I could sit with Jacob's family. I imagine Lucien expects me to talk to him before the second half, but I would rather avoid that. We could use your help. Papa said I could go to Jacob's for a reception for Jason if I take Edward. He's over there. Do you think you could ask him to come here?"

Margaret laughed. "I can't believe they thought taking Edward was a good idea."

"Aunt Rose suggested it. How could they refuse?"

"Sometimes I wonder about your good luck."

Margaret left on her mission and soon came back with Edward, who quickly agreed to go with them. "Wait for me at your seats. I'll find you afterward."

When the concert ended, Jacob told his parents he'd be bringing Julia and another guest with him. Raised eyebrows were their only response.

It didn't take Edward long to find them. "We need to go as soon as possible. I gave our regrets to Ben, and I'm sure he'll pass the news on to Lucien." He hurried them toward the door. "Lucien isn't in a good mood. We don't want to run into him."

It didn't take long for Jacob to locate the carriage he'd hired for the evening and they left for his house.

Julia's head drooped. "I've probably ruined the truce I had with Lucien."

Jacob looked at her, confused. "Do you want me to take you back?"

26

Jacob didn't want to take Julia back to the concert hall, but felt he should at least offer. At the suggestion, Julia's head snapped up. "No!"

"All right, I won't." He held his hands up in surrender.

She stared at him, wide eyed, chuckled, then laughed until she fell back against the seat.

Jacob didn't know what was funny, but he couldn't help laughing with her. She leaned back with one arm across her stomach and dabbed at her eyes with a handkerchief. He wanted to scoop her up in a hug.

He glanced at Edward, who had joined in, then turned back to Julia.

She straightened in the seat and made an effort to get herself under control. Finally, she said, "I wish you could have seen the look on your face when I said no." She giggled, and hiccupped. "I'm sorry. I didn't mean to scare you. I want to tell Jason what a good job he did. To use one of Momma's words, the concert was marvelous."

"He did well, didn't he?" Jacob didn't try to hide the pride he felt for his brother.

"You may not be seeing as much of him at the store," Edward said.

"We haven't seen a lot of him anyway. If he's not practicing with the orchestra, he's practicing at home."

When they came to a stop at Jacob's house, Julia asked, "Did your parents mind you bringing me?"

"You'll surprise them again." Julia being willing to come to his home would help his parents see her differently. "You're changing some of their notions tonight. We're proving the upper and middle class can mix."

She turned to Edward. "You're okay with this, aren't you?"

"Yes, the kind of person you are is more important than how much money you have." He grinned. "And anyway, have you ever known me to turn down a party?"

Jacob introduced Julia and Edward to his aunt and uncle and the friends who were there to congratulate Jason. Everyone was polite, but she felt most comfortable with Jason and Joel. The brothers didn't seem to have the same class prejudices as the older people. Eventually Jacob's father made his way to their corner of the room and sat to visit with them.

"Mr. Harrington," Jacob's father said, "what do you do to keep yourself busy?"

"I'm finishing my last year at Harvard, so mainly my classes and studies occupy me right now."

"And what will you do after school, work with your father?"

"I have the opportunity to go to Europe and travel for a year or so. I'll get involved with the business when I get home."

"My son is talking about traveling west, to Iowa." He gestured toward Jacob with his glass of punch. "Has he told you?"

"Yes, and I wish him luck." Edward smiled at Jacob, then turned back to Jacob's father. "It's a different kind of adventure, but an adventure just the same."

"Different indeed. His adventure will include a lot of hard work." He looked pointedly at Julia. "What about you Miss Phillips, what does your future hold?"

His focused attention caused her mouth to go dry. She took a sip of punch before answering. "That's a good question. Since women aren't as free to decide their future as men, for right now, I can't give you a definite answer."

Jacob's mother joined their group. Edward quickly stood so she could have his seat. "I would imagine you hope for marriage and a family."

Julia smiled at her. "Yes, I'd like that. Did you hope to have your family on a farm, Mrs. Anderson?"

"I was raised on a farm. It's the life I knew. But I have to tell you, I like city life much better."

"We had a good childhood, Mother," Jacob said, from his chair on the other side of Julia. "You must not have been too unhappy."

"Oh no, I wasn't unhappy. When we moved here I realized the difference. It's not something I would choose to go back to."

"If you're trying to scare Miss Phillips and Mr. Harrington away from the idea of farming, let me add my penny's worth." Joel focused on Julia. "Farming is something you do only if you truly love the land, or love the person who loves the land. If you do it for any other reason, you'll be miserable."

Julia relaxed her stiff posture as he talked. She smiled and he gave her a quick wink. It looked as if they had one more person on their side.

❦

On the way home Jacob said, "I hope you don't think my parents were too hard on you. They seem to feel the need to impress you with how hard we had to work on the farm."

"I'm impressed," Edward said glibly. "It won't be on my list of things to do."

"I hate to think my father may have implied you don't work hard, Edward. I'm sure your family does, or you wouldn't be where you are."

"It's a different kind of work." He gave a dismissive wave of his hand. "Don't worry, I wasn't offended."

"Good. Uh, do you mind if I take you home first?"

"I'm afraid I wouldn't be doing a good job as chaperone if I said yes. You know your parents will ask, Julia."

"You're right. They will." She sighed.

"Well, I'm glad you came. Julia wouldn't have been able to otherwise."

When the carriage stopped at Julia's house, she gave Edward a hug. "Thank you for coming."

Jacob helped her out of the carriage and walked her to the door. "It meant a lot to me that you were willing to come tonight. I know my parents don't make it easy."

She gazed into his eyes. "I like to be with you."

He smiled and took her hands in his for a moment. "I'll see you after church tomorrow and at your sister's." After she went inside the house he went back to the carriage.

As they started, Edward said, "If you'd like to have a fairly private conversation with Julia, I have a suggestion."

"I'm listening."

"Have you noticed the gazebo at the pond in the Public Garden?"

"I've seen it."

"It can be a good place to find a few moments alone."

Jacob grinned. "Are you speaking from personal experience?"

"Nothing serious." Edward chuckled. "I never wanted to give a girl the wrong idea. The last thing I want is some papa herding me toward the altar."

"I used to feel the same way."

"You've had another year or two to think about it. I'll consider marriage when I get to be your age."

"Ha. The ripe old age of twenty-four?"

Edward glanced at him out of the corner of his eye. "I guess it depends. The right woman has a way of making a man change his mind."

"That's true." Jacob sighed. "I wish she didn't come with so many obstacles.

Tuesday, Jacob met Julia at the corner of Katherine's street and they strolled, arm in arm, from there. Even though puddles dotted the street, the beautiful spring day provided mild breezes and warm sun on their shoulders. Even the horses clip clopping along and the birds singing in a near-by park seemed to appreciate it. Along the way, he asked, "How did it go with Lucien? He looked pretty upset Sunday."

"We took a ride that afternoon and had a chat. He couldn't decide who he was more angry with, you for asking me, or Edward for being willing to go, which allowed me to go." She chuckled. "It seems you two are a bad influence."

Jacob rolled his eyes. "Everything's the same between you?"

"Yes, although he did remind me that once our engagement is public, he doesn't want me to spend time with you and Edward. The party is two weeks from Saturday."

He sighed. "I know. I wish there had been some way to change his mind. At least he doesn't expect you to announce it one week and get married the next. You'll still have some time."

"That's true, but it will be harder for us to see each other without it getting back to him. And in the middle of June, our families go to our summer homes. We won't be back until mid-September."

A knot formed, making his chest ache. "We don't have much time left to see each other. May I write to you?"

"I'll get you the address."

"Will Edward go with you, or wait in the city until it's time for him to leave?"

"He'll come, then we'll all come back to the city for a sendoff. The families will stay a few days, then go back to the country."

If Julia planned to go with Edward, she certainly didn't act like it. They'd have all that time together, though. Maybe she hoped he'd take her west? He wanted that to be true more than anything. But the way things stood financially, it would be another year or two before he'd have enough money. And even if he wanted to settle down in the city, which she seemed to prefer, he wasn't in a position to do that, either. If he had nothing to offer, she'd only have one option.

"Jacob, we're here." Julia pulled him to a stop. "Are you all right?"

He blinked and focused on her. "I'm fine. Let's go see your sister."

Katherine waited for them on a gold velvet settee in the drawing room. She smiled when they came in.

Julia led him forward for introductions.

"I'm glad to finally meet you. Please have a seat." Katherine indicated a matching settee across from her. "I've heard about you for some time now, and told Julia to bring you over so I can see what all the fuss is about."

"Thank you for inviting me, Mrs. Harrison. I hope it won't cause you any trouble."

"If you're referring to Margaret's husband, don't give it another thought," she said, with a wave of her hand. "His family is especially pompous. Alexander is much more open-minded. And please, Mr. Anderson, call me Katherine."

Her genuine spirit warmed him. He smiled. "Thank you. I will if you'll call me Jacob."

Katherine turned to Julia in delight. "You're right, he does have adorable dimples."

Jacob chuckled when Julia blushed.

"Well, I guess the secret's out," Julia said. "How are you feeling, Katherine? You look stronger today." A maid brought the tea tray and Julia got up to pour.

"Some days are better than others, and this is a good one. But I don't want to talk about me. I want to find out about Jacob. Tell me," Katherine said to him, "what is there about farming you like better than our fair city of Boston?"

He took a deep breath and let it out slowly. Here was his chance to explain it in a way he hoped Julia would understand. "To be honest, I feel closed in here. I like open land around me, where I can plant a field and watch a crop grow. I enjoy sitting under a shade tree next to the house listening to the birds sing. There are a lot of reasons, but mainly I want to own a place, and know my hard work is providing for my family."

"It sounds as if there's no question in your mind what you want to do." Katherine took a sip of tea. "Talking about shade trees and bird song makes me long for our summer home. I know Julia feels the same."

"As a child, Momma let me help the gardeners." Julia smiled at the memory. "They would leave a space for me to plant when we came. I loved seeing the seeds turn into flowers. It must be remarkably satisfying to see a whole field growing."

"It is, but of course a lot can happen between planting and harvest. A farmer doesn't feel truly satisfied until the crops are gathered in. I can't help thinking he's a little more thankful for the food on his table, than those who buy it at the market."

Katherine gave him a gentle smile. "You can certainly appreciate the work that goes into it, but God provides the rain and sunshine to make it grow, just as he provides city people the income to buy it."

"I never thought about it like that. Please forgive my arrogance." He wouldn't make that mistake again.

Katherine took another sip of tea, then asked, "What do you believe about God?"

"Well..." He glanced at Julia and she gave him a sympathetic smile. She'd warned him Katherine would talk about God.

He looked back at Katherine who waited patiently for an answer. "I believe God watches over us. He created the world, so he has some interest in it. When we were children, mother taught us to pray and give an offering when we went to church. I like to sing the hymns."

Jacob gave Julia a helpless look, but Katherine surprised them with an apparent change of subject. "So, you'd like to go to Iowa. When would you do that?"

"It depends on how long it takes to save the money I'll need. Right now, it doesn't look like any time soon." He snuck a quick look at Julia, but if she was disappointed, she didn't let it show.

Katherine set her teacup aside. "May I tell you what I believe about God?"

"Of course." This kind woman could tell him anything she wanted.

"I believe He takes more than a passing interest in us. He provides for our needs and gives us protection. If you go to Him in prayer, and tell him the desire of your heart, He'll hear you."

That sounded too good to be true. "Are you saying all I have to do is pray, and I'll get the money I need?"

She chuckled. "No. I'm saying, if you're willing to put your life in God's hands, and trust him to provide what's best for you, I think you'll be surprised at what he brings about, whether it be money for Iowa or an opportunity here in Boston."

"I'll think about it," he said, and shrugged. "I guess I don't have anything to lose."

With a slight shake of her head, she said, "You have much more to lose if you don't. But we can talk about that another time. I'd like to hear about your family. Julia says you have two brothers, and you're all different."

"That's true." He relaxed and smiled. "It's hard to believe we all had the same upbringing."

Jacob went on to tell Katherine about his family and farm in New York, and the things he enjoyed about Boston.

Julia had listened to the exchange between Jacob and Katherine with great interest. Could she turn control of her life over to God? It didn't make practical sense, but when had she been practical? She would definitely think more about it. In the meantime, she enjoyed watching Jacob talk. His eyes sparkled and he smiled often, giving her a glimpse of those adorable dimples.

Before they left, Alexander surprised them by coming home to meet Jacob. They took an instant liking to each other and Alexander made an appointment with Jacob for lunch the next day.

As they got ready to leave, Katherine said, "I'll be praying for you Jacob. I'm sure God has a plan for you."

"I'll let you know as soon as he lets me know."

27

Alexander asked Jacob where he lived and offered his carriage for their ride home. On the way, Jacob said, "Your sister and brother-in-law are wonderful."

Julia's eyes shone. "Yes, they are. I love Katherine dearly and care for Alexander like a brother."

"I like Margaret, too." Jacob smiled and took Julia's hand in his. "That leaves one more to meet."

"I think we should stop while we're ahead." Julia wrinkled her nose. "Of the four of us, Priscilla is most like Momma."

Jacob reveled in this opportunity to be alone with Julia. He would have been happy doing nothing more than gazing into her eyes and holding her hand all the way to her house, but he had to ask, "How do you feel about Katherine's thoughts on praying?"

"I've seen a change in her life," Julia admitted. "My sister has always been a sweet person, but tended to be a worrier. Now she says no matter what happens, God will take care of her."

Jacob mulled it over for a while. "Maybe I should pray about money for a farm."

A line appeared between Julia's brows. "Remember, Katherine said to pray about your heart's desire, not money. I suppose you

228

could tell God you want a farm and let him work it out. In the meantime, I'll pray for nice weather on Thursday. I don't want to miss seeing you again because of the rain."

He grinned. "I guess praying for weather is all right. Farmers do that all the time. Let's meet at the Public Garden."

"Okay, I'll wait for you at the fountain by the main entrance."

The carriage came to a stop in front of Julia's house and Jacob helped her out, keeping her hand in his. "Thank you."

Julia gave him a puzzled look. "For what?"

"For sharing your sisters with me. For sharing your time," he added with a smile.

Her warm smile lit up her eyes. "The time shared has been a pleasure."

Jacob let go of her hand with reluctance and watched her go into the house. On the way home he decided he would try praying. His heart had two desires and he planned to pray about both. First, he wanted Julia to be his wife. And second, he wanted a farm to raise their family on.

Julia started up the stairs as her mother came in. "Did I see you talking to Jacob?"

"Yes, we had a wonderful visit with Katherine. She likes Jacob and so does Alexander."

As they made their way upstairs to change for dinner, Momma asked, "Why was Alexander home?"

"He came home to meet Jacob, and invited him to lunch tomorrow."

"That sounds like him. There are few people he doesn't get along with."

Momma stopped in the hall outside her bedroom door and

turned to her. "You know, Jacob seems like an intelligent young man. Maybe Alexander could find a position for him. Didn't you say he doesn't enjoy working in the store?"

A sigh slipped out. "He wants a farm, Momma. He doesn't like living in the city."

Momma waved away Julia's statement. "It's just different. I imagine he'll get used to it. I think I'll talk to Alexander about it next time I see him."

Julia watched her go into her room, then turned and went into hers. She wished Momma could see the Andersons as more than a project.

She sat in her rocking chair thinking about her situation, as she waited for Millie to come help her get changed. Each of her sisters had gotten a nice sum of money when they married. If they would approve of Jacob, the money could help toward a farm. But it would never happen. If she married him, they'd be on their own. She needed to do some serious thinking, *and*, she decided, some even more serious praying.

When Jacob arrived home from the store on Wednesday, his father called him into the living room. "Have a seat, son. I want to talk to you." Jacob sat in an armchair close to his father, with no idea what might be on his mind. "I want to let you know I've sold the farm to our tenant, Homer Swift. I didn't think your Uncle Jared should have to oversee things there if you weren't going back. I understand your desire to start with a place of your own." His father leaned back in his chair with a chuckle. "I'll admit old Henry makes Iowa sound mighty tempting."

Surprise washed over him. "I knew Mother liked it here, but I wasn't sure about you."

"I believe this has been an excellent move. I have no regrets about coming here or selling the farm. My only regret is none of you boys wanted it. The land has been in our family for generations."

"Uncle Jared doesn't want it?" Jacob swallowed hard and fought the guilt threatening to make him blurt out he'd made a mistake. Everything would be so much easier if he went back to New York.

"He feels he has enough to do. His son will take over his farm and the girls are already settled. Swift sent his agreement to the price return post."

Jacob slumped forward. He'd considered going back if there were no other way to help Julia before October. Now it wasn't an option.

"I'd like for you to go to New York as my agent and handle the sale. You can stay with Uncle Jared, and he'll give you any help or advice you need. If you're going to buy a place, it'll be good experience to have been on this side of the sale first."

"When do I need to go?"

"Within the next day or two, and you should plan on staying for three weeks to a month. I've had a lawyer look over the deed and draw up a contract for the sale, but I imagine Swift will want someone there to look it over before he signs." His father held out a packet of papers.

"Also, I want you to negotiate the sale of the equipment. That's not included in the contract, so you'll want to get a fair price for everything. Since you don't want the farm, I feel the least I can do to help you get your start is let you have the proceeds from the equipment."

Jacob straightened. "Thank you. That will help. But why do you think I'll have to be there so long?"

"You know Swift. His name doesn't describe him." His father shook his head. "I've never seen anyone move so slowly and still get things accomplished. He's also thorough, so he'll have a lot of questions."

Jacob shifted in his chair. "Maybe it won't take as long as you think."

"I'm sure Miss Phillips will get along without you for a while. She's not going anywhere."

"Actually, she is. She and her mother are going to their country home in mid-June and won't be back until September." Panic clawed at his chest. How could he lose so much time with Julia?

"Maybe it's just as well." Mr. Anderson rested his elbows on the arms of his chair and steepled his fingers. "Some time apart may help to get her out of your system. You know you're only fooling yourself if you think her father will approve of her marrying you. I wouldn't be surprised if he has some rich young man lined up right now."

Jacob clenched his fists in his lap. "She's not interested in some rich young man."

"It doesn't matter what she's interested in. She'll do what her father tells her. I don't know what woman wouldn't want to marry money anyway. It only makes sense."

"She said money isn't important to her."

"Time will tell." His father gave him a knowing look. "When will you be going?"

"I'll leave Friday," he said with a sigh. "Julia and I plan to see each other Thursday. I want to tell her I'll be leaving."

"Friday morning will be fine." His father stood, came around the desk and clapped a hand on Jacob's shoulder. "I'm sure this will all turn out for the best."

When Julia arrived at the theater with James and Sophia, she saw Jacob pacing back and forth. As soon as they made eye contact, he gave her a heart-melting smile and headed their way.

As Jacob reached her, Lucien came up on her other side, and took her arm. "Hello Jacob. Julia, we should find a seat. There will be quite a crowd tonight."

Julia pushed down her annoyance. "Edward and Aaron came early to get seats for everyone. Let's look for them."

The five of them hadn't gone far down the aisle when Aaron greeted them. "We have a row toward the front. Edward and Lily are waiting for us." Aaron offered Sophia his arm and she took it with a smile.

A frown crossed Lucien's face. Julia felt a little guilty about Sophia giving Aaron the wrong idea, but Aaron had a lot of admirers. He wouldn't lack for female attention.

When they found their row, James immediately went to Lily, and Edward stood to greet them. "Hello, everyone. I think we have plenty of seats."

Aaron and Sophia went in the row and sat next to James and Lily. Lucien stood back to allow Julia to go in next, but she said, "Why don't you go ahead. That way I can talk to both you and Jacob." He hesitated for a moment, then went in and sat beside Sophia.

Once they were all settled, Edward said, "Oh, Lucien, I almost forgot to tell you, Harry Jones said he wants to talk to you before the program starts."

Lucien frowned. "He wants to talk to me now?"

"That's what he said. It sounded as if it might be important." Edward pointed to the far side of the theater. "He's sitting over there."

"All right, but I can't imagine what couldn't have waited until tomorrow." Lucien excused himself and made his way through the stream of people coming down the aisle to find seats.

As soon as he left, Edward got up and took Lucien's place.

Julia was speechless. Edward didn't usually make up stories to get his way, but this looked pretty suspicious.

Everyone in the row stared at him, so finally he said, "Okay, so it wasn't important, but I did see Mr. Jones, and he said he wouldn't mind talking to Lucien."

Sophia frowned at him, but Julia couldn't hold back a giggle.

"Hey," Edward said, draping his arm casually across the back of Julia's seat, "I only have until August, and I didn't want to argue with him."

Julia shook her head. "You won't be able to get away with that after the party. Once the announcement is made and everyone knows...."

"Don't worry about it," he said, waving off her concern. "Once we get to the country, Lucien won't be around to complain."

Julia laughed again, and turned to Jacob. "You're awfully quiet. Is everything all right?"

"Have you been praying about the weather?"

"Yes. Have you been praying about a farm?"

"I did last night. Pray for no rain again tonight. I need to talk to you, but not here." Jacob gave her an anxious look. "Do you think there's any way we could have some time alone?"

Butterflies fluttered in Julia's stomach. She didn't know whether to be excited or worried, and no way would she find out tonight. There were too many people around to hold a private conversation. She and Jacob were talking far too loudly to be considered polite, just to hear each other above the crowd.

"I'll see if James can come with us. He can keep Sophia company while we talk. Do you still want to meet at the same place?"

"Yes."

When Lucien returned, he looked at Edward and sat next to Jacob with a sigh. "Have you seen a stereopticon presentation?"

"Yes, I saw a "magic lantern" show before I left New York. Very entertaining."

"It brings another dimension to the talk."

"I agree," Julia said. "I'm especially interested to see how they present Egypt." Edward leaned around her and asked Lucien, "Did you find Mr. Jones?"

Lucien glowered at him. "Less than three weeks."

A shiver ran up Julia's spine. The look on Lucien's face when he sat back made her wonder if she should be concerned for Edward.

28

When the lights in the theater dimmed for the program, Julia tucked her hand through the crook of Jacob's arm. He covered her hand with his. If the program were about earth worms and went on for hours, she'd be content. But of course, it felt more like five minutes and the small physical contact of hand on hand came to an end. The lights came up and everyone stood to leave.

Julia turned to Jacob. "We're going to my house for supper tonight. Will you come?"

He gave her a half smile. "I appreciate you and your friends being willing to include me, but I don't think your parents would like it."

"I think you worry too much, but I don't want you to feel uncomfortable."

The group made their way to the doors, where Jacob said good-bye. "Remember, no rain."

She smiled and nodded.

"What's that supposed to mean?" Lucien asked.

"Jacob and I are tired of the rain, so we're praying it will stop."

Lucien's eyes widened, then he frowned. "That's ridiculous. Praying won't change the weather."

"It hasn't changed your mind, either," Julia mumbled.

"What's that?"

"How about taking me home?"

Lucien's eyebrows shot up, then he glanced around as if she might be talking to someone else. "Are you sure you didn't mean to ask Edward?"

She laughed. "I hardly think I would confuse the two of you. Let's go."

Later that evening, Julia managed to get James alone in the hall outside the drawing room. "I need to ask a favor. Will you go to the Public Garden with Sophia and me tomorrow? Jacob wants to talk to me privately and if you're there Sophia won't be left alone."

James took a minute to think about it, then sighed. "I'll do it, but I'm not sure it's a good idea. You know your parents won't approve of you meeting Jacob alone."

Julia put her hand on his arm. "Thank you, James. I appreciate you wanting to look out for me, but try not to worry."

◦◦◦◦◦◦◦

Julia had a hard time paying attention to her supper guests. They were all talking about the stereopticon show they'd seen that evening, but all she could think of was what Jacob wanted to tell her. Judging by his troubled expression, she doubted it would be good news. Or, maybe she'd misjudged his mood. She would simply have to wait until tomorrow to find out.

Later, when her friends said their good-byes, James stepped close. "I'll see you tomorrow."

Lucien lingered in the drawing room until everyone left, so Julia walked him to the front door. "The contractor said they hope to have the foundation in by the first of the week. We'll go by and look as soon as it's done."

"Fine. Good night, Lucien." She took a step toward the stairs, but he reached out and caught her hand, pulling her to him. When she looked up at him in surprise he bent down and kissed her lightly on the lips.

"Good night."

He turned and left, leaving Julia to stare at the closed vestibule doors. That was definitely in violation of their "friends only" agreement. She'd have to watch for it in the future.

Turning, she started again toward the stairs.

"Julia, wait a minute."

She whirled around and almost cried out when Edward stepped out of Papa's study.

"It's just me," he said, coming quickly toward her.

Julia put her hand over her racing heart. "Why were you lurking in the study?"

"I want to know what's going on. You were obviously distracted tonight, and for some reason James knows why and I don't." Edward sounded miffed. "And I wasn't lurking. I was waiting for Lucien to leave." He grinned. "He finally got around to kissing you, didn't he?"

"Don't remind me." Julia wiped her mouth with the back of her hand. "He needs to save his kisses for Sophia."

"What's wrong?"

Julia pulled Edward into the study and spoke quietly. "Jacob wants to talk to me alone tomorrow. He looked troubled about something, and I have no idea what it is."

"What is James doing about it?"

"He'll keep Sophia company while I talk to Jacob. We couldn't leave her wandering around the park by herself."

"Of course, that's a good idea. Don't worry about tomorrow, though. The last time you did, it turned out to be a misunderstanding."

"I know, but I'll feel better after I talk to him."

"Promise you'll send a message to the school if you want to talk tomorrow night." Edward tilted her chin up so he could make eye contact. "Okay?"

"Okay." She gave him a hug.

"Julia, are you still down there?" Momma called, causing her and Edward both to jump.

"I'm in Papa's study. I'll be up in a moment."

"All right, Dear."

Edward whispered, "I'll see you tomorrow or Friday at Grandmother's."

"Thank you." She watched him slip out the door, and went upstairs.

Jacob knew without a doubt the morning had been the longest in his life. The familiar jittery tingly feeling he got when he saw Julia washed over him, which didn't help his nerves. She, James, and Sophia joined him by the fountain. From there the four of them headed into the park toward the pond.

Jacob gave her hand a quick squeeze. "I'm glad God answered your prayer for sunshine. I'll know who to ask to pray when my fields need sun instead of rain."

"Are you responsible for this nice day?" James asked. "Be sure to ask for another one for Saturday, Julia, so we can all go on a picnic."

"That sounds fun. Do you like picnics, Jacob?" Julia's eyes sparkled.

"Yes, as long as I'm not responsible for the food. I'm afraid I'm not a good cook."

"Don't worry about that," Sophia said. "The ladies bring the food, and there's always plenty."

When they arrived at the arbor leading to the gazebo on the pond,

Jacob stopped. "Do you mind if Julia and I go on alone?"

James glanced at Julia. "That's why I'm here. We'll meander over this way."

Jacob and Julia strolled through the leafy arbor and into the gazebo. He stepped over to the railing and gripped it with both hands. How would Julia react to his news? The question had kept him awake last night and dogged him all morning.

"Jacob, come sit with me."

He turned and joined her on a bench. Jacob took a deep breath and prepared to give Julia his news, but before he could start, she spoke. "I forgot to ask how lunch went with Alexander."

Releasing the breath, he said, "It went well. He seemed genuinely interested in getting to know me. He'd be a good friend."

"Momma would like for him to be an employer."

"What do you mean?"

Julia bit her bottom lip. "It looks as if she's made you her next project.

She thinks it would be perfect if Alexander gave you a job. I'm afraid she's of the opinion that staying in the city to work is a better idea than farming."

Jacob thought about it. He didn't like to imagine the next month without her, let alone a lifetime. Maybe he should consider the offer if Alexander made one. "If I did work for Alexander, would it change my status in your parents' eyes?"

"I'm afraid it wouldn't." Julia covered his hand with hers. "Anyway, you shouldn't give up your dream."

Jacob looked out at the puffs of clouds reflected in the water. A pair of swans glided by, causing small ripples in their wake. If only he felt as calm as his surroundings. He took both of Julia's hands in his, and when he met her eyes, she gazed back at him, a small line between her brows.

"Tell me what's wrong."

He took another fortifying breath and blurted it out. "Father sold our farm. He wants me to go to New York to handle the sale and everything involved. I leave tomorrow morning and may not be back until June. I'm afraid I'll have to miss the picnic and everything else for the next month." He squeezed her hands a little tighter. "But I'll miss you more than anything.

"When you told me about Lucien, I wanted to rescue you. My parents told me I shouldn't keep seeing you because nothing could ever come of it. But I haven't wanted to stop. Being with you makes me happy, and I've continued to pretend there might be some way I could help you.

"Now I have to face reality. Father plans to give me some of the money from the sale, but it still won't be enough to go west." He released her hands in frustration and went to stand by the rail again. "I want more than anything to be your knight in shining armor, but I can't. I don't even have the right to be."

Julia came and stood behind him. "Jacob, you must realize by now that your social class means nothing to me. You have every right to be my knight."

He turned and pulled her into his arms, holding her tight for a few moments, then released her. "Unfortunately, I'm a knight with no horse."

"Keep praying, Jacob. Katherine believes God will show you what to do and so do I. When you come back, you can tell me if he gave you your heart's desire."

Wonder filled him and he gave her a slow smile. "You're giving me permission to hope for another month?"

She returned his smile. "Yes. I'm giving myself permission, too." She took his hand. "Come back and sit down. Tell me everything you'll be doing while you're gone."

Julia listened to Jacob, wondering how she could feel so happy and sad at the same time. He'd as much as said he wanted to take her away with him, but there wasn't enough money to do it. A month might be enough time for God to work things out, whatever it would be. What a relief to leave it in God's hands.

After a while, Jacob said, "We better find James and Sophia. James probably wants to get back to work this afternoon."

"You're right." She kissed him on the cheek. "I'll miss you."

Jacob lifted her hands and kissed the back of each one while gazing into her eyes. "I'll think of you every day."

When Julia got home, she debated whether to ask Edward to come over. He'd be comforting and encouraging, but it could wait until tomorrow. She refused to be upset about Jacob leaving despite the tears stinging her eyes. He would come back and maybe he would have good news.

As soon as Edward and Lily saw Julia at Grandmother's Friday evening, they cornered her in the drawing room. Lily spoke first. "Edward told me Jacob had news for you. Was it good or bad?"

"He left for New York this morning. His father sold their farm and wants Jacob to handle everything."

Lily gripped her hand. "Is this good news or bad? He's coming back, isn't he?"

"Yes, he should be back by no later than the middle of June." She tried to keep her tone light to sound positive, but she already missed him. The month ahead would be the longest of her life.

"That wasn't all though, was it?" Edward asked.

In spite of her good intentions, a sigh slipped out. "He's discouraged. Even though he'll receive some money from the sale it won't be enough to go west. When he does go, he wants to take me with him." She straightened her shoulders and looked from Edward to Lily with a smile. "You never know, though. Something could happen. Katherine talked to Jacob and me about praying for God's will in our lives, so that's what we're doing. She's praying, too."

Edward and Lily's eyes met, then returned to her. Edward asked, "Are you serious?"

"Yes. Katherine is very convincing. You should talk to her about it some time."

"Maybe I will, but for right now, it sounds like I get to have you to myself again." He wiggled his eyebrows at her.

Julia laughed. "Don't forget about Lucien. I'm sorry to say he's not going anywhere."

"Don't worry about him. He's only a temporary fixture." Edward winked. "We'll just continue to go around him."

Monday morning, Lucien folded his newspaper and laid it on the table by his plate. A quick look at his watch showed he had time to relax with another cup of coffee in his formal dining room before heading to the bank. He smiled as he refilled his cup from the silver pot left for him on the table.

The news Julia shared with him when he asked about Jacob after church yesterday couldn't have been better. He'd been wracking his brain to think of a way to get him out of the picture and Jacob's father did it for him. By the time Jacob came back from New York, Julia would be out of the city. Hopefully, by the time she came back she'd be over her idea of friendship with him.

Edward, on the other hand, was a different problem. He frowned and drummed his fingers on the table. Edward had until the engagement dinner to start acting like a gentleman, but since that didn't seem likely, Lucien had a plan to make Julia push Edward away on her own.

29

Jacob looped his horse's reins around the porch rail and waited for Homer Swift to return from putting his horse in the barn. He studied his former family home. Even though ready to move on, a touch of melancholy settled in at the idea of leaving this place in the past.

These last two weeks had moved at a snail's pace. Homer was every bit as slow as his father had said. Jacob had given him the deed and contract the day he arrived. Homer took three days to read the documents before taking them to a lawyer for his opinion. A few days later, he went into town to hear what the lawyer had to say.

This was a big step, Jacob understood that, but he'd never met anyone as careful about making a decision as this man. Finally, after several more days of waiting, they'd both gone into town this morning and Homer signed the contract.

Jacob stuffed his hands in the front pockets of his blue denim trousers and sauntered over to the shade of a maple tree. He'd tried to convince Homer it would be a good idea to look at and decide on which pieces of farm equipment he wanted to buy while he went over the sales contract, thereby speeding up the process. He should have saved his breath. The fact that Homer had gotten around to having a family surprised him, but the man had a wife and four children.

Homer plodded back from the barn and came to a stop beside Jacob. "Why don't we talk about the wagons and tools on Monday? I probably ought to get a little work done this afternoon."

Jacob breathed an inward sigh of frustration. "I'll be here Monday morning."

When he got back to his uncle's farmhouse, he took care of his horse then dropped in a chair on the porch and propped his feet on the railing.

Aunt Ruth came out of the house and handed him a cookie. "You get anything done this morning?"

"He finally signed the contract." Jacob patted his shirt pocket to reassure himself he actually had it. "He doesn't want to talk about anything else until Monday."

"Your Uncle Jared gets frustrated with him, too. He gets things done around there though. The place has been kept up."

"It looks like he knows what he's doing, all right. It just takes him so long to make a decision." Jacob took off his hat and raked his fingers through his hair.

Aunt Ruth chuckled as she sat in a rocking chair next to Jacob. "You haven't said anything, but I get the feeling you're in a hurry to get back to Boston. Have you met someone special?"

He hadn't talked about Julia because from this distance she seemed like even more of an impossible dream. He didn't want to hear another person tell him he should forget her. But he'd been praying every night.

"Yes, I have," he finally answered. "Her name is Julia, and she's beautiful and intelligent and fun. I enjoy visiting with you and the family, but I'm afraid I would rather be with her. I had no idea I could miss someone so much."

"She sounds wonderful. Is she willing to go to Iowa?"

Jacob brought his feet to the porch floor and leaned his elbows on his knees. "I believe she would, but it will be a while yet before I'll have the money to go. Unfortunately, her father is pressuring her to marry before the end of the year."

His aunt frowned. "Your father is giving you money from the sale, isn't he?"

"Yes, but I don't think it'll be enough, not for two of us. I want to make sure I can take care of Julia if she goes with me."

"What about your mare? Jimmy would buy her."

"My cousin always has had his eye on her." He chuckled. "As a matter of fact, he already asked me. I'll sell her, and that'll help, but not enough."

"Have you been praying about this?"

Jacob sat up and looked at his aunt, surprised. "Do you believe I should?"

"God wants his children to be happy, and it sounds like Julia would make you happy."

"Two weeks ago, her sister recommended we pray. I do every day. But I don't know how much time God needs."

She reached over and laid her hand on his arm. "He does everything in his own time. If you and Julia are meant to be together, he'll work it out."

"Thank you, Aunt Ruth, I needed to hear that. Would you mind mentioning it when you talk to him? And maybe you could ask him to hurry Homer up a little."

"I'll be happy to include you in my prayers. Now, how about going with Jimmy and the other young people on a picnic today. It seems you've done nothing but work since you got here."

He relaxed and smiled. "Maybe I will. It'd be nice to see everyone again."

⚬⚬⚬

Julia looked at her friend from all angles and smiled. "The hat looks perfect on you, Sophia. You should get it."

"I believe I will." Sophia handed the hat to the clerk. "Will you have this delivered to my address please?"

"Certainly, Miss Howell."

Before they could turn to leave, the bell on the door rang and Julia heard Clara Pennington. "Look, Momma, there's Julia. She'll solve the mystery for us."

Julia groaned inwardly, but put on a smile and turned to face the Penningtons. "Hello, Mrs. Pennington, Clara."

Mrs. Pennington smiled at both Julia and Sophia. "Hello, girls."

"You simply must tell us, Julia," Clara gushed. "The rumors are flying about your dinner party next Saturday. Will there be an announcement?"

Julia manufactured a patient smile. "I'm afraid I'm not at liberty to say." If only she could go out just one day without everyone questioning her.

"She means yes," Clara told her mother. "Now we only have to guess who, as if it's any secret."

Mrs. Pennington put a hand on her daughter's arm. "Now, Clara, Julia didn't say anything to confirm the rumor."

"Well, it's the same thing as a confession. I can't believe I spent all that time making a fool of myself over Edward."

Clara put her hands on her blushing cheeks. "I'm so glad you stopped me, Julia. It looks as if you two are more than friends after all."

Julia tried to keep annoyance out of her tone. "Clara, your momma's right. I'm not confessing to anything." She noticed the other customers, as well as the clerks, doing their best to listen in without appearing to do so. "My parents give a dinner party or a ball every spring. Why should this one be special?"

"I overheard Mr. Jordan telling Papa he was getting worried about losing his bet with Mrs. Jordan. It sounded as though you and Edward are the couple in question this year."

Mrs. Pennington's eyes widened and her face flushed. "Clara, you shouldn't be listening to your papa's conversations."

"I couldn't help it. Mr. Jordan is loud. But he's not the only reason I'm suspicious. Ben seems to have some inside information, and he won't say what." Clara huffed. "He can be infuriating."

Julia could no longer maintain her patient smile. "Well, I'm afraid you'll have to wait until next week to find out."

"Oh pooh, why can't you tell us," Clara pouted. "What difference will one week make?"

"That's a good question. One more week to wait shouldn't make a difference. If you'll excuse us, Sophia and I have more shopping to do." When they got outside, she said, "How about some tea?"

"Would you like to go to your house or mine? Those are the only places we can go without someone asking you about the rumors."

Julia sighed. "I know, but I told Edward we'd meet him. He'll wonder where we are if we don't show up."

"Meeting Edward for tea will only make the rumors worse."

"I know, but he cheers me up." She headed for the tea shop and Sophia fell into step beside her. "These last few weeks of school have kept him so busy, I'm lucky to see him on the weekends. Thursday afternoon is unusual."

The girls sat in a cozy tea shop full of small tables. Before long, Edward joined them "Are you keeping count of how many people have questioned you?" he asked Julia with a grin.

She frowned at him. "No, I'm not. I don't know why they can't mind their own business."

Edward chuckled. "It sounds like we better get a pastry to go with our tea. Someone needs sweetening up."

"We can't go anywhere without someone asking her what to expect next Saturday." Sophia gave her a sympathetic pat on the arm.

The waitress stopped at their table, and Edward ordered cakes and a pot of tea.

When the waitress left, Julia said, "Apparently, Boston's old families have nothing better to do than speculate on who's getting married next."

"If you're cranky, I can just imagine what Lucien must be like."

Julia waved away the idea. "I doubt he's hearing any of it."

"He has to have heard something. My parents have. I spent yesterday evening at home, trying to evade questions I couldn't answer."

Shame burned in her. "I'm sorry." She reached over and put her hand on his. "I'm acting as if I'm the only one involved. You've put yourself in this position for my sake and I'm not being appreciative."

He turned his hand over and held Julia's. "You're just having a bad day. But I'll tell you what you can do to make up for it. Go with me to the picnic Saturday, and bring all my favorite food."

"Will I be allowed to talk about how much I miss Jacob?"

Edward gave an exaggerated sigh. "If you must, but only for the first half hour."

Her face relaxed into a smile. "You're a good friend."

Mrs. Jordan bustled over to their table. "How's my favorite couple today?"

"We're fine, Mrs. Jordan," Edward said. "How are you?"

"I'm doing well, thank you. I'm in a hurry, but I wanted to stop and say I'm looking forward to next Saturday." Mrs. Jordan turned a cheerful smile on Sophia. "Aren't they wonderful together? Well, I must run. I imagine I'll see you at the Franklin's ball. I believe there may be an announcement there, too."

"Well, what do you think, Sophia? Aren't we wonderful?" Edward asked, imitating Mrs. Jordan.

Sophia gave Julia an "I told you so" look and ignored him.

Julia took her hand out of Edward's. "Maybe we should tell her. She seems so happy. It would be nice if she were warned ahead of time."

"As soon as you tell her, you might as well tell everyone else," Sophia said. "She's a good-hearted person, but Momma says she can't keep a secret."

Edward nodded. "I'm afraid Sophia's right. She'll have to be surprised along with everyone else."

"Let's change the subject. Tell me how classes are going this week."

She relaxed as they chatted. As always, Edward made her laugh.

Before they left, Edward reminded her, "Don't forget about Saturday. I'll come by for you at noon."

As the two girls rode home, Julia said, "You should bring some of Lucien's favorite food to the picnic."

"I might do that." As they got out of the carriage, Sophia said, "I'll be over tomorrow to help with your embroidery."

When Julia went into the house, her mother greeted her. "We need to have a talk. We'll go to your room."

What could she have done to upset Momma this time? Before this afternoon, she hadn't seen Edward all week, so it couldn't be about him.

She didn't have long to wonder. As soon as they were in her room and the door closed, Momma said, "Priscilla came by this afternoon to tell me she'd seen you at the tea shop. Really, Julia, why do you continue to encourage Mrs. Jordan, and everyone else for that matter, to believe you and Edward are a couple?"

Julia mentally reviewed the afternoon and couldn't imagine what she'd seen that would send her hurrying over to tattle, unless it was Mrs. Jordan's comments. "Momma, I can't help what Mrs. Jordan thinks. Everyone will know what you and Papa have planned for me when the announcement is made."

"Holding hands and gazing into each other's eyes are reasons why Mrs. Jordan thinks as she does." Her mother crossed her arms. "That simply has to stop."

Julia wanted to throw her hands up in frustration. "If that's what Priscilla saw, she mistook the intention. Too bad my sister didn't come over and talk to us instead of running to you." Julia went to the window then turned to her mother. "Have I told you how much I miss Jacob?"

"Jacob?" Her mother closed her eyes for a second and shook her head. "He's not our concern right now. You'd best let that friendship drop anyway."

"He means a lot to me. I'm not going to forget him just because he's not from one of the old families."

"Well you might as well get used to missing him, because you won't see him this summer. And once you're married, Lucien may not allow it."

"I can't marry Lucien, Momma." Tears blurred her vision, and she worked to swallow the lump forming in her throat.

Momma dropped her arms to her sides and took a step toward her, then stopped. Julia could almost see her mother's conflict. Offer comfort or stick to the plan? The moment of indecision passed and Momma said, "You can dear, and you will."

30

Saturday, Edward came for Julia in his carriage, and they set out for the countryside. "I'm surprised your parents let you go with me. They don't seem to like me much anymore."

Julia chuckled. "They like you. It's because Papa has his heart set on Lucien and he and Momma both know he can't compete with you." She looped her arm through his, took a deep breath and slowly exhaled. "I love spring. The air smells sweet, flowers are everywhere and the trees look alive again." Tilting her face to the sky she closed her eyes. "And the sun feels wonderful on my skin."

Edward smiled, glad he'd remembered to fold down the top. "You can't go ice skating when the sun's warm."

She didn't open her eyes, but her mouth turned up at the corners. "Every season has its highlights. I'm glad it's spring."

He enjoyed seeing her relaxed and happy. Should he ask or not? He debated for a few moments then said, "I almost hate to bring this up, but have you heard from Jacob yet?"

Julia wilted and stared at the road. "Jacob asked if he could write and I gave him my address. I thought I'd hear from him. I've been praying every day like Katherine told us, but I'm afraid my faith isn't very strong." Turning to him, she said, "Not hearing from him makes me wonder if he's still thinking of me. I wonder what he's doing right now?"

Edward gestured to the scenery around them. "On a beautiful day like this, I'd say going on a picnic. Country people do that, don't they?"

She narrowed her eyes and pulled away from him. "What do you mean, 'country people?'"

He couldn't hold back a grin. "I mean people who live in the country, of course. We like to go to the country to get away from the city for a while. People who live in the country are already there."

"Oh, I didn't think about that." She relaxed and watched the scenery. "I imagine people enjoy getting together with their friends, no matter where they live."

He gave her a side glance then focused on the road. "Do you honestly think you'd like living on a farm?" Edward had a hard time picturing it.

After a few moments, she said, "I honestly don't know." She turned to him. "I want to ask you something, Edward, and I want a truthful answer."

"Always."

"If I do become a country person, will you still love me? Will you think less of me?"

What? He pulled the carriage off the side of the road and turned to face her. "I can't believe you asked me that. If I decided to become a sailor and spent all my time on the ocean or at the harbor, would you still love me?"

"Of course."

"Would you worry about me?"

"Yes, I'm sure I would, but I wouldn't try to keep you from your dream."

Edward rested his arm along the back of the seat and looked in her eyes. "I won't try to keep you from your dream either, Julia. If living on a farm makes you happy, I'll probably worry about you, but I'll never stop loving you or think less of you."

Moisture beaded on her lashes. "I'm sorry, I shouldn't have doubted you." She threw her arms around his neck.

He held her as she cried against his shoulder, while he willed the sting of tears away from his own eyes. When she slowed to a stop, he dug out his handkerchief and wiped the tears from her cheeks. "Do you feel better?"

"Yes and no." She sniffled. "I still miss Jacob, but I suppose I needed a good cry."

He put his arm around her shoulders, kissed her on the temple and gave her a hug.

A carriage came to a stop beside them. "Do you need any help?"

"We're fine." Edward turned to see Ben and Samantha looking at them with open curiosity. "Julia had something in her eye. I think we've got it."

"Thank you for stopping to ask," she said, from behind him.

Ben nodded. "No problem. I imagine everyone else is there, so we should get going."

"We'll follow you," Edward said.

They watched Ben's carriage disappear up the road. Julia sighed. "Do you think he'll talk to Lucien?"

"Maybe."

Edward kept an eye on Ben while he, Julia and their friends spread picnic blankets under some shade trees beside a stream. The ladies unpacked the baskets they'd brought and everyone shared. When they'd finished eating, Ben stood and headed his way, which was also Lucien's way since he sat close by. Edward figured Lucien would get an earful.

Instead, Ben squatted beside him. "There's something I'd like to ask you privately. Do you mind if we go to the other side of the stream?"

"No, I don't mind." He stood and followed Ben over a foot bridge.

As soon as they were out of hearing range, Ben said, "You must be aware Julia is betrothed to Lucien."

He almost laughed. Did Ben plan to give him a 'stay away from Julia' talk? "She told me her father agreed to the marriage."

Ben frowned and stepped toward him. "Then what are you doing? I've been debating whether to talk to you for some time now, but that display on the side of the road is what convinced me."

Edward leaned his shoulder against a tree and crossed his arms. "I know you and Lucien are close. Do you think Julia is the best person for him?"

"Frankly, no, but he's made up his mind. You should respect the fact that she's no longer available. And she needs to stop behaving as though she's still unattached."

"I don't want to make you angry, but this isn't your problem."

"Lucien is my friend. I know he'd speak up for me."

Edward straightened but kept his arms crossed. "As Lucien's friend, the best thing you can do is talk him out of this marriage."

"I've tried." He pointed his finger at Edward. "My advice to you, as Julia's friend, is to think about her reputation." He turned and Edward watched as he almost, but not quite, stomped away.

When Julia arrived at the Franklin's ball with her parents, she immediately looked for Edward. Since Lucien took her home from the picnic, she hadn't had a moment alone with him after Ben's little talk, and she wanted to know what he said. Unfortunately, Lucien found her first.

"You look pretty this evening. You must have had time to rest from our excursion this afternoon. I enjoyed it. Did you?"

"Yes." She smiled but continued to scan the arriving guests.

"It was nice of Sophia to include my favorite picnic food. Maybe you could remember that next time."

"She's a thoughtful person. Speaking of Sophia, there she is."

Lucien looked in the direction Julia indicated. She watched him from the corner of her eye and was satisfied with his reaction. How could he not be aware of what Sophia's smile did to him?

"Hello, Lucien, Julia."

"Hello, Sophia. Have you seen Edward?"

"Not yet."

"Oh, you can be sure he'll be here," Lucien said with disgust. "He never misses an opportunity to monopolize your time."

Julia laughed. "I don't know why you mind. I leave you in good company."

Lucien smiled at Sophia. "That's true."

"There's a handsome couple if ever I saw one," Mrs. Jordan said, patting Sophia and Lucien on the arm. "I believe Edward is looking for you Julia. I saw him when I came in. Here he comes now."

When Edward reached them, Mrs. Jordan said, "It's so satisfying to see my couples together. You young people have a nice time. To Edward and Julia, Mrs. Jordon said in a stage whisper, "Next week it'll be your turn." She left them and found another couple to talk to.

Julia and Edward looked at each other and then at Lucien. He frowned, but didn't say anything.

The first chance Julia had she asked Edward about Ben. "He wants me to respect Lucien's claim to you and he wants us to behave ourselves. He's concerned about your reputation."

She rolled her eyes. "He's probably more concerned about how something might reflect on Lucien. He's typical of most men in our class."

"I assume I don't qualify as 'most men.'"

Julia smiled. "You, my sweet Edward, are definitely an exception. You and Alexander. Of course, Jacob would be an exception in any class."

In her bedroom a week later, Julia couldn't decide whether the past week had gone fast or slow. She was in no hurry for the dinner party tonight, so in that respect it seemed as if time had flown. On the other hand, she still hadn't heard from Jacob, making the days drag by.

Maybe after spending these last three weeks on his uncle's farm he had decided she wouldn't be able to handle that life. Or maybe Jacob had given the idea up as hopeless. He didn't have the money and she was an upper-class city girl.

Would love be enough to overcome those things? Julia's heart, her romantic side said yes, but her head said maybe not. If Jacob was thinking with his head and not his heart, she may never see him again. Had all her prayers been for nothing?

She sat at her dressing table and watched tears roll down the cheeks of her reflection. What would she do if Jacob didn't contact her? And what about Edward? He'd been her rock and companion all her life. She'd come to realize her feelings for him had gone beyond friendship, but he hadn't mentioned Europe again.

Could it possibly be God's will for her to marry Lucien? If she were serious about letting God have control of her life, she would have to accept it. "Lord, if Lucien is your choice for me, please give me strength to be obedient, because it doesn't feel right in my heart." She dropped her head on her arms and cried until there were no tears left.

Later, when Millie came in to help her get ready, Julia realized she'd cried herself to sleep. "Come on now, Miss Julia, there's no need for tears yet. This is only the announcement. The wedding is still almost five months off," Millie said kindly. "You have a whole summer of fun stretched out in front of you. Try thinking about that."

The best she could manage was a wobbly smile. "I'll try, Millie. Thank you for reminding me."

By the time Millie finished fussing over her no one would know she'd spent the afternoon crying.

Momma and Papa beamed at her as she came down the stairs. "You look charming my dear," Papa said. "We want you to know we're happy you've accepted Lucien. He'll take good care of you."

Her stomach clenched, but Millie's words helped steady her. Tonight was only the announcement.

31

Julia clenched her fan in one hand and curled her other into a fist at her side. Her head pounded, just as she'd predicted to her father a few weeks ago. In the five minutes before the event started, she listened as her parents discussed again whether to make the engagement announcement during dinner or have a break in the dancing, as the Franklin's did at their ball last week. They finally decided on dinner. Julia imagined Momma may have considered the possibility she would be hard to find if she weren't already sitting at the table with them.

Guests began to fill the hotel's reception area. Momma turned to her and frowned. "Try to smile, for goodness' sake. This is a party, not a funeral."

She made an attempt, but it felt more like a grimace. "Momma, do you suppose…" The expression on her mother's face said, "No." Julia sighed. When she became a mother would she be able to do that?

Everyone who received an invitation came, which made for quite a crowd. If felt as if their voices combined into a wall of noise pushing against her. Her parents kept her close by their side as they greeted each one. She didn't get to talk to Sophia or Lily, but they gave her sympathetic looks as they came by and that brought stinging tears to her eyes.

Lucien approached and stood beside her, smiling with warm approval. But Julia found herself searching for Edward. She needed the encouragement he could give her with his good humor and optimism.

The next time Momma looked her way, her brow furrowed. "You're pale, dear. Are you feeling all right?"

Papa peered at her from the other side of Momma. "She's fine. It's probably the excitement."

"Actually, I could use some fresh air," Julia said, fanning herself.

Momma put a restraining arm around her waist. "You'll be fine once you've had something to eat. You stay right here."

"I could get you something to drink," Lucien offered. "Do you think that would help?"

"That's kind of you, Lucien," Momma said, "but I believe we can go into the dining room now. Why don't you go ahead and escort Julia?"

The faces of those around them as they led the way to the dining room had wide eyes or raised eyebrows. This wasn't going the way everyone anticipated.

Once they'd all been seated at tables lined with candles and bouquets of spring flowers, the servers placed a bowl of mock turtle soup before them. Julia got Momma's attention. "Have you seen Edward?"

"No." She frowned. "Talk to Lucien."

Julia sighed and turned to Lucien. "How is the house coming along?"

He laid his spoon down. "I'm glad you're finally interested. They're making remarkable progress. We'll take a look tomorrow afternoon."

She couldn't think of anything else to say. Lucien attempted several topics, but she was too distracted to carry on a conversation.

Finally, he asked, "Will it make you feel better to know Edward's here?" Julia turned to him, her eyes wide. "I heard you ask your mother. You're not eating and you're not talking, so I assume you must be worried whether he's here or not."

She couldn't think of an appropriate way to respond, so he went on, "Maybe it finally occurred to him to leave us alone. This is our night, and it's about time he had the decency to step aside."

A factual tone from a factual person. Julia stared at her bowl and continued to stir her soup, while blinking back tears. Lucien covered her hand where it rested on the table.

"I'm not trying to upset you, but I'm tired of pretending to be casual friends. Tonight, we're done with that."

She raised watery eyes to his, and whispered, "It's not too late to stop this."

Lucien's eyebrows jumped to his hairline. "I can't believe you're still resisting."

Julia pulled her hand away. "Believe it, Lucien. I can't marry you."

"Yes, you can." Lucien spoke through clenched teeth. "In a few minutes, your father is going to stand up and make the announcement. You will then have until October to stop being childishly stubborn."

"If anyone is stubborn it's you."

The silence in their vicinity made Julia aware of guests surreptitiously listening. They went through the next two courses without speaking. Then Papa stood and tapped on his glass with a fork.

All conversation ceased and everyone gave him their attention.

"I would like to thank you all for coming. This is a special evening for us and we're glad to have friends here to share it. I'm proud to announce the engagement of my daughter, Julia, to Lucien Harris."

Her father raised his glass in Lucien and Julia's direction. "May they have a long and happy life together."

After a moment of stunned silence, most of the guests recovered themselves and joined her father by raising their glasses. He sat down, looking pleased. Momma and Papa received congratulations from those seated around them.

Julia didn't want to look at anyone else. She knew the murmuring she heard was speculation about Lucien and her. If only she could stand and shout it had all been a horrible mistake.

"Julia, your parents want us to lead the way to the ballroom."

She lowered her head with eyes shut tight for one, two, three seconds, then stood and allowed Lucien to escort her, aware that every eye in the room was on them. The others soon followed and filled the dance floor. After the first dance, she said, "I'm done. I want to find Sophia."

"Fine, I'll help you look." Lucien tucked her hand in the crook of his arm.

As they left the floor, several people stopped them for congratulations. Lucien thanked them and answered questions about where they'd live, if they planned a wedding trip and when they were getting married. Julia felt like telling them they ought to be congratulating her parents for orchestrating all this.

After half an hour, the closest she'd gotten to Sophia was seeing her go by with one dance partner after another. Edward still hadn't made an appearance, and if one more person told her how surprised they were but hoped they'd be happy, she would scream. So far, Lucien had made all the responses, but the next person to say something to them would hear the truth of the matter.

Julia saw Mrs. Jordan coming toward them. If anyone deserved to know the real story, this kind woman did. Then she wouldn't have to tell anyone else because Mrs. Jordan would.

"Julia, you and Lucien have certainly managed the surprise announcement of the season. I confess I would never have put the two of you together."

Before Lucien could respond, Julia said, "It surprised me, too, Mrs. Jordan. I came home from shopping one day, and discovered Papa had made an agreement with Lucien. If I had been allowed any say, I would never have put the two of us together either. I believe Lucien and Sophia are much better suited."

Mrs. Jordan's smile disappeared and she blinked a few times. "Well dear, I hope things work out for you." She patted Julia on the arm and hurried away without looking at Lucien.

"Why did you tell her that?" Lucien faced her, his brows scrunched together. "It's bad enough you've made no attempt to be gracious to those offering good wishes. Now you want to spread the idea you're being forced into this? Can't you at least pretend to be happy for your parents' sake, if not for mine?"

She narrowed her eyes. "No, I can't. You said tonight we're done pretending."

"Fine, but you're not to give that story to anyone else. Are we clear?"

Sophia came over to where they stood glaring at each other. "You two don't look like a happy couple. Maybe you could use a little time apart. How about dancing with me, Lucien?"

He looked at Sophia as if she'd thrown him a lifeline, and left without another word.

Someone took her hand and she turned to see Edward smiling at her. She wanted to throw herself in his arms and weep, but instead she said, "Where have you been? I've been looking for you."

"I'm under orders to stay away from you this evening." His eyes twinkled. "Come dance with me."

She gladly followed him onto the dance floor, but frowned. "Who gave you orders?"

"I believe your papa made a request, and mine passed it along. Now I want you to cheer up. I've brought you an engagement gift."

Julia shook her head. "You can't be serious. Why would you get me a gift?"

"I am serious, and I think you'll like it. At least I hope you will." He took a quick look around, and danced her through an open French door leading to the terrace.

It was a beautiful spring night. The stars sparkled in a black velvet sky. Shrubs and small trees in pots dotted the terrace, as well as flowers, filling the mild air with their sweet fragrance.

Edward took her to a shadowed area and pulled a slim packet from an inside coat pocket.

"What is it?"

"It's your ticket to Europe." He smiled and put it in her hand. "I booked passage for both of us yesterday."

Julia stared at the envelope. Earlier in the day she'd been afraid he wouldn't take her, so where was the relief she should be feeling?

Edward lifted her chin with his finger. "What's wrong? I thought you'd be pleased."

"I *am* pleased. The fact that you'd do this for me means more than I can say. But it's not fair to you."

He dropped his hand. "What's not fair?"

She held the envelope between them with both hands. "Not too long ago you were terrified of the consequence of taking me with you."

"I've come to realize I'm more terrified of leaving you here, not knowing what's happening to you." He put his hands on her waist and drew her closer. "We'd be happy together, Julia. I have no doubt."

"I'm in love with Jacob. I can't just forget him."

Edward huffed. "Can he take care of you? The last time I talked to him he wasn't in a position to do so."

She stared at the flagstone they stood on and shook her head. "I don't know. I still haven't heard from him." Julia leaned against Edward, her ear against his chest. His heart beat a steady rhythm, and at that moment in his arms, her world felt safer.

"I'll tell you what. If there's still no change by the middle of July, you can plan to go with me. Will that be all right?" he asked, kissing the top of her head.

"Yes," Julia said gratefully. She slid the ticket into his pocket. "Keep it safe for me until then."

She put her hands on his shoulders, stood on tiptoe and kissed his cheek.

He pulled her into a hug. "No more worrying about the future. I'll take care of you."

Julia relaxed her hold. "No more worrying."

"We better go back in before we're discovered."

They stepped out of the shadows and headed for the door as another couple came out. Edward quickly pulled her behind him, his muscles tense. Then he relaxed and said, "Are Momma and Papa aware you're out here alone with a gentleman?"

James and Lily both had wide eyes, when Julia stepped up beside Edward. Lily tilted her head and put her index finger on her chin. "And what do you suppose they would think if they knew you were out here alone with a woman engaged to another man?"

"I won't tell if you don't."

"You know I never would. Julia, this is the first time I've seen you smile all night. It looks as though my brother has been able to cheer you up."

Julia gave Edward's hand a squeeze. "We had a nice talk."

"Good. Edward, Papa is looking for you."

"Okay, see you two later."

They slipped back into the ballroom and went different directions.

It didn't take long for Lucien to find Julia. He took her hand and led her to an unoccupied corner of the room. "Let's sit," he said, indicating the chairs along the wall. She had barely settled when Lucien started. "A little while ago, I stepped out on the terrace for some air, and what did I see but you and Edward step out of the shadows."

"We did run into each other."

Did the blush on her cheeks come from the heated room or the embarrassment of being caught? "I need to ask you a question. Do you remember when I told you that as your husband, I would be faithful?"

"Yes, I think so."

"I'd like to know if I can expect the same from you?"

She leaned toward him and spoke softly. "In light of the fact that you saw Edward and me together on the night of our betrothal announcement, are you inclined to end our engagement?"

He gazed at her, considering the possibility of walking away. The idea of pursuing Sophia tempted him. But in only a few months, he'd achieve the goal he'd planned years for. If life with Julia got too aggravating, he could leave when the debt had been paid to his satisfaction. He'd find another woman with Sophia's qualities.

Time to take the next step. He stood. "Come with me. I have something to tell you."

Lucien led her into the hall outside the ballroom where doors to offices lined the opposite wall. The third doorknob he turned opened the door.

Julia crossed her arms. "I'm not going in there. If you have something to tell me it'll have to be out here."

He stepped close. "It's about your father. I don't want anyone to overhear." Lucien backed into the room and waited.

She studied him a few moments, then stepped inside. "What about my father?"

"The uncle who raised me contacted me from Philadelphia the first of this year. He found out a distant cousin of ours holds a grudge against your father. My uncle believes if I marry you and am part of the family, I can prevent the man from carrying out whatever retribution he has in mind. When I approached your father with the option of possible scandal and financial ruin or allowing us to marry, he chose the latter. I assured him I care for you and would have asked his permission to court you anyway."

Julia sank into a chair, her hand pressed to her heart. "Why didn't Papa tell me?"

"We believed it would be safer if you didn't know. Your resistance took us by surprise, but we must continue on this course or expose your family." Lucien pulled a chair up beside her. "It's best if you don't say anything to your father or anyone else about this. The less it's spoken of the safer it will be."

She turned to him, tears shimmering in her eyes. "You're saying the only way to protect my family is to marry you?"

"I'm afraid so, but I hope you won't always think of it as a hardship. We can settle into a congenial relationship and if you're willing, it can be something more."

When she blinked a tear rolled down her cheek and she pulled a handkerchief out of the handbag she wore around her wrist. He gently took it from her and wiped the tear from her face.

"There's one more thing you should know. Our engagement and marriage must look real. From now on you'll have to limit your company to me. I know Edward cares for you and would want to protect your family as much as you do." Lucien returned her handkerchief. "It's best if you tell him he'll no longer be part of your life. After that you shouldn't have contact. Will you do that for your father, your family?"

She took a shaky breath. "I'll do what I have to."

Julia dried her eyes and they went back to the ballroom. Momma spotted them and hurried over. "Julia, Lucien, you should be dancing and mingling. Everyone is asking where you are."

Lucien held out his hand. "We don't want to disappoint the guests." She took it and they joined the color and movement on the dance floor. "Let's pretend for one more night we know how to be civilized to each other. We can begin again tomorrow to work out our differences."

She nodded, but couldn't bring herself to smile.

When the last guest had gone, her father declared the party a success. The musicians packed away their instruments and the hotel staff worked quickly to clean things up.

As they left, Papa said, "I noticed you and Lucien had a bumpy beginning, but things seemed to have smoothed out. Everything will be just fine for the two of you." Turning to her mother he asked, "Don't you think so Elizabeth?"

Momma gave her a weary look. "I certainly hope so."

As soon as Millie left her room, Julia climbed into bed and pulled the blankets up to her ears. The things Lucien told her bounced around in her head like a rubber ball. Was it true or did he make it up to ensure she'd do what he wanted? What could the man have against Papa? Why would it matter to a distant relative of Lucien and his uncle, if Lucien was in her family?

She rolled to her side. How did he expect her to stop having contact with Edward? Not seeing him would be hard even if she *didn't* want to. The families got together often, they attended the same church, had the same circle of friends. What kind of believable excuse could she give for separating herself from him? And what about Jacob? Lucien hadn't mentioned him.

Julia rolled to her other side and hugged a pillow, using it to soak up the tears that kept coming. Surely someone could figure out a way to help. How hard had Papa and Lucien tried to find a different solution? She couldn't let her father, her family, be ruined.

Her throat and head ached from crying. She started to turn again and heard, 'God will take care of you'. She stilled. Katherine's advice replayed in her mind. Pray. Julia slid out of bed onto her knees. "Dear Father in heaven. I don't want my family in harm's way. If your plan is to use me to safeguard their safety please give me strength. If Jacob is still interested in me, I pray he'll understand and be comforted. Bless and keep Edward, too. He's a good man. I'm trusting you to show me what to do. Amen."

32

This secret was too big to hold inside. Julia's head ached with thinking about it. She debated with herself on the way to Katherine's Monday. Should she tell her sister what Lucien said?

On entering, Julia saw this wasn't one of her sister's good days, so she sat next to her bed to talk to her. Katherine sat propped against several pillows and her maid had arranged her hair, but she appeared as pale as her bedclothes. "Are you sure you want me to stay? Maybe I should let you get some rest."

"Please stay." Katherine put her hand on Julia's. "I won't feel any better if you leave, and I want to hear about the party."

"All right." She drew in a deep breath and blew it out. "Momma and Papa felt it went well. I think they expected me to do something rash, so when nothing happened, they were relieved. I can tell Momma is still holding her breath, though. She won't relax until there's a wedding."

"Will there be a wedding?"

Julia moved from her chair to sit on the edge of the bed facing Katherine. "That's one of the reasons I'm here. I need your advice. Lucien told me something I'm not allowed to repeat. I'm not even supposed to ask Papa about it."

Katherine's eyes widened. "My goodness. Can you at least give me a hint?"

"Without giving details, the message confirms what Papa and Lucien have been telling me all along. I never had a choice. I have to marry Lucien."

Katherine's forehead creased. "This sounds ominous. Is Lucien blackmailing Papa?"

Julia sucked in a breath. If her sister guessed the truth it wouldn't be the same as if she told it. "No, but this marriage won't be what it seems."

"Ah." Her sister smiled. "Do you want to play twenty questions?"

A smile bloomed as relief filled her. "Yes. That would be perfect."

"Is the marriage Papa's idea?"

"No."

"Is Lucien forcing the issue?"

Julia closed her eyes and replayed the conversation. Lucien had made himself out to be a hero, but it didn't add up. "He didn't say so."

"You're not sure."

"True."

Katherine relaxed against the pillows and patted her fingers on the coverlet. In a few moments she returned her focus to Julia. "Will the marriage protect you or Papa?"

Excitement bubbled up. She's going to get it. "Both of us."

"Mama, too?"

"Yes."

"Is Papa the main target?"

"Yes."

Her sister went back to patting the coverlet. "If the marriage is Lucien's idea, then the threat must be something he found out and told Papa. Why does Lucien believe being a part of the Phillips family will protect it? More importantly, what or who is the threat? Did Lucien tell you what the threat is?"

"Yes."

"Does it come from someone we know?"

"No."

"Hmm, even more curious. I assume it has something to do with banking. Some customer isn't happy and has a grudge. If being part of the family will bring protection it makes me think the person is someone Lucien knows or is even part of his family. Did he give you a name?"

Julia laced her fingers together and squeezed. "No, but you're close."

Her lips quirked up. "Lucien convinced Papa that someone with a grudge is out to ruin him. But if Papa would give his blessing to marry you, the family would be safe. That seems like a lot of work to trick Papa into making you marry him. I believe the threat is someone in Lucien's family. We need to find out about his past. Who would want to harm any of us?"

"You're brilliant!" Julia leaned forward and gave Katherine a hug. "I need to do some detective work."

"I'll see what I can do from here. Before we start, though, we need to pray for God's guidance." Julia held Katherine's hand while her sister prayed. "Dear Father, you know exactly what's going on here. We're thankful you have a plan and will show us what we need to do. Thank you for peace that comes with trusting. Please give Papa wisdom as well. In the name of Jesus we pray, amen."

Julia squeezed her sister's hand. "Thank you."

"You're welcome. Now, pour me a cup of tea and tell me about the choices I believe you still have."

Julia got up and lifted the tea cozy off the pot, filled a cup and handed it to her sister. She returned to the chair by the bed. "Jacob is first in my heart, but I don't feel I can trust it where he's concerned."

"Why do you doubt your heart?"

She lifted her hands in a helpless gesture. "Because it doesn't make sense. There's nothing logical about Jacob and me being together. Edward and I, on the other hand, make perfect sense."

"What does your heart tell you about Edward?"

"I care a great deal for him." She laughed a little. "Three weeks ago, I explained to Lily that Edward and I only loved each other as friends. But since Jacob has been gone and I haven't heard from him, I've become aware of how much Edward means to me."

"Can you tell if his feelings have changed?"

"At the party Edward told me he booked passage to Europe for both of us. He wants to take care of me."

Katherine lifted a brow. "I'd say that goes beyond friendship."

"The thing that troubles me is why I wasn't more excited when he told me. I worried he wouldn't take me and when he showed me my ticket, all I could think is, it wouldn't be fair to him."

"Not fair in what way? Aren't you physically attracted to him?"

Her cheeks warmed and she twisted her ring. "I don't think it would be an issue. The problem is, the love I have for Jacob is different. It feels wild and out of control. I have no doubt Edward would keep me safe and secure. A future with Jacob seems risky, uncertain, to say the least. Does that sound crazy?"

Katherine reached for her hand. "No. I'd say Edward feels safe because you know what to expect. A future with Jacob is unknown and therefore a little scary. It also sounds as if your feelings for Jacob are more passionate." Katherine smiled weakly. "Don't tell Momma I used that word."

"I won't." Julia laughed. "She might not let me see you again."

"Tell me about Jacob. Have you heard from him?"

"No, so I don't know if God has answered his prayer. Edward said we could wait until the middle of July for Jacob to have the means to take me west. After that he wants to know for sure if I'll go with him." She scooted to the edge of her chair. "Should I go with Edward when I feel passionate about Jacob, or should I stay and hope things will work out for Jacob before October? Or maybe it *is* God's will for me to marry Lucien."

Katherine shook her head. "If Lucien was the man for you, I believe God would have softened your heart toward him by now. As for Jacob and Edward, I can't tell you what to do. It sounds as if you'd be happy with either of them. You're going to have to trust God and your heart to make themselves clear."

"But you have a preference, don't you?"

"Of course, I'd like to see you choose a life that would be easier on you. A life that would keep you close to me, once you got done traveling." Katherine smiled. "But the important thing is to be where God wants you. If you and Jacob belong together, he'll take care of you no matter where you are."

Julia slid back on her chair with a sigh. "Are you telling me to keep praying?"

"Keep praying. Trust God to do what's best for you."

"Okay, I'll try. Waiting for an answer is hard though."

"Tell me more about the party. I hate missing out on everything."

Julia spent the next hour telling her sister about the party and all of the other social activities going on.

Alex came home from school before she left, and rushed in to tell his mother about his day. Julia enjoyed watching the two of them together for a while, then left for home.

❧

Later that afternoon, Lucien went to the top floor of the bank to pay a visit to his future father-in-law. Mr. Phillips offered him a seat and closed the door. He came back around the desk and sat facing him, his hands folded on the desk top. As usual, his expression was neutral, other than the occasional tick in his right eye. "What's on your mind, Lucien?"

"I want you to know what I told Julia the night of the engagement party, in case she asks you about it. It's painfully obvious she doesn't want to marry me. I even spotted her on the terrace with Edward. Because this betrothal is supposed to look genial, I told her our marriage would protect all of you. I gave her a story about a distant cousin with a grudge and Julia's marriage to me would keep him at bay. She is now willing to behave in a way that will keep her family safe." He didn't try to hide his smug smile.

Mr. Phillips stared at him a full minute without speaking. For the first time since he'd put his plan in motion a tremor of fear passed through him.

In a conversational tone, Mr. Phillips said, "I'm tired of seeing Julia unhappy. Keeping constant pressure on her to accept she has no choice but to marry you makes me weary. My wife has questioned me and I've lied to her. I don't like that."

He put his hands flat on his desk and pushed to his feet. Lucien quickly stood as well, not knowing what to expect, but Mr. Phillips stayed behind his desk, his hands clasped behind his back.

"When you first came to me to announce your betrayal, my nightmare about what could happen became a reality. You have no idea how much sleep I've lost over the years. I gave your father the best information and advice I had at the time. Hearing about his financial loss and knowing it happened because he followed my advice shook me badly. And then to hear he'd killed himself over it…"

He looked down and shook his head. "My heart broke for your mother and you. I wanted to offer help, but couldn't find you."

Lucien swallowed hard when Mr. Phillips raised his eyes and focused on him again. He didn't want to feel sorry for the man. If it wasn't for him his father would be alive. Mr. Phillips deserved to pay. He turned on his heel and hurried out of the office.

Mr. Phillips sat in his desk chair with a sigh. Time to do what he should have done all those years ago. He pushed the lever on the intercom. "Mrs. Turner. Please make an appointment with my lawyer for me."

33

Tuesday morning Julia watched for Lucien from the drawing room window, her insides jumpy with nervous excitement. She couldn't wait for this opportunity to question him about his family. As soon as he appeared in front of the house, she hurried downstairs and stepped out the door as he reached for the bell.

"Good morning, Lucien. I'm ready." He stepped back with a quick intake of breath, eyes wide. The door closed behind her with a bang.

For a second, he stared at her, then blinked. "I don't believe I've ever seen you this excited to go look at the house."

Julia stepped around him to the sidewalk and held out her hand for assistance into the carriage. "I believe you're right. Shall we go?"

The carriage creaked as the two of them settled on the seat. They soon moved forward, the horse's hooves clip-clopping in rhythm with the other horses when they joined traffic on the brick pavement. The ride wouldn't be long so Julia didn't wait to ask her first question. "It came to me I don't know much about your family, other than you were raised by your uncle in Philadelphia after your parents passed. Did any of your relatives live in Boston?"

For a moment, Lucien's jaw tightened and his lips pressed into a straight line, but when he turned to her, she couldn't tell what his emotions might be. "There's no point trying to guess who the relative is who holds a grudge against your father."

She frowned. So much for trying to be subtle. Might as well be direct. "You can't blame me for being curious about the person who has denied me my heart's desire. Did he do business with my father here in Boston?"

Lucien sighed before answering. "Yes, I believe so."

"Have you ever met him?"

"No."

Impatience filled his tone, but she forged ahead. "What makes you think he'll care if you're part of my family?"

He pulled the carriage off the street by the Public Garden and turned to face her, brows furrowed. "There is nothing to be gained by talking about the situation. My uncle, who is a friend of your great uncle, gave me the news about my cousin. I don't think he would have mentioned it if I couldn't help in some way."

Julia laced her fingers together in her lap and squeezed. "I think you know what happened, and I have a right to know."

Lucien scowled and spoke through clenched teeth. "How about being grateful I'm giving up what I wanted for my life to protect your family? Or would you rather take your chances?"

She stiffened at his tone. "What are you giving up?"

A trolley went by on the other side of the street, its bell clanging. After it passed, he said, "I've been working toward a goal for most of my life. I now find myself in a situation where I need to make some decisions."

He got the horse started again and they pulled onto the street. Without looking at her, he said, "I'm not saying any more about this. I'm afraid your curiosity will have to go unsatisfied."

Julia fumed beside him. She'd learned nothing, well, not much. Why couldn't he tell her everything she wanted to know? Maybe between the two of them they could figure out a way for both of them to have what they wanted.

Lucien continued toward the new house, his hands squeezing the reins. He should have known Julia wouldn't meekly accept the explanation he'd given her Saturday night. She'd probably spent the last two days thinking of ways to save the family without his help. Of course, she could do nothing if she didn't know who to guard against, but that didn't mean Julia would stop trying to get an answer.

The aroma of cinnamon rolls wafted out to them from a bakery on the corner. Normally it would make his mouth water and he might even stop to get one. Today his queasy stomach rebelled at the idea of eating anything. His visit to Mr. Phillips yesterday had left him unsettled. What did Julia's father plan to do? Announce what happened twenty-five years ago? That would take away Lucien's hold over him. The rest of his plans depended on being married to Julia so he'd be closer to the money.

"Lucien! You passed Fairfield Street."

He blinked and focused on his surroundings. "I'm sorry. My mind wandered. I'll turn around up here."

"Humph. I wonder where your mind wandered."

A side look showed her frowning, arms crossed over her chest. He sighed and directed the horse back the way they came, then made the turn onto Fairfield. Seeing his plan put in motion filled him with satisfaction, but he'd had no real peace for years. It didn't look like something he'd have going forward either.

They could hear construction sounds before they saw it. Hammer on nail echoed against the housing around the site. As they got closer, they heard the shusha shusha of hand saws and the men calling to each other.

Lucien pulled to a stop beside the house and waited for Julia to say something. The workers had made good progress since the rain let up last week. They'd finished the foundation and laid the subfloor. Now, they worked on framing the first floor. He turned to Julia. It surprised him to see her taking in all the details.

She glanced at him then back at the construction. Speaking above the noise, she said, "I'll have to admit I can start to imagine this being a house."

"The framing goes fast. It won't be long until they have the second floor on. Maybe they'll be up to the third floor before you leave for the country."

Julia's eyebrows rose. "That's only a little more than two weeks."

"If the weather stays fair, they might be able to do it."

Her shoulders rose in slight shrug. "Do you think it'll be done by October?"

"The contractor isn't promising it, but we can live in my townhouse until it's finished." He shifted his gaze back to the house and the men working on it. "We don't want to rush the builders. We want it done right."

"I have an idea. Let's postpone the wedding until the house is done."

"No." He pulled the horse away from the curb and headed toward Julia's house.

"Why not? A Christmas wedding would be pretty."

"No." Lucien kept his eyes on the road and tried not to clench his teeth. "Why would you want to postpone when you know what's at stake? We should elope before you go to the country so everything is settled. I'll pick you up Thursday morning and we'll tell your parents when we get home." Since he'd committed to this course why should they wait? Hopefully her father wouldn't do anything to prevent him before then.

He turned to see her reaction. All the color had drained from her face.

"Hello!" They looked ahead and saw Edward coming toward them. "I thought I'd find you two in the neighborhood. Checking on the progress?"

Lucien stopped when the carriages were beside each other. "Yes. It's going well. Have you been by much?"

"Now and then. Do you have to go back to work, Lucien?"

"I planned on it. Why?"

"How about if I take Julia home for you. I finished classes today and I feel like celebrating. Do you want to get some ice cream, Julia?"

Lucien angled his back toward Edward and spoke softly. "You haven't given him the message, I see."

"I haven't had a chance. I can now."

"All right, but I'm serious about Thursday. I'll come by for you at ten o'clock."

She leaned around him. "I'd love to, Edward."

Edward jumped down and helped her from Lucien's carriage and into his. Julia didn't make eye contact as they rode past.

Lucien briefly closed his eyes, then urged the horse through traffic as quickly as possible. A sense of impending doom clung to him. He needed to be in his office, his sanctuary. Solitude would help to get his thoughts in order.

◦──◦

Julia took a handkerchief from her beaded reticule and dabbed her upper lip and forehead. If she'd been with Lucien even a moment longer, she would have lost her breakfast. A bitter taste lingered at the back of her mouth. He couldn't force her to go with him, could he? What if she didn't come to the door or stayed in bed all day Thursday?

"Hello. Can you hear me? What happened?" Edward waved his hand in front of her face.

She blinked, drew in a shuddery breath and turned toward him. What could she say? She'd been talking about postponing the wedding until Christmas and suddenly Lucien wanted to elope on Thursday?

Edward kept glancing at her as he directed the horse through traffic. "Ice cream can wait. We need to talk."

Julia nodded and rested her head against the back of the seat. The sights and sounds of the city melted away as they rolled into the countryside. The carriage rocked and jostled them when he pulled it off the road, parked under the shade of an oak tree and turned to her. "What is going on? You were white as a ghost when I met you and Lucien in town."

She heaved a sigh. "I'm supposed to tell you we can't have contact anymore. Lucien and I are now exclusive."

Edward's eyebrows shot upward. "That's it!? It looked as if you were going to faint or throw up, or…something. That directive isn't even realistic. What really happened?"

Julia almost laughed at his reaction, but in truth, there was nothing funny about the situation. "Stop shouting. You're scaring the cows."

He looked past her to the flower dotted meadow on the other side of the fence. Several cows stared at them. He took off his hat, held it over his heart and spoke toward them. "I apologize if I startled you."

The spring winding tight inside her began to loosen. She grinned when he turned back to her. "I can count on you to make me smile."

Edward raked his hand through his hair. "That's nice, but—"
Julia held up her hand palm out.

"At the end of the engagement party, Lucien told me our marriage would help protect my family. I'm not supposed to tell details, but I'm not sure I believe him. His behavior doesn't always make sense. Take today as an example. He has never rushed me regarding the date for the wedding, but when I suggested postponing until after the house is finished, he said he'll pick me up Thursday morning so we can elope. That's when you saw us."

Edward shook his head. "No wonder you didn't look well. You need to talk to your father."

"Lucien told me not to, but I think you're right. I will tonight." With the decision made she fully relaxed. The weight of trying to know what God wanted her to do lifted. She felt light enough to float off the seat. *Thank you, Lord, for speaking to me through Edward.*

Julia wiped the moisture from her lashes and gave her friend a hug. "Thank you for the advice. Now, if you still want to celebrate, ice cream sounds good."

He stared at her, then slowly smiled. "You're all right? That almost seems too fast. Are you sure you don't want to worry about it some more?"

She laughed. "I'm sure. God told me what I need to do through your advice."

"That's great." Edward grinned. "There's something I'd like to talk to you about if you can wait a little longer for ice cream."

She relaxed against the seat with a smile. "I can wait."

"It's about last Saturday. I've been thinking about it, and, well, have you heard from Jacob yet?"

"No, but he didn't think he would be gone more than a month. Surely, I'll hear from him by next week. Why, what are you thinking?"

"I want you to know we don't have to keep this a secret. If you decide next week it's not going to work out with Jacob, I'll talk to your father." His expression sobered. "Of course, you'll have to figure out what Lucien is up to. Or, we could beat him to it and find a justice of the peace this afternoon." He grinned and wiggled his eyebrows.

She laughed and shook her head. "Let me talk to Papa to see what's what. I know he won't want me to marry Lucien on Thursday, but we've had the party and the announcement has been in the papers. There's some pride involved." Julia paused and sighed. "This is going to be a long day. I hope Papa will tell me what's going on."

"I hope so, too. I've hated watching what Lucien is putting you through."

"Edward, you've been a life saver through all of this, but I'm sorry for any distress it's caused you. Instead of worrying about me you should be thinking about graduation on Sunday, and the fun you'll have this summer. You should be looking forward to a tour of Europe as a bachelor."

"Don't be sorry, Julia. I'm not." He relaxed back in the seat and ran his hand through his hair. The cows, grazing on wild flowers in the meadow held his interest for a few minutes, and then he turned back to her. "We've been together all our lives, and to tell you the truth, I believed we always would be. Life is more fun when you're with me. That's why I asked you to go to Europe in the first place."

He took her hand in his. "I know you'd rather be with Jacob, but if it doesn't work, I promise you'll never regret coming with me."

Her heart sat like a lump of lead in her chest. "I believe you. If I'd never met Jacob—"

"I know." He put a finger to her lips. "Remember this, I want you to be happy. You do what your heart tells you."

She took his hand and laid it against her cheek, then kissed his palm. "It's hard for me to imagine life without you." She blinked back tears.

He pulled her close and held her for a while. When he released her, he said, "I have something to give you." Reaching into his jacket pocket, he pulled out a jeweler's box and opened it. Nestled inside was a small gold cross with a diamond in the center hanging on a fine chain.

"It's beautiful." She took the box in her hands and gazed at it. Her heart swelled to overflowing with thankfulness for her sweet friend.

"No matter what decision is made, I hope you'll wear it often and that it'll remind you of me."

"Thank you." Two fat tears rolled down her cheeks. "Will you help me put it on?"

"I will if you stop crying." He smiled as he lifted the necklace out of the box and fastened it around her neck.

"I don't need anything to remind me of you, but I'll cherish it as long as I live."

He leaned over and kissed her on the corner of her mouth. Then he picked up the reins and turned the horse around. "We better get back to town. Ice cream awaits."

She smiled, not wanting him to see the turmoil churning inside her. *Lord, please show me what to do.*

John Phillips sat across the desk from his lawyer and college friend, Jackson Turner. The relief he felt over finally making the decision to talk to Jackson made him calm in a way he hadn't been in a long time. Last night he'd had his best night's sleep in twenty-five years. "It's good to see you, Jackson, but I wish we were meeting over dinner rather than the unfortunate situation I need your help with."

"I'll take a raincheck on the dinner," Jackson said with a smile. "I'm having trouble imagining you in a situation of any kind. Even at Harvard you stayed on the straight and narrow."

John dipped his head. "Yes, well, this has nothing to do with pranks or pushing limits."

His portly friend grew serious. "I'll do whatever I can to help. What's going on?"

Drawing in a breath, John started at the beginning. How bad he'd felt when he heard, his search for the family, wanting to protect his father, who still lived at the time, and the integrity of the bank, nightmares and finally Lucien's betrayal and blackmail threat.

Jackson leaned back in his desk chair and listened to the entire story without interruption, his expression showing interest until Lucien came into the picture. Brows lowered over narrowed eyes indicated his opinion of him.

John leaned forward. "This has to end now. I want to protect my family from scandal, but not at the expense of our future wellbeing. No doubt marrying Julia is only the beginning, and she doesn't want to marry him at all."

"I agree." Jackson sat forward and rested his arms on the desk top. "But let me ask how you feel about the young man? Is he redeemable? Does he deserve a chance even after what he's put you through? Or should we turn the tables and ruin him?"

"Good questions." John relaxed in his chair, rested his elbows on the armrests and tapped his fingertips together. "Before all this nonsense I believed Lucien to be intelligent, hard-working and considerate. Now that I know he's been lying to us for the last five years, I wouldn't trust him as an employee or around my family again."

"We can ask Lucien to come to my office and tell him you plan to put out the information yourself along with the fact that he is trying to blackmail you. Or, he could drop everything, leave Massachusetts and never come near you again."

"Do you think someone who has been planning revenge most of their life will give up that easily? Even if he leaves, which I hope he will, I wouldn't want him to think there's nothing left for him and take his life as his father did."

"Even if he does, John, it won't be your fault, just as his father's actions weren't your fault. You can't control what other people do."

"Good counsel, Jackson. Thank you."

"My pleasure. I'll send a message this afternoon inviting him to a meeting tomorrow morning. You'll receive a note informing you if he's coming."

The men stood and shook hands. "I hope for his sake he comes."

34

Lucien kept the door to his small office closed all morning and into early afternoon. He tried to work, but couldn't concentrate. Letters and numbers shifted around on the documents until they made no sense. The image of Mr. Phillips' face when he told Lucien he was tired hovered at the front of his mind.

He stood, took a couple steps to the window, raised the sash and looked at the sidewalk below. His father died jumping from his office window. Beads of sweat broke out on Lucien's forehead. He stepped back and quickly closed the sash. He wouldn't do that. His hands clenched and unclenched at his sides. All the plans he'd made were coming together. No need to worry about a bump in the road.

Lowering himself into his desk chair, Thursday came to mind. Eloping had been an impulsive decision, but if Julia cooperated it would solve everything. A knock sounded at the door and he flinched. He took a fortifying breath. "Come in."

His secretary entered. "I'm sorry to disturb you, Mr. Harris, but this arrived for you and the messenger is waiting for your answer."

He tuned over the envelope and his stomach cramped. The return address was The Law Firm of Turner & Turner.

Jacob watched farms and forests go by the train window as he rode back to Boston. He'd spent the last two weeks dickering with Homer Swift over every piece of equipment on the farm, from wagons to garden tools. At last Homer had been satisfied he was paying a fair price, and went to the bank to withdraw the funds. Jacob shook his head at the memory. At least the part of the sale going to him would help. It wouldn't take as long to make up the rest.

Each mile that brought him nearer to Boston raised the level of his excitement along with a nervous jittery feeling. How would it go when he saw Julia again? Did she still care or did she have a change of heart? Hopefully she received the letters he sent. Even with a slow mail service, he'd hoped for one in return.

The whistle sounded as they got close to the station and the train slowed. Steam hissed from the engine as it pulled in and a black sooty cloud rose from the coal burner's smoke stack.

Jacob spotted his father and Joel in the crowd on the platform. After hearty handshakes he asked, "How can the shop spare both of you at the same time?"

"Jason's there," his father said, as they headed for the baggage car. "Tell me how the rest of the sale went. Your last letter sounded as if Homer would never agree on anything."

"I think we did well. You were right about Swift being slow to make decisions. If I didn't need the money so much myself, I'd have given it all to him just to be done with it."

"It's a good thing you didn't," Joel said, slapping him on the back. "I imagine you'll want to head west as soon as you can."

Jacob collected his bag while his father hired a carriage to take them home.

When they'd gotten away from the clattering of horses' hooves and the crowd of people at the train station, Jacob asked Joel, "Have you seen anything of Julia?"

Joel and his father exchanged looks. "I've seen her from a distance."

He couldn't keep the excitement out of his voice. "How did she look? Who was she with?"

"She looked fine. Whenever I saw her, she was with a group of people. The gentleman you brought to the house with you after Jason's debut is always close by."

"Why don't you tell us about the farm, son? Is Swift doing a good job?"

Unease gnawed at him. Why were they being so evasive? "The farm looks good considering one man is running it. He does have one hired hand, but it couldn't possibly be the same as when there were four of us."

"It doesn't sound as though you have any regrets about not taking the farm yourself," his father said.

"I think I'll like it out west." *Too late now for regrets.* "Has Julia been into the shop at all?"

"No," his father said, as he and Joel's eyes met again. "Your friend Mr. Harrington has. He bought a gift for a friend."

Jacob did his best to remain calm. "Did he mention Julia?"

"Well, yes," Joel said. "That's who he bought the gift for."

"Oh, what did he get her?"

His father cleared his throat. "Jacob, I wonder how well you actually know this girl. She seems to have more than enough admirers."

Jacob frowned. "What are you talking about?"

"There's something we need to show you when we get home."

He couldn't help noticing Joel avoided eye contact. "Why can't you tell me now?"

"We're almost home, son. You can wait a little longer."

When they went into the house his mother hurried down the stairs to greet him with a warm embrace. "It's so good to have you home again. Dinner will be another hour. Would you care for some coffee now?"

"That sounds good, Mother. And I need to tell you before I forget, Aunt Ruth says to give you her regards."

"I'm glad you remembered, dear, now let's all go up to the drawing-room and have a chat."

Once they were settled, he asked, "Is something wrong, Mother? You seem nervous."

"Oh well, it's just that I feel bad for you, but it's for the best," she said, patting his arm.

"What's for the best?" He was tired of the mystery.

His father picked up a newspaper lying on a table near his elbow. "We saw this two weeks ago." He passed Jacob the paper.

Engagement announcements headlined the top of the page. Right below that was the information regarding Julia and Lucien. He should have known it would be in the paper, and that his mother would see it. Everything upper class fascinated her.

She broke into his thoughts, "It says they had a grand dinner party. All the old families of Boston were there. It also says a fall wedding is planned. I'm afraid she led you on a merry chase. I'm sorry, but it's better to know sooner than later."

Jacob's father rested his hand on Jacob's shoulder. "You might remember me telling you Mr. Phillips probably had someone picked out for her. It looks as though I was right."

Jacob tossed the paper on the floor. "She doesn't love him. Just because it's in the paper doesn't mean it's going to happen."

His father snorted. "Do you still think she might run off to Iowa with you? You need to face facts, son. She's out of your reach."

"I'm not in any hurry for you to go, Jacob," his mother said gently, "but maybe you should consider heading west with what you have. It would be better than taking the chance of running into her here."

He heaved a sigh. "I'll think about it." No wonder Joel and his father had been acting so strange. They believed they were giving him information he knew nothing about. He didn't believe Julia would go through with the marriage to Lucien, but he didn't know what might have happened between her and Edward in the past month. Why would he buy her a gift?

"Jacob, are you all right, dear?" His mother put her hand on his arm. "Obviously this has come as a shock. We don't have to talk about it."

He turned to her, "I appreciate your concern, but I'm all right. Julia told me her father wanted her to marry, so this isn't a total surprise. I can tell you she's not happy about the man her father's chosen for her."

Jason entered the room. "Hello everyone." He paused and took in their serious expressions. "You must be talking about Julia."

"You're right, son. We've been trying to encourage your brother to forget Miss Phillips and think about moving on to Iowa." Turning back to Jacob, his father said, "If you've known about this other man all along, I have to wonder what happened to your common sense. Surely she doesn't plan to defy her father's wishes."

"She asked him to reconsider."

"Well, obviously he hasn't." His father pointed a finger at him. "My advice to you is to stay away from her."

"I'll think about it," he said, for the second time. "If you'll excuse me, I'd like to go to my room and clean up before dinner."

Jason watched Jacob leave the room. As soon as he was out of ear shot his mother turned to his father. "This is worse than we thought. I'm sure Jacob must want to rescue her from a marriage she doesn't want. He's not thinking about what's best for him, and apparently he can't see she would never stay on a farm."

"If he does something foolish it won't be good for our standing at Mr. Phillips' bank." His father turned to him and Joel. "Has he talked to you boys about this? Do you think you could help him see reason?"

"He's talked to me," Jason said, sitting down across from his father, "and I can tell you this is not a rescue mission. He's in love with her, and from what I've seen, she cares for him, too."

"Well, what about this man she's engaged to, and Mr. Harrington? She seems to be involved with him also," said his mother. "Does this look like a good situation to you?"

He sighed. "I'll talk to him. You might be right. Maybe heading west would be the best thing."

❦

Wednesday morning Jacob found Jason alone in the dining room. Time to get some answers.

"How did it feel to sleep in this morning?" Jason asked, pouring himself a cup of coffee. "Getting up at dawn is something I don't miss in the least."

"I'm glad we have a chance to talk alone," Jacob said, ignoring Jason's attempt at small talk. He sat down and reached for the coffee pot. "Tell me what you know about Julia."

Jason sighed. "I'm afraid she's become a favorite topic of conversation. It seems everyone at the concert hall has some inside information on the old families, and they want to share it."

"What are they saying?"

Jason pointed at the platter by Jacob's elbow. "Would you mind passing the eggs and sausage? Help yourself first, of course."

He had no appetite, but took some of the food and passed it on. "What are they saying, Jason?"

"Did Julia tell you about a Mrs. Jordan?"

"Yes, she's the official match maker or something along those lines."

"Right, well she practically guaranteed Edward and Julia would be the subject of the announcement two weeks ago. I'm sure you already knew Lucien would come as a big surprise to everyone." Jason paused to take a bite. "Since then, the talk has been about all the times Edward and Julia were seen together before the party.

"Julia didn't give any indication she was about to become engaged to someone else. It's even been rumored the two of them were seen on the terrace in a compromising position at the party."

Jacob frowned, and Jason reminded him, "These are stories that are being repeated. I don't know if they're true. Also, no one seems to think Julia and Lucien looked particularly happy together. It seems they spent a good part of the evening quarreling." Jason turned his attention to his breakfast.

Jacob raised his eyebrows. "Is that it?"

Jason looked at him reluctantly. "Are you sure you want to listen to a bunch of rumors?"

"Yes. I'm sure." He crossed his arms and leaned back in his chair, never taking his eyes off Jason.

With a sigh, Jason continued, "Well, there's also speculation about whether there will be a wedding in the fall. Some people believe Julia will take off with Edward. I've even had a couple of people ask me if they hadn't seen her spending time with you."

"Her parents must be upset with all the talk." Jacob took a gulp of coffee. It upset him, but what could he do?

Jason shook his head. "I'm sure nobody's talking in front of them."

"Joel said Edward bought Julia a gift. Do you know what it was?"

"I wasn't in the store at the time, but Joel told me he bought her a necklace." Jason's eyes widened. "Are you thinking she might actually go with Edward?"

"If she feels her choice is between him and Lucien, she will. They care a lot for each other." Jacob put down his cup and began stabbing at the food on his plate with his fork. "I wish I could offer her a life with me. Before I left, that appeared to be what she wanted."

He put the fork down, hesitated, then went on. "Her sister told us we should pray about what we want, and I have been. Something could still work out before fall," he said, trying to convince himself as much as his brother.

Jason cleared his throat. "I know this isn't what you want to hear, but it would probably be a good idea to go to Iowa and find someone else. Even though you both care about each other the situation doesn't look any more possible now than it did in February."

"You're right, it doesn't, but I have to talk to her at least one more time. If we can't be together, I want to know she'll be all right."

"I understand. When will you see her?"

"I don't know." He stood and paced to the window. "Sometime within the next two weeks. After that, they leave for their house in the country."

35

The next morning, Lucien sat at his breakfast table and stared at the wall across from him without seeing. He dreaded the coming meeting, but was afraid not to go. His newspaper lay to his left. A plate of ham, eggs, tomatoes and toast sat untouched before him. A cup of coffee sat close to his right hand growing cold. Even though the cook prepared his favorite breakfast and the maid arranged the table to his liking, none of it mattered.

Little sleep left him bleary-eyed and exhausted. Mr. Phillips said he hadn't slept well for twenty-five years. Is this how he felt every morning? How had he gone on day after day?

The hall clock chimed nine. Time to go. He pushed away from the table, took his hat and walking stick from the hall tree and left the house. In no time the hansom cab he'd hired dropped him off in front of the building housing the law firm of Turner & Turner.

Lucien dried his damp palms on a handkerchief as he rode the elevator to the eighth floor. On arrival to the lobby, the secretary ushered him into Jackson Turner's office. It had the musty odor of old books. Mr. Phillips had already made himself comfortable in a brown leather wingback chair.

Mr. Turner introduced himself, then said, "Come join us, Mr. Harris."

Lucien crossed the dark blue patterned carpet and sat in the armchair offered him. Could he possibly bluff his way through this?

The attorney sat and started the conversation. "Mr. Harris, Mr. Phillips and I had an interesting talk yesterday. I invited you here this morning to hear your side of the story and discuss how to proceed. Why don't you start with the conversation you had with Mr. Phillips in February?"

Lucien hesitated and a trickle of sweat ran from his armpit to his elbow. Maybe he should confess the whole story and hope Mr. Turner would be sympathetic toward him. After all, it was a terrible thing to happen to a little boy.

Both men waited, their eyes focused on him. He swallowed hard. "If you don't mind, I'd like to start at the beginning." Mr. Turner motioned for him to continue. "My mother wasn't well so my father helped her as much as he could. When I turned five, he took us to my maternal uncle's house. He said he loved us, but we would be living there from then on. Mother died not long after Dad left, and I never saw him again."

He shifted in his chair to see if his story was affecting Mr. Turner. The man looked interested. "At twelve my uncle adopted me, making me his heir and my last name Harris. Then he told me what happened to my father."

Lucien turned narrowed eyes on Mr. Phillips. "This man intentionally gave him bad financial advice, because he feared my father might become a competitor in the real estate market. Father lost everything and couldn't live with the shame."

Mr. Phillips shook his head vigorously and sputtered, "That's not true. He wanted to invest in railroads. I've never had dealings with them."

Leaning back in the chair, Lucien spoke in a cold voice, "That's the story my uncle gave me. He made sure I had the best schooling so I could come to Boston someday, work my way into your family and make you pay for my father's life."

Now both men reacted. Mr. Turner looked at him with pity. Mr. Phillips stiffened and scowled, his face flushed. "If you're telling the truth, which I question considering you've lied to us these last five years, we need to speak with your uncle. He's wrong."

Lucien relaxed and allowed himself a small smile. "I'm afraid you're out of luck. He passed away two weeks ago. So, you see, it's your word against mine. Your best course of action is to continue as planned. I won't tell the world you're a murderer and you'll share your wealth with me."

Mr. Turner asked, "How will that pay for your father's life?"

Feigning surprise at such a silly question, Lucien said, "I'll have all the advantages due me if my father had lived."

A vein pulsed in Mr. Phillips's neck. He started to speak, but Mr. Turner held up his hand. "Mr. Harris, this is how we'll proceed. You will never come into contact with any member of the Phillips family again. You will leave Boston by tomorrow evening and never return. If you don't comply with these two directives, Mr. Phillips, a man whose family has lived in this area since before the revolution, will tell your story on his terms and reveal your plan to blackmail him. Are we understood?"

Lucien's eyes widened and his jaw dropped. How could that have gone so wrong? It was a great story, and he would not submit. He'd play along. Hanging his head, he said, "I'm sorry. I've been misled. I appreciate the mercy you're showing me."

They all stood, and Lucien plodded to the door, hoping he appeared a beaten man.

"Lucien," said Mr. Phillips. Lucien stopped, but didn't turn. "Please clean any personal items out of your office before you go home."

He left the building, but didn't stop at the office as it held nothing he wanted. Another plan formulated in his mind, and he'd been given until tomorrow evening to carry it off.

Julia hadn't realized how anxious she'd been until last night when Papa told her not to worry about Lucien any more. He planned to give Momma and her full details tonight. She relished the ability to draw in a deep breath with ease and didn't miss the pressure weighing down her shoulders. God had answered her prayer and she couldn't thank him enough.

Later that morning, Sophia answered Julia's knock. They went to Sophia's bedroom and settled into chairs by the bow window. Julia tried to contain her giddy excitement. Her friend would be disappointed to learn about Lucien's real identity.

Sophia gave her a broad smile. "You look like you're bursting with good news. Has your father called off the engagement?"

"Yes!" Both girls jumped up. Sophia let out an uncustomary squeal as they hugged each other.

"Tell me how it happened. Does that mean Lucien's available?"

Julia sobered. "I have bad news about that. It turns out he's a con artist trying to blackmail Papa. That's all I know right now, but thank goodness he's been found out."

Sophia slumped in her seat. "How could I have been so wrong about him? You even told me once that you felt something was off. How did I not see it?"

Julia reached for her hand and squeezed it. "Don't feel bad. He had everyone fooled. I'm glad you didn't get caught up in it."

"I am too." Sophia straightened and clenched her fists in her lap. "Lucien Harris is despicable. Your life and your family's lives would have been ruined. How can a person do such a thing?"

"I believe Katherine would say it's because, sin, not God's love, rules his life. Lucien cared only about getting what he wanted. God watched over me through all of this. He has a plan for each of us and I know I've learned some things because of it."

Sophia gazed at her for a while, as though coming to a decision. "You aren't the same person now as you were in February, and I believe it's God who has made the difference. What do I need to do to have him in my life?"

Julia was tempted to take her friend to Katherine so she could tell Sophia what she needed to know. Julia didn't want to mess up something this important, but peace filled her and gave her confidence. "Ask him to forgive you for the things you've done or said because of your human nature, then invite him to take control of your life. He loves you and has a plan for you. Trust him to lead you in the way you should go and he'll give you peace. We can pray right now if you want."

"I'd like that."

Julia held Sophia's hand as they prayed. When they said amen, Julia's eyes misted at the expression on Sophia's face. Her sparkling eyes and beautiful smile testified to the joy that filled her.

❦

After lunch, Julia watched from the window in the drawing-room for Edward to come take her to the Common. She planned to tell him Lucien was no longer in the picture, but that meant she no longer needed a rescue, even if Jacob didn't contact her again. He'd be free to go on his trip as a bachelor and from their conversation the other day, she knew he hoped she'd go. *Dear Father, please be with Edward. I don't want to hurt him.*

When they got to the park, Julia and Edward strolled arm in arm by Frog Pond. Edward talked about the things they'd do when they got to the country, while Julia gave him noncommittal answers.

Finally, he stopped and turned to face her. "You're here," he said, moving his hands up and down on either side of her. "But it doesn't feel like you're here." He tapped his temple with his index finger. "What's on your mind?"

She smiled at his description. "I have news about Lucien."

Edward held up his hand palm out. "Don't tell me. Lucien came to his senses and broke off the engagement."

"No, but—"

"I've got it." He closed his hand and held up one finger. "Your father came to his senses and broke off the engagement."

Julia chuckled. "Yes, he told me last night. But it's more than that. Papa and his attorney had a meeting with Lucien this morning and Momma and I will get the details tonight." Relief and thankfulness filled her tone. "God answered my prayer."

Edward led her to a bench. When they sat, he turned so they were face to face and laid his arm along the top behind her. "What made your father change his mind and why is his attorney involved? Did he catch Lucien embezzling from the bank?"

"No." She paused in case he wanted to jump in again with another possibility. When he said nothing, she continued. "It's worse than embezzlement, if you can imagine. Last night Papa told me Lucien had been planning all along to blackmail him. At this morning's meeting he'd tell him not to bother me or our family ever again."

Edward shook his head. "I never would have guessed that. Something didn't seem right about him, but I could never put my finger on it."

He straightened around and leaned against the back of the bench, his gaze on the pond. "This is wonderful news for you. No more pressure, no ticking clock forcing you to make a decision."

Julia put her hand on his briefly. "This is good for everyone. Jacob won't have to feel as though he can't help me if he doesn't have enough money by a certain time. You can plan your trip without wondering until the last minute whether you'll be free to travel as a bachelor or have a wife in tow."

He took his hat off and raked his hand through his hair. "You know I want you to go."

"I know." Her heart ached. It'd be nice to know the future, but she still had to wait, even though she no longer had a deadline.

Edward turned to her. "If Jacob contacts you, will you let me know?"

"Yes, of course"

He squeezed her hand and smiled. "Let's take a swan boat ride."

"All right." She smiled as he assisted her to her feet and looped her arm through his. "And then we can get ice cream."

Edward grinned and gave her a wink. "I like the way you think."

Jacob turned and took a different direction. He hadn't expected to see Julia and Edward, and he certainly didn't want to follow them. The fact that he'd allowed himself to stand by a tree and watch their conversation felt like spying on them. It made his skin crawl. He hurried down the sidewalk, oblivious to the summer sights and sounds around him. Edward and Julia looked happy. Maybe he was supposed to see them so he'd know what to expect. She'd decided to stay in her social class.

36

The next morning, Julia sat alone at the breakfast table when Millie came in with an envelope. "A messenger just brought this for you, miss."

Julia set her tea cup in its saucer and accepted it with a trembling hand. Did she dare hope it came from Jacob? "Is he waiting for a reply?"

"No, Miss."

"Thank you, Millie." The maid turned and left her alone again. It was rare to be in the dining room without at least her mother for company, so she took advantage of the opportunity to open the envelope without being questioned or given advice about the contents.

Flutters filled her middle. The back revealed only her name written in a hand she didn't recognize. She picked up a knife and slid the blade under the flap close to the fold. Halfway across, she froze. What if Lucien sent it?

Indecision held her until the possibility of it coming from Jacob won out. She opened it, and pulled out a single sheet of paper.

Dear Miss Phillips,

I've returned to Boston with exciting news. Please meet me
at the bench close to the willow near the lagoon at 10:00.
Come alone. This news is for your ears only.
Ever your great admirer,
Jacob Anderson

Julia's breathing quickened. She pressed her hand over her racing heart and reread the note. It had to be from Jacob, but why would he ask her to come alone?

A smile formed as she relaxed. The exciting news must mean he had enough money to go west and wanted to propose. If they were alone, they could leave without anyone knowing. He wouldn't know they no longer needed to rush.

A glance at the grandfather clock in the corner showed five minutes past nine. Plenty of time to get ready. She picked up the envelope and headed to her room.

She went to her wardrobe, but anticipation made her too jittery to stand still, let alone focus. Everything looked the same.

Julia made herself be still, took a deep breath and blew it out slowly. She needed Sophia. Her calm and steady friend would be a big help right now. She wrote a quick message asking her friend to come over and had it delivered. Julia picked up the note she'd tossed on the bed and sat in a chair by the window to wait.

She jumped up when Sophia knocked on the half-open door and came in. Julia waved the sheet of paper in the air. "Guess who I heard from?"

Sophia chuckled. "It has to be Jacob."

Julia handed her the note. "You have to help me decide what to wear. He wants to meet at ten o'clock."

Her friend quickly read the note and frowned. "He wants you to come alone. I don't think that's wise."

Julia put her hands on her hips. "Don't be a worrier. I think it's because he has enough money to go west. He's probably going to propose. How many people would you want around if someone were proposing to you?"

"Wellll…" Sophia laid the note on the secretary. "Do you think it's safe? What did your father tell you last night?"

"Let's sit down." Once settled, Julia told her friend about Papa's secret and how he'd apologized for the unpleasantness she'd endured for the past few months. "Lucien is supposed to leave town by this evening, so I doubt he has time to come to the park."

"You have a point, but if it's him pretending to be Jacob, you'll be in danger. Someone needs to keep an eye on you. I'll be sure to stay out of sight."

Some of Julia's excitement evaporated at her friend's sudden departure from common sense. "You can't skulk around behind trees and bushes alone."

Sophia brought her a piece of paper and pen and ink. "See if Edward will go."

"Good idea. I'll tell him to meet us here as soon as possible. We don't have much time."

Julia dashed off a note and gave it to Millie while Sophia picked out a dress for her. She was ready by nine forty-five when Millie told her Edward had arrived. As soon as they reached the hall, Julia gave him a quick hug. "Thank you for coming so fast."

"You're welcome, but what's the rush?"

"I'll tell you on the way to the Public Garden." She herded them out the door and into the waiting carriage.

As soon as they started, she said, "I got a note from Jacob at nine this morning asking me to meet him at the bench close to the willow at ten o'clock. Sophia is afraid it might be Lucien pretending to be

Jacob and wants to make sure I'll be safe."

She glanced at her friend who nodded. Edward looked to Sophia then back to Julia, his brows drawn. She leaned closer and lowered her voice. "Sophia suggested she follow and hide in the bushes to make sure it really is Jacob."

"I can still hear you, Julia."

Edward guffawed and slapped his leg. "You two had me going for a moment. I was a little perturbed at being dragged away from my leisurely breakfast, but it's turned out to be entertaining."

Julia stared at him. "We're not trying to entertain you." She pulled the note out of her purse and handed it to him.

His frown returned. "Why would he ask you to come alone? I see Sophia's concern."

Julia's heart beat faster as they got closer. "I think I'll be fine, but I suppose it doesn't hurt to be careful."

Edward's face held no trace of amusement now. "We'll make sure it's Jacob."

The carriage stopped at the park entrance on Arlington Street and they got out. Julia started out first. Excitement filled her with energy. She had to remind herself to walk like a lady when she wanted to run.

Edward and Sophia should be following, but now that they were at the park, she could see there wasn't much for two people to hide behind. Once she passed the statue of George Washington on his horse, a straight path led to the lagoon.

Colorful flower beds arranged in patterns and leafy trees and bushes strategically planted in the green areas didn't offer much cover. Staying nearby without being seen would be a challenge.

As she got closer to the lagoon, Julia scanned the other side. No one waited at the bench by the willow. Her footsteps slowed as doubt crept in. She could be early or he'd been detained like the day they met at Deer Park.

As she started across the bridge a commotion arose behind her. She turned to see a group of boys in knickers and short jackets, who looked to be around ten or twelve. They shouted, pushed and jostled each other as they came.

Julia spun around and quickly made her way to the other side where a group of frowning adults headed her way. Hopefully they planned to take the boys in hand. The shouts and scuffling shoes sounded as if the boys stayed on the bridge. She stepped to the side to avoid the coming adults and turned back to see what would happen.

When a smaller boy shoved his way into the middle of the fray, the biggest of the boys picked him up and tossed him over the railing of the bridge. Her jaw dropped. He hit the water with a splash and she reached for the end pillar of the bridge for support. People brushed against her in their hurry to get to the edge of the lagoon, while the boys on the bridge ran back the way they'd come, ducking out of reach of the men racing toward them.

The hair on the back of her neck rose at the awareness of someone right behind her. Before she could turn a man's arm wrapped around her waist pulling her tight against his body, and a sickly-sweet smelling cloth covered her nose and mouth. Darkness closed in as the scene slipped away.

⌁

Edward watched Julia walk away from them. The more he thought about it the more apprehensive he became.

Sophia took his arm as they followed Julia along the path. "This is madness."

Edward looked at Sophia, surprised at her forceful tone. "I agree. I don't like any of this."

Sophia turned to him. "I tried to talk her out of it, but she wouldn't hear it. She had to come rushing out here without thinking it through."

She pointed at herself. "I say we forget staying out of sight. If Jacob is the one who sent the note, he won't care that we came along to ensure her safety. If it's not him, we'll be right there to prevent something bad from happening."

He picked up the pace. "I like that plan. Running from a hiding place to save the day isn't realistic. If we keep up this speed, we should catch up with her before she crosses the bridge."

As they got closer to the lagoon, Edward saw a group of boys heading for the bridge. He spotted Julia already halfway across. The boys caused a ruckus by pushing each other and yelling out insults. She turned to look then hurried to the other side.

"We need to go faster, Sophia."

She nodded with grim determination.

They arrived at the bridge behind a small group of men, who wouldn't let them pass. Suddenly one of the boys sailed over the side of the bridge, splashing into the water near a swan boat. Sophia gasped and squeezed his arm. The next thing he knew the boys were pounding back their way, eluding the grasp of the men in front of them.

Edward hurried Sophia to the other side and quickly scanned the area. "I don't see her, do you?"

"No. She's not at the bench where they were supposed to meet either."

Edward tensed. "If she did see Jacob, I don't believe she would have gone anywhere without making sure we knew she was safe."

Sophia's face turned ashen. "That means Lucien has her."

Edward's chest tightened until it felt as if it would cut off his air. Where would Lucien take her?

Sophia laid her hand on his arm. "Dear God. Please show us what to do."

He drew in a deep breath and exhaled with relief. "Let's take a quick look around. If we don't find her, we'll go see her father."

Until Jacob saw Julia with Edward yesterday afternoon, he'd held out hope that the things his brother told him concerning Julia were nothing but rumors. He wanted her to be happy, but his chest felt like an anvil had dropped on it. His mind had been in such a fog he was no use at the store, so his father sent him home where he'd been moping in his room.

The clock on his chest of drawers showed five minutes until twelve. He'd wasted the whole morning slouched in a chair brooding. A knock at the bedroom door made him jump.

Jason stepped in, looked him over and shook his head. "You need to stop feeling sorry for yourself. You're worrying our parents. Is there a chance you could be wrong about what you saw?"

Jacob's brow furrowed. "You think I'm mistaken?"

Jason raised his hands, palms up. "It's possible. Stop hiding in your room and find out." He slapped Jacob on the back. "Let's eat lunch."

After lunch, Jacob went back to his room and did what he should have done in the first place. He knelt by his bed and poured his heart out to God. Someone cleared their throat and he looked up to see his father in the doorway, gazing at him with pity.

"I'm sorry to disturb you Jacob, but I'd like to have a word before I go back to the store."

Jacob quickly stood. "I didn't hear you knock," he said, his face warm. "Come in and sit down."

His father pulled up the one chair in the room, and Jacob sat on the edge of the bed. "Son, your mother and I feel badly about how things have gone with Miss Phillips. You know we think she's a nice young woman, but not the best choice for a farmer's wife. So even though it's hard to believe now, things have worked out for the best."

"I know how you feel—"

"Yes, well, what I want to say is, your mother and I have talked it over, and we'd like for you to have half of the proceeds from the sale of the farm. It should be enough to get you a good start. You can leave as soon as you want." His father watched him closely. "How does that sound?"

Jacob stared. Did he dare believe what he heard? With the added money, he would have enough to ask Julia to go with him. That is if he was wrong about her and Edward. "That's very generous. Are you sure you and Mother won't need it?"

His father's serious expression relaxed into a smile. "I think we'll be fine. We just need to know if you want it."

"Yes!" He jumped to his feet, his smile wide, and reached to shake his father's hand. "Thank you."

"You're welcome. Now you better start thinking about how you're going to get there. Going by train would be quickest, of course."

"I'll look into it this afternoon." As soon as his father left, Jacob got back on his knees and said a prayer of thanks.

When awareness came back to Julia, she lay flat on her back with a pounding headache and no idea where she was. She lifted her hands to rub her forehead and temples, then eased her eyes open. Turning her head carefully, she saw she lay on a sofa in a stuffy darkened room. A man who didn't look like Jacob sat with his back to her several feet away. She closed her eyes and stifled a groan. Sophia had been right, but why hadn't she and Edward saved her?

37

Julia struggled to a sitting position causing a spring in the sofa to squeak. The man in the chair turned to face her. Lucien. That put her mind at ease a little. She'd rather face an enemy she knew.

Lucien stood, carried his chair to the sofa and sat so close his knees almost touched hers. She scooted back to put more space between them and he chuckled. Maybe she didn't know him as well as she thought. Her stomach clenched at the maddening smirk on his face.

"I'm glad you're awake, Julia. We have some things to discuss."

"Yes, we do. I'd like to know where we are and how I got here. What did you do to me? I have a terrible headache."

"You're full of questions, aren't you?" He put one arm across his body, propped the elbow of his other arm on his hand and tapped his chin with his fingers. "Let's see, I think I'll answer the last one. You breathed in chloroform from the handkerchief I put over your nose. One of the side effects is waking up with a headache."

Her eyes flew wide. "You kidnapped me! That's despicable." She crossed her arms over her chest and frowned, which only served to amuse him.

"Yes, you guessed it." He gestured toward her. "I knew you were an intelligent young woman. I'm sure your Papa explained what a bad man I am and how I'm to leave town without ever making contact with the family again."

"Surely you can see this will ruin your life when you're caught. Why allow your father's misfortune to dictate how your life will go? If your uncle passed, shouldn't you go settle the estate?"

"Ah, my uncle. Now there's the problem." He scooted the chair away from her, stood and paced to the writing table, then turned to face her, his hands behind his back. "My uncle is still very much alive. I told you he died because it served my purpose." He leaned toward her when her mouth dropped open. "I'm bad. Remember?"

Her throat tightened, making it hard to swallow. Lucien must have been lying to them the whole time they'd known him. She held her hands toward him, palms up. "If he's alive, then go to him and start a new life."

He gave a mirthless laugh. "My uncle has informed me I'm not to come back until I have certain assets." Lucien came back to the chair and sat. "Since our marriage has been called off, I have to get what I need another way. Unless you'd like to reconsider?"

Julia studied him. "How can I know if you're telling me the truth? Does any of this have to do with your father?"

Lucien stood to his feet so quickly the chair tipped over behind him with a clatter. He stood rigid, hands fisted at his sides. "Here's the truth, Miss Phillips. If it weren't for your father we never would have met. And I never would have had to live with my uncle."

This was the real Lucien, and God help her, she felt sorry for him. He appeared to wilt as he bent over, set the chair up, then sagged into it and stared at the floor.

Speaking softly, Julia asked, "What are you going to do now?"

He lifted his eyes to hers. "I wrote a nice letter to your father while you were sleeping, asking for a certain amount of money. When that's been delivered, you'll never see me again." Lucien straightened in the chair. "I'm afraid this will involve some inconvenience, but as long as your father acts quickly you'll be home again before you know it."

Lucien stood, crossed to the door and took his hat from the coat stand. "There are a couple of things I need to do. In the meantime, you won't be able to leave, so don't wear yourself out trying to open the door." He pointed to a table she hadn't noticed. "There's water, and some bread and cheese if you're hungry. I won't be gone long."

He stepped out and a key turned in the lock with a click. She crossed the room and tried the door, just in case. Julia wasn't surprised when it didn't open, but disappointment still nudged at her. She'd have to think of something else.

Jacob entered the train station and headed for the ticket window. He hoped the agent wouldn't mind giving information instead of selling him a ticket right now. Four people stood in line, so he sauntered over. No need to hurry just to stand around, even though he'd like to tell everyone to clear out of his way.

He stopped behind a man wearing a black jacket, tan trousers and a bowler hat. The man held a satchel in one hand and an umbrella in the other. In front of him stood a woman in a large hat, holding the hand of a small child dressed in a sailor suit.

When the gentleman at the window finished, they all stepped forward. Jacob shifted to the left to see around the hat. The next man in line glanced to either side before leaning in to tell the agent his destination. The customer didn't look as though he'd take long.

Jacob stepped back and slid his hands in his pockets. A shriek rent the air. He and the man in front of him jumped. The source of the sound turned out to be the child ahead of them. He yanked on his mother's hand, apparently done with standing in one place. His mother's face glowed crimson. "Shhhhh."

The ticket agent said to the man at the window, "I'm sorry sir, I didn't hear you."

As the man leaned in, the child wailed. His poor mother frantically searched through the bag hanging over her arm, pulled out a lollipop and stuck it in her son's mouth. In the same moment silence settled over them, the man at the window yelled, "Two tickets to Philadelphia."

Jacob resisted the urge to laugh out loud. The situation had played out like a comedy show. But the man's shoulders hunched forward, as if his whole body cringed. He paid for the tickets, then hurried toward the door. Jacob's eyebrows shot upward when he saw the man's profile. Lucien Harris. But why did he buy two tickets to Philadelphia?

Now that he thought about it, everything about Lucien's behavior appeared suspicious. When he reached the window, Jacob got the information he wanted then asked, "Which train is the man from a few minutes ago taking to Philadelphia?"

"He's taking the last train out this evening, nine o'clock."

"Thank you."

Jacob stood outside and leaned against the front wall of the train station. If he could talk to someone who knew the latest news in the upper-class it would answer a lot of questions. He shook the thought off as impractical. The likelihood of being invited into the home of one of Boston's old families for a gossip session was zero.

He pushed away from the wall and hired a hansom cab to take him to Beacon Hill. Maybe he could get a message to Sophia. She'd talk to him. He drummed his fingers on the seat as they made their way through traffic. Halfway there he remembered the last place he'd seen Julia was the Public Garden. He gave the driver the change in address and tried to be patient.

As they got closer to the garden, he saw an unusual number of policemen. He hopped out and headed for the lagoon. Navy blue uniforms were everywhere. They appeared to be searching for something.

Jacob scanned the people milling around, hoping to see a familiar face. When he spotted Mr. Phillips approaching Edward on the other side of the lagoon, he hurried over the bridge and jogged toward their location.

Edward removed his hat and raked his hand through his hair. When Mr. Phillips got close, he asked, "What did you find out? Has the house been searched? Has anyone talked to the staff?"

"The police are doing that now. The officer told me if I wanted to help, I should stay here and continue the search."

Edward threw up his hands. "Well, she's not here. We've already looked everywhere. There has to be some clue to tell us where he's taken her."

Jacob stepped closer. "Excuse me." Both men turned toward him with a frown. "Can you tell me what's going on?"

The men blinked at him a couple of times before recognition dawned in Edward's eyes. "Jacob! You're back."

"Oh yes, Jacob." Mr. Phillips rubbed the back of his neck. "Julia is missing, quite likely kidnapped." He turned to Edward. "I should go home and see if a ransom note has been delivered."

"Good idea. I'm going with you. You'll recognize Lucien's handwriting, won't you?"

The men left Jacob, taking long strides toward the park entrance. Jacob's mind struggled to process what he'd heard. Julia. Kidnapped? Lucien? There must be some mistake. He took off after Edward and Mr. Phillips, catching up to them as they got into a hansom cab.

"May I come?" They made room for him and Edward filled him in on the way to the house. "What time did this happen?"

"A little after ten," said Edward. "Why do you ask?"

"I saw Lucien at the train station ticket window around one o'clock. A few people stood between us in line, but I still heard him ask for two tickets to Philadelphia. In light of what you told me, his behavior makes sense."

Mr. Phillips leaned toward him. "What did he do? Did he see you?"

"No, and it looked like he didn't want to be seen. He kept glancing to either side. It made him look like a criminal. Once he had the tickets, he hurried out with his head down."

Both men watched him intently, their hands folded tightly in front of them. Edward asked, "Any chance you know what time his train is supposed to leave."

"Yes, nine o'clock. If we arrive early, we should be able to catch him."

"Thank goodness you showed up today." Mr. Phillips took out his handkerchief and wiped his forehead. "We need to alert the police."

Edward took off his bowler and ran his hand through his hair. "With all the talk Julia's been doing about God it makes me feel as though he had a hand in this. Jacob, it's hard to believe you just happened to be in the right place at the right time."

Jacob replied, "I agree, but I'm confused. Why would Lucien kidnap Julia when he's supposed to marry her?"

Mr. Phillips grimaced. "Recent events brought about the necessity of breaking the engagement. This must be Lucien's way of trying to force my hand. My attorney and I told him to leave town, but it appears he doesn't plan to leave without a substantial sum of money."

The cab stopped in front of the Phillips' townhouse and the men climbed out. When they entered, Jacob saw Mrs. Phillips hurry to her husband with red rimmed eyes.

"John, what's going on? We got a letter from Lucien demanding money if we want to see Julia again."

Mr. Phillips put his arm around his wife's shoulders. "We're going to get this straightened out." Their butler approached Mr. Phillips with a tray holding a letter. "Thank you, Sanders. Will you please notify the police? We have some information for them."

Jacob followed the group to the drawing room where Mr. Phillips read the letter aloud.

Mr. and Mrs. Phillips,

Julia is here with me in fine health and good spirits. If you'd like for her to remain so, you will put fifty thousand dollars in a black attaché case and deliver it to the address I'll send you tomorrow.

If you love your daughter, you'll follow my instructions.

Lucien Harris

The housekeeper stepped in to see if they needed anything and Mr. Phillips asked for tea. While Mr. Phillips comforted his wife, Jacob took Edward aside. His need to know details about the situation had raised his internal pressure to the boiling point. It took all his self-control to use a civil tone when he asked, "What is going on?"

Edward sighed and shook his head. "I knew something was off about him. If only I'd figured it out."

Jacob threw his hands in the air. "What are you talking about?"

"It turns out Lucien is a con man. He's been trying to take advantage of an unfortunate incident that Uncle John happened to be involved in. Lucien threatened to tell all of Boston my uncle was responsible for the death of his father unless he agreed to let Lucien marry Julia."

Edward's eyes narrowed and he clenched his hands. "When I

think of what Julia endured because of that man…" he blew out a breath. "He better hope I don't get my hands on him."

A man would have to be blind not to see how much Edward cared about Julia. Jacob turned toward the window. His lips pressed together. No matter who Julia chose to spend her life with, he'd make sure she was safe.

Sanders came to the door and announced the arrival of two police detectives. They all sat and worked out a plan to rescue Julia at the train station, or on the train if the two of them managed to slip by them.

Jacob headed home on foot to give himself something to do while waiting for the hours to pass. His emotions churned inside him. Thinking about what might be happening to Julia put him on edge. He needed to get on his knees and give it to God or he'd go crazy.

38

Julia heard footsteps approaching and ran to stand against the wall by the hinge side of the door. She gripped the knife she'd picked up from the table, while her heart beat painfully against her chest. Julia held her breath when the key scraped into the lock and clicked. The door opened and Lucien stepped in.

"Julia. I know you're in here. Come out from wherever you're hiding."

She leaped from behind the door and rammed him with her shoulder. He staggered back a few steps as she ran into the hall, her shoes clacking on the ceramic tile. Light shone through the side lights of the front door, but it looked a mile away. Sucking in another breath she managed to run two more steps before Lucien grabbed her arm, spun her around and threw her over his shoulder.

"Put me down!" Julia kicked her feet and pounded on his back with her left fist. "I have a knife. You better put me down."

Lucien laughed and continued the short distance back to the room. He shut and locked the door, then set her on her feet. She stood, her muscles tense and held the knife in front of her, blade toward him. Through clenched teeth, she said, "Unlock the door and let me out."

He crossed his arms and grinned. "Or what, you'll spread butter on my jacket? You know that's a butter knife, don't you?"

Julia stared at him, unsure of what to expect from this Lucien. He'd never been light hearted before. Would he suddenly turn mean?

She relaxed her stance, took the knife back to the table then slumped onto the squeaky couch. It had seemed like a good plan. She sighed and lifted her eyes back to his. "What's next?"

He reclaimed the chair he'd used earlier. "I'm glad you asked. Tonight, we're taking a train to Philadelphia and a coach from there to a country house my uncle owns. We should be quite comfortable there until your father answers the letter I sent him."

Her eyes flew wide and she sat up straight. "Will a chaperon go with us or be at the house? We can't go about unattended without causing a scandal." Her brows snapped together. "Or is that what you really have planned? Once father believes I've been compromised, he'll have to let you marry me, then you'll have what you wanted in the first place."

He shook his head and chuckled. "I've spent enough time with you to know we wouldn't have a happy marriage. If society is upset, then that's too bad. I'm sure Edward or Jacob would marry you regardless. You'll be fine and I'll have the money I need to satisfy my uncle."

She leaned back against the sofa and crossed her arms. Maybe there'd be a way to escape at the train station. Of course, that depended on her moving under her own power as opposed to being chloroformed and carried in.

Julia watched Lucien wander over to the table. He pulled what looked like the handle of a knife from his pocket. She drew in a quick breath when a blade popped out the end. He used it to cut off a piece of cheese and some bread, then he stabbed the cheese with the point of the blade and brought it and the bread over to her.

"You should eat something. It'll be a long time before we get another meal."

She took the cheese from the blade he held out and accepted the bread. He turned and went back to get some for himself. When he finished, the blade slide back into the handle with a snick and he put it in his pocket.

He sat in the chair near the sofa and watched her as he chewed. Julia avoided eye contact but could feel his gaze on her. She wanted to brush it off.

Taking small bites made the strong flavor of the cheese and the dry bread go down a little easier. When he finished, he poured a glass of water for each of them. She drank, grateful for the moisture on her tongue and throat.

"The train leaves at nine o'clock tonight. Will you cooperate by walking in with me without a fuss? The alternative is to get another sniff of my handkerchief and sleep for the journey."

Julia held her hands up in front of her. "No, no. I'll do what you say. I don't want another headache." She folded her hands in her lap. "To be honest, I feel bad for you. It sounds like you had an unhappy childhood and your uncle has some kind of hold over you. Have you ever considered asking for God's guidance?"

He drew back from her with a grimace. "God! He's never done anything for me. Why would he start now? Especially after some of the things I've done."

"Because he loves you and wants to help you. He's waiting for you to ask." Lucien didn't look convinced. "How about if I pray right now. You don't have to do anything, but listen. Actually, you don't even have to do that." She gave him a smile.

Lucien shrugged and motioned with his hand for her to go ahead. She bowed her head and closed her eyes. "Dear Father in heaven. Thank you for loving each of us. I'm grateful for your desire to hear our praises and requests. Right now, I'm asking for wisdom. Please help Lucien and me to make good decisions and follow the path you have for us. Amen."

When Julia opened her eyes, Lucien gazed at her with an expression she couldn't identify. Puzzled, skeptical, maybe a little hope mixed in.

The grandfather clock in the corner chimed once to mark the half hour. Julia took a deep breath and stood. Half past eight. Time to go. She'd keep her word by cooperating. God would take care of the rest.

Lucien turned off the gas lamps and shifted aside the heavy velvet curtain to make sure the cab had arrived. He went to the door and helped Julia with the hooded cloak he'd gotten her. She left with Lucien and allowed him to assist her into the cab.

Every muscle in her body tensed when the cab started forward. She reminded herself to breathe. Never in her life would she have imagined she'd find herself in this situation. She glanced at Lucien. He frowned while pressing on the fake mustache he'd found somewhere.

Julia didn't think he'd hurt her, but she didn't like the idea of waiting in a strange house in another state. Maybe a person could appreciate this kind of thing more when they looked back on it. Going through it was nerve wracking.

Jacob met Mr. Phillips, Edward and six plain clothes policemen at the train station at eight o'clock. Some travelers had arrived already. They sat on the chairs and benches in the waiting area. The police scattered out among the seats and opened newspapers.

Many large pillars stood about the room. Jacob stepped behind one not far from the front entrance, then watched to see where the other two went. Edward slid into an alcove next to the platform entryway and Mr. Phillips stopped on the other side of a large potted plant near the seating area.

Jacob pulled out his pocket watch. Five minutes past eight. Lucien probably wouldn't arrive until boarding time, so he could blend in with the other travelers. Jacob snapped the cover shut. It looked as if they had around forty minutes to wait and he hated to wait. What seemed like fifteen minutes were only five. *Aargh. Stop looking at the time.*

The door opened to admit more people leaving on the nine o'clock train. He stepped back as they filed past, but could easily see Lucien and Julia weren't among them. The noise level grew as more people congregated in the waiting area. The high ceiling and marble floor amplified the sound. Jacob clenched and unclenched his hands. It felt as if a spring inside him wound tighter with each passing minute.

The next time the door opened, a man and woman came in. Jacob couldn't see the woman, but got a look at the man's profile. He wore an old-fashioned floppy felt hat pulled low over his head and held two fingers below his nose as if holding on his mustache. This had to be Lucien in a bad disguise. Jacob stepped out behind him at the same moment the woman looked over her shoulder.

Even though the hood shadowed her face, a zing of joy swept through him. Julia. Her blue eyes widened. He put his finger to his lips and she faced front again.

⚬⚬⚬

Julia's heart pounded in double time. Jacob had returned and stood right behind them. Lucien bent his head to her. "Everything all right?"

"Yes. I'm nervous."

The double door to the loading platform opened and the conductor stepped out. "All aboard!"

Lucien picked up the pace, causing her to trot to keep up. All but a few men in the waiting area stood and moved toward the platform door. Those men made their way toward her and Lucien. He tried to angle around them, but they matched their movements until the two of them were surrounded.

Lucien said, "What is the meaning of this? We need to board the train."

A familiar voice spoke. "No. You're not going anywhere."

Julia pushed back her hood and saw Papa standing with the men to her right. Edward stood to her left and Jacob behind. Relief washed over her.

Lucien dropped her arm and instead put his arm around her waist, drawing her close. He let go of the ridiculous mustache, which fell to the floor, and slid his hand into the pocket with the knife. She sucked in a breath and her body tensed.

"Julia has agreed to go with me. You have no right to stop us."

Edward stepped closer and held out his hand. When she reached for it, Lucien moved her in front of him and pulled out his knife. He pushed the button making the blade shoot out the end and held it to her neck.

"If you want this to have a happy ending, you will all step away and allow us to board the train. Mr. Phillips, if you follow the instructions I send, you'll receive your daughter back safe and sound."

The men looked at Mr. Phillips and he gave a grim nod. The ones standing in front of them stepped aside. She hardly dared to breathe as Lucien led her awkwardly forward.

When they reached the door, Lucien activated the button drawing the blade back into the handle and held it at his side. He loosened his grip so they could move more easily toward the coach in front of them. He spoke quietly in her ear, "Don't forget your promise."

She closed her eyes and nodded, then accepted the graying conductor's assistance up the steps. On the second step she heard a thump and "Oof!" Julia turned to see Jacob trying to hold Lucien down on the platform. She stepped back to the doorway as the conductor rushed toward them. "Here now! You can't do that."

Passengers who hadn't boarded yet stopped to stare. Papa, Edward and the others clattered toward the scuffling men. A scream pierced the air and a man yelled, "He has a knife!"

Julia gasped and held tightly folded hands against her breast bone. *Dear God, please don't let Jacob get hurt.*

Edward arrived just before the others. By then Jacob had Lucien's arm pinned down and Edward wrested the knife from his grasp. The policemen hauled Lucien to his feet and led him away.

It was over. Julia drew in a deep breath and blew it out. Passengers went back to what they'd been doing as if nothing had happened, but she couldn't get her feet to step down to the platform. Her father, Jacob and Edward looked around, probably wondering where she was. Jacob spotted her, strode to the door and reached up to lift her down. Suddenly her knees buckled and she fell into his arms.

Julia hugged his neck and burst into tears of relief. He held her tight until Papa cleared his throat. Jacob loosened his hold and she turned to put her arms around her father. He held her close and kissed the top of her head. "Are you all right? Did he hurt you?"

She stepped back and gazed up at him through watery eyes. "No, but I'm glad this is over." She sniffled and dug in her purse for a handkerchief. Before she found it, one appeared in her line of vision. Julia took it, lifted her eyes to Edward's and the tears came again. They held each other until she finished crying for the second time.

"Thank you for rescuing me." She squeezed Jacob's hand and Edward's. "You were both brave. But how did you know we'd be here?"

Papa put his arm around her shoulders. "Jacob says God put him in the right place at the right time." She looked at Jacob with a smile. Papa steered her toward the door. "Let's go home. We'll tell you about it on the way."

Julia savored the security she felt with her three favorite men. God had truly blessed her. When they arrived at Jacob's house, she reached for his hand and squeezed. "Thank you, again. Let's get together tomorrow. I want to hear about your trip."

"I'd like that. Send me a message with the time and place."

Jacob watched the cab leave before going in. Thank you, God, for keeping Julia safe, and for allowing me to be part of bringing her home. When he reached the parlor, the family surrounded him, all asking questions at the same time. He laughed and held up his hands. "Let's sit down. I'll tell you the entire story."

Later, Jacob had time to think about Julia's feelings. As far as he could tell, they hadn't changed, even though his had grown stronger. Things looked the same between her and Edward, too. Since she didn't have to marry Lucien, would she be interested in marrying anyone? He hoped his questions would be answered tomorrow.

39

The next morning, a plan to share and the aroma of coffee, bacon and eggs drew Jacob to breakfast with his family. He enjoyed the companionable table banter. He'd never take it for granted again.

His father handed him the basket of biscuits. "You're quiet this morning. Something on your mind?"

Jacob took a deep breath and let it out. "Yes." He smiled at his parents and brothers. "I did a lot of thinking and praying last night and have come to a decision. I'm going to ask Julia to marry me and go west as soon as we can get ready. If she says no, I'll go anyway."

"Sounds like a good plan," said Joel. "No point in dragging it out."

Jason chimed in. "I agree. It would be better to have most of the summer to get ready for winter on a farm."

"My thoughts exactly." He knew he'd be able to count on his brothers. "Mom, Dad, I hope you can be happy for me if she says yes. I'm sure God will take care of us if she does."

His father rested his hand on Jacob's shoulder. "Son, sometimes love doesn't make sense. It's clear to me, after what happened last night, you'd give your life for her. I'm not going to stand in the way."

"Thanks, Dad. I'm glad you feel that way. It's good to know I'll have your support, and advice, if I ask for it. No offense on the advice part."

Everyone chuckled, including his father. "I understand."

Jacob turned to his mother. "What do you think, Mom?"

"Oh, Jacob." She fished a handkerchief out of her pocket and dabbed at her eyes. "I want you to be happy. If, at some point, Miss Phillips would like my help, I'll come on out to see what I can do."

His mother's declaration took down the last barrier, allowing peace to flood in. His family was with him. Jacob got up and went to her. She stood and he hugged her close. Stepping back, she said, "My only concern is that a society girl can't get married this quickly."

"I'll find out this afternoon. In the meantime, I'm going to buy a ring." When they all stood to leave, Jacob asked, "Anyone know a good jeweler?"

Joel put on his hat. "Follow me, Jacob. I'll take you to the best establishment in town."

Jacob laughed, plucked his hat from the coat tree and left with Joel and his father.

Julia woke and stretched. She'd slept well considering the events of the night before. Her body and mind felt refreshed and ready for a new day. She sat and hugged her knees to her chest. There'd be no point denying her enthusiasm for the day had to do with Jacob.

Her nerves hadn't allowed her to truly identify how seeing him made her feel last night. She swung her feet over the side of the bed and rang for Millie. Her maid arrived with a message from Sophia asking Julia to have tea at her earliest convenience. Julia smiled at her friend's use of formal language. As far as she was concerned, they could have tea right now, but she'd better get dressed and have breakfast with Momma first.

Momma and Papa were in the dining room when she arrived. Her mother poured her a cup of tea. "How did you sleep, dear? No bad dreams, I hope."

Before she could answer, Papa spoke, "Are you sure you're all right, Julia? If Lucien hurt you, the police need to know. As it is, I don't know if I'll be able to forgive myself for what he put you through."

Julia sat on Papa's left and across from Momma. The circles under his eyes showed he had little sleep. She laid her hand on his. "I'm fine. This wasn't your fault. You made the decisions you felt were best."

Papa turned his hand over and gave hers a squeeze. "I appreciate you saying that."

She switched her focus to Momma. "I slept well, thanks in large part to knowing God was with me during the ordeal. My nerves were frazzled, but no physical harm came to me. I'm ready to put all of this behind me.

"Please pass the milk." While she stirred milk into her tea her parents looked at each other, then back at her. That meant they had something to tell her. She sincerely hoped it would be better than the last announcement they'd made concerning her future.

"Julia, dear." Momma hesitated, then continued. "We didn't want to say anything about this last night, but there's something we want you to know." She paused and gave Papa a slight nod. "Go ahead and tell her, John."

Julia raised her eyebrows and turned to Papa.

"Yes, well, since Lucien is out of the picture, we want you to know you're no longer under pressure to marry, unless you want to."

She smiled and released the breath she'd been holding.

Papa continued, "It hasn't escaped anyone's notice that you and Edward seem to be a couple without benefit of the formal title."

"Has he said something to you?" She couldn't hide the surprise in her voice.

"No. We just want you to know, even if we do think Edward is still young and unsettled, if he's the one who will make you happy, we won't oppose it."

Julia blinked back tears. These were the parents she'd known and loved all her life. She stood and gave her father, then her mother, a hug. "Thank you for allowing me to choose the man I marry."

She returned to her seat, took a deep breath and spoke from her heart. "I love Edward. He's a dear friend and I imagine we'd be happy together, but my heart's desire is someone else. So, I have to ask. Will my freedom to choose include someone who isn't a member of one of the old families?"

Momma and Papa both wore a blank expression. She and Edward had done such a good job, they hadn't suspected Jacob of being more than a friend. "I'm talking about Jacob Anderson."

"Oh." Momma blinked and a small line appeared between her eyes. "But he doesn't have a position, unless you count clerking in his uncle's store. Didn't you say he wants to go west to start a farm?"

Papa leaned back in his chair with a sigh and rubbed the back of his neck. "This is a surprise. Have you talked about a future together? Do you have any notion of what it takes to be a farmer's wife?"

Julia took a sip of tea then pushed it aside and rested her folded hands on the table. "We talked before he went to New York a month ago. At that time, he didn't have enough money saved to take me west with him. I don't know if anything has changed. As far as knowing how to be a farmer's wife..." She lifted her hands, palms up. "I don't, but I can learn."

Momma sniffled into her handkerchief, then said, "If you go all the way out there, we may never see you again."

"Trains run both ways, Momma. We can come back to visit or you could come to see us."

Papa harrumphed. "I think we're getting ahead of ourselves. We'll talk more after you've seen Jacob."

"I'm excited to see him, but Sophia and I are having a chat first. She sent me a message first thing this morning." She stood. "Please excuse me."

Thirty minutes later, Julia sat in Sophia's drawing room. "I should have listened to you, Sophia. You were right on every count."

Sophia shook her head. "It's in the past. There's no point dwelling on "'if onlies."' I'm happy you're safe and unharmed. And I'm glad Lucien didn't get away. He should pay for all the grief he put you and your father through."

"My mind is still unsettled about him. Either he's an excellent actor or someone has him under their thumb and he's been following orders."

The tea arrived and Sophia poured for Julia and herself. Julia set her cup on the rosewood table beside her chair and reached for a scone. She picked up the conversation while applying strawberry preserves. "I hope they'll look into it. Lucien was never mean and some of the things he said about his uncle made me feel sorry for him."

Sophia gave her a fond smile. "You have a tender heart. We'll pray for justice."

Julia took a dainty bite of her scone. After she'd swallowed, she said, "I'm excited to see Jacob and I have an idea." She set her plate down and smiled. "There will be no more going to meet someone alone, so I hope you'll be willing to go on a picnic lunch today."

Her friend's eyebrows lifted. "Today? That's short notice."

"I know." Julia scooted to the front of her chair. "But there's no way I can wait until this evening or some other day to talk to him. It would be good if one more could join us."

Sophia chuckled. "I don't blame you. I'll contact Edward." She sobered. "Maybe I shouldn't ask him. It seems unkind or at the very least, awkward."

"Oh, Sophia, you're right." Julia sighed and dropped her head. In her excitement about Jacob she'd forgotten Edward. A wave of guilt rolled over her. She squeezed her eyes shut for a moment then straightened. "Tell him the purpose of the trip, to hear about Jacob's time in New York, then he can decide what he wants to do.

"I'll get a message to Jacob and tell Mrs. Smith to make us a basket."

Jacob got Julia's message at the store and had been smiling ever since. Joel had even told him to tone it down. He studied the rings in the case, finally selecting the one he hoped she'd like best.

Joel finished with a customer and came to see what Jacob had decided on. "Nice choice. Good luck. I look forward to hearing the result at supper tonight."

"Thanks." Jacob told his father goodbye and headed home in a cab. On the way, he ran over a timeline in his mind. If Julia agreed to marry him, he'd like to have the ceremony in no more than one week and leave soon after. As soon as they had a date, he'd buy the train tickets. Julia could handle the wedding details.

Suddenly, he realized he was being awfully optimistic. Other than the kidnapping, this seemed like a direct answer to his prayer, but in the month he'd been gone, she may have changed her mind about him. Or her friends and family might have convinced her to stay in her own social class. It could be that God had only answered his request for a farm. His initial excitement dissolved into anxiety.

Julia passed the time pacing from one end of the drawing room to the other. One minute, excitement filled her with bubbles, the next, apprehension threatened to overwhelm her. Would Jacob ask her to marry him or tell her his feelings had changed?

About fifteen minutes before they were to leave, Edward stepped into the drawing room and her emotions took another turn. Her heart ached to see he wasn't wearing his usual confident smile. They met in the middle of the room. "Hello, Edward. Do you want to talk about it?"

He raised his right eyebrow. "That's usually my line." He took her hand, led her to a sofa and they sat. "Yes, I do want to talk. I've been telling you these last several months that your happiness is what matters to me. That hasn't changed. If Jacob has everything worked out and asks you to marry him, I won't stand in the way if that's what you want."

Tears sprang to her eyes at his declaration of selfless love. He still held her hand so she lifted his and kissed the back of it. "Thank you."

"You're welcome. Now I want a promise from you that I'll be invited to the wedding."

She hugged his neck. "Of course, if there is one."

Sanders cleared his throat from the doorway. "Miss Julia. The carriage is here and Miss Howell is already aboard."

Julia and Edward stood and hurried downstairs. When they got to the bottom, Millie handed Edward the requested picnic basket and they joined Sophia. It didn't take long to reach Jacob's house then go on to the Public Garden.

Edward led them to a grassy area under some shade trees near the lagoon. "How does this look, ladies?"

"Perfect." Julia and Sophia spoke at the same time. They looked at each other and laughed. Edward spread out the purple and gold paisley blanket and Julia unpacked cold meats, bread, cheese and cakes. Mrs. Smith had even included a bottle of lemonade.

Julia's gaze rested on Jacob more often than not. Most of those times he was looking her way, which caused little ripples of happiness. While they ate the men told their version of what had happened the night before.

Edward smiled and jabbed his thumb toward Jacob. "He knocked Lucien down and sat on him while I wrestled the knife out of his hand. It was a two-man effort."

Sophia appeared suitably impressed. "I'm glad you were both there."

Julia shuddered. "Jacob, tell us about New York."

Jacob wiped his fingers on a napkin as he spoke. "First of all, it took longer than I expected." He leaned his back against a tree with his legs stretched in front of him, ankles crossed.

"The man I had to deal with took ten times longer than any one I know to make up his mind about anything. He had already agreed on the price for the farm, but it took two weeks for his lawyer to look at the contract, him to hear his lawyer's opinion and finally decide to sign. After that we had to look at every single piece of equipment and every tool, then discuss their value."

Edward lounged back on his elbows. "Do you think it was worth the time?

"Absolutely." Jacob chuckled. "At one point I was ready to give him everything just to be done with it. My aunt encouraged me to hang on, and I'm glad I did."

He turned to Julia. "Will you walk with me? I have some information to share with you."

"Yes, I'd love to." She looked at Sophia, then Edward. "Do you mind?"

Sophia gave her a wide smile. "We don't mind, do we Edward?"

"No, of course not."

Edward's smile wasn't convincing and it made Julia sad. She had to hold onto what he'd told her before they came to the park. As soon as Jacob got to his feet, he helped her stand and said, "We'll try not to be too long."

Sophia made shooing motions. "Take all the time you need."

Jacob offered Julia his arm and they strolled toward the lagoon. Her emotions swirled inside her. Would he declare his love or tell her it wouldn't work between them?

40

Jacob led Julia to the white gazebo on the peninsula in the lagoon. The water, the swans, the trees and flowers, all made for a perfect scene, but they could have been black and white for all he noticed. Julia glowed with color. The shades of pink in her dress, her cheeks and her beautiful golden hair… He could gaze at her all day. That wasn't why he brought her here, though. "Come sit down. I have to tell you something."

As soon as they were seated on one of the benches, she asked, "Has God answered your prayer?"

He smiled and tried to ignore his jittery nerves. "I prayed for two things. One has been answered. I have enough money to go west."

"That's wonderful. When do you plan to go?"

Jacob swallowed hard. Did she want to hurry him off? "It depends on the second prayer." He took her hands in his and looked into her eyes. "I know we've known each other only a short time, but you've had hold of my heart from the first day I saw you. I think about you constantly."

Don't stop now. "Julia, what I'm trying to say is, I'm in love with you. I want, more than anything, for us to be together for the rest of our lives. I know I can't offer you the kind of life you're used to, but

I promise I'll never stop trying to make you happy." He paused, searching her eyes for a reason to continue.

Her smile softened. "You know how I feel about money, Jacob. I'm far more interested in a person's heart."

Relief eased the tension holding him, and he went down before her on one knee. "Now that you know what's in my heart, will you consider becoming my wife?"

She swiped her fingers at the moisture under her eyes. "Yes. I'd be proud to be your wife."

Jacob jumped up and let out a whoop, sending the gliding swans flapping to another part of the lagoon. He pulled a laughing Julia up into his arms and swung her around. They both sobered when he set her back on her feet.

Love and trust shone in her eyes. He drew her toward him and she lifted her face to his. When their lips met, Julia slid her hands up around his neck and his arms tightened around her for a kiss filled with promise and a future.

Jacob reluctantly released her and put his hand on his forehead. He felt as though he needed to get his bearings. Then he remembered the ring in his pocket. "I have something to give you." He stepped back to the bench and they both sat.

He fished in his pocket, pulled out the ring and slid it on the third finger of her left hand. "Oh, it's lovely." She held out her hand to admire it. The ring had a cluster of small pearls and tiny pink rubies set on a band with a lacy design worked into the gold on either side of the pearls. "Thank you, Jacob." She kissed his cheek.

He kissed the back of her hand and then the palm. "Thank you for making my dreams come true. We've got a lot to discuss. When can I talk to your father?"

⁂

Julia's brain buzzed with excitement, making it hard to focus. She closed her eyes and breathed a prayer. *Thank you, Lord. Help me to think clearly.*

"You should send him a message today, asking to meet with him. This morning at breakfast, Momma and Papa told me I no longer have to marry a man of their choosing. They weren't expecting me to name someone who's not in our social set, but in light of all I've been through, I think Papa will consider it. He already knows and likes you."

Jacob blew out a breath. "All right, that sounds hopeful. Here's another question. Do you think we could marry before you leave for your country house? It doesn't give you much time, but leaving from here will be easier."

She laced her fingers together in her lap and squeezed. "I think I could be ready in a week." Ideas flitted through her head. "The first thing I want to do is talk to Katherine. We might be able to use their house for the ceremony."

"As soon as we have a day set, I'll get the train tickets." Jacob pulled a piece of paper out of his pocket and handed it to her. "I picked up this schedule yesterday afternoon. It looks as though it will be a four-day trip. My uncle's friend lives on the east side of Iowa, so we should stop there first."

Julia tingled with anticipation. "This is going to be an adventure."

Jacob hesitated. "A better adventure than Europe?"

Her smile softened. "A different adventure."

He looked at her necklace. "Maybe this is none of my business, but I have to ask you about Edward. If I hadn't asked you to marry me, would you have gone with him?"

Her hand went to the cross on the necklace Edward gave her. Jacob deserved nothing less than honesty. "Yes, if Lucien was still in the picture, and if things hadn't worked out between us, I would have gone with him."

His shoulders slumped. "So, you have feelings for him, too."

She looked into his troubled eyes. "I care a great deal for him, and I always will. But I have no doubt you're the right choice for me." She covered his hand with hers. "I love you, Jacob. My heart is yours."

He exhaled. "I'll never ask about it again."

"All right, I have something to ask you. Why didn't you write to me while you were gone?"

Jacob's eyebrows jumped up. "I wrote several letters. You didn't get any of them?"

She shook her head. "Momma must have kept them from me. Maybe she hoped I'd forget about you."

He took both her hands in his. "I'm sorry you didn't get them."

"I am too, but her tactic didn't work. And now you won't need to write because we'll always be together."

Jacob gave her one of his heart-melting smiles. "I love to hear you say that." He hugged her. "We've left Edward and Sophia waiting longer than I expected. Let's head back."

As they got close to the blanket, Julia smiled at the sight of Edward stretched out on his back with his hat over his face and Sophia sitting against a tree reading a book. Sophia looked up at their approach and grinned. "It looks like congratulations are in order."

Julia laughed. Her big smile had given it away. Edward stood and assisted Sophia to her feet.

Jacob cleared his throat. "Thank you, but it's not official. I still have to talk to Julia's father."

Julia nodded. "Based on what Papa said at breakfast this morning, I think he'll approve."

Edward avoided eye contact as he shook out the blanket and folded it. "It sounds like we need to get you two home. I'm sure there's a lot to be done."

Later in the afternoon, Julia went to Katherine's house. She found her sister in the drawing room with Alex.

Katherine's face lit up when she saw Julia. "What a surprise. Can you stay for dinner?"

"Yes, thank you." Julia sat with her sister and nephew. "I hope you don't mind me dropping in at this hour. I have something to share with you."

"Sounds interesting. Will Alexander be included or is it a sisters only talk?"

"Alexander too. We may need his help."

"Now I'm really curious, but I suppose we'll have to wait until after dinner."

"That would be best."

"You mean I'm not allowed to hear," Alex complained.

"Not yet." Julia reached over and ruffled his hair. "But, you will soon."

After they'd eaten dinner, Julia waited in the drawing room while Alexander and Katherine tucked Alex in for the night. When they joined her, she told them her news. "We truly love each other and want to be married. I know I'll be giving up a lot, but I believe it'll be worth it." She raised her hands, palms up. "And, how could we ignore what seems to be an obvious answer to our prayers?"

"I'm not surprised you made this choice." Katherine settled more comfortably against a pillow on the sofa. "It certainly sounds as if God has opened the door for the two of you to be together, and you can count on him to help you with your new life."

Alexander brought his wife a cup of tea and sat beside her. "Jacob's a good man. I have no doubt he'll take care of you."

"Including Momma and Papa in our plans is a big relief. I hated the idea of going behind their backs."

Katherine nodded her agreement. "This is much better. I'm glad the Lucien business is behind you. When do you plan to be married, and where?"

Julia leaned forward in the armchair, where she sat close to her sister. "We need to marry within a week. If you're up to it, I'd like to use your drawing room."

Her sister beamed. "Of course, you can use our drawing room. I'll have the cook make a special wedding lunch for you. You just let me know what day."

Julia turned to Alexander. "Will Friday be all right? I want it to be when you can be here. And do you think your friend who is a justice of the peace might be able to perform the ceremony?"

"I can do it any day you want. I'll be glad to ask my friend if he has Friday available. Has Jacob spoken to your father yet?"

"He sent a message today. Hopefully Papa will see him right away. We're on a tight schedule, but I think I can be ready in time."

"Oh." Katherine's eyes flew wide. "What about a wedding dress? You have to have a special dress."

"Well…" She needed to make a list. "I hadn't thought about that yet."

"You can wear mine." Her sister's smile lit up her face. "I had it wrapped and stored in case I had a daughter who'd want to wear it, so it should be in good shape. You're welcome to it."

"Thank you, Katherine." Julia gathered her into a hug. "I'd be honored to wear your beautiful dress."

❧

Jacob stepped out the front door of the Phillips' home as Julia got out of her brother-in-law's carriage. The sight of her filled him with warmth and excitement. Now he wouldn't have to wait to share the result of speaking with her father.

The driver asked, "Will the gentleman need a ride?"

Julia turned to Jacob, and he said, "I'd be grateful for a ride if I can have a moment to speak with Miss Phillips."

"Certainly."

Jacob closed the distance between them and reached for her hands. He raised them to his mouth and kissed them both. She quirked an eyebrow. "What did he say?"

"He started a sentence and stopped, then started to say something else and stopped." Jacob chuckled. "He's more unhappy at the prospect of you going far away than marrying a man from the merchant class. In the end, he said we have his blessing."

She closed her eyes and sighed. "Thank you, Jesus."

"We have one more obstacle."

Her eyes flew open.

"Your mother."

<h1 style="text-align:center">41</h1>

The next morning, as they talked in the drawing room, Julia gained a new understanding of the word obstacle.

"Julia, we simply can't put together a decent wedding in less than a week. We need to make arrangements with the church, send out invitations, order flowers, plan a menu. And what about your dress?"

"Please try to relax, Momma. You're going to give yourself a headache." Julia handed her a cup of tea with two lumps of sugar. "It will be a small wedding in Katherine's drawing room. We're inviting only immediate family and close friends. We can write those today. Katherine's cook will handle the meal."

Momma looked only slightly assured. "Yes, well, that still leaves your dress, flowers and a minister."

Julia left her chair and sat beside Momma on the loveseat. She put her arm around Momma's shoulders and squeezed. "I'm going to wear Katherine's dress, Alexander is getting a justice of the peace and flowers can be ordered on short notice."

"Humph. Katherine shouldn't be hosting this in her condition. I insist we have the ceremony here." Momma set her teacup aside, crossed her arms over her chest, and gave Julia her best "I have spoken" look.

With a sigh, Julia went back to the armchair. "I think it will be easier for her if she doesn't have to leave her house, but I'm sure she'd appreciate your help. Maybe we can go for tea tomorrow afternoon and talk about her plans."

Momma relaxed her rigid posture. "I suppose you're right, but with this schedule, we better see her today. We don't have time to waste." She went to the secretary and pulled out stationery and ink. "Let's start on the invitations now."

Julia settled at a table across from her mother and made the list. Before they could get the first invitation written, Momma folded her arms on the table, rested her head on them and wept. Julia stared. She'd never seen her mother cry like that. She pulled her chair around beside Momma, and gently rubbed circles on her back.

After a while Momma calmed and lifted her face to Julia. "Do you know what people are going to think? You're getting married in a hurry and going far away. I don't want people talking about you."

Julia sat back in her chair. Momma was right. That's exactly what people would think. "I understand what you're saying and I certainly don't want to leave a scandal for you to deal with. We need to think of a way to let everyone know the reason for our quick departure. If they understand our need to acquire land in time to prepare for winter, maybe they won't be so judgmental."

"Some will believe it, most won't. I don't know why people would rather think the worst."

"There has to be something we can do." Julia tapped her lips with her index finger. "I know. How about an announcement in the paper about our marriage and the purpose for going west? Or maybe you could have a dinner in our honor and tell the guests where we are and why."

Momma nodded. "Those are possibilities. People will also wonder what happened to Lucien. A gathering where we could talk to a lot of people at one time would be convenient. It's not as if we can pretend the whole thing never happened. The papers carried the story two or three days."

"That's perfect. You can deal with two issues at one time." Julia knew her mother would be able to manage the situation. She didn't have the reputation for being a problem solver for nothing. Most people were glad to stay out of her way and let her handle it.

"I'll have to talk to your father, but I think we can work something out."

Julia embraced her mother. "Thank you."

"You're welcome." She sat back, but held one of Julia's hands. "You asked me when I first told you about Lucien if I cared about your happiness. I cared that you would be protected and provided for. Seeing you and Jacob makes me realize what true happiness is and I'm glad you found it. The only thing that upsets me is he's taking you so far away."

Wednesday evening Julia and Jacob went to Katherine's for dinner. Alexander started the meal by raising his glass to toast their engagement. She swallowed down a lump in her throat. She hadn't expected to get teary, but it hadn't hit until now how much she would miss them.

Alexander said, "Sam White, the Justice of the Peace, confirmed again today that he'll be here by ten o'clock Friday morning."

Jacob set his water goblet down. "All right. I'll get tickets for a late afternoon train."

"No, you won't." Katherine laid down her soupspoon and looked at them. "We won't let you spend your wedding night on a train. We want to book a room for you at a hotel. You can leave the next day, if you want."

He turned to Julia and when she smiled, he said, "Thank you."

Alexander addressed Jacob. "I don't know what all is involved in moving west, but I assume there must be things that need to be organized. Do you have everything set?"

"All but the train tickets. I'll get those tomorrow. Julia has been a lot busier than I have."

Katherine motioned toward Julia. "That reminds me. We've received a response to all the invitations. Everyone invited plans to come."

When they finished eating, Alexander said, "If you ladies don't mind, I'm taking Jacob with me for a little talk. We'll join you later, in the drawing room."

Julia made sure Katherine was settled comfortably on the sofa and then sat on a nearby settee. "What does Alexander want to talk to Jacob about?"

"I imagine he plans to make sure Jacob understands what it means to be a loving husband. He probably also wants to share information on limiting the number of children you have. Because of my experience, he's protective. He wants to protect you too, so it's something Jacob should know."

Julia pointed to herself. "What about me? I'm involved in this. Shouldn't I know what's going on?"

"I'll tell you everything you need to know Friday. Come over early, so we can talk while you get ready. I promise I'll do a better job preparing you than Momma did me."

Presently, the men joined the ladies. They talked until Julia could see Katherine was tiring. She gave her sister and Alexander a hug. "Thank you again."

"We appreciate everything you're doing for us," Jacob said, shaking Alexander's hand.

"We're happy to do it." Alexander clapped Jacob on the back.

Jacob put his arm around Julia as they started for her house. "I spent four months wishing you could be mine, and in just two more days we'll be married. It's hard to believe."

She snuggled closer to him. "I can't wait."

Friday morning, Julia awoke to the sun shining around her curtains. She mentally checked the list of things that needed to be done and felt satisfied all tasks were finished. A lot of her time had been spent sorting through her clothes to determine what would be appropriate to take. She'd closed the lid on her final trunk last night.

Millie came in and pulled back the drapes, letting the light pour in across her bed. Thank you, God for a beautiful day. She bounced out of bed and slipped into the dressing gown Millie held for her.

"Your momma is already having breakfast. You better hurry down. I'll help you with your bath when you come back up."

Julia had a sudden awareness of doing things for the last time. The last morning she'd have breakfast with Momma. She'd spent her last night in this room, in this bed. After today, nothing would be the same, but she wasn't afraid. Instead, bubbles of excitement filled her, making her want to laugh.

After breakfast, Julia enjoyed a warm bath in violet-scented water. She closed her eyes and relaxed while Millie massaged her scalp as she washed her long hair. After being toweled dry and brushed out, it lay in golden waves down her back.

Millie met Julia's eyes in the mirror of the dressing table. "It seems like a shame to put all of this pretty hair up. I'd like to do something different for your wedding. Will that be all right?"

"Yes. I know I'm in good hands."

Millie pulled Julia's hair up on the sides then arranged it to fall in waves and ringlets from the top of her head. She gave Julia a hand mirror so she could see the back.

"It's beautiful. Thank you, Millie." Julia took one of Millie's hands and pressed it between hers. "I don't know what I'll do without you. Not just because you're an excellent lady's maid, but because you've been kind and understanding and supportive my whole life."

Millie's eyes shone with unshed tears. "Serving you has been my pleasure. Now you best get going. I'll see you at Miss Katherine's in an hour."

At Katherine's, Julia and her sister had a woman-to-woman talk. Her excitement bubbles came to a stop as she considered what Katherine told her. Then Millie came and Julia pushed it to the back of her mind. In an hour and a half, she'd say her vows and become Mrs. Jacob Anderson.

Katherine gave her a bottle of lotion to apply before layering on the undergarments. Julia stood behind a modesty screen, poured some in her hand, then smoothed the silky liquid on her skin. She inhaled deeply then sighed with a smile. "The fragrance is lovely."

Her sister sat in a chair nearby. "I agree. It reminds me of the sweet roses by the porch at our summer house."

Next came the dress. The satin and lace gown fit as if it were made for her. The veil, secured with jeweled combs made the finishing touch. "You look lovely," Katherine said with a catch in her voice.

Julia gazed at her reflection in the full-length mirror with a pleased smile and a quivery stomach.

A knock sounded at the door and Millie let Alexander in. "Everyone is here, including the nervous groom."

Sophia and Lily followed him in. "We had to see you one more time as Miss Phillips." Lily hugged her. "You look beautiful."

Sophia hugged her, too. "Yes, and very happy."

"Thank you, I am happy. I'll confess I'm a little nervous too."

"That's only natural," Margaret said, as she came into the room.

Her sister crossed the room and took Julia's outstretched hands. "I feel somewhat responsible for all of this, so I want to make sure you still believe you're doing the right thing."

"I'm sure." She squeezed her sister's hands.

"I suggest we go downstairs before the men start coming up," Katherine said. "I don't plan to hold a wedding in the bedroom."

Everyone filed out of the room with Katherine and Alexander in the lead.

Papa stepped in the room and held out his arm. Julia's smile wobbled as she slipped her hand around her father's elbow. They stood at the top of the stairs waiting for Margaret to start the *Wedding March* on the piano. While they waited, Papa said, "I want you to know if you ever need anything, you can contact us. We'll always be willing to do what we can."

She looked up at her father's misty eyes. Tears stung hers in response. "Thank you. I hope we won't have a problem we can't handle, but it's good to know you're here for us if we do."

The music began and Papa escorted her down the stairs.

When they entered the drawing room, she glanced around at her family and friends standing on either side of the aisle. Pink roses and baby's breath sat on every available surface. They were her favorite, but it was Jacob who drew her eyes and held them.

He waited for her at the end of the room with love shining in his eyes. His smile warmed and calmed her.

The ceremony went by in a blur. She and Jacob pledged themselves to each other, he put a wedding band on her finger, gave her a sweet but short kiss and it was over. They received hugs and congratulations from everyone. Her sisters cried, but they assured her it was only because they'd miss her.

In the midst of all that, the butler announced Mr. Pickering had arrived. "Wonderful," Alexander said. "Bring him up."

Mr. Pickering came in carrying a large box accordion camera. A young man followed carrying a tripod and a square box with a handle on top. Alexander smiled as they had their picture taken.

Gratitude filled Julia when she saw the way everyone made Jacob's family feel welcome, but she could see their look of dismay when they entered the dining room. Each place setting had a bewildering array of silverware and cutlery. She quietly told them, "Start on the outside and work your way in. If you get confused, check to see what the person beside you is doing."

After a delicious lunch the servers entered the dining room with a beautifully decorated white frosted, cake. Through all of it, Julia kept looking at her wedding band, trying to reassure herself this was real. Her family and friends were there. The man she loved sat beside her. She could safely declare this her happiest day ever. So, why did she keep having the urge to cry?

When they'd finished eating, Julia led the ladies to the drawing room while the men stayed behind to talk business and politics. As soon as she sat on the sofa, Sophia brought her a package and sat next to her. "I got you something you might need."

Julia tore off the wrapping and discovered a cookbook. She laughed and held it up for the other ladies to see. "Practical, as always, Sophia. I'm sure Jacob will hope I'm a quick learner. To tell you the truth, cooking hasn't even come to mind."

"I have a book for you too." Margaret got up and handed it to her. "Mine is of a practical nature also, but won't be needed right away."

"What will I need besides a cookbook?" Julia removed the paper to find Mrs. Sara Hale's, *The Nursery Basket*. Her cheeks warmed. "Oh." The ladies chuckled when she showed them the title.

Lily jumped up. "I have something for you too." She went to a nearby table and picked up a wooden box. The lid had a lovely flower design inlaid with mother of pearl. When Julia lifted the lid, she found it full of stationery, envelopes and a pen with a bottle of ink. "I want to hear from you as often as you can write. We'll all wonder how you're doing."

"Thank you, Lily. I promise I'll use this as soon as I can."

"My turn." With a smile, Katherine passed her a package that Julia knew had to be another book. She removed the paper to reveal a beautifully bound family Bible. "It has places for keeping family records and I've taken the liberty of recording your marriage. You can add the names of your children as they come along."

"Thank you, Katherine. It'll be a family treasure."

Jacob's mother gave her a box filled with family recipes. "If Jacob gets to missing home, one of these dishes is sure to cheer him up."

"Thank you. What a thoughtful idea."

Momma passed her a heavy box. "I want you to have something my mother gave me on my wedding day. I hope it will remind you of home."

Julia removed the paper and lifted the lid. Two crystal candlesticks, nestled in soft linen folds, shone in the sunlight coming through the bay window. She gazed at Momma. "Are you sure? These are the ones great grandmother got from Ireland, aren't they?"

Her mother smiled. "I'm sure. It's always been my plan to pass them on to my youngest daughter."

"Thank you, Momma. It means a lot." Julia turned her gaze on each of the ladies. "Thank you all. Each gift is special and when I use it, I'll think of you."

Julia smiled as the men came into the drawing room, and Jacob sat beside her. The rest of them found their wives or an empty seat on the furniture arranged in a conversation group. When Julia showed Jacob her gifts, Jason grinned. "If our cousins are anything to judge by, you'll need that baby book within the year."

"Maybe," Jacob said. Julia felt her cheeks warm and noticed Jacob had blushed, too.

"There's no need to rush things," Alexander said. "I imagine you'll want to settle in first."

"If you'd had more time, you could have had Henry Palmer scouting out some land for you," Joel said.

"I sent him a telegram. If there's something available in the area, he'll be able to tell us."

"What will you do while you look?" James asked. "Are there towns big enough for you to find work?"

"The east side of Iowa is fairly well settled. There are a number of large towns or small cities. Nothing like Boston, of course." He included everyone when he said, "I'm sure we'll be all right."

Edward cleared his throat. "I hope it won't take you too long to find a place. I'd like to know you're settled before I leave."

Katherine smiled. "We'll have to see what God has planned for them."

42

The wedding guests chatted a while longer before leaving. Now that the time had come for good-byes, Julia couldn't stop the tears. Sophia held her tight for a long time, and then quickly left the room. James hugged her and shook Jacob's hand. "I wish you both the best."

Joel and Jason shook Jacob's hand and hugged her. Jason said, "Welcome to the family, Julia."

Mr. and Mrs. Anderson embraced them both and wished them well. Mrs. Anderson gripped Julia's hand. "You let us know if you need anything."

"I'm happy for you." Tears pooled in Margaret's eyes again. "I hope all goes well for you both." One more hug and she and her husband left.

Lily squeezed Julia tight. "I'll be thinking about you. Remember to write."

Julia smiled through her tears. "I will, and maybe you'll have good news to tell me when you write back."

Edward shook Jacob's hand. "I'm counting on you to take care of her."

Jacob put his hand on Edward's shoulder. "You can trust me."

Edward turned to her and pulled her into his arms. "Be careful and stay well."

"You, too," she said, hugging him tightly. He kissed her on the cheek, and then he and Lily were gone.

Priscilla approached her for the first time that day. Julia held out her arms and her sister stepped forward, held her tight for several seconds then stepped back. "I'm happy you got to marry a man you love, and I hope you'll never have regrets." Priscilla brushed at the moisture under her eyes. "This is my gift for you." She handed Julia an envelope. "Keep it for the future. There might be a time when you find yourself in need of it."

"Thank you, Priscilla."

Momma and Papa gave them another hug. Momma said, "We'll make sure your gifts get packed and sent to the station with your trunks."

Papa started to speak, cleared his throat, then said, "Jacob, take care of our little girl."

"I will, Sir."

He turned, and put his hands on her shoulders. "Julia, I want to give you a little advice. You're embarking on a life filled with experiences you've never had before. Don't give up if things don't work out the first time or two you try them. Ask for help when you need it. And take care of yourself."

"I will." She squeezed Papa around the middle and then her parents left.

Julia turned to Katherine and Alexander. "I don't think I can stand one more good-bye."

Katherine tilted her head toward the sofas. "Come back and sit down for a minute. There's something I'd like to say."

When they were seated, Katherine sat on Julia's other side. "I hope you two will never forget how God made it possible for you to be together. Your road ahead is uncertain, but God can take care of that, too. Tell Him your needs and trust Him to take care of you."

Jacob nodded. "We will. I have no doubt He answered our prayers."

"Good. I'd also like to say I hope you won't use the Bible we gave you as nothing more than a decoration for a table in your drawing room. Please read it. You need to understand more about who God is and what He's done for us. Will you do that?"

Julia squeezed her sister's hand. "Yes, Katherine. We will. I promise."

Alexander sat in an armchair catercorner to Katherine. "We're both glad to hear that. The success I've had is because I'm committed to following God's plan for our family."

"All right then." Katherine smiled. "I suppose you two should get your things together and head for the hotel. Come on, Julia, let's get you ready to go."

Julia and Katherine went to the guest room where Katherine's maid helped her out of the wedding gown and into the dress she'd brought with her. When she had changed, Katherine gave her a hug and a kiss on the cheek. "Have fun on your adventure."

Downstairs, Alexander hugged her and Katherine embraced Jacob.

Jacob turned to her. "Are you ready to go, Mrs. Anderson?"

A sudden shyness swept over her, but she took his arm and they left for the hotel. When the bags for the trip were secured in their room they went to the Public Garden. Julia tried to soak it all in. The beauty of the landscape, the water, the swans, the people. This was another last thing to do, maybe not the last time ever, but for a long time.

Jacob pointed to the lagoon. "How about a ride in a swan boat?"

Julia smiled up at him. "I'd like that." After that they walked on the Common and reminisced about the times they'd met there. "I feel as though these parks had a lot to do with our relationship."

"I do, too." Jacob grinned. "I wish I could find someone to thank for having the foresight to put them here."

They enjoyed a wonderful evening meal in the hotel dining room, then went to the room Alexander had reserved for them. It was large enough to include the usual bedroom furniture as well as a sitting area. The kindness he and Katherine had shown them overwhelmed her. Julia blinked back tears of gratitude. "They're wonderful, aren't they?"

"Yes, and so are you," Jacob said, coming to stand in front of her. He cupped her face in his hands and kissed her, then ran his hands lightly down her arms to her hands and brought each one to his lips. "You're beautiful. When you came into the drawing room on your father's arm, I had to keep telling myself you were real."

All thoughts of Katherine and Alexander evaporated, replaced with the quivery feeling she'd had earlier in the day. "You'll turn my head saying those kinds of things," Julia teased.

"I don't think that's possible. You're too sweet. And I want to tell you. I like the way you're wearing your hair today." He turned her around. "It's pretty."

"Thank you, but I can't take credit. Millie has always done my hair. I'm afraid you'll find I have a lot to learn."

"Did she brush it for you too?" asked Jacob, playing with her curls.

"Yes."

"Well, I can do that." Jacob pulled out hairpins. Once free, the rest of her hair tumbled down her back in silky waves. He ran his hands through it, then lifted it to his face and buried his nose. "It's as soft as it looks and smells wonderful."

A thrill ran through her. She didn't know what to think, but she happily found her hairbrush and sat on a footstool in front of the chair he'd gone to sit in. He carefully pulled the brush through her hair in long even strokes and the nervous excitement of the day began draining out of her.

"I don't remember being this relaxed when Millie brushed my hair." She yawned. "I feel as if I could go right to sleep."

He stopped. "You do? Why don't you tell me what other things Millie did for you? Maybe I can help you with something else."

Julia turned on the stool, and faced him. "Millie prepared a warm bath every day and helped me wash my hair. She helped me dress in the morning, at night before bed, and with every change made during the day. I'm not sure you could do all of those things." Julia tried not to smile, while shaking her head doubtfully.

He laughed and pulled her up onto his lap. "I've never been a lady's maid, but I think I could manage those tasks. I might be better at helping you take things off than putting them on, though."

She smiled and laced her hands behind his neck. "We'll figure it out together."

THE END

ACKNOWLEDGEMENTS

First and foremost, I want to thank Jesus Christ my savior for giving me the opportunity to share the stories he's laid on my heart. The ladies in the Scribes 200 critique group get a huge shout out. Your suggestions, corrections and encouragement helped to make Heart's Desire the book it is. Thank you to my beta readers. You gave me great feedback.

My copy editor had her work cut out for her. Thank you, Penny for your hard work. To my friends and family, thank you for your support and belief in me. And, Earl, my loving husband, thank you for allowing me the time and space needed to bring a story to life.

ABOUT THE AUTHOR

Linda lives in west central Ohio with her husband, daughters, grandson, two cats and a dog. She earned a degree in psychology from Anderson University where she learned the voices in her head were actually characters from stories waiting to be told.

Linda recently retired from the county's public library system. It was the perfect place to indulge her love of young adult and Christian fiction. It was also a good place to build a long "To Read" list. These days she enjoys being a fulltime author in her home office, despite interruptions from family members and pets. Linda is a member of American Christian Fiction Writers.

To learn more about Linda and the books she writes visit her website: http://www.LindaHooverBooks.com

Or stop by her Facebook author page: www.facebook.com/LindaHooverAuthor

www.ingramcontent.com/pod-product-compliance
Lightning Source LLC
Chambersburg PA
CBHW021725110726
47902CB00005B/1354